Praise for *USA TODAY* bestselling author

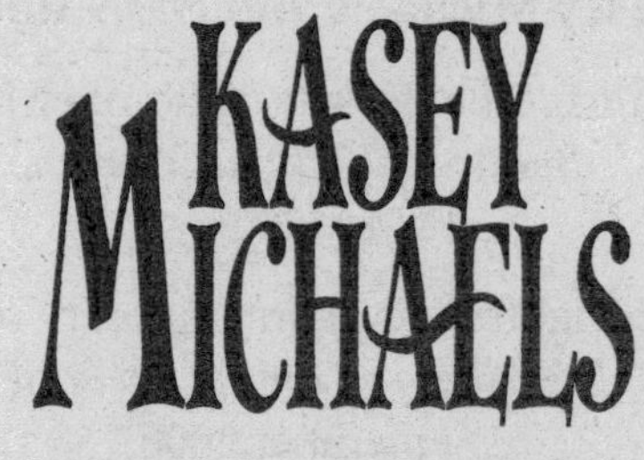

"Michaels has done it again....
Witty dialogue peppers a plot full of delectable details exposing the foibles and follies of the age."
—*Publishers Weekly*, starred review,
on *The Butler Did It*

"Michaels demonstrates her flair for creating likable protagonists who possess chemistry, charm and a penchant for getting into trouble. In addition, her dialogue and descriptions are full of humor."
—*Publishers Weekly* on *This Must Be Love*

"If you want emotion, humor and characters you can love, you want a story by Kasey Michaels."
—*New York Times* bestselling author Joan Hohl

"Kasey Michaels creates characters who stick with you long after her wonderful stories are told."
—*New York Times* bestselling author Kay Hooper

"Kasey Michaels aims for the heart
and never misses."
—*New York Times* bestselling author Nora Roberts

Coming soon from
Kasey Michaels and HQN Books

The next title in The Beckets of Romney Marsh series:
Beware of Virtuous Women
May 2006

And a delightful new contemporary romance:
Everything's Coming Up Rosie
September 2006

Also Available
A Gentleman by Any Other Name
Stuck in Shangri-la
Shall We Dance?
The Butler Did It

KASEY
MICHAELS
The Dangerous
Debutante

HQN™

ISBN 0-373-77151-7

THE DANGEROUS DEBUTANTE

This edition published by arrangement with Harlequin Books S.A.

www.HQNBooks.com

Printed in U.S.A.

Dear Reader,

In the midst of the war with Napoleon, Romney Marsh is far removed from the remainder of England; not geographically, but in the minds of its inhabitants, who believe the English Crown cares little that the area's precarious economy is being devastated by that war.

At the same time, those on the Marsh are grateful for this neglect, as this leaves them free to pursue that time-honored enterprise of Marshmen: smuggling.

Ainsley Becket had come to Romney Marsh to live in peace, raise his family and keep the dangerous secrets of their past well buried. But the winds of war blow where they will, and before long Ainsley and his sons are caught up in helping the Marshmen in their nocturnal pursuits, protecting them from a large, dangerous gang out to destroy any competition. The Black Ghost, so carefully hidden by the Beckets for more than a dozen years, has been resurrected, opening the family to danger that cannot be avoided.

When Morgan Becket is found riding out with the Black Ghost, Ainsley knows it is time for his headstrong daughter to leave Romney Marsh and discover the larger world that awaits, which hopefully is big enough to contain her strong will and even banish her own lingering demons.

As England looks to wage war on yet another front, Ainsley Becket's carefully constructed new world faces danger and discovery yet again...and this time it is Morgan who unwittingly brings that danger home in the person of the man she loves.

I hope you enjoy this second book in The Beckets of Romney Marsh series. Don't miss *Beware of Virtuous Women,* Eleanor's story, available next month.

Sincerely,

To Bob and Maryjane Daday.

CHAPTER ONE

11 March 1812

My dearest Chance and Julia,

Warmest greetings from Becket Hall, my children.

It seems so long since your visit at Christmastime, but we understand how occupied you must be at the War Office, Chance, what with our new Lord Wellington so busily preparing to storm Badajoz now that he has at last dispensed with opposition from Ciudad Rodrigo. Wellesley now an English duke, and even Duque de Ciudad Rodrigo into the bargain? *¡Madre de Dios!* How we reward men for the efficient killing of other men in this upside-down world.

I wonder, do the honors change him, or will his good common sense prevail? With the rumblings we hear about Bonaparte possibly setting his sights on Russia, Wellington would be wise to let the Little Corsican have his head, and concentrate on the Peninsula, as I have a great respect for the Russian spirit. No one, as we both know, fights with more determination than a man with his back to the wall.

But that is a discussion for another time.

There continue to be no red skies at morning, and only clear black nights, all of them without incident, and we rejoice in the fair weather. Courtland keeps himself busy about the countryside.

All else remains quiet here, or will be as soon as Morgan is dispatched to you on Friday. She'll be heavily accompanied until well into civilization, and should be with you by dinnertime on Sunday, unless she bedevils Jacob into some mischief along the way. I have commissioned Jacob to guard her because the poor besotted boy would die for her.

I have, however, yet to decide whether this makes the lad eminently suited for the position, or fatally flawed.

Cassandra, of course, is exceedingly jealous of her sister, and has demanded I remind you that she will be needing a Season of her own in a few years, a truth this father greatly wishes to ignore.

Fanny has not asked for the same consideration, as she remains more invested with her horse and Romney Marsh, and you know that Eleanor has made it quite plain she has no intentions of traveling to London, much less considering marriage.

I say this only in the hope you will not envision the whole of the thing at once, this continuing sponsoring of your sisters, and decide to pack your bags in the middle of the night as you and Julia flee to America.

As to America. Forgive this recluse his interest

in the world. What hear you at the War Office about the possibility of war between our countries? Someone here has heard rumblings, although you, of course, cannot mention your most unreliable source if you speak to your superiors.

Were I a betting man, however, I would place my wager on the rumor becoming fact before summer.

Spencer and Rian keep themselves busy, with Jacko and some others beating in their heads with knowledge that should have been theirs years ago, while I have, as you know, made Courtland my special project for the nonce. So I suppose I should correct myself. All is not quiet here at Becket Hall, and I must say, life grows more enjoyable by the day.

Monsieur Aubert, the dancing master you were so kind to dispatch, has left here a fortnight past, contemplating the pursuit of another calling, and with the protective *gad* a sympathetic Odette fashioned for him. But Morgan has learned her steps, if she does tend to move with a bit more flamboyance than the good *monsieur* felt he could countenance. *Mon Dieu,* but that Frenchman could weep!

I do feel I also must tell you that I have just yesterday received a rather impassioned note from the good *monsieur,* apologizing most profusely for allowing Morgan to tease him (the man said *tease,* and I shudder to consider the implications!) into teaching her the steps to the Viennese waltz, supposedly considered quite acceptable in

Paris, yet, mourns Monsieur Aubert, totally offensive to London society.

Yes, son, this all comes to you in the way of a warning. If, at a ball, you hear the strains of anything you believe even vaguely Bavarian or German in tone, you might wish to grab Morgan by the ear and drag her to the nearest refreshment table, so that she cannot disgrace you in public.

Although I must tell you that Eleanor and I are pleased with the modiste that accompanied the *monsieur,* and Morgan's wardrobe should be most fitting for a London debutante with aspirations to set the ton on its collective ear.

It is Morgan herself, as you know, who is not quite so demure, as she is, physically, her mother's daughter. Clad in fine silks or sackcloth and ashes, our Morgan remains impossible to overlook.

But I need not tell you any of this. I know Morgan is in good hands, thanks to my dearest Julia, who could most probably whistle a herd of stampeding elephants to heel.

You will see us all soon enough, God willing, and your siblings send their love, with Courtland adding a special message that he fully expects you to pop Morgan off on some unsuspecting Romeo before the man has a chance to see her with both eyes open.

Keeping you both to your promise to accompany Morgan back to her family at the end of the Season, I look forward to regular reports of the girl's progress. Do think to spare this old man's blushes, however, and don't tell me everything my dear daughter might do. My imagination is terrifying enough. I shall hold out only faint hope there exists a man in London who will be up to the challenge she presents.

A grateful parent's thanks, blessings, and prayers on you both.

Your loving father,
Ainsley G. B. Becket

"YOU'LL BE DELIGHTED to know that my father remains the master of understatement," Chance Becket said, then handed the two-page letter to his wife before heading to the drinks table in the drawing room of their Upper Brook Street town house, to pour himself a glass of wine. "Would you care for some lemonade?"

"No, thank you, dearest," Julia said, quickly scanning both pages, then putting them down beside her. "Ainsley never worries about the cost of postage, does he? I'll read this later. Why don't you tell me what he has to say—and what you believe he was really saying."

Chance sat down beside his bride of nearly a year and took her hand, raised it to his lips. There was no sense in lying to her. "I believe, sweetings, he was warning us that Morgan could present a problem."

Julia rested her head against her husband's shoulder and sighed, for she knew Morgan, and believed Chance's words also to be in the way of a gross understatement. "Oh, is that all. I'm already expecting problems, and I'm certain the last thing Morgan would want to do is to disappoint me. What else did he say?"

"The Red Men Gang is still happily absent from Romney Marsh, Court's still in charge as the Black Ghost, and everything continues to run smoothly on that head."

Julia straightened, thoughts of their time spent at Becket Hall rising to the surface, bringing back old memories, old fears. She'd first met Chance, met the Beckets, when she'd answered an advertisement and became nanny to Chance's young daughter, Alice. And her life had never been the same. "He actually said that?"

"No, not in so many words. But he did say it." Chance put down his wineglass and became occupied in twirling a lock of his wife's blond hair around his finger. "He also sees a defeat in Bonaparte's future and an English war with America. Why a man who never leaves Romney Marsh is still so interested in the rest of the world amuses me. That he can know so much, analyze and deduce so much, amazes me. I wish he'd come to London, join me in the War Office."

Julia squeezed Chance's hand, the secrets they shared about Ainsley Becket, all of the Beckets, already holding them fast. "But he won't. He doesn't dare be recognized, or else everything he's so carefully built will come tumbling down."

"I'm not sure even he believes that anymore. He's been safe for more than a dozen years. Well, we'll soon have Morgan, at least. That's a start. Then possibly Spence and Rian will come for a visit, and I can chase them out of every gambling hell and whorehouse in the city."

"They wouldn't do that," Julia said, then bit her bottom lip for a moment. "Yes, they would, wouldn't they? I think I'll allow you to be in charge of your brothers when they visit, and I'll watch over the girls. Do we have a bargain, sir?"

Chance grinned, then kissed her cheek. "If I'd known how easily I could be shed of responsibility for Morgan, madam, I would have been a happier man these past months. So it's a promise? You're in charge of bearleading Morgan, and any of my sisters who want to cut a dash in society, and I'm in charge of my brothers?"

Julia saw her husband's smile and reached for Ainsley's letter. "Before I agree to that, I think perhaps I ought to read your father's warnings for myself."

Chance rolled his eyes dramatically and picked up his wineglass again. "So much for my hopes. Did I tell you, dearest, that I'll be needed at the War Office almost continuously for the next three months?"

Julia's eyes had already widened as she read about Monsieur Aubert. "Oh, I doubt that, Chance. I doubt that *very* much. The waltz? She wouldn't dare. I may be new to society myself, but I know the waltz is frowned on—why, even Lord Byron condemns it."

"As being unchaste. Yes, I know. While Byron himself, of course, is virgin as a new-fallen snow." Chance took a sip of wine. "Ainsley seems to want Morgan married off quickly. I think that's fairly clear. Do you think we should be drawing up a list of eligible bachelors?"

"And then steer her toward them? Oh, I don't think so, darling. It's the one we'd steer her away from that she'd most likely find interesting. That said, yes, I believe I've reconsidered, and will join you in a glass. And *not* lemonade."

CHAPTER TWO

JACOB WHITING WAS SO upset he could barely keep from wringing his hands like some fretful old lady as visions of disaster evilly danced in his head. He'd thought this would be such a grand adventure.

Just once before in his twenty years had he been anywhere interesting, when he'd been taken to Dymchurch to have a tooth drawn. Traveling up to London-town had come to him unexpectedly, like a special treat from Father Christmas, and traveling there with Morgan Becket was like all of Christmas and his birthday combined.

And now, not even two days into his grand adventure, Morgie was ruining everything and he wished himself back at Becket Hall, or snug in his bed above The Last Voyage in the small village Ainsley had built for everyone, listening to the old sailors telling tall tales as they drank their rum in the tap room below him.

"Morgie—that is, Miss Morgan, please. Your papa will have my head on a pike if anything happens to you."

Morgan Becket frowned at Jacob, who was proving unusually uncooperative, not to mention melodramatic. She was much more used to having him twisted neatly around her finger, as he had been from the first day he'd laid eyes on her, more than a dozen years ago.

But this time, smiling hadn't worked. Teasing hadn't worked, either. Her papa must have truly put the fear of God in the poor fellow. "Very well then, timid-toes. I'll saddle her myself. I *can* do that, you know."

"No!" Jacob protested, then quickly ran after Morgan, who was grinning as she marched, chin held high, across the dusty inn yard toward the stables. She'd been waiting for this moment, when the outriders her papa had sent along with them had been dispatched back to Becket Hall, and only Jacob stood between her and adventure.

"*Please,* Miss Morgan," he repeated, fairly dancing along beside her as she ate up ground easily with long, fluid strides that might look distressingly mannish on some females…females with less curves, that is. "You can't be riding into Londontown on Berengaria, you just can't."

And then Jacob winced, because he knew immediately that he had made a fatal mistake.

"*Can't,* Jacob?" Morgan asked, turning to include him in her grin. "Well now, that fairly settles the matter for us, doesn't it?"

She put her gloved hand on his upper arm, and Jacob's country-fresh complexion turned beet-red as he felt his resolve fleeing out the back door of his brainbox.

"Morgie, don't. Please?"

"Think about it, my friend. The entire *world* goes to London for the Season. Am I to be just one more country bumpkin sent off to snare a husband? I don't think so. I don't think I'd be able to countenance that. Besides," she added, when her childhood friend seemed ready to weep, "Chance and Julia will be expecting something outrageous. We wouldn't want to disappoint them, now would we?"

"Odette said you'd behave, just like a little lamb." He reached inside his shirt and pulled out a small brown bag tied up with multicolored ribbons, looked at it in some disgust. "This is what I think of her voodoo!"

"Stop!" Morgan, genuinely alarmed, caught his wrist before he could throw the bag to the ground. "Are you out of your mind? *Odette* made that for you."

Jacob nodded, wide-eyed as he wondered if Morgan had just saved him from having a lightning bolt reach out of the sky to explode his intestines. "She said I could control you with it. I didn't believe her, not really. I've heard the stories. About how she's been wrong before, how she promised safety all those years ago when you all were on some island, and—"

"Jacob Whiting, shut your mouth," Morgan warned tersely, then looked about to see if anyone was watching, had overheard. She moved closer and continued, "God gave you a brain, or at least one could hope so. *Use* it. And use your mouth less, or you'll be on your way back to Becket Hall before you can so much as plant a foot on the cobbles of Upper Brook Street—and you'll be walking all the way, my friend, still with the feel of my boot on your backside."

"I'm sorry, Morgie. I know I shouldn't have thought to throw… And I shouldn't have said what I said about," he lowered his voice to a whisper, "the you-know-what. You've got me so I don't know if I'm on my head or on my heels. I thought we'd be just fine for these last few miles. Only two more hours, after all, and in the light of day, with plenty of other folks on the road to keep us company. I wasn't counting on trouble from you the moment the others left us. I'm sorry, I'm so sorry."

Jacob knew as well as she did that the outriders had been sent back to Becket Hall because tempting fate by allowing any of their faces to be seen so far from Romney Marsh would be foolish in the extreme. It would mean certain destruction, allowing any of them who had been fully grown and fully formed when they had all "died" and come to England, to be recognized.

Morgan and her siblings were safe, except perhaps for Courtland, who had already gone ten and seven when they'd arrived in Romney Marsh. Chance had also been older, but he'd changed so from who he had been that no one had yet made the connection between the gentleman he'd become and the man he'd been.

No, there was little fear that the child Morgan had been would be remembered, or recognized in the young woman she was now.

"It's all right, Jacob," Morgan assured him quickly. How could they be nearly the same age—with Jacob the elder by two full years—and yet him still so much the child? "But no talk of times past, remember?"

"It…it's not like I know anything, anyway, is it?" Jacob's complexion, a moment before so colorful, had paled dangerously. "You won't…you won't tell anybody?"

"Not a soul, I promise." And then, to take the look

of worry from his face, she asked, "Did Odette actually promise that little bag would give you control over me?"

He shook his head. "She said it would keep me from being trampled." And then he smiled, his humor restored. "And, thinking on it, if I stand back out of the way when you have the bit between your teeth, I suppose she might be right. But you will be wanting the *new* saddle? I don't think my heart could take anything else."

Morgan laughed, and the two of them headed toward the stables once more. She'd been in the coach all day yesterday, acting the lady, and for most of today, and she didn't believe she could stand another moment of being so confined. Especially now, when they were so close to London.

Which was why she had asked Jacob to bring her second largest trunk into the inn while she dined in a private room that had been arranged for her, then quickly dressed herself in one of her new riding habits. The marvelous dark green creation, with its tight-fitting, short velvet jacket held closed with braided frogs, and the shako hat with the dyed green feather, seemed perfect for the day and her mood.

The skirt was split, but daring as she was, she was not foolish enough to believe riding astride to be an option. Besides, she rather enjoyed the sidesaddle, which had been a parting gift from her brother Spencer. He'd told her he doubted he could sit a horse half so well if he were forced to ride in skirts and with both legs dangling over the same side of the animal.

She'd known her brother's compliment had been meant to cajole her into not arguing about the sidesaddle, but she'd allowed herself to be flattered.

She'd also made sure Jacob had sneaked out to the traveling coach before dawn yesterday, to hide her usual saddle in the boot.

"I thought Papa's guard would never leave us, you know. Berengaria must be itching for a run as much as I am," she commented as she stopped outside the stables, allowing Jacob the face-saving gesture of ordering one of the ostlers to fetch the mare.

"Not a run, Miss Morgan," Jacob said, for once looking as if he meant what he said. "You said you wanted to ride right out in front of the coach for a ways where we could see you, that's all. There'll be no runs, or else—"

"Don't say any more, Jacob," Morgan warned cheerfully, "because we both know how difficult it would be for you to carry through on any threat."

Not caring who saw, because Morgan never cared a snap for what anyone else thought of her as long as she was happy with herself, she raised her arm and draped it around Jacob's shoulder, then leaned her head against him. "Ah, Jacob, we aren't children anymore, are we? Isn't that incredibly sad?"

He turned adoring blue eyes on her for a moment, then quickly put some distance between them, his heart aching. "We could go back, Morgie. We don't have to go on. You don't need no London gentlemen to be looking at you, pawing over you. You know I—" He stopped, appalled at himself for almost saying the words. "That is…you shouldn't have to do anything makes you unhappy, Miss Morgan, so if you want to turn back to Becket Hall, I—"

"Oh, Jacob," Morgan said, hating herself for upsetting her friend, who only meant the best for her. But now, almost overnight, she was Miss Morgan, not his playmate, his cheerful nemesis, and the sudden transition was proving troublesome for both of them.

She would be a terrible person, indeed, to make the situation even more difficult. "Please stop apologizing, Jacob. I'm the one who's sorry. I'm horribly selfish, and I'm mean. What's worse is that I know I am, and I still behave so badly to people who certainly don't deserve such treatment. But, truth to tell, and only between us, I'm nervous, too. I don't want to disappoint everyone who believes I'm going to have such a brilliant Season."

Jacob's slow smile was Morgan's first warning that she'd almost talked herself into behaving. "Then you'll ride into London in the coach?"

She jammed her gloved fists against her hips and glared at him. "Jacob Whiting, when did you get so smart? What do you think you just did?"

"I *handled* you? Well, almost," Jacob said, his smile fading as he realized perhaps he'd been just a tad too proud of himself. "At least that's what Mr. Courtland called it. 'She seems heartless, but she wouldn't hurt a fly, not on purpose,' he told me, 'so just fold on under like a blanket on a bed, and she'll come around and stop her nonsense.'"

Morgan tried to raise a wave of anger, but found that, try as she would, humor was winning out. "I'll kill that stick of a brother of mine," she declared without heat, and then began to laugh. "Oh, Jacob, I don't know which of us is the worse. You for being so truthful, or me for being so bad. And here I am, going from worrying Papa and my meddling brothers to yet another meddling brother. Why do men think they are here to protect us fragile females? How I long to be in charge of my own life."

"There's many who'd say you already are," Jacob said, his smile wide as he felt that, just this once, he'd had the final word with her.

"Not really, Jacob, but I soon will be, I promise you that. Starting now. That ostler's taking forever. What do you say we saddle Berengaria together?"

Jacob shook his head. "No, Miss Morgan," he said, suddenly very serious. "I know my place, and you have to be learning to know yours. You just stand yourself there and be a lady while I go take care of Berengaria."

"Yes, Jacob," Morgan said with mocking obedience, lowering her head so that she could look up at him from beneath her dark lashes. "I'll be very good, I promise."

Jacob sniffed. "And I'll be very quick, because you won't be very good for very long."

Morgan watched him go, idly tapping the riding crop against her gloved hand, and wondered if perhaps it was time to stop teasing Jacob as if they were still children. He'd almost said something they would both regret forever. He didn't love her, not *really.* But he might think he did, and that would be too bad, because her affection for him was real, but quite different in nature. She could never be *in* love with Jacob. It was much too easy to control him.

Feeling rather ashamed of herself—yet unable to help rejoicing that she would get to ride Berengaria into London, which had been, after all, the point of the entire exercise—she turned on her heel and began to stroll around the yard of the country inn. Perhaps someone would see her in her lovely new riding habit and be impressed all hollow. She'd like that, and it would be a good omen perhaps, a hint of how she and her wonderful new wardrobe would be received in London society.

Except, she realized, frowning, she was very much alone, save for a man just now leading his mount into the yard. No, not leading the stallion, for the reins were loosely tied up on the saddle. The horse was *following* him like a faithful hound, not looking at all subservient, but more as if he accompanied the man only because it pleased him to do so.

Morgan laughed out loud at the sight, then concentrated her attention on the animal.

The stallion was magnificent. Beyond magnificent. Nearly white in the sunlight, its hindquarters dappled-gray, with a thick silvery mane that flowed to its shoulder, and a proud tail that nearly skimmed the ground.

Not a huge stallion, although the chest was fairly massive for its size, which had to be between fifteen and sixteen hands. Probably closer to fifteen. The ears were small and perfect, and when the horse turned toward her, as if aware she was admiring him, Morgan saw huge, intelligent eyes in a finely shaped head with a slightly convex nose.

Without a thought to convention—something she was definitely unaccustomed to considering at the best of times—Morgan set out across the yard, calling out to the man as she neared, "What a beauty!"

CHAPTER THREE

ETHAN TANNER LOOKED TO his right at the sound of the female voice, and was quick to agree. A definite beauty. He watched, caught between amusement and fascination, as the young woman advanced toward him, walking with the confident, long-legged stride of a man, except that she was most amazingly female.

Lush. Tall, but far from angular. The breeze whipping through the inn yard all but plastered her divided skirt against her long thighs with each step she took, clearly delineating them, and Ethan unexpectedly felt a familiar stirring.

He continued his inspection of this exotic beauty whose appearance was so at odds with the current fashion, which centered on petite, blue-eyed blondes.

Her nearly black hair was brushed sleekly back from her head, probably twisted into a knot at her nape. God, he hoped so, because a man should be able to see that dark silk tumbled over her bare breasts and back before he lowered her onto his bed. The green shako hat was set at a provocative tilt on her forehead, while a thick, sleekly curved lock of almost shoulder-length hair caressed the creamy ivory skin of her flawlessly beautiful face.

She came closer, and Ethan's inspection continued unchecked by any thought he might be staring like some starving fool with his nose pressed against the pastry shop windowpane.

Dark winglike brows over unusual gray, smoky eyes that seemed to hint at all the sensuous mysteries of the ages. High cheekbones that gave her a slightly exotic look. A wide, full mouth that lifted faintly at the corners.

Her riding habit was of the first stare, although it was doubtful any modiste had ever dreamed any of her creations could be so flattered, or look so circumspect and so wanton at one and the same time.

As a package, taken altogether, Ethan decided, this woman was Original Sin. And Adam had his full empathy.

He amazed himself at his almost embarrassingly poetical mental impression of the female, although he was not surprised to feel eminently attracted to her face and form. This female was fashioned to be alluring. This female who, he finally realized, was so blatantly ignoring him.

"Alejandro, you're being admired, you lucky bastard," he drawled quietly. "Bow to the lady."

Morgan, still fairly oblivious to anything save the magnificent horse, stopped short when the stallion turned toward her, then slowly, gracefully, bent his left knee to the ground as he extended his right leg and lowered his head.

"Oh, you brilliant, handsome boy!" Morgan walked straight up to the horse and placed her gloved hands on either side of its muzzle before planting a kiss between his ears. "What's his name?" she asked, looking adoringly at the stallion.

"Alejandro," Ethan answered. "And damn me if I don't find myself jealous of a horse. Here now, *up*, you toadeating sycophant."

Alejandro smoothly stood up once more, and swung his handsome head toward Ethan, showing his teeth in a horsey smile.

Morgan laughed in genuine delight, neither seriously considering the hinted flattery nor insulted by the swear word. After all, she knew who she was, how she looked, and she had grown up at Becket Hall, with brothers who rarely watched their words around her. "It's as if he understands you," she said.

"If so, he's got the advantage of me," Ethan said, his gaze still drinking in the sight of this gorgeous woman. This gorgeous, well-dressed, *unchaperoned* woman who didn't seem to entertain the slightest hesitation to speak with an unknown man.

"Is he Andalusian? I've seen a few drawings, but this is the first time I've ever—"

Morgan had at last drawn her attention away from Alejandro, to speak with his owner. Whatever she'd planned to say—had she planned to say anything?—became lost as she looked at him.

Simply looked at him. As if she'd never seen a male of the species until that moment.

His eyes attracted her first. Nearly straight brows, low over long, green eyes, with the whites accentuated by thick, dark lashes, those eyes seemed amused and unreadable at one and the same time, as if the laugh lines that fanned from the outside corners could be genuine, or were just a clever facade meant to keep anyone from looking any deeper.

His nose was magnificent. She'd never thought a nose could be described that way, but this one could be—so wonderfully straight, the nostrils slightly flared above a most…a most *intriguing* mouth. Even his ears seemed perfect, lying flat against his head and visible because his darkly blond hair had been ruthlessly combed straight back off his only slightly lined forehead to brush at the collar of his shirt.

His long, leanly muscled body was clad seemingly carelessly in that open-necked white shirt, a dark leather vest, fawn buckskins and high-topped riding boots.

Her brothers dressed much the same way at Becket Hall. But this was different. This was…this was dangerous. *Personally* dangerous.

And she was being silly! She wasn't intimidated by a man. Why would she be? Men were intimidated by *her.*

But not this one. He was the most *man* she'd ever seen.

A dangerous man. Definitely dangerous; a clear warning positively radiated from him. She could all but see it, an aura of deep red ringed with yellow surrounding him, which could be some trick of the sun but she was certain was not.

Years earlier, Odette had told her about such things, how certain creatures, human or beast, stood apart from others merely by being alive. Their power was stronger, for good or for evil, and a wise person who encountered one of these creatures recognized that and made subsequent choices, decisions, accordingly.

Odette had told her that Ainsley Becket was one of the dangerous ones. Odette had seen that in an instant and she had followed him, because to be with him was much preferred to being against him, as she had also sensed his good heart.

"But he's only Papa, he's not dangerous to me, not at all. What should I do, Odette?" Morgan remembered asking the voodoo woman. "If I ever see one of the dangerous ones, I mean? What should I do?"

Odette had laughed, that deep, rich laugh that came from somewhere deep inside her. "Child, you already know the answer. *You* are one of them, one of the dangerous ones. You do not pick the danger, it chooses you, and only a foolish woman would deny that truth. But, inquisitive child, to answer your question...the good Virgin only knows what would happen if you ever came up against one of your own kind, one with your own powerful will."

Morgan wondered what the good Virgin might be thinking if she chanced to be looking down from heaven at this moment.

She really should stop staring at him. But he was staring at her, and fair was only fair.

He waited, watching her look at him, enjoying the luxury of looking at her, then finally broke the silence. "You were about to say something?"

Morgan raised her chin slightly, refusing to be embarrassed that she had been staring, and instinctively went on the attack. "And who, sir, are you?"

"Me?" His grin was boyish, unaffected, carving long, slashing dimples into his lean, tanned cheeks—which made him seem even more dangerous than before.

"Why, I'm abashed," he drawled, slowly advancing toward her. "Bedazzled. Enchanted. And, for my sins," he added, bowing from the waist, while keeping his amused green gaze on her, "I am also Ethan Tanner, Earl of Aylesford, at your service and your every command, madam."

"Really," Morgan said, wishing her heart would show some sympathy and slow from its furious gallop. She'd already half expected him to be somebody important, as he was dressed well, if casually, and his horse was not the possession of a simple country squire.

As the stallion nuzzled her shoulder, she schooled herself to calmly raise one hand to stroke Alejandro's strong neck, never realizing how striking woman and animal looked together. "How wonderful for you."

Ethan tipped his head slightly to one side, looking at her quizzically. How wonderful for him? Harriette Wilson wouldn't be so bold, and she was a practiced courtesan. And damn Alejandro for the traitor he was.

Who did this luscious woman belong to? And how much would it cost him to take her away from any fool so stupid as to let her roam free? Half his fortune didn't seem too much to pay.

"Yes, thank you," Ethan said, "I am rather pleased my mother had the good sense to marry well. And, if I may be so bold, as no one else seems to be present to do the honors, may I ask your name, beautiful lady?"

Should he have called her a beautiful lady? Morgan doubted that he should. She more than doubted it, after enduring long hours of Eleanor's lessons on how one behaves in society. Still, he intrigued her, and she'd never backed either away or down from anything or anyone that intrigued her.

She'd play his game to see where it might take her, but she'd be damned if she'd curtsy. "I suppose turnabout is only fair. I am Morgan Becket, of Becket Hall. That's in Romney Marsh, so you probably won't have heard of us or it." And then, before she could bite her tongue, she added, "I'm on my way to London for the Season."

"Is that so?" Ethan said, hastily attempting to reshuffle his initial conclusion that she was a kept woman. "Unaccompanied, Miss Becket? How…very original."

Morgan blinked at this, at the earl's tone that suddenly seemed entirely too familiar, as if, in the blink of an eye, the game had turned serious. She suddenly wished the six outriders back. She looked toward the stables just in time to see Jacob leading Berengaria out into the yard.

Yes, there he was. Her remaining "accompaniment." And here she was, having disobeyed her papa's strict orders to stay as private as possible and for God's sake not cause any disasters between Becket Hall and Upper Brook Street. "I can rely on you to do this one thing," Ainsley Becket had asked her, "can't I?"

Obviously her papa had overestimated both her limits of obedience and Jacob's power to control her.

But if she was in a pickle now it was through her own fault, and she couldn't allow Jacob to become involved, try to defend her honor or any such nonsense. Not with a man like the earl, who could easily chew up Jacob and spit him out again before the younger man could count to three.

She quickly looked at the earl once more.

He was still smiling at her. As if he knew something she didn't know, and delighted in that fact.

Damn. This was no longer even in the least amusing. Now she truly understood why she was supposed to stay in the coach, or in her private dining room when they stopped for meals, and in her private bedchamber at the inn where she'd passed the single night they needed to be on the road.

Bringing a maid from Becket Hall had been out of the question, partly because Morgan didn't actually *have* a personal maid there, partly because no one at Becket Hall had the faintest idea of how to properly dress a lady's hair or such things…and mostly because the fewer tongues hanging about and liable to flap, the better.

Careful. Through years of practice, the Beckets had learned how to be careful. Too careful, Morgan had always believed, which was one reason she'd always tugged so hard on the reins. After all, the island had been so many years ago….

Yet now here she was, alone and seemingly unprotected, strutting about as if she had an army at her back, when Jacob was her only soldier—and with no reason for the earl to believe her better than it had to appear she was.

How different from Becket Hall, where everyone knew her and every last man there would stand in her defense against any danger. Why, if Jacko or any of the others had heard the earl's words, even seen the unnervingly familiar way he was now smiling at her, Ethan Tanner's life wouldn't be worth a bucket of warm spit.

But Jacko wasn't here. The outriders weren't here.

Nobody was here. And Morgan couldn't simply stand here and brazenly stare back at the earl while waiting for Jacob to do something that would probably get his nose broken. She had to talk her way out of the predicament she'd created.

"My maid has taken ill, my lord," she improvised quickly, "and therefore is on her way back to Becket Hall in the company of my outriders. I know my position to be precarious at the moment, except for the fact that my groom, Jacob, along with my coachman, would skewer anyone who dared to so much as look at me crookedly or take insulting notions into his head. You wouldn't be addlepated enough to do either of those things, would you, my lord?"

Ethan bowed again, amused by her sudden vehemence, and very much pleased that he would appear to be without competition. Miss Morgan Becket wasn't a kept woman, a high-flying concubine. She was simply badly managed by her keepers and more accustomed to free and easy country ways. In short, she was marvelously unencumbered, and his for the taking if he played his cards correctly.

Until she showed her face, and that body, in London society. After that, she would set her own style, and he could end up as one of many vying for her favor.

The devil he would! He'd noted the way she'd looked at him. He knew how he'd felt when he'd first caught sight of her, would not easily forget that figurative punch to the gut that had all but bowled him over. The attraction had been instant, and definitely mutual. Even Alejandro seemed to know, for God's sake. The horse also appeared to be smitten, which simply showed how a man could never quite trust other males when a beautiful female was added to the mix.

In fact, there was now only one new problem to supplant what he'd believed his previous problems. Miss Morgan Becket, if truly a hopeful debutante, was also most certainly a virgin. He'd always made it a point not to come within ten yards of a virgin.

Then again, in exceptional circumstances, exceptions could be made. In this case, the exceptional circumstance was that he felt reasonably sure he'd never want another woman until he'd first had this one beneath him.

Ethan searched for something to say, anything that couldn't be misconstrued.

"Far be it from me to reprimand you, Miss Becket, and you must be sad about the loss of your maid—but you should not be standing out here alone. People, some people, could not be faulted for thinking you less than you should be."

All right, she was standing on firmer ground here. She knew a veiled insult when she heard one, and was not the sort to pretend she hadn't. She much preferred to take the gloves off and lay them on the table—challenge him to either say what he meant outright, or shut up. "You wouldn't be one of those people, now would you, my lord? Or would you? Come, come, my lord. Have you been thinking me less than I should be?"

Ethan scratched at his temple, trying to hide his surprised smile with the gesture. "Polite ladies don't as a rule confront gentlemen, Miss Becket."

Morgan shrugged. Her heart was pounding hard again, but this time with excitement, delight, because she wasn't backing down, and doubted he would, either. "I've never been accused of being polite, or overworried about rules. Although I'm quite convinced you've often been accused of being quite rude."

"Guilty as charged, madam," he said, bowing to her.

Then he looked past her, to watch as a dainty, high-stepping black mare was led toward them, the groom holding the mount's bridle looking like a fellow caught between recognizing his betters and contemplating mayhem. And mayhem appeared to be winning.

Morgan, watching the earl's eyes, turned to see what had caught his attention, and nearly groaned aloud.

"We're less than two hours from London, my lord, and well into civilization," she pointed out quickly as she faced Ethan once more. As she spoke, she put one hand behind her back, waving Jacob away, while hoping her childhood friend wouldn't go making a cake of himself. "I will be safely under my brother's roof before dark.

"Not that my traveling plans are any of your concern, you grinning idiot," she added as she pointedly turned to say goodbye to Alejandro, stroke his mane, her temper beginning to rise past levels she knew to be controllable. But she had every reason to be angry. After all, *she* wasn't the one who was looking at *him* as if he were a particularly tasty plate of mutton chops, was she? Had she been?

Possibly, she realized.

"I've fetched Berengaria for you, Miss Morgan," Jacob said from behind her, his voice unnaturally deep, as if he wanted to sound menacing and, if he believed the ploy successful, deluding only himself. "I took the liberty to order the carriage horses ready, and told Saul to haul himself out of the common room and back up on the box, so we can be going now. Don't even have to wait so much as a minute, Miss Morgan."

Morgan didn't have to turn around to know that Jacob had his free hand resting lightly on the pistol tucked into his waistband, the romantic fool. They'd practiced shooting pistols together over the years, and Jacob still would have to consider himself lucky if he could hit the Channel if he was already standing knee-deep in the water.

"Yes, thank you, Jacob. If you'd please lead Berengaria over to that mounting block?"

Ethan had been enjoying himself, watching varying emotions pass across Miss Morgan Becket's expressive face, but now he was actually concerned. The chit was going to *ride* into London? And with that hot-headed halfling as her only protection? Not that he saw a second horse. No, the idiot thought he could guard her from his seat on the traveling carriage now being led out into the yard.

There was no more time for bantering, for relishing the situation. This was serious, and now that Ethan was in it, he knew he could not walk away. He didn't want to walk away.

"Forgive me, Miss Becket, but I'm afraid that I, as a gentleman, cannot countenance what you seem to be planning."

Morgan glared at him. "*You* cannot countenance?" And she'd thought the man handsome? Even intriguing? He was only any one of her tiresome brothers, looking at her as if she was being fractious on purpose.

Which, she knew, she usually was. And, over the years, she had become very, very accomplished at it. But that had nothing to do with the moment. She wanted to ride, and she would ride.

Before she could say anything else, Ethan stepped past her, leaving her to stew where she stood. "Jacob, is it? I am the Earl of Aylesford, although you may feel free to look upon me as your temporary savior. It is my understanding that Miss Becket's maid—chaperone—has been dispatched home, leaving her under your, I'm convinced, well-intentioned protection. Is that correct?"

Jacob was rapidly reconsidering his ability to beat this man into a jelly. An earl? What was he supposed to do with an earl? "Um…"

"Yes, I thought I'd concluded correctly," Ethan drawled as he took the lad's arm and led him out of earshot. "You may not be aware, Jacob," he continued quietly, "that such an arrangement is wholly unsuitable, or that I, as a good friend of Miss Becket's brother in London, would be remiss indeed, even criminally so, if I did not step in and rescue both you and Miss Becket from what is only to be termed an untenable situation. I'm sure you'll agree."

Jacob held up one finger as if to lend emphasis to whatever he planned to say in response, but he didn't say anything, as his brain had begun to cramp halfway through the earl's statement. He simply stared…not at the earl, but past him, to Morgan. He looked positively petrified, which he was, because Morgan was staring at him as if he should be counting the remainder of his life in minutes. "Um…"

Ethan leaned closer, deliberately placing himself between the nervous groom and his view of his glowering mistress. "Women can be so headstrong, can't they, Jacob? Leaving us men to either be brutes, or give in, hoping for the best. And, of course, then praying that the lady in question does not toss her reputation to the four winds with a single, unintentional mistake brought on by pure female bullheadedness. And all of it inevitably to end with some poor, well-intentioned fool forced to take the blame. In this case, my friend, that poor, well-intentioned fool taking the blame? Well, I'm very much afraid that would be you."

Jacob frowned in confusion. "You say you know Mr. Chance Becket. But it sounds like you know Miss Morgan, too."

Ah, a name. Jacob was proving quite helpful.

"We're men, Jacob, you and I," Ethan said, winking conspiratorially, purposely placing himself on the same side with the groom, the side that needed to find a way to make the contrary Miss Morgan Becket behave. "We all know women. We just don't understand them, which, rather happily, accounts for much of their charm. Now, you help Miss Becket mount, and then order the coachman to follow us to Tanner's Roost, where I will change into something more suited to town wear, and provide one of my maids to accompany Miss Becket to her brother. He still lives in—damn, I've quite forgotten his direction."

"Upper Brook Street, my lord. Just on the right, three doors off Park Lane and Hyde Park. That's what they told me. Told me his number, too, but I'm not so good with numbers. Three doors off Park Lane, on the right," Jacob repeated helpfully, already more relaxed.

Or at least he was, until Morgan Becket approached, her fists jammed on her hips.

"What do you two think you're doing?" she asked, not caring that the lordship was a lordship and the groom was her good friend. Not caring about anything save that she had been summarily dismissed by both of them. Even Alejandro had ambled off to a nearby water trough. "Jacob—I want to mount Berengaria."

Unspoken were the words, *And if you don't help me I'll do it myself, damn your eyes, you traitor.*

Ethan bowed to her. "I'll be more than happy to assist you, Miss Becket, while Jacob attends to other matters. Jacob and I, and we do apologize for keeping a lady standing out here in the sun, have just been debating how best to handle the logistics of the thing."

"What *thing?* There is no *thing,* my lord. And I don't care a fig about standing in the sun. Now go away."

Jacob made a short, strangled sound, handed Berengaria's reins to Ethan, then hastily trotted off, to climb up on the traveling carriage.

Morgan, sudden confusion mixing with her anger, watched him go. "What does he think he's doing?"

"He's behaving with good common sense," Ethan told her, taking her by the elbow and leading both her and the mare to the mounting block beside the stable yard fence. "Now come along. We're a good two miles from Tanner's Roost."

"Tanner's—what's that?" Morgan asked, digging in her heels. "What did you say to Jacob?"

"Nothing I should have liked to have said," Ethan told her, leading her forward once more, not terribly delighted in her reluctance, yet happy to know she wasn't featherwitted enough to easily go off with just anybody.

After all, she had only his word that he was an earl. He could be an out-and-out rotter. In fact, there were many among his wide acquaintance who might consider him so. "If he's the one who agreed to send your maid packing, I should have torn a strip off his hide, in fact."

"*You,* my lord, have no right to say or do anything where I am concerned."

"Oh, how wrong you are, Miss Becket. It would be my good friend Chance tearing a strip off my hide, if I were to wave you merrily on your way as you go riding off to be murdered—or worse."

Well, that stopped her. At last.

"You know Chance?"

The lies unrolled like silk from Ethan's tongue, even as he marveled that she had gone slightly pale at the mention of her brother's name, and not the broad hint of murder, or worse. "Yes, of course. I didn't make the connection at first. Becket. Chance Becket. Resides in Upper Brook Street, only a few steps from the Park. Good man."

"Oh." Morgan considered this as she accepted his assistance when she put her foot on the mounting block. "All right. You know my brother, so I suppose I should be gracious if I don't want to have him bring his wrath down on me, which would be stultifyingly boring, to tell you the truth. Now, what about this Tanner's Roost? It sounds like a thieves' den."

Ethan smiled as he watched Morgan mount the mare. "An interesting observation, Miss Becket, and so eminently *gracious.* I must remember that, next time my mother tells me how much she admires the name."

CHAPTER FOUR

THEY HADN'T GONE a half mile before the thrill of being on Berengaria's back, even on a sidesaddle, had faded enough for Morgan to wonder what on earth was wrong with her.

What had caused her to so easily agree to ride off willy-nilly with this man she did not know, to go to a place she did not know, to do—well, nothing was going to happen. The man was an earl, for pity's sake.

Or at least he had said so, then had convinced Jacob to trust him. Which wasn't much of an endorsement, for Jacob trusted her, too.

At least they were still on the main road, or what she believed to be the main road.

When she got straight down to it, she didn't know much of anything. Except that Chance was probably going to ring a peal over her head that her papa would hear all the way back in Romney Marsh.

No longer able to enjoy her view of the countryside or the fresh, sweet smell of the country air, Morgan slid her gaze toward the earl—if he really was an earl.

He sat Alejandro as if born to the saddle, controlling the stallion simply by being in that saddle, moving effortlessly, as if the two had become one, man and horse looking so stunningly complete together.

Morgan felt heat running into her cheeks as another thought struck her. Alejandro and Berengaria also looked good together, the bright and the dark.

But not as good as she and Ethan Tanner would fit together. Her dark to his light. He, so very English. She, so very Spanish, at least the parts of her she'd taken from her mother. Her true father could have been English, for her skin was lighter than Spencer's, at least. But her sire could also have been Austrian, or Russian, or any one of the mongrels that had relieved himself of his seed inside her two-penny-a-poke mother.

No. She wouldn't think of that. She was Morgan Becket, of Becket Hall. Ainsley Becket was her father. She was who she believed herself to be, and now that she was grown she would become what she wanted to become. A person in her own right, free of the past.

And what did any of this matter now? She had to keep her concentration on the moment, and this moment seemed terribly important.

"How do I know you're really the earl of wherever you said you're the earl of?" she heard herself ask, her lips moving before her brain could even hope to catch up, let alone shove a gag in her mouth.

Ethan, who had been amusing himself imagining Morgan Becket's reaction to meeting his mother—he could learn a lot about her when he saw that reaction—found her question highly amusing.

"You doubt me, Miss Becket?" he asked as he looked over at her, one eyebrow raised speculatively. "Are you saying that I don't have the presence, that ineffable air, of a peer of the realm? And that's Aylesford, by the by. Aylesford's not much in the great scheme of things, I'll grant you, but we're rather proud of it nonetheless."

"I'm sure you are," Morgan said, knowing he meant his words as a bit of a setdown, even a reprimand, and then ignoring that fact as unimportant to the moment. "So, *my lord,* you were simply out riding?"

"And then stopping for a cold mug and a slice of ham, yes. Which reminds me, I'm hungry. I believe you've made me miss a meal, Miss Becket."

"How terrible for you. I seem to have been nothing but trouble to you, my lord. Perhaps we should simply part ways now?"

Ethan smiled, finally understanding her problem. "You're afraid of me, Miss Becket? How wrong of you. And, although it's unconscionably rude to point this out, how very *tardy* of you. You should have run screaming from me some time ago. It's miles too late now to think about your possibly precarious position."

Morgan laughed, in real delight. "Whose precarious position, my lord? I am quite safe. It's you who should be concerned. Out here, alone with my protectors."

Ethan laughed along with her, happy to see that she was far from missish and wasn't going to suddenly go all hysterical on him. "You mean that unwashed cub up behind us on your coach?"

"No, not Jacob. You have him thoroughly cowed, and you're even proud of your achievement, which you shouldn't be, because Jacob could be cowed by an angry ladybug. I meant one of my papa's most trusted men for more years than I'm alive. Saul."

Ethan frowned, trying to remember who Saul might be, and then smiled as he recalled a gray-haired hulk of a man who had climbed up into the box with some difficulty, as he carried the weight of too many large dinners with him. "Your coachman? You consider *him* your protector?"

"Indeed, yes," Morgan said, barely able to keep from bouncing in the saddle, because she was about to take that smug, satisfied smile off his lordship's handsome face. My, how she loved to win! She really ought to consider scraping up some maidenly modesty from somewhere, now that she was to be a debutante. But how boring that would be....

She turned on the saddle, calling back to the coach, which was no more than twenty yards behind them, as Jacob knew to keep close. "Saul! His lordship would very much like to see Bessie."

"Bessie?" Ethan also turned in his saddle, looking back over his shoulder, toward the coachman. "What's a—my God."

Saul, still with the reins wrapped around his beefy hands, had reached down into the depths of the box, to come up with Bessie—a short, lethal-looking cross-bow, loaded and ready to loose an equally short, lethal-looking arrow straight into Ethan's back.

"Thank—thank you, Saul!" he called out, waving to the man. "Bessie's...quite beautiful. Truly impressive."

Saul, his expression still fierce, lowered the weapon. Ethan couldn't hold back the relieved sigh that escaped his lips as he looked at Morgan, although he was fairly certain he'd have an itch directly between his shoulder blades until they'd arrived at Tanner's Roost.

"Do you have any idea how *far* one of those arrows can travel?" she asked him, her glee so clear Ethan wondered briefly if Adam hadn't possibly had second and third thoughts before he took that apple. "I've seen Saul put one neatly through a—"

"Yes, I'm sure you have," Ethan said quickly, then attempted to turn the conversation to something she'd said earlier, something that interested him very much. "Where did you say Becket Hall is located, Miss Becket?"

"Romney Marsh, directly on the Channel. Only a few dozen miles from Maidstone as the gull flies, as they say. Or an entire world away from here or anywhere else, as others say."

"I've been to Camber, if we can really consider that a part of the marsh," Ethan said, struggling with himself to not take another peek over his shoulder, to see if Saul seemed happy, pleased with his place in the world, and not liable to want to shoot anything at the moment. "That was a few years ago, for an uncle's interment. I don't know which was more depressing, the young widow trying to corner me in the morning room, or the cold, gray weather. And it was July, I believe."

"I've never been to Camber," Morgan said, ignoring the rest of what the earl had said, considering it wiser to ignore most anything he uttered, as a matter of fact. She'd much rather look at him than listen to him, because what he said was often nonsense or provocative, or both, but looking at him could become a lifelong obsession.

"Ah, but now you'll be able to say you've been to Tanner's Roost, just as one day, perhaps, I will be able to say I've visited Romney Marsh and even Becket Hall," Ethan said, indicating that she should turn her mount to the right, head between two huge stone pillars and onto a smaller roadway that was, all in all, in much better condition than the main highway.

He didn't realize he had been worried that she'd balk at the last minute until he felt his shoulders relax when she turned her mount onto the drive.

Saul followed, but even Saul and his crossbow didn't serve to contain all of the butterflies now fluttering inside Morgan's belly as they proceeded along the twisting lane cut through the trees, the branches overhead so dense they nearly blocked out the sunlight.

Romney Marsh was open. A person could see for miles and miles; a person could *breathe* there. Most importantly, strangers approaching Becket Hall from either land or sea would be noticed—and prepared for—a good quarter hour before they arrived.

"Are you certain your house is in here somewhere?" she asked, trying to sound faintly amused, when all she could think was that a person could ride into these woods, never to be seen again. Not only that, but Tanner's Roost would be almost impossible to defend. Didn't that bother the earl? Or perhaps only those who knew they needed protection ever considered such subjects.

"As this is my property we're riding through now, I'm fairly certain the Roost is still here, as it was here at breakfast time, which seems so long ago now, Miss Becket, thanks to you," Ethan answered lazily, knowing he could barely wait to see her reaction to his family home.

Morgan blinked. "What sort of a man blames a

female for his empty belly? Oh, never mind, you all do, don't you, just as if feeding you is our purpose in life. And you're saying that this is all yours?"

"Again, with gratitude to my mother, for marrying so well. You'll be meeting her, you know, when we get to the Roost, which you should be able to see just as we get past this final curve in the drive."

"Uninvited guests aren't welcome at Becket Hall," Morgan said, beginning to worry about his lordship's mother, and the reception she'd get when she was introduced to the lady she'd call…*what* did one call the mother of an earl? She knew the answer, had been well drilled by Eleanor in all the titles, but her mind had gone suddenly, frighteningly blank.

If her sister were here now, she'd probably not even say, "I *did* warn you." Because Elly was a good person, with a good heart. Morgan knew she should strive to be more like her. She also knew she'd have the same luck with that as she would in an attempt to fly up to the moon.

"My mother feels quite the opposite when it comes to visitors." Ethan ran his gaze over Morgan's gracefully erect upper body. Would he be doomed to hell for wishing his mother away from Tanner's Roost, so he could be alone with this intriguing woman? Probably. "She's always happy to welcome guests, and there are usually several of them wandering about the hallways."

Morgan shook off her worrisome thoughts and concentrated on the earl once more, feeling that paying him any less than her full attention could end with her deep in trouble. "And now there's one more, although I won't be staying above an hour, unless you are an inordinately slow dresser, as I've heard that society gentlemen can spend several hours just in tying their neck cloths."

"Gentlemen don't arrange their own neck cloths, Miss Becket, any more than they would take the pressing iron to them. We pride ourselves in being exceedingly and unremittingly useless. I know I do."

And then, as Morgan struggled for an answer to such a damning admission delivered so joyfully, they were out from under the nearly quarter-mile canopy of trees and into the sunlight once more. An enormous expanse of lawn appeared, with a castle sitting on a gentle rise of earth smack-dab in the center of it.

Morgan was instantly diverted by the sight. "A castle. It's an actual castle! All those turrets, and all with flags flying from them. How…how *extraordinary!*"

Ethan grinned, even as he had planned to remain expressionless, no matter what her reaction. "I ordered the moat filled in with dirt soon after I came into the title, which has cut down some on the damp but, yes, Miss Becket, a *real* castle. I take it you're impressed? I'd been wondering about your reaction. Now, if you'll please walk your mount in while I rush off to alert my mother? She enjoys guests, but hates being caught unawares. I'll alert one of the staff, and he'll arrange care of the horses and escort you to the drawing room."

Before Morgan could answer, Ethan was gone, and she was dealing with Berengaria, who wanted to follow. Morgan pulled on the reins as her black mare danced in a full circle, then watched as Ethan and the magnificent Alejandro abandoned the drive, to ride across the freshly scythed acres of lawn toward the castle.

The sight had her breath catching in her throat. The snowy horse, its mane and tail caught by the breeze, its hooves throwing up green-and-black clumps of earth. The rider, the full sleeves of his white shirt billowing in that same breeze. Both outlined so clearly, first against the lush green of the grass, then against the dark, cold gray stone of the castle.

And she'd been wondering why she'd so blithely followed this man? How could she be, when the answers were so obvious?

Morgan hadn't even noticed that Saul had brought the traveling coach up beside her until she heard Jacob say, "It's like the drawings in the books in Mr. Ainsley's library, isn't it, Morgie. A fairy castle. Not even real. Morgie? You hear me?"

Morgan swallowed with some difficulty, then nodded, not trusting her voice. Lightly tapping her heel against Berengaria's flank, she moved forward. She followed the path set by the earl, allowing Berengaria her head, just a little, so that they approached the castle at a maidenly, if eager trot. Her mount's shod hooves made sharp, echoing contact with the thick planks of the lowered drawbridge that spanned the now wildflower-and-grass-clogged moat, and Morgan delighted in the sound.

Once she was inside the castle walls, a young boy wearing scarlet livery and a powdered wig approached, and reached for the mare's bridle. "Afternoon, miss. His lordship says you're to be taken straightaways to the drawing room, if that's all right, miss."

"Yes, thank you." Morgan raised her leg slightly,

lifting it out of the sidesaddle, then leaped gracefully to the cobblestones of the large courtyard, not even considering that she should wait for assistance, let alone that anyone would think she needed it.

As Berengaria was led away, Morgan turned in a slow circle, attempting to drink in her surroundings. She wasn't an expert on medieval architecture, and had never wished to be, but this castle seemed awfully… *young.*

Castles, Morgan felt sure, should look ancient, and weathered. With moss perhaps, and definitely with ivy. And there should be more castle, too. Things like keeps and bailiwicks, whatever they were. And an array of stone outbuildings. This was just a huge stone box topped with fanciful turrets on all four corners, and with a sort of half house, half castle stuck inside.

New, if stones could look new.

A very large toy. A plaything. A child's fantasy. As Jacob had said, a fairy castle…

"This way, miss," the footman prompted her.

Morgan looked behind her, to be sure Jacob and Saul and the coach were on their way across the drawbridge, then followed the servant beyond the flagstone courtyard and up a few wide steps, into the castle.

The stone hallway was huge, and seemed to go up and up forever, until it disappeared into darkness. Morgan had a moment of silliness, wondering if there was an echo in the hall, and what the footman would do if she cupped her hands around her mouth and yelled "Bally-hoo!"

"This way now, miss."

Biting her lips to hold back a giggle, she had only a

few moments to take in the huge wooden tables and straight-back chairs that lined the hall, barely enough time to gawk at the dozen or so suits of armor, and no time at all to wonder if a retreat wouldn't be prudent, before following the servant.

And it only got worse…or better, if she had set out on a hunt for the ridiculous. The drawing room had stone walls, and window embrasures that had to be four feet deep. The walls were hung with huge tapestries, and when she sat down, the furnishings, completely wooden, proved as uncomfortable as they were ugly.

Morgan shivered, the riding habit that had been just perfect for the day suddenly feeling thin and inadequate, because the castle interior seemed to have its own weather, a very different temperature from the outside. With no sun to warm her, she looked longingly at the huge stone fireplace that was, alas, without a fire.

The man lived like this? He forced his mother to live like this?

"I've blundered into a madhouse," Morgan whispered to herself. "And no one in my family will be the least surprised."

She then picked up her gloves and riding crop, deciding a hasty escape would be the only way to maintain her own sanity. She was halfway to her feet when the earl entered the room, stopping not six feet inside the doorway.

Ethan lifted a finger to his lips for a moment, warning Morgan to silence, then smartly turned to face the doorway.

This was the moment. Morgan Becket would either

delight in his mother, or run screaming from her. You could tell a lot about a woman from the way she reacted to a man's mother. Especially *his* mother.

Another liveried servant, this one older, thinner and terribly bent, entered the huge chamber, loudly tapped the floor with the long staff he carried, and announced in a rusty voice, "Hear ye, hear ye, presenting her ladyship, Druscilla, Dowager Countess of Aylesford!"

Ethan executed a rather elegant bow, and held it, then turned his head toward Morgan. He gifted her with a smile and a wink before turning his attention back to the doorway, which she then did as well…just in time to see the dowager countess make her appearance.

"God's teeth," Morgan whispered under her breath as she blinked, blinked again, and then hurriedly dropped into a curtsy.

She hadn't run, screaming, from the room. Ethan grinned. So far, so good.

The woman who'd swept into the large room had once been very beautiful, and still was, in a faintly faded sort of way. Her son very much resembled her, as far as it went, and it didn't go far, because the dowager countess seemed to have come from another time, one long since passed.

She was dressed in a sort of costume, her crimson brocade gown finished with huge, puffed velvet sleeves slashed through with ivory silk. A matching brocade beret covered most of her pale blond hair, and there was a huge emerald-and-diamond pin in the shape of a dragon attached to the very front of the thing. Her neckline was clogged with what could be a dozen different necklaces, and she had a heavy gold chain around her waist, from which hung a two-foot-long painted stick that ended in a clutch of red-tipped ostrich feathers.

She looked wonderful. She looked ridiculous. And when she winked at Morgan, just as her son had done, she seemed very aware of how bizarre she must appear.

"Welcome to Tanner's Roost, my dear," the dowager countess trilled. "How wonderful to have a fresh victim!"

Morgan looked to Ethan, who merely shook his head and scolded his mother. "*Maman,* don't scare the girl off now that I've just found her."

"Oh, stuff and nonsense, Ethan. Look at that chin, that proud carriage. This one doesn't frighten easily—do you, dear? Now go away and clean up your dirt, if you really plan to desert your poor mother and ride to London, and Miss Becket and I will have a little natter. Won't we, Morgan—I will call you Morgan, because it's such a lovely name. Except perhaps for Morgan Le Fay, or whatever that harridan's name was. Ethan? You're still standing there. Shoo!"

"He looks like any guilty son, doesn't he?" Morgan commented as Ethan quit the room, enjoying herself again. She should have agreed to leave Becket Hall sooner, and would have, if she'd known being out and about in the world could be so very amusing. Then, waiting until the dowager countess had seated herself before sitting down beside her, she added, "Now, what is this about a new victim, my lady?"

"Druscilla, my dear. Just call me Druscilla. Everybody does. I do hope you'll have time to meet some of my friends, although I doubt that, as Ethan warned me that you are pressed for time if you are to beat dusk to London. We're practicing for tomorrow night's performance—my guests and myself, that is. Not that you'll be missing a marvelous treat by not lingering here to watch us. Poor Algernon makes for a very timid Henry, I'm afraid. Shall I tell you a secret? If Algernon had really been the king, he would have sent Anne Boleyn off to her chambers with no more than a mild scold and cold porridge for her dinner."

The earl's mother lifted the painted stick, pushed on a small button near the base, and the lush feathers opened into a fan, which she then began waving under her chin.

"Warm in here, isn't it? I don't know how the ladies of old Henry's court stood it, I really don't. All this heavy velvet? And you'd positively *weep* if you saw the ridiculous underpinnings those poor creatures were forced to endure, although I was thoroughly shocked when I realized what they *didn't* wear. Perhaps a welcome breeze up under their skirts cooled them somewhat. In any case, it must have come as at least a little something of a relief when Henry chopped off their heads—took a bit of the weight off their shoulders, as it were."

Morgan wasn't used to being at a loss for words, but found she had nothing to say to her ladyship's statements. So she merely smiled, fairly convinced that this strange woman was the sort who could hold conversations all by herself, if the other person just smiled or nodded in the right places.

And she was right, for Druscilla was off once more,

barely taking a breath before saying, "You're probably wondering if I'm a wee bit batty. Or prodigiously batty, and I suppose some would say I am. But I'm happy, and Ethan indulges me just as his dear father did before him. Neither of them cared a scrap about the scandal, which is just as well, because what is done is done, and can't be undone. Oh, the marriage, yes, that could have been undone. God knows George's family tried, insisting their poor boy had lost the reins on his brains. But not Ethan. Difficult to undo Ethan, don't you think? And he makes a splendid earl, even if society still pretends to be all aghast about his dreadfully inappropriate mother."

This time Morgan nodded, schooling her expression to one of mingled sympathy and disgust. Or at least she hoped so. Mostly, she wanted the woman to keep talking.

"It was a love match, you understand. George and me. We took one look at each other and that was that, and me only fifteen to his eight and thirty. We cared not a snap what the world would think. Well, George didn't. I had no idea the fuss it would make, as George had somehow neglected to tell me he was, at the time, a viscount. And his title wasn't really important, then or now, because we loved each other dreadfully. So we built our castle, and put up our walls, and never bothered about anyone. It's been five years that he's gone, and I still miss him so."

The bright light in Drusilla's eyes faded as she shrugged, sighed. "Well, enough of that. My only regret is that Ethan seems always to pay the price for his parents' happiness. It can't be comfortable being the son of a soft-headed fool and a common strumpet. But, still, the ton accepts him, if only on sufferance. Ethan says that's because of the title and all the money, but I think it's because he's so pretty. What do you think?"

"I…uh…" Morgan hadn't counted on being asked a question, so she quickly, and none too tactfully, responded by asking one of her own. "You weren't really a strumpet, were you?"

Druscilla patted Morgan's hand. "No, dear, but I certainly wasn't acceptable, either." She leaned closer. "You see, I was a *performer.*"

"An actress?" Morgan asked, rather excited to hear such a romantic story, certainly a happier story than that of her own parentage. Although, if London society looked at Ethan askance, what on earth would they do if anyone ever learned about her beginnings?

"Not then, no," Druscilla said. "I had aspirations, yes, but I was still young, and was forced into company with a band of jugglers and magicians and miracle-sellers and their ilk. Would you like me to read your palm? I can, you know. Not correctly, but definitely convincingly. I would have done much better if I'd looked like you. I'm much too pale, too watery. You've the look, the fire, of a real gypsy. I had to wear a huge black wig, and it itched horribly, almost as badly as this horrid gown. Next year, and so I told my friends, we'll perform a more *modern* play."

"*Maman?* Have you quite talked Miss Becket's ear off in my absence?"

Morgan watched as the earl reentered the room, looking every inch the London gentleman, and refused to acknowledge the small skip her heart gave at the sight of him. She could still see the raw power in him, but that power had been somehow leashed with the addition of finely cut clothing. It was the sure knowledge that the leash could be easily snapped that intrigued her. Almost challenged her, as if he had somehow flung a glove at her feet, daring her to try.

And all he'd done was walk into the room, smile at her.

Imagine what would happen if he ever touched her....

"Of course I did, Ethan, just as you knew I would. All our ancient scandal revealed. Why else would you have all but dragged me away from our rehearsal?"

"Yes, of course, *Maman.* Forgive me." It was true he had counted on his gregarious mother to run her tongue on wheels, say everything that needed to be said. But did she also have to say, within Morgan's hearing, that he had wanted her to do precisely that? No head for intrigue, his mother, much as he loved her.

The dowager countess turned her back on Ethan and took Morgan's hands in her own, squeezed them. "He'd much rather, you see, have me tell the story, and not have you hear any nastiness about his mother from some muckraking dragon in London. At least, this way you know you've heard the right of it and can make up your own mind."

She leaned close, whispered, "He's a very sensitive soul, my dear, sweet Ethan is."

"Oh, ma'am, I think you may worry yourself too much on that head. I may have only just met him, but I already believe your son more than capable of taking care of himself," Morgan whispered back to her, smiling.

"Placed in uncaring hands, my dear, anyone's heart

can be broken." Druscilla squeezed Morgan's hands one more time, and got to her feet. "And now, if you don't mind, Algernon is waiting, probably sharpening his ax down to a nub. Do come see me again, Morgan, as I'm sure you will, as Ethan has never before brought a young lady here. You must be very special."

"Umm, thank you...Druscilla." Morgan dropped into another curtsy, then watched as Ethan first bowed over his mother's hand, then leaned in to kiss her on both cheeks, his mother holding him close as she whispered something in his ear.

He laughed, kissed her again and then watched her go before turning to Morgan. "My mother reminded me that I should ask if you wish to freshen up before we continue our journey."

"Really," Morgan said, tipping her head to one side as she considered this. "I doubt she was reticent to suggest such a thing to me directly, and had to beg you to ask the question. What did she actually say?"

Ethan stepped closer. Morgan was as beautiful as he'd remembered while he'd harried his valet into rushing through the quick change of clothes, then set the man to having his entire wardrobe moved to town by morning. Ethan had half hoped he'd had too much sun, and his reaction had been temporary...but this woman only improved on second sight, and his interest only deepened.

But that didn't mean he'd tell her that his mother had suggested he should waste no time in having Morgan for his own as "you two would give me splendidly beautiful grandchildren. And she didn't turn tail and run from this silly pile or your strange mama, Ethan. The girl's got bottom!"

No, he wouldn't tell her any of that. "Nothing important," he said, offering his arm and leading her back into the cavernous foyer. "So. Did my mother produce a deck of cards from that fantastical costume and ask you to pick one, any card at all?"

"To tell my fortune, you mean? No, she didn't."

"No, not to foretell your future, although I'm sure she wished to. I was referring to her showing you one of her card tricks. She's quite good with sleight-of-hand, but we've already seen all her best tricks a thousand times. It's why she was so glad to see a new victim, as she calls anyone who has yet to watch her perform."

Morgan withdrew her hand from his arm, pushing ahead of him through the doorway once the footman had opened the door for them. "Now you're making fun of her. Your own mother. That's despicable. I found her to be very nice...extremely interesting. People shouldn't all be alike, or just what we expect. It's our differences that make us so intriguing."

Ethan relaxed, not realizing he'd been holding himself so tightly. She'd passed his impromptu test, more than passed it—she'd actually defended his mother to him. "Oddly enough, I believe you. Now, ask me your questions."

"I have no—oh, all right." Morgan stood in the courtyard and gave an all-encompassing sweep of her arm. "All...all *this*. Why?"

"Fair enough question, I suppose. Because my mother told my father that she'd always wanted to be swept up by a prince and taken to his castle. He wasn't a prince, but he could build her a castle, so he did, although some might quarrel with the way it turned out—me, for one, because it's wickedly drafty. I've set about correcting that, but the work is a slow process, I'm afraid. I'm drawing up plans for a second house on the estate, quite on the other side of the park. Brick, not stone, in case you might wonder. And there will be no moat. Tanner's Roost will become the dowager's residence."

"Because your mother adores her castle."

"Very much so, yes. Unfortunately, Tanner's Roost also has become one of the many reasons anyone in London will be more than happy to tell you that the late Earl of Aylesford was a lunatic who eloped with a common piece who'd worked her dark magic on him. Right before they warn you away from the couple's sure-to-be unstable progeny."

Morgan thought about all of this for a moment, then said, "And you wanted me to know all of this. You brought me here especially to hear it, to see everything, to be introduced to your mother, and to have her tell me the story. You didn't have to do that. You're Chance's friend. If he's accepted you, nothing anyone else could say would mean anything to me. Besides, I make up my own mind."

Ethan looked toward the pair of grooms leading Alejandro and Berengaria toward them, composing his thoughts. "Ah, yes, your brother. Chance. Would it bother you overmuch if I told you I've never met the gentleman, never had the pleasure?"

Morgan turned on him, her glorious gray eyes opened wide. "You *lied?*"

He grinned at her. God, she was gorgeous. Fiery. "Blatantly, yes."

"But…but you said Upper Brook Street. I heard you. Only a few steps off Park Lane."

"Your groom is quite gullible, and inordinately helpful. I'd slice out his tongue, were I you, if you have any secrets you don't want told."

Morgan shot a glance toward Jacob, a small smile beginning to play about her lips. She'd been fooled, tricked. Lied to. And she didn't care. "I have considered that, from time to time." Then she turned back to Ethan. "It isn't just what people may think, what they might say. You really are reprehensible, aren't you? You may even enjoy what must be your terrible reputation."

"Oh, there's no *may* about it, Morgan," Ethan said, cupping his entwined hands so that she could use them as a mounting post as he all but threw her up onto the sidesaddle.

Morgan looked down at him from atop Berengaria, who had begun to dance in place, eager to be on her way once more. "Please be certain to behave yourself when you deliver me to my brother, *Ethan,* because I believe you and I could become very good friends over the coming weeks."

He bowed to her in agreement, then swung gracefully onto Alejandro's back. "There are many things in this world and out of it, Morgan, many questions to which I don't know the answers. But there is one thing I do know, and that is this—you and I are destined to be *very* good friends. We'd both have it no other way, and I will greatly enjoy introducing your unique self to the ton. Shall we ride, take our first steps in shocking the good citizens of Mayfair?"

Morgan, being who she was, knowing who she was, didn't bother to dissemble, and certainly did not even consider acting coy or missish. Odette hadn't given her any suggestions on how to handle a dangerous man like Ethan Tanner, but Morgan had already made up her mind. She would be straightforward, would never back down, and she'd challenge him to be the same.

"You can't wait to stand London on its ear, can you? But what makes you think I should be such a willing partner to what is most probably your ongoing assault on the ton?"

"You were about to ride into London, unescorted, straight into Mayfair. And, if I may be so bold—and I'm always bold—if I ever saw a young woman ripe for mischief, it's you. I imagine there's little you'd shy from, Miss Becket."

"My father, as I understand it, has already sent my brother his condolences as he attempts to steer me through the Season, if that's what you mean. But all I wanted to do was make clear, from the outset, that Chance might be my host for the Season, but he will *not* be my keeper. And it's Morgan. I'm Morgan, remember? And you're Ethan."

"With each other, Morgan, yes, we are, but not in public. Then we would be wise to play by some of the rules, even as we bend or break many more of them. I will address you as Miss Becket, and you can simply call me Aylesford. Agreed?"

"So your mother isn't the only one who enjoys play-acting," Morgan said. "Very well. I suppose I've played my own share of games."

"Meaning?"

"Meaning you may have made a point to have your

mother explain at least something of you to me, but I'm convinced she doesn't know the half of it. Oh, and that, much as you may have hoped I might, I'm not returning the favor by confessing my own possible shortcomings, either in part or in whole. After all, *Aylesford,* I barely know you and, from what you have said, I have to think you at least slightly scandalous in your own right."

"Only slightly?" Ethan's full-throated laugh shooed several birds from the canopy of trees above them. Moments later, the two riders turned onto the main roadway once more, already a good fifty yards ahead of Jacob and the coach.

"Jacob will be having fits if we get much farther ahead of him," Morgan said, looking back at the vehicle.

"Really? How very unfortunate for Jacob. It's a straight run from here to Birling, and with little traffic to get in our way. Shall we?"

Morgan and Berengaria were a full three lengths ahead of Ethan and Alejandro before he'd finished speaking....

CHAPTER FIVE

"I, AS A GENTLEMAN, hesitate to point this out, but I believe you might be sulking, Morgan," Ethan said as they rode side by side through the streets of London. The loud, crowded, definitely not perfumed streets of London.

He'd tried, not successfully, to convince her to return to the coach for this last short leg of their journey, to sit with the maid he'd stationed in the coach—amazing himself with his concern for her reputation—but when Morgan had refused, he'd decided that the best education often comes from lessons learned by one's own experience.

He'd been amused by her obvious delight when they'd first approached London and she eagerly pointed out steeples and tall buildings she recognized from books in her father's study. Her eyes had shone, and she'd been as excited as any child. But she'd grown more and more silent, withdrawn, as they'd moved into the metropolis.

"I'm fully aware that I'm sulking, thank you," Morgan retorted, longing to lift a handkerchief to her nose, for the smell these last ten minutes or so had gone from annoying to faintly sickening, to perfectly vile.

She wasn't eager to separate the odor into all its contributing smells, but she could tell that they were near the Thames, near the docks. And town docks were docks, here or in the islands.

All Morgan knew was their own small, isolated island, their safe paradise that, to her, was only a vague memory of sand, and heat, and clear, blue-green water. Of laughter, of freedom. And from the time they'd left the island, she'd never traveled more than five miles from Becket Hall.

This street, this place, was so alien to her. Had she been born into squalor like this? If her papa hadn't bought her the very day she'd been born, and taken her to the island, would she still be living in a sorry, desperate place such as this? Would she even be alive now, to wonder?

For the first time, Morgan thought about her mother as anything more than the uncaring whore who had given her life. Maybe she hadn't wanted to sell her child. Maybe she had seen the purchaser as the only way out for her daughter, the only chance she could give her.

What if her mother hadn't sold her, had instead kept her? Would Morgan have fought, or would she eventually have made her own living on her back? How strong does a person have to be, to fight such poverty, such squalor, such hopelessness? How long does someone struggle before she gives up and simply lies down?

Morgan would like to think she would have been strong enough, even angry enough, to have found a way out. But she also knew she could never really know that, never know what choices that child would have made. If there even were choices for women in places like this.

Without knowing anything about her, Morgan knew she had judged her mother, and damned her. This new knowledge wasn't easy to swallow.

"How can people live like this?" Morgan demanded of Ethan, as uncertainty was alien to her, and she much preferred the familiarity of anger, of attack. "And why would they want to? Crowded together, living in the midst of their own filth? And these houses? They're all falling down. Surely they don't choose to live this way."

Ah, yes, he was an evil man. There were many ways to enter London, make their way to Mayfair, and when Morgan had declined riding inside the coach yet again, Ethan purposely had chosen one of the least palatable routes. She would be uncomfortable, but she would be safe. He was with her, after all, and his reputation rode with him, even in this god-awful section of the city.

Besides, although he knew himself to be reckless, he wasn't so full of himself he thought he was above being attacked simply because his face and reputation were known here. There was also the trio of heavily armed outriders he'd brought along to make up their small procession. And Saul. And Bessie.

But Ethan had meant only to shock Morgan back into the coach with the smells, the dirt, the squalid surroundings. Instead, she seemed angry. Angry and profoundly sad. There were depths to this woman, something he hadn't considered when he'd looked at, immediately desired, her.

In his own defense, he knew he had never looked very deeply at any of his women.

Ethan felt the sting of the mental slap that thought provoked: *And you're proud of that?*

He'd try again, pretending he'd noticed Morgan's distaste, but had failed to sense her distress. "Perhaps you'd like to reconsider riding in the coach? We've still some minutes to go before we reach Upper Brook Street, and I'm certain your brother would be happier to see you arrive…how should I say this? Oh, yes, I know. In the manner of a young lady."

Morgan shot him a chilling glance, eager to be angry with someone other than herself. "I'll say this for you, Ethan, you don't give up easily. But neither do I. Could you have picked a worse route? Or do you really labor under the misconception that I don't know what you're trying to do?"

"I had thought of another street even worse than this one, then decided this was bad enough," he said, grinning at her. "But, now that you've seen through my plan, let's say we desert this area for a wider street. One where we won't have to worry about the slops being flung out the upper storys of these fine establishments and down onto our heads."

"Thank you," Morgan said, maneuvering Berengaria past an overturned apple cart and the two angry men screaming at each other, blaming one another for the accident. She smiled as she saw that a growing number of young boys dressed in rags, their feet bare, were busily stuffing spilled apples into their ragged shirts, unnoticed by the arguing men.

Then she laughed as, moving very quickly, Ethan bent from his saddle and neatly scooped up one of the apples still balanced precariously on top of the pile in the cart.

He rubbed it against his sleeve and then handed it to her. "Please accept this as a peace offering. I'm forgiven?"

Morgan felt a flush of delight lick through her as he bowed to her from Alejandro's back. She didn't believe in wasting this moment, or any moments of her life, by holding on to anger. A person said what she said, did what she did, and then the moment was over, and the next one was upon her. Fresh. New. Every moment was a new beginning. Morgan had made that promise to herself long ago.

"Yes, I suppose you're forgiven. And I understand that you meant well, really. Just never do it again, all right? We're supposed to have cried friends, as far as things go, at least. And, to tell you the truth, I'm glad I saw this. Everyone at Becket Hall seems to think the streets of London are littered with gold. Now I can tell them that at least a few of those streets are spread with substances not quite so grand."

"You'd have to tell many who live in Mayfair the same thing, as they rarely venture outside their own insular area, where the gold may not litter the streets, but is definitely present in abundance. An acquaintance of mine once told me he'd gotten horribly lost in Piccadilly, after residing in Mayfair for fifteen years. Piccadilly, you understand, is only about five blocks from his residence. Are you sure you want a Season, Morgan? As I've already warned you, by and large, we're a worthless lot."

Morgan relaxed somewhat as the street they entered seemed more open, and definitely less odiferous. There were even a few trees gamely lining the flagway, although they were rather sad specimens. "You can't all be useless. Look at Wellington, all our officers. And surely you've served?"

Ethan laughed. "Oh, surely not. As the only son, and with the knowledge that my completely unsuitable cousin would assume the title if I got myself killed, not to mention make my bereaved mother's life a horror, I've kept myself safely on this side of the Channel."

Morgan began to feel uneasy. "My brothers Spencer and Rian are all hot to go to the Peninsula, and will get there one of these days, I'm sure, when our father decides they're not still too wet, and agrees to buy them commissions. Chance is involved at the War Office here in London. Courtland's the oldest after Chance, and has all the responsibilities of the estate, but I know he'd otherwise be standing as close to Wellington as he could get, sword in hand. It's only natural, only to be expected."

Ethan shook his head. "So speaks the young and romantic. No, Morgan, not every man is anxious for the chance to sleep in cold mud, be bitten to near madness by fleas, and given the opportunity to either die in that mud or return home inconveniently missing one or more bodily parts. I have not served, I do not serve and I have no intention of serving. Feel free now to call me nasty names."

What Ethan was saying was so very alien to anything Morgan had ever heard. They had come to England, and England was their country now. A person defended his country, even if it was only to keep his own family, his own home, safe. "You don't care about England?"

Ethan shrugged, more than happy to pursue the conversation, and to witness her reaction. "I speak English,

I speak French. My king is mad, his heir a spendthrift profligate—can Bonaparte be that much worse? I can always sail to America, as the title means little to me, anyway. The money, of course, is another matter. That would go with *Maman* and me. And perhaps my valet, as a gentleman shouldn't stray too far from any fellow who knows his way around bootblack."

Morgan looked at Ethan for long moments. Just looked at him. And then she grinned. "You *liar!* Is that the sort of thing you say to tip society over onto its ear? But do you really expect *me* to believe such nonsense? You're English to your toes. What a bag of moonshine!"

Ethan was quite impressed. And only a little uneasy that she seemed to so quickly and easily see what so many others did not. "A liar, Morgan? Society believes me, why shouldn't you?"

Because I grew up amid a family that has had to live by its wits, and its lies. "Like recognizes like, I suppose," was all she said, all she'd admit this early in the game. Not that anyone outside the family would ever know more than the Beckets chose to tell. "So many turns, so many huge buildings—and so much cleaner. Are we getting closer?"

Knowing he'd been figuratively slapped down, and feeling more intrigued than ever, Ethan brought himself back to his surroundings. "Look straight ahead, Morgan. We're nearly at the park. We'll arrive in Upper Brook Street momentarily. To which end, I suggest you attempt to brush some of that travel dust from your skirts."

Morgan looked down at her riding habit. "It's only

dirt," she said, not concerned in the least, and quickly redirected her attention to the vast expanse of greenery that had sprung up so unexpectedly in front of her, as if ripped from the countryside by some giant hand and then carefully placed in the middle of London. "I've read about this. It's Hyde Park, isn't it? Where everyone goes to see and be seen?"

"At the fashionable hour of five in the afternoon, yes. We, however, are somewhat tardy, it having gone at least seven by now. Luckily, there's not too many of the ton out and about, and you might even make it to your brother's door without setting off a small scandal."

"That shouldn't please you," Morgan reminded him.

He would have to tread carefully here. What had begun as a lark, and a definite interest in bedding this beauty, had, somewhere between coercing her into traveling to Tanner's Roost with him, and arriving in London, become eminently more important to him.

"Truth to tell, Morgan, I've had second thoughts. I don't think you should be so eager to shock society. After all, you might enjoy the Season. You could be a Sensation, you know."

"Oh, yes, I know that," Morgan answered without conceit, and Ethan bit the inside of his cheeks to keep from laughing. "But it isn't as if I was going to go very far in society anyway, so that won't happen. We're mere commoners, you understand, and I won't have to bother with the rules of Almacks and the like, or the queen's drawing room. And it's not as if I'm here under orders to capture myself a husband."

"Really?"

Morgan busied herself brushing at the velvet of her

jacket. Why did she keep talking to this man, babbling like some ridiculous twit? Why couldn't she feel comfortable with him, as she did with Jacob? Even superior to him, as she did with Jacob, with any man who'd ever come into her orbit?

She was *aware* of Ethan Tanner, and that, she'd been discovering these past few hours, was something totally alien to her. She'd never considered trying to impress any man. Her looks had always done that for her, with little or no effort on her part.

And she couldn't seem to shock him, which was highly disconcerting, because she liked her admirers feeling off balance, and herself in command. She'd try again.

"Oh, all right, Ethan. They may not have said anything, but I know they want me married off. Quickly. Before I do something horrible, such as deciding to set myself up independently, so that someone isn't always saying 'Morgan, you shouldn't,' and 'Morgan, ladies don't do that,' and 'Morgan, for God's sake, behave.'"

She raised her head, grinned at him. After all, since she couldn't seem to stifle herself, better to tell him truths that would keep him from searching for other truths she could never share. "I'm quite a handful, and they want me to be someone else's handful, I think, preferably before the poor bugger figures out that his life will never be in his own charge again."

"Poor bugger, is it? I don't even know this eventual poor bugger, but I already feel sorry for him."

"And it's not that they don't love me, because they do," Morgan hastened to add, rolling her eyes at his last statement. "And I understand. Really. I'm not an...an *easy* person. Why, much as I believe you'd be rather formidable, I'm reasonably certain I could have you as much under my thumb as poor Jacob in, oh, less than a fortnight. And that's after forewarning you!"

Ethan heard the words, the jovial warning—that he saw as a challenge—but felt fairly sure that he also heard some hurt Morgan tried to hide with her smile, her casual shrug as she admitted she wasn't an "easy person." He certainly did believe her to be a complicated person.

The question that had been nagging at him these past few hours, however, had been did he need another complication in his already complicated life? Morgan Becket was an unexpected delight, unlike any woman he'd ever met. Open, a little too honest, and with a native intelligence that was often missing in other females, or else carefully hidden, because debutantes, God forbid, would never wish to appear smarter than the men they were out to trap.

But Morgan, he suspected, could prove to be his torment if he let her, if he indulged himself in her luscious body, her active mind. Could he afford to find himself thinking of her as more than a titillating diversion, an added confusion to anyone who might look at him and suspect him of being anything more than he'd carefully taught them to believe?

Was nothing simple in these trying times? Not even bedding this incredible beauty he felt sure he could quickly convince to become a willing partner, no matter that she'd all but challenged him to believe he could tame her?

As their horses slowly walked along the cobbled

street beside the park, as if even their mounts were reluctant to put an end to this fairly intimate interlude in the midst of the metropolis, Ethan said, "Perhaps we should part ways once I've safely delivered you to your brother's door."

Morgan turned startled eyes on him, shocked to think she could win so easily. Was having him go away *winning?* She didn't think so.

"Why? What did I say? I thought we were going to be friends, enjoy London together." Then her gaze dropped, and all she felt was disappointment to learn that Ethan wasn't the man she'd begun to believe he was. "It's because I told you that we Beckets aren't very important, isn't it? You say you don't care what anyone thinks of you, that you even go out of your way to be outrageous, but when it comes straight down to it, you're still the earl, and you still want to be accepted by…by your *peers.*"

"Not accepted, Morgan. Tolerated is all I've ever aspired to over the years. I'm more surprised than I can tell you, but it's *your* reputation I'm thinking of now. And now we turn onto Upper Brook Street and your brother's residence, which may be all that will save my life, considering the way you're staring daggers at me."

She did long to slap his face. "*My* reputation? So how *had* you planned for our *association* to play out, Aylesford, before this attack of conscience, or perhaps vanity? Or, because of what I've told you, are you simply afraid Chance will see me as compromised and demand you marry me, see your title as a real coup for his sister?"

"So many questions. Depending on my answers, I

would have to be a hardened seducer, a socially conscious twit or a bloody coward. Why not all three?"

Belatedly, Morgan realized that, while she had been testing him, he had been testing her. And, damn his eyes, she was fairly certain she had been bested in their contest to see which of them was the worst, the most unsuitable—or which of the two of them was to be in charge of their association.

Well, he might have put her down, but she was far from out, and was more than ready to begin again. "Why not, indeed. All three. Since that's what you want me to believe."

"Added to all the things you want me to believe about you," Ethan told her as he motioned for her to turn toward the flagway. He quickly dismounted, and took Berengaria's reins in one hand as he stood on the cobblestones, looking up at Morgan.

Yet again, Ethan understood, she'd seen through him, judged him correctly.

And she *knew.* She knew, just as he knew. They'd been going round and round since the first moment they'd looked at each other. And all to no effect. They could never be friends. They would have to be so much more than friends, or nothing at all.

"You've warned me away. I've warned you away. And now we're here, at your brother's door. What next, Morgan? We can't keep on fencing like this, or we'll exhaust each other. So, does it end here? Do you believe we should end here? We've both certainly given each other enough reasons to have it end here, whatever in hell it is we seem to have begun between us."

Morgan fought back the urge to run her gloved

fingers through Ethan's dark blond hair. She'd known, from the first moment she'd seen him. And he'd known, as well. She wasn't congratulating herself, being prideful in thinking that. He'd also known, from that first moment.

Dangerous Ethan. Dangerous Morgan.

Like recognizes like.

She wet her lips, spoke carefully. "Together, we could be very dangerous, to society, to each other. Mostly to each other. Couldn't we, Ethan?"

He put a hand on hers as Alejandro gracefully stepped to his right, bumping up against his master, pushing him closer to Morgan.

"Damn horse," Ethan said mildly, near enough now to see the deeper gray rings around Morgan's pale gray irises. "I swear, he's worse than my mother."

She relaxed, only then realizing how frightened she'd been that this man, this so very different, so very intriguing man, had almost walked out of her life as quickly as he'd walked into it. Giving in, just this once, couldn't be called total defeat.

She leaned down, her face within scant inches of his, and whispered, "You won't leave now. Will you? Please."

"I was only fooling myself if I thought I could. No, I'm not going anywhere, unless we go to hell together." Ethan's attention was now fixed on her full, slightly smiling mouth. "If I were to kiss you right now, could you promise Saul won't loose Bessie on me?"

Something inside Morgan relaxed. Lose a battle, win a war. "I can't promise that, my lord Aylesford. I suppose you'll simply have to decide if the kiss would be worth taking that chance."

Ethan's slow, knowing smile served to curl her toes inside her riding boots. He cupped his hand around the back of her neck and gently pulled her closer. "Oh, that decision was made long ago, on the road to Tanner's Roost. By both of us. Bessie, do your worst…."

Morgan allowed her eyelids to flutter closed as she waited for the touch of Ethan's mouth against hers. Not her first kiss, but she knew this one would be different. She didn't know *how* it would be different…but she was eager to learn.

"Experiencing some difficulty in dismounting, Morgan? That isn't like you."

At the sound of Chance's deadly calm voice, Morgan sat up straight on Berengaria once more, sparing a quick smile and shrug of her shoulders for Ethan before saying, "Peeking out from behind curtains now, Chance? That isn't like you. Or is that, Lord forbid, what marriage does to people?"

"Hush, Morgan," Ethan warned her quietly. "Your brother's attempting to pretend he doesn't have grounds to call me out. Be grateful, even if you can't be gracious."

"Call you out? Don't be ridiculous. We Beckets aren't that civilized. He'd just knock you down, right here in the street. Several times."

"Don't sound so delighted, imp," Ethan said, then left her still atop Berengaria, and mounted the flagway, his right hand outstretched, the most recent shock in a day littered with them carefully hidden behind a genially smiling face.

How could he have known, even though Morgan had told him that her brother worked at the War Office?

The War Office was immense. And yet, at this moment, the world seemed dangerously small.

Amazingly, either Chance Becket didn't recognize him, or he was as accomplished at concealing his emotions as was Ethan himself.

"Mr. Becket, please allow an explanation if you will. Your sister and I came upon each other out on the road, and I offered my services in escorting her into London once I ascertained that she had planned to abandon her coach and insist upon riding into the city. Ah, and I am Ethan Tanner, Earl of Aylesford, and I extend my sympathies, sir, as your sister would appear to be a rare handful with a mind very much her own."

Chance Becket accepted Ethan's hand, squeezed his around it with more force than a gentleman would consider necessary, and held on, drew Ethan closer.

Ethan considered returning that pressure, but what point would it serve? He had been caught out, about to kiss the man's sister. Besides, if either of them physically pressed the matter, the situation could vault above the uncomfortable and into recklessness that would serve neither.

"Aylesford, is it? Your reputation precedes you, my lord," Chance said flatly, looking over at his sister. "I'm now attempting to understand what I've done to make God so anxious to punish me. It would please me if you were to tell me that you have now completed your gentlemanly duty and are eager to be shed of my troublesome sister, to whom you may not have taken an instant dislike, perhaps, but to whom I suggest you would be wise to feel a very definite indifference."

Ethan kept his expression neutral as Chance Becket

released his grip, although he inwardly damned the poor reputation he'd so carefully built these last years, if only because Chance Becket obviously was aware of it. Of that, and probably of much more. "You're warning me away, Becket?"

"Let's be polite, Aylesford, but not that polite. I'm *ordering* you away," Chance countered. "I owe you my thanks and a drink, I believe, and then you will oblige me by forgetting you ever met my sister."

He looked past Ethan again. "Morgan, get yourself down here, now. No one is present who doesn't know you're more than capable of dismounting on your own."

Ethan watched as Morgan lifted her leg over the pommel and slid gracefully to the cobblestones. She brushed off her gown, stripped off her gloves and advanced on her brother with a bright smile on her incredibly gorgeous face.

"Don't frown so, Chance. I come bearing gifts." Reaching into the pocket of the riding habit, she then held out her hand to her brother. "Apple?"

The imp! Was she afraid of anything? Ethan stepped beside Chance, knowing when to take his opportunities. "My advice, friend? Don't take it. That little Eve has already landed us both in enough trouble. Our only hope now is to join forces."

Chance looked at Ethan, one eyebrow raised in question, before he sighed, nodded and gave in to the inevitable. "As long as you know…"

"Oh, I know. So does she. And now you do, as well. It's going to be a very *interesting* Season with Miss Morgan Becket as one of its debutantes."

Morgan pushed the apple, hard, into her brother's stomach. "Soon you'll be hugging, and drooling all over each other's shoe tops. Enough of the both of you. I'm going to see Julia and Alice."

Both men watched her go before Ethan said, "Now, having been duly warned and threatened, how about we all step inside in case there are other curtain-twitchers about, and discuss how I am going to procure your sister's voucher to Almacks, hmm? Because, no matter what you do or say, even a brother can't be so blind about that magnificent creature. Steel yourself, Becket. I am not going away."

CHAPTER SIX

AFTER RATHER HASTY introductions, Morgan was whisked off upstairs by her sister-in-law, Julia—a polite, minor beauty who nonetheless looked more than prepared to drag Morgan out of the room by her ear if she didn't have the good sense to go willingly.

Leaving Ethan alone with Chance Becket in the tastefully appointed drawing room. "Julia's taking her up to the nursery, to see our daughter, Alice. And probably to ask a dozen questions about you. I don't think you have to worry about me, Aylesford, half as much as you have to worry about my very astute wife. If she decides you're a rotter, you won't get within fifty yards of Morgan again."

"Thank you for the warning."

Ethan had been given only a few moments to visually inspect the man he'd judged to be two or three years his junior, and had come up with no familial resemblance between Chance and Morgan Becket. Absolutely none.

Chance was blond, like his wife, like Ethan himself. Tanned, but obviously fair-skinned, a well set up gentleman who seemed more than capable of knocking Ethan down. At least once.

Both Chance and Morgan were tall. Other than that, they appeared to be as "related" to each other as chalk was to cheese.

But Ethan did recognize the man, remember him. Just as Chance had recognized and obviously remembered him. Now to discover if this would make things easier for Ethan, or even more complicated. He'd much rather have Chance Becket as an ally, although if the man knew precisely what Ethan planned for his sister, Ethan felt certain he would already be a dead man, and Becket wouldn't bother about the consequences.

Strong-willed people, these Beckets of Romney Marsh. Perhaps it was something in the air there, at the back of beyond.

"Thank you," Ethan said, accepting the wineglass Chance offered. "I'll speak honestly here, Becket."

"Is that so, Aylesford? You know how to do that?"

Ethan answered without rancor and, in fact, with some humor. "I'm making an exception here, Becket, and being quite unusually jovial and forthcoming. But don't push, and neither will I. I failed to make any connection between you and your sister, as we've never been formally introduced. My mistake entirely. Not that you and your father can be held blameless as, while Saul and his Bessie are both quite formidable, the young man she calls Jacob is so thoroughly enamored of, and cowed by, your sister that he's of no worth at all."

Chance gave up his slightly threatening stance, since it didn't seem to have any affect on the earl in any case. "I've been worried about that from the moment I received my father's latest letter informing me that

Jacob would be accompanying her. Jacob's a good enough lad, but that's rather like putting the pigeon in charge of the fox."

"You do seem to know your sister very well. I'd like to add that, had I realized your relationship to her, I would have made other arrangements to get her back into her coach and safely to Upper Brook Street, and gone on my way. Looking back, I would say those 'arrangements' would have been to bind and gag her before tying the coach doors closed."

Ethan took a sip from his glass. "I repeat, I would like to say that. But that last little bit would be a lie, and we both know it. Your sister is the most extraordinary woman I've ever met. And she seems to see straight through me, which is as unique as it is unfortunate. I'll need to keep her close these next weeks."

"Or I need to truss her up as you suggested, and send her back to Becket Hall," Chance said, sitting down in the facing chair, resting his elbows on his knees. "But she'd only run away, find her way back here, as Morgan always most wants to be where she shouldn't be, so I might as well not dream of such an easy solution. But what do you mean, she sees straight through you? I don't know what's going on. She can't possibly know what's going on."

"And she doesn't. But while the rest of London believes me to be fairly worthless and more than a little base, your sister's reaction to my well-rehearsed patter was to grin and call me a liar. She then added that like recognizes like, or some such thing. That shocked me. Is there something else I should know, other than the fact that your sister would make a far better ally than an enemy?"

"You mean, other than that I'd hang parts of you from every lamppost in London if I thought you'd touched her, and damn the minister if he thinks you're indispensable. Or so he said when he warned me to silence about your presence in the War Office that night."

Ethan smiled. "He called me indispensable? Well, now I am flattered."

"Don't be. The last man the minister termed indispensable was sent off on a sure suicide mission three months ago. He came back to us last week, packed in pickle juice. I may not have to worry overlong about you and my sister."

"Really. I can see you and I are going to have an interesting relationship these next weeks. And we won't mention the minister again after this conversation, will we?"

Chance sighed, pushed his fingers through his long hair, which was tied at his nape. "Then this conversation is over. I can't say what I don't know. It was late, supposedly everyone was gone, and you were stepping out of his office as I was stepping in. We weren't introduced, but still I was told—in no uncertain terms—to forget I'd seen you. That's all I know on that subject."

"And it's more than enough, I think we'll agree," Ethan said, lifting his wineglass in a small salute. "Suffice it to say the gentleman and myself are involved in a small…project."

"Yes, I'd worked that out for myself, thank you. And now that I've got the name to go with the face, and know the reputation that is common knowledge throughout Mayfair, I can keep myself up nights, wondering what the devil the *gentleman* is up to this time, or I can pace the floors worrying about what you think *you* might be up to with my sister. Either way, I see little sleep in my future."

Ethan smiled, liking this honest, forthright man very much. And it was time to leave the subject of the minister, and Ethan's connection to him. "You and Morgan had different mothers? I don't mean to be overly curious, but she has a rather exotic look about her that, frankly, you lack. Spanish, I'd say."

Chance gazed at Ethan for long moments, during which neither one blinked.

"She could be. Our father adopted most of us. All of us, actually, save our sister Cassandra, who is the daughter of Ainsley Becket and his deceased wife. We can trace our lineage to our own parents, some of us, but that's as far as any of us can go. You're the twelfth earl, aren't you? Steeped in family and tradition?"

One corner of Ethan's mouth twitched in amusement. "Obviously your knowledge of me, although most probably damning, is also limited, Becket. When it comes to matters of bloodlines, the only ones that interest me are those of my horseflesh. So I was right? Spanish?"

"Does it matter?

Ethan shook his head. "No. Not at all. What matters is that Morgan seems to believe she won't be welcomed too deeply into society. She could be right, you know, which begs the question as to why she's here. She told me it's to marry her off, turn her into someone else's problem."

Chance sat back in his chair, blinked. "She said that?" He began rubbing the back of his neck. "She couldn't mean it. Morgan knows we would never... And she wanted to come. I think she wanted to come. Seasons are for women. Gowns, balls, all of it. I really wasn't paying attention. Damn. Maybe I should at least offer to send her back to Becket Hall."

It suited Ethan to keep Becket talking. "You're merely thinking out loud, I'm sure, and aren't seriously considering chasing the girl home to the wilds of wherever it is you all live, to marry some stammering country lad she'd be forced to murder in a week, if only to break the boredom. And where is Becket Hall, again? Romney Marsh, I believe she told me?"

"The far end of the earth. Another few hundred feet, and we'd be floating in the Channel," Chance said, still with his mind on other things. "No, she has to stay here. There's no future for her at Becket Hall, no future there for any of the girls. We all agreed."

"You *all* agreed? This is so utterly fascinating," Ethan said, and meant it. "Tell me, just how large is a clutch of Beckets?"

"Hmm? Oh, I'm sorry. Woolgathering. How many of us are there? Eight, actually, and our father, Ainsley. Four girls—Eleanor, Morgan, Fanny and Cassandra. Four boys—Courtland, Rian, Spencer and myself."

"So you have three more sisters to marry off? I don't envy you that, Becket."

"Two. Eleanor...she doesn't want a Season." Chance drank down the rest of his wine. "And why am I telling you any of this?"

"I have no idea, other than the lure of my trusting face," Ethan said, smiling, "although I'm finding it all extremely interesting. A man who would take on seven children not his own. A rare individual, I'd say. I should like to meet him one day. Does he often come to London?"

Chance Becket's expression closed, became noncommittal, and Ethan knew he had somehow gone too far. Ah, but a simple answer to a simple question, even if a lie, would have worked much better for the man, because now Ethan found himself becoming even more intrigued with Becket Hall and, most especially, one Ainsley Becket.

Being who he was, Ethan smiled politely and asked, "Have I said something wrong?"

"Not at all," Chance answered, deciding he would like very much to go upstairs and throttle his sister for introducing this dangerous man into their midst. "I'll see what's keeping the ladies. Morgan will want to thank you again, as do Julia and myself. And we don't want to keep you."

"You don't want anything to do with me at all," Ethan said, getting to his feet as Chance stood up. "Let's take the gloves off here, all right? I've had the pleasure of your sister's acquaintanceship for less than a half day, and I already can say with some certainty that, left to her own devices, and beautiful as she is, she's certain to make a shambles of her come-out."

"You can't know that."

"But I do, Becket. She's too intelligent, for one, and has a wild, independent streak in her that society may admire from a distance, but will publicly condemn. Oh, and she's much too exotically beautiful not to gain the intense animosity of every petite, blue-eyed, watery blond nincompoop currently believed to be all the fashion. You're a good man, Becket, and I'm sure your wife is a good woman. But you and your wife, forgive my immodesty, cannot take your sister where I and my title can, present her where I can, and, yes, protect her along the way. As I can. Do we understand each other?"

"You're saying that the Earl of Aylesford wishes to assist in sponsoring Miss Morgan Becket for the Season. Yes, I understand the language. And I'm not a fool, my lord. What you're saying without saying it is that you want her for yourself—and by that, my lord, you had better mean marriage, or the minister will be mourning the loss of yet another indispensable agent."

"I believe you, Becket. Marriage it is, although I don't think Morgan needs to hear that as yet."

"God, no. She'd either leap at the idea or run a hundred miles, and at the moment, I don't know which would be worse. You know, I should be delighted to think my sister has met and conquered an earl, no less, in a matter of a few hours. Not surprised, because nothing she has ever done could possibly surprise me, but delighted. That is, if the earl had been anyone save you. But fair warning, Aylesford, on two heads. Hurt her and you're a dead man. That, and don't count on her affection next week. She's only today gotten her first small bite out of London society. Her tastes may run elsewhere once she gets a few more bites."

"I believe you can safely leave those worries to me, thank you."

"Sure of yourself, aren't you?"

Ethan smiled, remembering the way Morgan had looked at him when he'd been about to kiss her. "Hopeful, Becket. I'm very hopeful."

"In any case, I'll be watching you, Aylesford."

"And, as I intend a rather hot pursuit of your sister's hand, that will be easy to do."

Chance shook his head, giving up the battle of words. "As long as we're speaking with gloves off, what in hell did Morgan do in the short time you two were together?"

Ethan shrugged, then told the truth, as sometimes the truth was the most confounding of all. "She has no airs about her, or false modesty, for that matter. She knows who she is and what she wants. She's honest."

"Morgan? We're talking about my sister Morgan?"

"Indeed, we are. And now, please give my excuses to the ladies as, doubting a dinner invitation to be forthcoming, I wish to ascertain if my valet has as yet arrived in Grosvenor Square to warn my chef that I'm in very distinct danger of starving."

"Then you'd better go, because you're right. At the moment, Aylesford, I am not disposed to offer you so much as a crust of stale bread."

Here was Ethan's chance to poke at the sore spot that appeared to be Ainsley Becket, and watch for Chance's reaction. "No London milksop, are you? Interesting. You make me wonder, sir, how you and Morgan can be unrelated by blood, yet seemingly cut of much the same cloth. Your father must be an interesting man. A very interesting man."

Chance said nothing.

Which said very much, indeed. Ainsley Becket had his son's loyalty, definitely. The question that begged, however, was why the man needed such fierce protection. Ethan loved puzzles.

"Yes, well, I've outstayed my welcome, if there ever was one offered. Tomorrow, Becket? If you'd inform your sister that I should be pleased if she will deign to allow me to drive her in the Promenade. Good evening."

Chance simply stood and watched as the Earl left the drawing room, holding his breath until he heard the footman close the front door on Aylesford's back. He then went to the drinks table to pour himself another glass of wine.

"Honest? Morgan is honest? Only to a point, my lord, only to a point—straight up to the line you'll never be allowed to cross." He lifted his glass in a mock salute to what he believed was the condemned man who'd just been in his presence. "Good luck to you, Aylesford. You're going to need it."

CHAPTER SEVEN

"MORGAN, I WOULD greatly appreciate it if you would stop prowling about like a caged beast, and explain to me what on earth you were thinking when you allowed the earl to accompany you here."

Morgan had been hugging her arms around her waist as she paced inside her assigned bedchamber, if only to attempt to hold in all the pent-up energy instigated by the kiss that hadn't happened, and the thought of how it could have been. She felt such a tension in her body, from her head down to her toes.

And no release. Just more tension.

When would she see him again?

What would she say? What would *he* say?

Would he still look at her the same way? Would she respond the same way?

She would ask Julia, but her sister-in-law surely couldn't know. Julia had Chance, and they might love each other, but they could never feel the way Morgan felt right now. No one had ever felt this way before, not since the beginning of time.

Did he feel the same way?

He had to.

What would she do if he didn't?

Morgan dropped her arms to her sides as she stopped pacing and turned to smile at her sister-in-law. "I already told you, Julia. I simply wanted to give Berengaria a run. Poor thing, once the outriders left us she was going to be tied to the back of the coach and *dragged* into London. I couldn't allow that."

Julia Becket looked at Morgan levelly. "So, of course, the mare would need to have her *run* all the way to your brother's front door. Has it been so long, Morgan, that you've forgotten you know me, or that I know you? Has it been so long that you've convinced yourself I've just come down in the last rain, and would believe that obvious clunker?"

Morgan hopped up onto the high tester bed. "Apparently I should have taken the time to make up a more plausible story," she said, grinning at Julia. "All right, I give over. *I* wanted a run. Do you know how stultifyingly *boring* it is to be stuck inside a stuffy, bumping traveling coach for days on end?"

"Two days, and yes, I know, and can tell you honestly that two days inside a coach with a young child may not be boring, but they definitely are no more pleasant," Julia said, smiling at an old memory.

"But there was more than being bored, wasn't there? You wanted to prove to Chance and to me that you might be here, but being under our roof and obeying our strictures would be two entirely different things. I can understand that, Morgan. You are used to having your own way at Becket Hall."

"Except when Eleanor *talks* to me," Morgan interrupted, making a face. They'd speak about Eleanor. Much better to speak about Eleanor than "strictures"—

at least until Morgan could get herself under control. "She's so little, so quiet, and yet she rules us all. How does she do that?"

Julia laughed. "I don't know. But she does, doesn't she. Now, let me finish. I understand that you don't much care for taking orders or following rules, and I was prepared to deal with that. However, I will be damned if I'll stand by and let you ruin yourself, then be forced to explain that ruination to your papa. Not if I have to strap you on my back and *carry* you back to Becket Hall. Am I making myself clear here?"

"As the bell in the church tower on Sunday morning, yes. But it wasn't my fault, Julia. He's the one who insisted on accompanying me. I didn't hold a pistol to his head."

Julia looked at her sister-in-law, now stripped down to her white cotton shift, but still wearing her riding boots, her night-dark hair hanging more than halfway down her back. "You hold a pistol to the head of every man who looks at you," she said, not without humor.

Morgan didn't bother to deny Julia's words.

"What's worse is that you know you do. Look at that smile on your face right now, for pity's sake. But this isn't Becket Hall or the village, Morgan, where everyone knows you, and where every last man jack knows what would happen if he dared too much. This, Morgan, my dear, is London, and when you play the flirt here, someone might take you very seriously."

Morgan braced her palms against the bedspread as she swung her booted legs back and forth over the side of the bed. "The Earl of Aylesford. That's who you mean. Don't worry, I already warned him."

"You already…oh, Lord." Julia subsided into the cushioned chair in front of the dressing table. She'd already fainted once, two days ago, luckily with her maid close by to catch her, but she'd rather not have to tell Chance he was going to be a father only after he'd picked her up off the floor. "You *warned* him? For God's sake, Morgan, what did you say to the man?"

"In a moment, Julia." Morgan hopped down from the bed as a maid entered from the dressing room and held out a dressing gown for her. "And what's your name? Louise? Isn't that a lovely name. I'm Morgan. I'll take that, Louise," she said, then did so, never realizing that the surprised maid was prepared to help her into the gown. Morgan would have pointed out that she didn't have two broken arms and could dress herself, thank you, if she had.

"I didn't *say* anything to him, Julia," Morgan said once the maid was gone.

"I suppose I should be comforted that you are for the most part conscious of your possible audience," Julia said. "Louise is fairly safe, but there's no one outside of Becket Hall who is ever to be considered entirely safe. You also remember that, don't you? Now, what do you mean, you didn't say anything to him?"

"Because I didn't. I merely admired his horse in the inn yard. He then introduced himself, graciously invited me to his castle, and then we came here."

"His castle. Oh, dear, it's even worse than I'd imagined." Julia lowered her head, rubbed at her forehead. Perhaps she should tell Chance now about the baby, while there was still time to send Morgan back to Becket Hall.

Because, what with being horribly sick every morning, these odd dizzy spells during the day, and the time she spent with their daughter, Alice, she might not be the best person to be riding herd on his sister. Wellington and his entire staff might not be enough to successfully ride herd on her.

Morgan sighed audibly. "Oh, don't say *oh, dear* that way, Julia. His *mother* met me there. I'm not a complete fool. I listened to Elly's lectures about proper behavior." She grinned. "Some of them. Enough, at least, to know that neither of us should be saying *damn* in public."

"Now you're correcting me?" Julia asked, wishing she could hold back her smile. She really did love Chance's sister. She was so…so *alive.*

"I'd never do that. I know how awful that can be for the person being lectured."

Now Julia laughed out loud. "I suppose I'm supposed to apologize for lecturing you?"

"Apology accepted, thank you," Morgan said, enjoying herself immensely, yet never quite able to forget for more than a few moments that Ethan had nearly kissed her. She tied the satin ribbons on her dressing gown, turning her back to Julia so that the other woman didn't see that her hands were shaking slightly. "Besides, I can handle the earl. He's only a man."

Julia was about to say *oh, dear* again, then realized that not only would she be redundant, but she'd appear weak. And nobody could afford to appear weak around Morgan. "I don't think your brother is delighted."

"Yes, I rather sensed that," Morgan said as she

turned to her sister-in-law once more, smiling, hoping that Julia hadn't noticed that her careful facade was beginning to show a few cracks. She really needed to be alone. Very much needed to be alone. To think, to plan, to remember, to anticipate. "The earl says he's tolerated in society, but that's all. Because of his mother being a…a very nice woman."

"Because she's a very nice woman? I'm afraid I don't understand."

Morgan shook her head. "Oh, what's the point. Chance will just ask somebody, and they'll tell him, and then you'll both ring a peal over my head, and then I'll tell you that I don't care, I'll see the man if I want to, and Chance will try to *reason* with me, and—we don't need to do all of that, do we? It seems such a waste of time, when we all know that, in the end, I'll do what I want to do."

"Yes, and the devil take the hindmost. As when you rode out on the marsh with Courtland and the others, without their knowledge. Chance threatened to turn you over his knee when you tried it with him. I know. And don't look so shocked, Morgan. Your brother and I have no secrets from each other. I'm a Becket now, too, remember?"

Morgan was surprised, although she immediately realized that she shouldn't be. "He's told you everything? About the Black Ghost? About us? About the *island?*"

"Everything," Julia said, looking at her levelly. "Nothing good, or lasting, can be built on a lie."

Morgan's smile bordered on triumphant, as she believed she was about to trump Julia's ace. "Becket

Hall seems to be standing fairly well for over a dozen years now."

"And it will continue to stand. We all will, unless some one of us brings the wrong person into our midst. Do you understand me, Morgan? You don't know this Earl of Aylesford. I saw him downstairs. I saw the way he looked at you, and the way you looked at him. He's dazzled you, hasn't he?"

"Dazzled me?" Morgan rolled her eyes dramatically, even as her stomach clenched at how clearly Julia saw what was happening to her. "As if I'm the sort to be dazzled. That's actually rather insulting, Julia. Either you think me competent enough for a Season, or send me home now, to play Snakes and Ladders with Cassandra."

"I'm sorry, Morgan. I apologize. Perhaps I'm being overly cautious. Neither Chance nor I ever dreamed that you'd have your own beau your first day in London—and we most certainly never dreamed you'd discover him on your own."

Morgan grinned, rather pleased with herself. "I did, didn't I?"

It was now Julia's turn to roll her eyes, and she topped that with a long-suffering sigh. "All I ask is that you don't rush to judgment, either for him or against him. Too many depend on who you choose to trust now that you're here, away from Becket Hall."

Morgan sat down on the carpet and began unlacing her boots, pulling them off and tossing them toward the corner of the room. "Well, and now *that's* the most insulting thing I've ever heard you say to me, Julia. That I'm a starry-eyed looby who'd whisper our secrets into my lover's ear."

"Your—your *lover?* You've only just met the man! First a castle, and now your *lover?*" Julia looked at the girl through narrowed eyelids. "Have you been reading novels? Oh, never mind. Morgan, I know. I saw him. He's definitely…dashing. But he's one man. You can't judge him against the men you know from the village. London has handsome titled men stacked up like cordwood, waiting for someone like you. You were sent here to have a Season, not a day."

Morgan was silent for some moments, weighing her next words very carefully before going to her knees in front of Julia, taking hold of her hands. "You have to promise, Julia. Promise you won't say any of this to Chance."

Julia hesitated, then gave in to the pleading look in Morgan's eyes. "I promise."

Morgan took a deep breath, let it out slowly, then said, "I think Odette saw him, Julia. I think she saw him a long time ago, and knew. He's my dangerous man, Julia. I feel it. I've felt it from the first moment I looked at him. He belongs to me. Much as I love you and Chance, and much as you hopefully love me, I'm going to have him. I don't think I have a choice."

"Does he?" her brother asked from the doorway.

Morgan let go of Julia's hands and leaped to her feet, to glare at Chance as he stood there, leaning nonchalantly against the jamb. Her chin lifting, she said regally, "I'll assume there's a key for that lock? If so, I want it."

"Really," Chance said, pushing himself away from the doorjamb, to fully enter the bedchamber. "And if there's a working chastity belt left in England I want the key to—"

"Chance! That's enough," Julia warned, trying not to giggle, because her husband was acting very silly. Just like an older brother, she supposed, and he didn't seem too comfortable in the role. "She's Morgan. Better she tell us the truth than lie to us, then do as she pleases."

"You can say that, Julia, my dearest, because you aren't aware of Aylesford's reputation. I may not be familiar with all of it, but I've heard enough at my club to know that he's no fitting suitor for my sister. For one thing, he's ancient, old enough to be your father."

"He is not! He can't be more than a few years older than you, *brother.*"

"Which still makes him more than ten years your senior. I…we can't allow that." He looked pleadingly at his wife. "Julia? Tell her."

Morgan turned to appeal to Julia. "Do you hear him? Making excuses, handing out trumped-up reasons."

Julia's expression was sympathetic. "Ten or twelve years are quite a few years…."

Morgan felt her own face grow tight, even as she began breathing evenly through her nose, calming herself. All she had to do was agree with them, placate them. Why was she fighting so hard? She forced her lips into a smile. "Very well. If you're adamant, I won't see him again. There. Is everyone happy now? Pleased with themselves?"

Julia gazed at her husband. "Chance? Remember what we talked about a few days ago? The day the letter arrived from Becket Hall? Something about lists…and *suggestions?*"

Chance looked at his wife, looked at his sister.

One appealed to him with her eyes. The other dared him with hers.

"All right, all right," he said, throwing up his arms in surrender. "Go to hell your own way, Morgan, you always do. I'd be a fool to think I could stop you, and anything I could tell you about Aylesford would only make him more interesting to you. Just be sure you don't drag the rest of us down there with you."

Morgan's smile was brilliant, if brittle. "Well. Finally. Thank you, Chance. I would have gotten my own way in any event, but it's wonderful to know that I now have your *permission* to make my own decisions, considering the fact that I'm a grown woman."

"Grown woman? You're *eighteen,* damn it, and you've got about as much knowledge of how things are for men like Aylesford as a turnip. I—"

Julia decided she'd heard enough. Nothing good could possibly come from speaking any more about the Earl of Aylesford. She pressed her palms against her knees and pushed herself to her feet. "Chance, darling? Please don't worry anymore, and come with me. I... I've got something to tell you...."

CHAPTER EIGHT

"MORGAN, PLEASE SIT DOWN. You're giving me a crick in my neck, watching you."

Morgan looked at her sister-in-law. "I can't, Julia," she said, as she continued to pace the drawing room. "What if I was wrong? What if he was just amusing himself at my expense?"

"Then, I suppose, you'll simply have to kill him," Julia said, smiling at her own small joke.

"You're not being helpful, Julia," Morgan said, stopping to glare at her.

"Forgive me. It's just that this is so unlike you, Morgan. You've changed your outfit from the skin out. *Twice.* You nearly drove poor Louise to despair about your hair. Anyone would think the Morgan I remember had been hidden in a closet somewhere, and someone who looks just like her has been put in her place—missing only the real Morgan's supreme confidence."

"I've never before had a reason not to feel confident," Morgan admitted, at last collapsing into a chair, a move that Julia approved by way of a small sigh and a whispered *thank God.* "After all, it doesn't take much to impress anyone at Becket Hall all hollow, now does it?"

"All those poor, adoring country bumpkins, you

mean, not to mention the occasional soldier who passes by and immediately becomes smitten with you," Julia said, shaking her head. "Morgan, you're an incorrigible flirt. Someone who didn't know you as I do would think you are quite shallow and vain."

Morgan shrugged, Julia's words not affecting her. "Elly doesn't bother to put herself forward, Fanny is mad for horses and doesn't even notice that there are men in this world, and Cassandra's still too young. I'm the obvious choice, that's all. But now I wonder if that's all I was—the obvious choice. But here? In London? Here I'm just one more hopeful debutante, lost among so many others. I don't like that. I really don't. I mean, I hadn't minded. Not until yesterday."

"Something changed yesterday?"

Morgan stared down at her leather-covered toes, then at Julia. "*Everything* changed yesterday."

Julia looked at her sister-in-law, whose expression proved the girl to be quite serious, if a bit melodramatic.

"Yes…I can see that," she said, then watched in bemusement as Morgan got to her feet and began to pace once more.

Morgan was dressed this afternoon in a buttercup-yellow walking dress accented in a lovely bright blue, and topped with a short, long-sleeved blue jacket. A simple enough outfit, but nothing remained simple once it was draped over Morgan's magnificent form. She could probably flatter rags used to wash the kitchen floors.

Louise had worked her wonders, even under considerable duress, so that now Morgan's thick black hair was pulled back to form an intricate knot that fell from her crown to her nape. Morgan's fine but exceedingly plentiful hair had no curl, and when she'd seen the curling stick she'd waved it away, preferring to lean toward the dressing table mirror, frown, and then pull a heavy lock of hair free, so that it hung from the slightly off center part, curving around her cheek and ending just below her jawline.

Julia doubted there was a man with a beating heart in this world who would see that lock of hair and not want to touch it, cup the cheek it caressed.

No artful, teasing curls for Morgan Becket. She didn't need them, for one, and any paltry little curls would have run away in fright when presented with that heavy mass of ebony glory that helped make Morgan unique, not just in London, but probably in most of the British Isles.

Combine the hair with the vibrant blue velvet, the way the soft buttercup muslin caressed her curves, the erect, I-dare-you carriage of the girl…add those amused, wickedly intelligent gray eyes, her fine, slightly golden complexion…and *magnificent* was the word that kept popping into Julia's head each time she looked at her. Along with *unique.* And, for anyone who didn't know the girl, *intimidatingly imperious.* Not a princess. No, not Morgan. Morgan was a queen.

And yet now, at this moment, while she awaited the arrival of the Earl of Aylesford, Morgan looked incredibly nervous, even vulnerable.

An odd sight, indeed.

"Morgan, you won't be lost among the other debutantes. You couldn't get lost in the middle of a battalion," Julia teased. "Now, the earl will arrive soon. He didn't mention an exact time—and yes, I've explained to your brother, in some detail, that he must learn to ask such questions—but the Promenade begins at five, so he has to present himself very soon. At which time, Morgan, you'll sit here with me, we'll greet the earl when he's announced, speak of nonsense for a few minutes, and then you can be on your—"

"He's here!" Morgan had been listening for the knocker to sound, and was already heading for the hallway.

Julia's amusement at her sister-in-law's nervousness vanished. "Morgan, sit down. Yes, he's here, but now he must be led upstairs and announ—oh, the devil with it," she ended, because Morgan had all but run from the room, leaving Julia to gather up the girl's gloves and bonnet and trail after her.

Morgan slid to a halt at the railing overlooking the staircase and foyer below, and watched as Ethan Tanner handed his hat and gloves to one of the footmen.

As she looked at him her nervousness fled, to be replaced by sheer excitement.

He was magnificent. Once again his dark blond hair had been brushed straight back from his forehead, and now gleamed golden in the sunshine filtering in through the large fanlight over the front door.

As her heart pounded, and her breathing became shallow, Ethan gave his name to the footman and said he'd "come to collect Miss Becket."

Trailing one hand along the banister, Morgan moved toward the staircase, calling out, "Collect her? You make me sound like a butterfly to be added to your collection, my lord. I don't think I'd like to have pins stuck through my wings."

Ethan looked up, to see Morgan slowly advancing toward him down the wide marble stairs. It had been a lifetime since last he'd seen her, but she had been well worth the wait.

"I agree, Miss Becket," he said, moving to the staircase, extending both hands up to her. "Beauty such as yours must be free to spread its wings, to fly." He added more quietly, almost fiercely, "My God, woman, why didn't anyone warn me that today would be the longest of my life?"

Laughter bubbled up inside Morgan. It was back. It had never left. Not for either of them. The feeling. The *knowing.* She stopped two steps above him, placed her hands in his. "There have been shorter years."

He drew her down the last steps, bent his elbows so that he brought her closer to him in the pool of sunlight, which seemed to have grown wider, warmer, since he'd entered the foyer. The whole world seemed to be washed in sunshine, even indoors.

He saw the laughter in her eyes, the joy…and the longing…and knew his eyes revealed the same to her. The man who hid his true feelings was some other Ethan Tanner, some poor creature only half-alive. His voice dropped to a whisper. "Let's get out of here before I do something that forces your brother to knock me down."

"Would you then get up and knock him down?" Morgan asked, so very aware of the warmth of his skin beneath her hands.

"No. I couldn't. I'd deserve every punishment, just for what I'm thinking right now. God, Morgan…this can't be happening. But it is, isn't it?"

Morgan nervously wet her lips with the tip of her tongue, and Ethan's grip on her hands tightened. "Yesterday…you were going to kiss me…."

"Morgan! Morgan, dear, you forgot your bonnet and gloves," Julia said, already halfway down the stairs, and wondering if she should send the footman for a bucket of water cold from the well, and throw it over these two near-to-boiling creatures.

Ethan reluctantly released Morgan's hands, to bow to the lady of the household. "Mrs. Becket, my esteemed pleasure."

"Yes, I'd gathered that," Julia said, handing Morgan her bonnet and gloves—nearly bowling her over as she all but jammed them into her waist. "To the Promenade, my lord? That is the plan?"

"And nowhere else," Ethan said, smiling in appreciation of this woman's unblinking frankness. "Yes, madam, to the very public, very crowded, exceedingly proper Promenade, where our combined behavior will be impeccable."

"I'm sure you'll both enjoy the spectacle," Julia said, knowing she and the earl understood each other.

Morgan hastily tied her bonnet ribbons to one side of her chin, then walked over to the door, eager to be on her way. "Julia? We're going to be late to the Promenade."

Julia looked at Morgan, and then at the earl once more, and mentally readjusted Chance's and her plans for a quiet, uneventful evening spent cuddling in their bedchamber. "My husband and I wish to extend an invitation to dinner with us this evening, my lord. We dine at seven."

"It would be my honor," Ethan said, bowing again, this time over Julia's gracefully extended hand. He looked up at her, into a pair of all-seeing green eyes, and added, "I'd never hurt her, madam."

"I'm sure you believe that, my lord," Julia said as he straightened once more. "I'm also sure she believes she'd never hurt you. But please remember, she's young, and fairly impetuous. What means the world to her today might be but dust beneath her feet next week."

Ethan looked toward Morgan, who had now pulled on her gloves and was looking at him worriedly. "I wonder, madam," he said, turning to Julia once more, "which of the two of us you most underestimate."

"Prove me wrong, my lord. And I suggest you begin by not being so terribly *intense* when you look at her."

"Point taken, madam," Ethan answered, feeling as if he'd just been disciplined by his tutor. "Your husband hinted that you are formidable."

"Thank you," Julia said with a small smile, then watched as the earl offered his arm to Morgan and the two of them walked down the few steps to the flagway, and the magnificent curricle that waited there.

Ethan's curricle was the envy of many a young buck who knew he'd never hope to aspire to such magnificence, but Morgan paid it little attention, preferring to inspect his lordship's horseflesh.

The matched blacks stood quietly in the traces, their fine, trim heads faced forward.

"They're as alike as two peas in a pod," Morgan said, marveling. "Hackneys?"

"Hackneys, indeed," Ethan told her, redirecting her

back to the curricle, and helping her up onto the seat. "But you're supposed to be impressed all hollow by my exquisite equipage."

He climbed up beside her, with a nod of his head informing the groom to take his hands from the horse's bridles—at which point the groom quickly leaped back onto the flagway.

"It's very nice," Morgan said offhandedly, then grinned as the pair smartly moved out into the middle of the street, their heads lifted proudly, their knees high with each exaggerated step, the motion snappy and extraordinarily disciplined.

"*Nice,* you say? Damned with faint praise. I believe I'll just toddle on home now and slit my throat."

Morgan still had most of her attention on the horses, which was so much more comfortable than allowing her thoughts to stray to the realization that she and Ethan were sitting so close together on the small seat that their bodies touched. Burned where hers touched his.

"Oh, hush," she said, putting a hand on his forearm, thrilled by the contact, yet comfortable with the act itself. "Don't you know? I have to talk about *something.*"

He turned to grin at her, those long slashes cutting into his cheeks. "Why?"

"Because I have to, that's all," Morgan told him. "It's only polite to talk."

"But you'd rather do something else?"

They'd joined the line of vehicles inching their way into Hyde Park. "I'd rather *be* somewhere else," she told him, keeping her gaze on him.

He adored her honesty, even as he felt sure she wasn't always honest. "Keep looking at me that way, Morgan, and in another moment we'll be the subject of dinner gossip all over Mayfair for a month. I don't mind, not for myself, but I think your brother and his good wife might have a word or two to say on the matter."

He faced forward once more, his pair obeying just the slightest flicker of the reins as the line of vehicles moved forward once more.

"Now, we are here, as someone may have already informed you, to see and be seen. We are most especially here so that I can spy out one of the hostesses at Almacks, and procure a voucher for you."

"Do I want to go to Almacks?"

"Many young ladies would gladly give up their hope of salvation to attend Almacks."

Morgan shrugged. "Well, in that case, I don't want to go. Why should I want to do what everyone else does? I never have before."

Ethan's delighted laughter caused several heads to turn and, once turned, many eyes began to stare. Female eyes. Definitely male eyes.

At another time, with another young woman up beside him, Ethan would be secretly pleased to have scored a coup, drawn such interest. After all, what was society if not one huge, unending game of tweaking your peers?

But not today. Not this woman. And when one ridiculously overdressed young cub on horseback leaned over to his friend and whispered something, and the friend made appreciative kissing motions with his mouth, Ethan knew what it felt like to experience the sudden urge to kill.

"This may have been a mistake," he said, even as the curricle was finally assimilated by the nearly endless line of vehicles making their way around the park.

But Morgan, who had wanted to be with the earl, though not necessarily in such a public place, was now looking around eagerly, utterly amazed by the crush of equipages, horseflesh and exotic people. "Nonsense. Is the entire world here? And what for, may I ask? Society, Julia told me, is fairly limited. Aren't they all out here, seeing the people they saw here yesterday and will see again tomorrow? Why do they do it?"

Ethan shrugged. "Because they always have?"

"But that's no reason. Perhaps they're hoping to see someone new." She grinned at Ethan. "Like me."

"Oh, I doubt the ladies have been hoping to see someone like you, imp," he said as Morgan sat up even straighter, and then waved to one young man who'd actually stood up in his stirrups to tip his hat to her. "And that fool's going to be facedown in the dirt in a moment, if his horse decides to move in any direction. I've seen him ride."

Morgan smiled, but said nothing. Why, he was jealous! And, while not unaccustomed to this sort of reaction from men who had entered her orbit in the past, she felt no great need to play on that jealousy, tease him, flirt with the other man.

Because no other man mattered to her, not a single soul in this entire huge park crammed nearly to bursting with what Elly had told her were termed "Exquisites." And "Corinthians." And even "Dandies."

For every gentleman she saw as the curricle inched along slowly, there were at least two females. Old ones, young ones, fat ones, chinless ones, overdressed ones... desperate ones.

Behind the bright smiles of the debutantes, the searching, assessing eyes of their keepers, there seemed to be an air of near desperation. As if failing to catch the eye of an eligible parti was a fate far worse than death.

Morgan leaned against Ethan's shoulder. "Do you smell it? The sun may be shining, and a fair breeze blowing, but all I can smell is fear. From both the hunted and the hunters. I'm so very glad I am here with you."

"Convenient, am I?" Ethan asked her. "That's rather lowering. And here I thought you might be beginning to care."

Now it was Morgan's clear laughter that brought outside attention their way, and this time very specific attention, from a quartet of matrons approaching from the opposite direction in an elaborate, open-topped carriage drawn by four aged horses.

"Aylesford, can you do nothing without causing a scene?" the largest of the four ladies asked. None of them had missed a meal in years, probably pushing slower people out of the way as they grabbed for the last pork chop, Morgan had already decided.

Ethan smiled as he tipped his hat to the ladies, even while drawing his slow-moving pair to a halt beside the carriage. "I don't think so, Aunt Tirrel, no. I should never want to disappoint your low opinion of me. But, alas, I haven't seen the Second Coming as yet. Is he home nursing another unfortunate carbuncle?"

Morgan watched as the woman's head snapped back

as if she'd been slapped. "Don't you dare speak that way about Fenton. I'll have you know that my son is tending to estate matters, which is more than you can say."

"True, Aunt. I haven't tended to your estate matters since last you applied to me for—"

The woman cut him off, saying, "Your lack of manners is showing, Aylesford. Introduce your companion. If you can," she added, her smile rather greasy, in Morgan's opinion. Why, if all the lace and feathers were stripped off her, to be replaced by an apron and a newly dead chicken in her fist, she'd be no better than Daisy, who worked in the kitchens at Becket Hall.

"No, that would be insulting Daisy," Morgan told herself quietly, then covered her mouth with her hand, to disguise a giggle with a discreet cough.

Ethan heard Morgan mutter, but couldn't catch her exact words. But he did hear "insulting." And he agreed. Aunt Tirrel was often an amusement to him, but not this time. This time, she would have to be put more firmly in her place.

"How remiss of me, Aunt," he said, very obviously placing a hand on Morgan's shoulder. "Miss Becket, I should very much like to introduce to you my aunt, Mrs. Tirrel, along with these other three delightful ladies whose names have escaped me at the moment. Aunt? If you'd do the honors?"

Mrs. Tirrel hastily introduced her companions, even while shooting daggers at Ethan, who had turned the tables, so that now the ladies were being introduced to Morgan, placing her socially above all four of them.

These were small things, but in a society as vapid as

the one in Mayfair, they weighed heavily, and Ethan knew it. He truly believed people like his aunt even kept score.

"Yes, yes, of course, I should have recalled the names on my own. So sorry, ladies, a thousand apologies. As for my companion, I am delighted to introduce you to Miss Morgan Becket." He leaned slightly toward the open carriage. "*The* Beckets of Romney Marsh, you know."

"Becket?" His aunt's face screwed up in concentration. "I don't believe I recognize the name."

Morgan had seen and heard enough. She put her hand against Ethan's chest, pushing him slightly back as she leaned forward and looked to the ladies on her left. "I should hardly doubt that, madam. Obviously, you and I do not travel in the same circles."

Then she sat back, raised her chin and said, "Aylesford, I believe the horses have been left standing long enough while you speak with your…relation." She said the last word with the same distaste one might reserve for having discovered a maggot in her bread.

Without so much as a hint of the amusement he was feeling, Ethan turned once more to his aunt and her companions. "Now see what you've done, Aunt. And here I'd been planning to invite you and my cousin to be a part of my small party next week, in honor of Miss Becket. I'm afraid you can put paid to that hope, madam."

"I…but surely—"

"Good day, ladies," Ethan said, and his team moved forward into an immediate trot, for there was sufficient room in front of them now, until they caught up with the other vehicles making the circuit.

Besides, he very much needed to laugh, and he was certain Morgan was suffering from the same urgency.

"'We do not travel in the same circles,'" he repeated, once the worst of his bout of hilarity was past.

"Well, we don't, do we?" Morgan retorted, delicately wiping at her streaming eyes with the corner of the handkerchief she'd pulled from her pocket. "I don't travel in any circles at all, unless we count this one, and I'd really rather leave the park, if you don't mind."

Ethan's smile faded. "She did upset you."

"Upset me? Really, Ethan, that sorry excuse, upset me? No. I'm simply bored, that's all. What is the sense of horseflesh like your pair, if all they can do is stand about, waiting to move a few inches at a time? I know I shouldn't pass judgment too quickly, but I must tell you that so far I find society to be damn silly. I can't for the life of me understand why anyone would think I'd find it otherwise."

"Don't say any more, Morgan, please, or I'll be forced to stop the curricle now, so that I can get down on one knee and propose to you. Because you're the most brilliant woman I've ever met."

She smiled at him, returning his own smile…until both those smiles faded, and all they did was look at each other.

The tension was back, twofold. Had they really believed they could go for a ride in the Promenade, be civil and polite to each other, behave as if they were nothing more than two people who had only recently met, and might possibly enjoy each other's company for an hour?

"Hold on, Morgan," Ethan said tightly. They'd neared one of the gates, and he skillfully directed his pair toward it, neatly feathering the off-wheel of the curricle to within an inch of the wheel of a larger equipage.

He turned the curricle into the street, his mind racing with all the reasons he should be heading straight to Upper Brook Street for all of the time it took him to turn into the mews behind his mansion in Grosvenor Square.

"Where are we?" Morgan asked, looking about at what had to be the servants' entrance to the building on her right, just as what stood to her left was most obviously a large private stable.

"Follow my lead," Ethan told her quietly as he hopped down from the seat, then assisted Morgan to the cobblestones just as one of his grooms rushed out to him.

"Somethin' amiss, milord?" the young man asked, looking toward the team. "One of 'em throw up a stone?"

"No, Harold, they're fine. Miss Becket has expressed an interest in seeing Alejandro."

The young boy looked at Morgan, then nodded. "He's sure somethin' to see, ain't he, milord?"

"If you'd be so kind as to stand with the horses?" Ethan offered his arm to Morgan, then added, as if it were an afterthought, "Isn't it time for your dinner, Harold?"

The boy's cheeks reddened as he nodded. "Didn't think yer knew that, milord, or cared. Yessir, it is. But, yer see, someun has to stay with the horses. The rest are all up in the kitchens." He straightened his spine. "But I'm good for it, milord, I am. Nobody nor nothin' gets past me."

Ethan tossed him a coin. "Good man, Harold. Let no one get past you while the lady and I are inside, and there'll be another coin like that for you later. We're simply going to visit Alejandro, if anyone asks."

Morgan looked anywhere but at the groom as the boy swallowed, his huge Adam's apple working its way up and down his throat. "That's what yer doin', all right, and so says me."

"Yes, thank you, Harold," Ethan said as he laid his hand against the small of Morgan's back, and they walked together into the well-kept stables. "Good man, Harold," he said as they went.

"Indeed, yes. I should think he is destined for great things," Morgan agreed, tongue-in-cheek.

"I'd say I was corrupting you, you know, but I think someone else has done that job for me."

"That would be me," Morgan said, grinning up at him.

The stables were of stone, with sweet-smelling straw on the packed-earth ground, and cool as well as comfortably dim.

Morgan felt very at home here, and admired how well-maintained everything seemed to be. The earl took pride in his horseflesh, and in how those animals were housed. You can tell a lot about a man from the way he treats those who serve him and his animals, her papa had told her.

"How many horses do you keep here? Isn't it expensive to house them in London?"

"Fifteen at last count and, yes, it's expensive. As is keeping two coaches, a curricle and my latest folly, a high-perch phaeton. Do you want to see it?"

"I'd rather see Alejandro."

"Of course you would," Ethan said, smiling, and he directed her to the left, as the vehicles were all stored to her right. "I have no idea why I even asked such a silly question, considering your reaction to my curricle."

Morgan walked deeper into the stables, down the wide aisle framed on either side by generous-size stalls, already fairly certain that Alejandro would have the last one, which spanned the entire width of the building. He probably had his own window, as well, and perhaps a huge, tufted pillow to lounge on if the spirit moved him.

She was nearly proved right. Alejandro's was the last stall. It was huge. It did have its own window cut through the thick stone, with its own wooden shutter fitted into the space.

"Hello again, sweetness," Morgan purred as the stallion moved toward her, for he hadn't been tied to any of the heavy iron rings bolted into the wall. "My, aren't you important. And you're not alone, either, are you?" she asked as she noticed the rather large collie dog sleeping in one corner.

"Alejandro doesn't like to be alone, so I ordered Jack brought here last night."

"Jack? I like that," Morgan said, smiling. "It's a fine name for a fine dog. My Berengaria is partial to birds, however."

"A bird?" Ethan was watching her closely, knowing they didn't have much more time, but also knowing that she wouldn't be who she was if she ignored Alejandro, who was now nuzzling at her neck like some fawning suitor.

"Hmm, yes," Morgan said, patting the stallion's cheek before walking back to Ethan. "Jolly. He's a parrot. Jolly Roger, actually. He must be fifty years old, we think. And not very nice, when he's upset." She smiled evilly. "I've learned quite a few words from him, as a matter of fact. Not that I'd ever repeat any of them."

"A sailor's parrot, obviously. I should have realized. Becket Hall is directly on the coastline, you said. Your family is made up of sailors?"

"Not at all," Morgan said, touching her hands to the lapels of Ethan's jacket, her gaze concentrated on her actions even as her mind was warning her to silence. "Papa simply prefers his privacy." She looked up at Ethan, smiled. "And you really can't get too much more private than the wilds of Romney Marsh."

"Or Alejandro's stall," Ethan said, taking a half-step closer to her. "You do know why I brought you here. Don't you, Morgan?"

Her gaze was steady on his. "Because walking me through the front door of your house would have destroyed my reputation, yes. My sister Elly was quite clear on what I should and should not do while in the company of a…gentleman."

Ethan tipped his head to one side, grinned at her. "Well, yes, that is one reason. But not the main reason. I brought you here, Morgan, because if I had to keep my hands off you for another hour, I would most probably have suffered irreparable damage to myself."

Morgan decided, there and then, that this probably was the moment she should draw back, reassess. Possibly even panic. But she felt no qualms. No fears.

And certainly no reluctance.

No need to tease, no reason to flirt.

But perhaps a moment to reassure?

"I have been kissed before, you know," she told him.

"Have you really?" Ethan said, one corner of his mouth twitching as he carefully slid his arms around her back. "Many times, I'm sure."

"Well, not *many* times," Morgan said, slowly sliding her hands up onto his shoulders. His mere proximity was making her breathless, slightly dizzy. "But most certainly more than once."

"Let me guess," Ethan said, his attention all on Morgan's mouth. "That halfling, Jacob?"

"Poor Jacob. And he's not a halfling. He's two years older than me, as a matter of fact."

Ethan began to wonder, not without humor, who was seducing whom in Alejandro's stall. "Sweetheart, that boy hasn't been older than you since you were in your mother's womb."

"Yes…my mother," Morgan said softly, then shook off a sudden thought that had a lot to do with *like mother, like daughter.* "And there were others."

Ethan's left eyebrow climbed on his forehead. "Really? May a gentleman ask how *many* others? Two? A half-dozen? A score?"

"Two," Morgan admitted, knowing he was laughing at her now. "Both gentlemen. In the Waterguard. Very dangerous soldiers."

Ethan rested his forehead against hers. "Will I be forced to call either of them out?"

Morgan sighed. "No. One broke his leg when he fell into a hole in the marsh, and was sent home. The other is dead."

"One of your brothers killed him?"

Her heart stopped for a moment, then began to beat again, faster than before. She dropped her arms to her sides and stepped away from him, making a great business of stripping off her gloves. "Why would you ask that?"

Ethan had sensed her sudden nervousness, had felt her muscles tighten beneath his hands before she'd pulled away from him. "I was teasing, Morgan. If they had seen him kissing you, you understand. I'm simply attempting to gauge my own odds on surviving the Season."

"Oh." Morgan relaxed, summoned a smile as she pulled at the fingers of her tight kid gloves, one by one. "I suppose you'll simply have to be very careful. Or… reconsider."

"I don't think I'll do that. After all, we've gone to all this trouble, hiding here in the stables like naughty children."

"I was always a naughty child," Morgan said proudly, feeling in control once more, as the subject of her brothers was dropped. "I'd tell you that I tried very hard to be naughty, but I can't say that. Naughty just came to me, quite easily. I think it still does."

"And that's why you can say that you've been kissed?"

Morgan frowned as she untied the ribbons of her bonnet and slipped it off, tossed it down on the clean, sweet straw before turning to face Ethan once more. "Among other things, yes. I just thought I should tell you not to worry that I'm afraid, or anything, because I have been kissed before."

Ethan took hold of her shoulders. "No, sweetheart, you have not."

"Are you calling me a—"

Ethan brought his mouth down on hers, even as he insinuated his thigh slightly between hers and cupped the back of her neck with one large hand, so that he could move her as he slanted his lips first this way, then that way. Teasing at her mouth, lightly suckling on her full bottom lip. Running the tip of his tongue across the front of her bottom teeth.

Retreating, but never completely. Advancing, assaulting and defeating her defenses, one by one, until she began to respond—which, he was delighted to learn, did not take above a few seconds.

Morgan felt his tongue inside her mouth, and it seemed the most natural thing in the world to her, even as she imitated his movements, attacking his lips when he withdrew, launching her own assault on him.

Excitement rippled through her, her blood heating, the rush of feeling caught somewhere between the mix of anxiety and exhilaration she felt when she rode out on the Marsh after midnight with the Black Ghost and a curiosity as old as time.

Ethan eased his knee more closely between her thighs, allowing her to feel his arousal, know what she was doing to him. She returned the pressure with her lower body, letting him take her weight against him, not backing away, but trading advance for advance.

He backed up, still holding on to her, until he could feel the cool stone wall behind him, and Morgan held him more tightly, so that their bodies were entirely outlined against each other while they exchanged deep kisses, pausing only to breathe.

It was madness. Kissing in the stables? Not since he

had been an eager young boy, and one of the dairymaids had offered to "educate you, sir, if you've a curiosity" had he felt such a driving need to touch, to explore. To experience.

Morgan moved him beyond anything he had ever felt, ever experienced, making all of his life before her a meaningless pursuit of paltry pleasures.

His hands skimmed her sides, his passion mixed with an odd, unfamiliar reverence that forced a sigh from his lips when he at last cupped her full breasts in his hands.

Their combined sighs met, mingled, and then passion slammed hard into both of them.

Ethan broke the kiss, burying his head against the side of her throat as Morgan dug her fingertips into his shoulders, threw back her head to give him access to her sweet-smelling skin as he ran the pads of his thumbs back and forth beneath her short jacket, across her taut nipples covered now only by the thin muslin of her gown.

Morgan couldn't breathe, didn't want to breathe, because that could mean this moment might slip away somehow, and she'd die if that happened, if there were no next moment that compared with this one.

And then the moment was over.

Ethan somehow regained control of himself, reluctantly, and not without personal pain, and slid his hands around Morgan's back, pulling her close, her head now against his shoulder.

Both of them were breathing heavily, as if they'd just run a long race, and he could feel Morgan's body trembling, only slightly, as she burrowed into him. She said something, but he couldn't quite catch the words.

"Were you just cursing me?" he asked, kissing her hair.

"No, of course not," she said, a slow smile curving her lips. "I was simply telling you that you were right. I've never been kissed before. Until now."

He lightly rubbed one hand up and down the smooth curve of her back. "And damn me if I'm not proud to hear you say that," he said, then gently pushed her away from him, looked down at her, smiled. "We're going to have to keep your face hidden as we pass Harold out there if we're not to corrupt the lad."

"Why?" Morgan asked, smoothing his neck cloth with her fingers, just to be touching him. She needed to keep touching him. She would never tire of touching him.

"Because, sweetings, you look well and truly kissed," Ethan told her, running a fingertip over her adorably pink and slightly swollen lower lip, "and only a blind man wouldn't notice, or know what we've been doing."

"Oh, God, really?" Morgan broke away, her hand to her mouth now as she walked across the stall, then turned to look at him. "Chance isn't blind."

"Neither, I suspect, is his dear wife." Ethan retrieved Morgan's gloves and bonnet, picking bits of straw from the latter before approaching her and carefully placing the bonnet on her head. "That's unfortunate. The brim is too short, and really doesn't conceal anything."

Morgan giggled, feeling very much like the naughty child she'd been, but now naughty for quite a new reason. A rather delicious reason. She threaded her arms up and around his neck once more. "You know, Ethan, as long as the damage has already been done…"

"Imp," he said, and pulled her close for yet another kiss. His mind might have been running ahead of him, composing exactly what he'd say to Chance Becket, but the words fled as a different hunger overtook him. Not to have her, which he most certainly wanted, but just to hold her, to kiss her. To never, never ever, let her go.

They stopped, kissed, several more times as they slowly made their way through the dim length of the stables, Ethan pulling her close one last time just as there was a mighty boom of thunder that seemed to shake the ground beneath their feet.

Morgan went up on tiptoe for yet another kiss. She'd been near tears, which was immensely silly, but just the thought of going back to Upper Brook Street, being without Ethan even for a moment, threatened to tear a hole in her heart.

It was madness. Needing someone so much, someone she hadn't until yesterday known existed. That one someone who made her complete, when she'd never known she'd been incomplete.

"Listen. It's raining," Ethan said, then kissed the tip of her nose as a wild inspiration struck him. "In fact, it's pouring. A wonderful, beautiful, drenching downpour. The weather gods are smiling on us, Morgan, if you're willing."

She frowned, looking out at the cobblestone alleyway, where rain was coming down so straight and so hard that it seemed to bounce a good foot into the air after it hit. "Harold's putting up the hood, but I'm sure the seat is already thoroughly wet. The weather gods smile when they get us wet?"

"They do if they're trying to help us. Morgan, how

do you feel about arriving back in Upper Brook Street looking as if you'd been dunked in the Thames?"

"What? And why are you grinning like that?"

"It's simple. The rain came suddenly, without warning. I made a valiant attempt to raise the hood, but the damn thing's broken, so that we had to make a dash for Upper Brook Street, entirely unprotected. Why, with the crush of other vehicles racing for cover, by the time we reached your brother's residence, we were both soaked to the skin."

"And I'd, of course, race inside and straight up the stairs, calling for a hot bath—and unseen by either Chance or Julia—while you, also quite naturally, have no choice but to come back here for a tub and change of clothes for yourself, as well." Morgan grinned in turn, delighting in the plan. "By the time we're both again presentable, my mouth will not look so…kissed. You're right, Ethan. The weather gods are smiling on us."

"Only if you promise you won't melt away in the rain, or mind ruining your gown," Ethan reminded her, taking her hand.

"I love the rain, love how it feels when I walk in it," she assured him. "As for this gown? I have others. More than I'll ever need." She squeezed his hand. "Are you ready?"

"In a moment." He kissed her again. God, would he ever have enough of kissing her? Then he headed out into the downpour, calling to his groom. "Harold, don't bother. The hood is broken."

Harold scrubbed at his face in an attempt to rid it of rain, and said, "Oh, no, milord. It works just fine."

Ethan held up two gold coins. "I say it's broken."

Harold grinned, showing a large gap between his top front teeth. "And it's truly sorry I am, milord, that it is. Couldn't get that there hood up iffen yer was to put a barkin' iron to me head."

"Definitely destined for great things," Ethan said, tossing the coins to the groom, then grinning himself as Morgan came running out into the rain.

She laughed as she held up her skirts, which instantly became drenched, and Ethan helped her onto the wet seat, vaulting up after her, his curly brimmed beaver at a jaunty tilt on his head.

He took the reins, blinking water out of his eyes. It was as if all the rain in the world had concentrated itself over Mayfair and was determined to fall in one huge torrent, even as the sun remained visible, high in the sky.

Morgan turned her face up to the flood, then pointed into the distance. "Look, a rainbow! Isn't it magnificent?"

Her straw bonnet had already given up the fight against the elements, and the brim now drooped over her face. Her thick black lashes were spiky around her laughing gray eyes, which shone with her delight. She was the most splendid, most *alive* person he'd ever met, even when soaking wet. Because she didn't care how she looked, not if she was enjoying herself.

"*You're* magnificent," he told her, meaning every word.

She playfully wiped at the rain dripping off his nose. "And you're very wet. One more kiss. Please? I want to taste the rain on you."

Ethan's gut tightened. He'd think he was being bewitched, but he doubted that. Or, if he was, he was a willing victim. "We'll corrupt Harold."

"Poor Harold," Morgan said, then pressed her smiling lips to Ethan's as the matched pair stepped forward smartly, in perfect precision, their hooves sending up sprays of rainwater, the droplets catching the sunlight and forming small, dancing rainbows ahead of the curricle…and the couple oblivious to all of it.

CHAPTER NINE

CHANCE REFILLED HIS GLASS at the drinks table, then rejoined his wife on the couch, lowering himself onto the cushions with a display of complete exhaustion. He felt like an old, a very old, man.

The earl had made his excuses shortly after their delayed dinner, begging a previous engagement that could not be ignored, and Morgan had then immediately made a great business of widely yawning and complaining that her hair was still damp inside its thick coil, so she'd like nothing more than to go upstairs and brush it in front of the fire, then have an early night.

Leaving Chance and Julia Becket alone in the drawing room.

"That," he said, lifting her hand to place a kiss in her palm, "was the most uncomfortable evening of my life."

Julia snuggled against her husband as she began untying his neck cloth. "Oh, it wasn't that terrible. The earl is very polite and entertaining."

"The earl, my dear, kept looking at my sister as if he was going to *pounce* on her at any moment."

"Before she could pounce on him. Yes, I saw that. I kept thinking it a good thing that the dining table separated them."

Chance sat up, dislodging his wife, who braced herself against the cushions and smiled at him in amusement. He pulled off his neck cloth, its length making the gesture more prolonged than impressive, then tossed it onto the table.

"And that business with the hood of his curricle? I can swallow that, if I have to, but explain to me why he didn't realize it was coming on to rain. Everyone else did, anyone with a brain. Anyone who was outside, actually *in* the park. And yet the pair of them showed up here looking like they'd been keelhauled."

Julia was no longer smiling. "Are you suggesting that Morgan and the earl were *not* in the park? Then where were they?"

Chance turned on the cushions to look at his wife. "I'm not sure either of us wants to know that. The question, Julia, is what in bloody hell are we going to do about it?"

Julia bit the side of her knuckle. "Tying her to the bedpost probably wouldn't work," she said, cudgeling her brain for an answer that actually might work. "I had foreseen problems having Morgan here with us, Chance, but nothing like this. And certainly not so soon."

"And not with Aylesford, definitely. It's as if she looked around her and found the one man I wouldn't choose for her. And then made a dead run at him."

Julia rubbed at her husband's back, feeling the tenseness in his muscles. "I know he's considerably older than Morgan, but that could be just what she needs. Someone steady. A…a sobering influence."

Chance, his shoulders hunched, swiveled his head

sideways to grin at his wife. "Are we speaking of the same Earl of Aylesford, darling? The one I'm speaking of is said to have walked up behind Beau Brummell and picked a bit of lint off his jacket, then held it up to the man as he suggested Brummell might take more care with his toilette."

Julia's eyes went wide. "He didn't do that. Beau Brummell is the most fashionable man in England. Everyone knows it."

"And the most fastidious, not to mention powerful, with the Prince Regent as his friend. Aylesford was deliberately tweaking Brummell, who, I'm also told, chose to laugh as if amused—probably because he's deep in debt again, and Aylesford undoubtedly holds a few of his gaming markers."

"Gaming markers or not, Brummell could have chosen to cut him, and the earl would have been socially destroyed. Wouldn't he?"

"Yes. Maybe. Nobody understands Aylesford. It's as if he courts disaster, daring society to turn its back on his title—and his considerable fortune. I wouldn't say he's a bad man, a *mean* man. I think he simply enjoys his outrageous reputation, enjoys proving the gossips right. I'm fairly certain he delights in pointing out that society, in general, is embarrassingly shallow, as it takes all he can dish out to them. Not that I understand why Brummell or any man would want to spend half his life dressing and undressing, and the rest of it posturing and preening."

Julia looked at her husband. His neck cloth was gone, the collar of his shirt now open, his waistcoat undone. His darkly blond hair, which had been tied at his nape, was now missing its black grosgrain ribbon and fell forward, so she pushed a lock of it behind his ear as she leaned forward to kiss his cheek.

This was the man she loved, the man she'd married. The London gentleman was fine, and served a purpose, but the real Chance Becket was freer, wilder, more vitally male.

"No, darling. You don't understand that. And yet I'd take you over a half-dozen Mr. Brummells."

He captured her hand and kissed her fingers, one by one, as he looked at her, and she felt the fire always simmering between them gaining strength. "You know, Julia, the more I think about it, the more I am beginning to believe you're right. Not about Aylesford being a sobering influence, because that, frankly, is insane, but about the rest of it. He might be exactly what Morgan needs."

"You don't mean that," Julia said, seeing the mischievous twinkle in her husband's eyes—so like Alice's, when she was trying to wheedle another few minutes with her toys before bedtime. "What are you thinking?"

Chance leaned back against the cushions once more, suddenly relaxed, his worries gone. He put his arm up on the back of the couch, and Julia tucked herself in beside him. Their daughter upstairs, the two of them here, a second child growing inside his beloved wife... His entire world, all he needed, all he'd ever wanted, and so much more.

"I'm thinking, wife, that Morgan is going to have a very short Season. Perhaps a week."

Julia frowned. "That's all?"

"Let me finish. A week, yes, that's more than enough, if I'm any judge of what the earl believes he feels for my sister."

"He thinks he's in love and that she's in love," Julia said rather sadly. "I can understand that from Morgan, but you'd think the earl would have more sense at his age. Love doesn't happen that quickly."

"No, but sometimes something else does," Chance said, "although the gentleman in me shouldn't remind you of our own beginnings."

"You're right, the gentleman in you shouldn't say such things. However, I didn't fall in love with the gentleman in you, and it certainly wasn't the gentleman in you that took me to bed that night. Earlier, I thought about dumping a bucket of water over the pair of them, you know, because I was afraid they were going to burst into flame at any moment. Is it…is it difficult for you to think about your sister as a woman with…with needs?"

Chance chuckled softly. "Morgan? No. Elly, Fanny, Cassandra. Yes, those three would be difficult to imagine. But not Morgan. She grabs at life with both hands, no question, wants to experience everything. I don't know why I would think she wouldn't be more… more…"

"Passionate?"

Chance winced, then smiled. "I was trying not to actually say the word, thank you. But, yes, passionate. Intense. But too young, and still too full of herself, I think, to know real love from…"

"Lust?" Julia supplied helpfully once more, delighted to see her husband so flustered. He was actually blushing, poor thing.

"All right. Yes, damn it. Lust. Which is why she

can't stay here, making a fool of herself with Aylesford, who seems more than happy to help her become a public spectacle like himself. She'd draw too much attention to herself, to all of us. God only knows who saw them today, riding through the rain like a fine pair of idiots. Damn! She was supposed to come here, attend a few select balls, be seen at the theater, a few country breakfasts. Find herself a suitable husband. It all seemed so simple, in theory."

"Most things do," Julia agreed. "But a week, Chance? How will you manage to convince her to go home? She won't leave him, you know. Not until and unless this fire between them burns out for at least one of them."

Chance got to his feet once more, pulled Julia up beside him. "I'm not going to convince her. Ainsley is, and I'll leave the *how* of the thing to him. I can have a letter to him by late tomorrow night with the right messenger, who can bring back a letter summoning Morgan home."

Julia sighed, shook her head. "Nothing is that simple, darling. Aylesford will want to accompany her."

Chance's grin was so near to evil that Julia laughed. "Possibly. But then they'll be Ainsley's problem, and whatever happens, it won't take place in the middle of Mayfair. Alice will want a Season one day, remember? That can't occur if we're all tossed out of society on our ears. So? What do you think?"

"I think we're either cowards or brilliant," Julia said as they walked, arm in arm, toward the foyer. "One more week, hmm? I think we should be able to manage that without the entire world tumbling down on our heads...."

CHAPTER TEN

ETHAN WAS HAVING SECOND thoughts. Away from Morgan, he could think more rationally, more reasonably, and he knew his behavior with her the day before had been far from proper.

He was older. He was experienced. He knew the rules, the strictures. He knew the boundaries, and when he'd exceeded them.

But that had been him. For him. In some twisted need to tweak the society that termed his father a fool and his mother a calloused fortune hunter. The society that had decided that any offspring of that pair couldn't possibly be more than another disgrace and disaster.

He'd enjoyed proving them wrong where it mattered, by not running through his fortune once he came into the title but increasing it; and proving them right, by being as outrageous as he wished to be.

The ball he'd hosted for the Society for the Aid and Solace of Rescued Doves—prostitutes who had hopes of a better life. That he had "forgotten" to mention the purpose of the ball when issuing the invitations to the cream of the ton was, of course, an unfortunate oversight.

Especially when several of the guests, in the company of their wives, recognized former mistresses sipping wine at the sides of the ballroom.

More of the short list of his calculated indiscretions marched in front of his mind.

The curricle race up Pall Mall one Sunday morning at dawn, with the winner then paraded through White's, held high on a chair and wearing a crown of gilded oak leaves.

A few carefully planned drunken brawls.

The day he'd fixed a tall pink plume to Alejandro's head before riding him in the Promenade, telling anyone who asked that he'd got the idea from the Prince of Wales. By the next evening, more than two score of young Fashionables had tied pink feather plumes to their unfortunate horses. Not only were more than a few society matrons bemoaning the loss of their treasured plumes, but the Promenade that day very much resembled a circus parade.

Alejandro's plume, of course, was now gone, and Ethan told anyone who asked that only a fool would trick out his horse in feathers unless he had lost a bet with the Prince of Wales.

Stupid stunts. Silliness. Anger, played out his way, on the stage of his choosing.

He hadn't done anything especially terrible in nearly six years, but the die had been cast, and his reputation had followed him into what he'd hoped might be his more sober thirties.

And now there was Morgan.

He knew his own demons. What demons drove her?

Like recognizes like. That's what she'd said, and he believed her.

Was that all there was between them? This nearly insane need to be together, to touch, to kiss. This hunger for so much more.

She was beautiful. More than beautiful. She was the most gorgeous woman he'd ever seen. Alive, vital. And as irresistible to him as the urge to take his next breath.

He'd have her body. He knew that. She wanted him, and he knew that, too. But once they'd made love, sated themselves on each other—what then?

Morgan was young, and probably hadn't thought beyond the next moment. But he was older, supposedly wiser, and couldn't claim the same excuse....

"Aylesford? It's done, and we all agree. The papers are genuine, completely in order and, for the main, in compliance with our conditions."

Ethan, who had been sitting with his chin in his hand for the half hour since he'd arrived and been ushered into the empty office, sat up in the uncomfortable chair facing the minister's desk as the self-important man himself entered the room.

The minister carried an ornately decorated silver tube and the tightly rolled parchment that had been its contents until someone elsewhere in the building had sawed off the top of the cylinder, which resembled three others Ethan had seen in this past year.

Knowing that at any other time he would have been sitting here wondering why the minister had broken with protocol and summoned him to the War Office in daylight, Ethan shook off thoughts of Morgan, and hoped he looked interested in what the man had to say.

"So we heard from them? I didn't think my friend would arrive for another few weeks."

"A fast ship and a favorable wind, I suppose. And a growing sense of urgency, unfortunately," the minister said as he lowered his bulk into the overstuffed leather chair behind the desk. "An answer, of course, is required."

"Of course." Ethan pushed any lingering thoughts of Morgan to the back of his mind. "When do I leave?"

The minister had unrolled the parchment and was in the process of securing the ends to the desk with an inkwell on one side and a brass paperweight in the shape of a peacock on the other. "Not as quickly as we'd hoped, unfortunately. We're in agreement in several areas, and have settled on several compromises. But they remain ridiculously adamant on one particular condition."

Ethan smiled ruefully. "Let me hazard a guess, my lord. They object yet again to the removal of American sailors from their ships."

"Their ships, Aylesford. *English* sailors. We do not recognize any trumped-up notions of a renunciation of nationality. Never have, never will. Do try to remember that when you speak with their representative, if you please."

Ethan spread his hands, palms up. "I'm only saying—"

"What you've said before, I know. You've been depressingly consistent in your objections, Aylesford. President Madison is pushing for war, but as long as we have the ear of our friends in the Federalist Party, there is still hope that sanity will prevail in their Congress, and he'll be voted down. And, damn me, if it weren't for the fact that this agent will speak with no one but you…"

"What can I say? I'm a likable fellow, and the friendship we struck up so many years ago is what has brought us this far, my lord. Unless you'd rather I withdrew?"

"You've got us by the bollocks, and you know it," the minister bellowed, bringing his fist down on the desktop, nearly oversetting the inkwell. "The day that the future of this country might rest in the hands of the unstable offspring of an unstable—"

Ethan was already halfway out of his chair. "And a good day to you, my lord. I'm off to my club."

"No! Wait, wait. I apologize. Sit down, damn it!"

"Certainly, since you asked so nicely," Ethan said, subsiding into the chair. "When will you have an answer ready for me to deliver to my friend?"

The minister sat back in his chair, propping his fingertips together beneath the second of his chins. "We've already requested an audience with the Prince Regent," he said, as if speaking to himself, "although God only knows if he'll take time away from his tailor to meet with us."

Ethan turned a short laugh into a cough. "Long live the king, my lord?"

"Why? He's no use to us, either. Padded the walls of his chambers, you know. To keep him safe, or to keep down the noise when he howls at the moon, who knows which? Mad as a hatter, all of them, with one no better than the other, and wars to fight."

"One to fight, one to prevent," Ethan corrected, hoping to get the minister back on point.

Another day, just one day before he'd met Morgan, Ethan would have enjoying bantering with the minister, baiting him. But he had other things to occupy his mind and his time with now. Thoughts about Morgan left little room in his brain to think about the failings of the royalty.

"Yes, yes, although I will tell you, Aylesford, I think we've already watched the horse run out of the stables on this one. Still, we must try. Now, the *Marianna* will be in our waters for only a week, and that began yesterday morning. We're holding the messenger for now, to finalize plans on this end. We can only chance one meeting, but not in Dymchurch this time, I don't think, after the close call you had in January."

"There was never any real danger, my lord," Ethan said, thinking back to the encounter between his friend and himself, and what had occurred when an officer of the local Waterguard had gotten too curious.

"Yes, and the clever fellow who followed you has been reassigned. Once his arm mends, that is."

"I honestly thought I'd only bent him, not broken him. I'm sorry."

"I'm sure he appreciates your concern. But we can't be too careful. Select another location, so we can send back the man who brought this with both a time and a place. All this damn secrecy. We should simply commandeer the *Marianna* and be done with it."

"My friend wouldn't like that."

"Your friend be damned!" The minister picked up the cylinder. "If a messenger can bring this, he can damn well carry back our answer. It would be a simple matter to follow him. We don't need you."

"One would think not, except that my friend doesn't agree. Besides, wasn't one failure enough for you?"

The minister had the decency to look ashamed. "We were only being careful."

Ethan hid a smile. He'd heard what had happened. The messenger who delivered the first cylinder to the

War Office and carried away the response had been only one of three heavily cloaked men who then rode out of London, each heading in a different direction. Even so, all three had been stopped on one pretext or the other…and none of them had the cylinder in their possession.

The next they'd heard from the agent, the message had been in the way of a warning: "Do not follow the man who brings this to you. In future, you will send your answers to Dymchurch with the Earl of Aylesford, and only the earl, else all communication stops. Once he arrives in the port, we will find him and complete the transaction at a place of our choosing."

It was, Ethan had told the minister at the time, so very nice to be needed, even if, it would appear, he was to be used as a sort of shield.

What he had never told the minister was that, when they had met for the first time, his friend had explained that the only way to believe the English communiqués were legitimate, hadn't been tampered with along the way, was to be able to trust the messenger without question. A messenger who couldn't be bribed or threatened. It made a curious sort of sense.

Three times he'd ridden to Dymchurch. Once to be stopped along the road and led all the way to Dover. Once to be met in the town, then quickly taken to the port of Hythe. Only on his last mission had he actually met with his friend in Dymchurch itself…with that meeting nearly ending in disaster.

"And the Prince Regent's answer?" Ethan asked, getting to his feet.

"We'll need as much time as we can get, every

moment of it, and all the arguing skills we can muster. No matter what, keep yourself ready, because you'll be leaving London in the next three to four days."

"Surely not four days to compose a reply. That's cutting a little too close to the bone, and exposing my friend for more time than usual."

"When politics begins to run smoothly, Aylesford, you'll be the first to know," the minister said with some heat. "For now, we muddle through the best we can. All right, I'll make the decision now, and then pray we can convince his royal highness. Saturday. You meet your friend Saturday night, which means I'll have everything ready for you by Thursday morning. Two days, Aylesford. And I'll need every moment of both of them, so go away and let me work. Get me that new rendezvous location by this evening, so I can send the messenger back with the information."

"There's no need to wait," Ethan said, an idea bursting into his brain, fully formed. "I already have a new location in mind, and a quite plausible reason for my face to be seen in the area. Do you have a map of southern England, my lord?"

The minister shook his head in obvious disgust at having to work with amateurs. "This is the War Office, Aylesford. Of course we have maps. We've got dozens of maps. What is it you want to see?"

"Precisely? A map of Romney Marsh, my lord."

The minister mouthed the words *Romney Marsh* silently a few times, as if Ethan had spoken in a foreign language, then snapped his fingers, a memory clicking in his brain. "I've got better than a map, Aylesford. I've got Chance Becket. Very useful man, very loyal. Just last year we—but that's not important. His family comes from Romney Marsh—somewhere in that mess of swamp and sheep. I'll have my clerk summon him."

Ethan's plan, although one he considered to be good, climbed into the realm of perfection, from any angle. "I have made Mr. Becket's acquaintance, my lord. To be perfectly truthful, I'm courting his sister at the moment. I'm certain we can gain his cooperation in this matter."

"Courting his sister? *You?* And Becket allows this? I may have to rethink my confidence in the man. I wouldn't let you within five miles of my daughter."

Ethan smiled, knowing he wouldn't care to be within ten miles of his lordship's daughter. "Yes, my lord. There's no limit to the man's folly, it would appear."

The minister rang the bell on his desk and directed the clerk to summon Mr. Becket to the office at once.

"You know, sir," Ethan said, as if speaking just as the idea came to him, "Becket's family estate is directly on the coast. I would imagine the *Marianna* could drop anchor off the shore at the appointed time, away from any port. I can deliver the communication aboard ship, and the agent can be at sea again almost immediately."

"Yes, yes, even better than any port, no matter how small, and with far less suspicion. Bad enough we have to worry about the French tooling about out there in the Channel, without problems from our own overzealous military on land. Yes, brilliant plan. I should have thought of it myself, eventually. Ah, Becket, you're here."

Ethan, who had remained standing, bowed slightly to Morgan's brother, whose expression was carefully blank.

"Mr. Becket, a delight to see you again, sir," Ethan said, informing him that, yes, the minister had already been told that they were acquainted.

"Aylesford," Chance said, returning the slight bow. "My lord," he said then, bowing to the minister. "You wished to speak to me, sir?"

CHAPTER ELEVEN

"NOW I CAN BE ALIVE again," Morgan whispered to Ethan, leaning back into him as he settled the cashmere wrap over her shoulders.

Ethan shot a quick look across the drawing room, to see that Chance and Julia Becket were concentrating on untangling the strings of her reticule from the tassels of her own shawl. A lovely, quite domestic scene that appealed to him only because it also served to keep the couple's attention away from anything he might do.

His hands still on Morgan's shoulders, Ethan bent to press a kiss just behind her ear. "The day only begins when I see you, when I touch you."

The very air in the large room should be crackling from the sparks that flew between them, this intense awareness of each other that had its own shape, its own smell, its own substance.

Could wanting another person like this be a sickness? If so, how was it cured?

"Yes, thank you, my lord," Morgan said, quickly stepping away from him as Chance lifted his head, looked in their direction, "I did spend a very pleasant day. I accompanied my sister-in-law and my niece to the park this morning. A very different place, the park in the morning. I noticed several people on horseback, as a matter of fact."

"Berengaria wouldn't get much of a run there, though, I'm afraid. The park being very circumspect, you understand. Isn't that right, Aylesford?" Chance had crossed the room and overheard his sister. "I warned her not to bring the mare to town but, being Morgan, she didn't listen. I ride Jacmel to Richmond Park in the early hours when we both need a run."

Morgan looked at her brother. "I'll go with you tomorrow morning. You, too, my lord. Your Alejandro certainly must be in need of some exercise."

Chance and Ethan exchanged glances, Chance trying very hard not to appear pained, and Ethan acknowledging that man's pain with a slight inclination of his head; both knew that a man needed some privacy in which to propose marriage. And, because he was not stupid in victory, Ethan did not smile.

"I'm afraid I can't, Morgan," Chance said as he continued looking at the earl, "as I'm needed early at the War Office. But perhaps his lordship would agree to accompany you? That is, my lord," Chance added in his frustration, "if you have ever seen the dawn."

"Oh, I've seen it many, many times, Mr. Becket. Usually on my way home to my bed."

Morgan bit back a giggle, then sobered. "So we can go? Exercise the horses, that is?"

Julia joined them, still adjusting the ends of her scarf around her forearms. "Only if you promise not to come home drenched." She turned to her husband. "I suppose I'm as ready as I'm going to be, darling. Shall we go?"

Ethan had arrived in Upper Brook Street shortly after dinner, having arranged with Chance to escort them all to the theater, as he had his own box for the Season.

He'd arrived in his town coach, so that all four of them could ride to the theater together—one of the concessions he had made to Chance Becket earlier. This was to be an evening spent in the decorous pursuit of tame entertainment, followed by Morgan's safe return to Upper Brook Street.

Morgan would see Ethan, Ethan would have the pleasure of her company, society would see them together as a couple—and Chance wouldn't have to lock anyone in her room or challenge anyone else to a duel.

It seemed a reasonable plan. But then, as Chance had days earlier admitted to his wife, when it came to Morgan most plans seemed reasonable, in theory.

Ethan entertained them on their way to Covent Garden, pointing out the sights to Morgan and delighting Julia with bits of harmless gossip, manfully ignoring the unexpectedly evocative smell of jasmine he was certain was emanating from Morgan's elaborately dressed hair. He held her hand only a moment too long as he assisted her from the coach.

"My box is on the third level, Mr. Becket. Number fourteen. In the event we are separated in this tangle of bodies, you understand."

"See that we're not, my lord," Chance answered, then turned to assist his wife from the coach.

"Take my hand, Morgan," Ethan told her quietly as they pushed their way through the crush of overdressed and heavily perfumed theatergoers on their way to the stairs, and his box. Chance and Julia were already some distance behind them.

"Will we be alone at all?" Morgan asked, disgusted with the amount of people pressed together like ants in a box, and all of them seeming to think this was a jolly good thing. "Is most of London here?"

Ethan looked back down the stairs, then pulled Morgan along more quickly, as he could see that Julia was climbing slowly, lamenting the torn ruffle on the bottom of her gown, where someone's errant foot had done considerable damage.

That the clumsy "someone" had been Ethan's trusted valet, acting on orders from his master, was not information he felt necessary to impart to Morgan. He'd be ashamed of himself, knew he should be ashamed of himself, but his desire to be alone with her, if only for a few stolen minutes, outstripped any shame.

For, if what he felt for Morgan was some sort of exotic sickness, Ethan knew at least a temporary cure. Holding her. Kissing her.

At the next half-landing, he broke to his right, pushing aside a burgundy velvet curtain and letting it drop once he and Morgan were behind it. They were now inside a narrow hallway used by servants bringing refreshments to their employers, but at this hour, not yet in use.

"One kiss," he breathed quietly, drawing her close. "Just to see us through."

Morgan pressed her palms against his fine black evening coat, her heart pounding with the nearness of him. "Until? I don't know how long I can survive on only your kisses."

"God, you had to say that," Ethan said, cupping her cheeks in his hands, his thumbs lightly tracing her full mouth. "You can't know what you're saying. This is a game to you, Morgan. Something outside your experience, and I'm a bastard for—"

"Oh, Ethan, please do shut up. It's already years too late for common sense or sermons," Morgan told him, pulling him toward her by the simple expedient of tugging on his neck cloth. Just before their lips met, she whispered, "We both want this. Like recognizes like, remember?"

Their kiss was anything but gentle. Because of their shared need. Because there could only be the one.

But its effect on Ethan would be noticeable if anyone in the crowd chanced to look, and at least Chance Becket would.

Ethan kissed Morgan twice more, quick, hard kisses, and then slid her shawl from her shoulders, folding it twice before draping it over his arm. The arm he would hold in front of him as they made their way up the remainder of the stairs and into their box…where he could sink into a chair, and blessed darkness.

"What are you doing?" Morgan asked him as she watched, and then she recognized his problem. The realization that she could do this to the man, with just the power of a few shared kisses, was intoxicating, and her smile was part pleasure, part triumph. "Oh, Ethan, I'm so sorry."

"No, imp, you're not," he told her sternly, then added, "and you're supposed to be ignorant of my dilemma."

"And have you think me stupid? I grew up in the

country, Ethan. All those sheep, all those horses. I mean, I do understand the…the mechanics of the process."

"You do, do you? Marvelous. And am I now to be compared to a ram, or a stallion?"

"Why, sir, how would I know that?" Morgan's eyes widened as she bit her lips, her beautiful face taking on a comic expression that had Ethan shaking his head as he wondered whether, if he just retraced his steps back to the inn yard where he'd first seen her, he might be able to locate his mind.

"I know you're a virgin, Morgan," he said at last, handing her back the shawl, which he most certainly didn't need now, after the sheep and horse comment.

"Do you? How?" Morgan asked him, a part of her knowing they shouldn't be having this strange conversation. Then again, that was the same part that knew she shouldn't ever have kissed this man in the first place. Why start listening to that part of her now?

"Some things a man just knows," he told her, pulling back the curtain very slightly, then taking a quick look down the staircase. There was no sight of the Beckets. Either Chance had escorted his wife to a withdrawing room, where someone would sew up her flounce, or they were already in the box, and wondering where he and Morgan had got to. Damn. He let the curtain fall, and turned back to Morgan.

"Besides," he said, smiling at her, "I'm willing to wager everything I own that, although anyone who sees you might want you, they're more afraid of you."

"Why? That's silly. Why would anyone be afraid of me?"

"You honestly don't know, do you?" he asked, tracing a finger down her cheek. "They're afraid of you, imp, because they know, deep inside themselves, that if they aren't strong, you'll devour them."

Morgan's temper flared. "Devour, is it? I'm hungry *now,* Ethan. Doesn't that worry you?"

His grin maddened her. "No, not at all. Like recognizes like, Morgan, isn't that what you say?"

She lowered her eyes for a moment, then looked at him. "We're warning each other off, aren't we? Pulling each other closer, and pushing away at the same time. Why are we doing that?"

"I don't know," he told her honestly. "I do, however, at last understand the moth's often fatal fascination with the flame."

Morgan nodded in agreement, not trusting herself to speak.

Ethan took her hand and, silently, they made their way up the staircase to his private box, where Chance was pacing back and forth in front of the door.

Too late to bar the gate, Ethan thought ruefully, remembering the minister's words of earlier that day. *This particular horse has already bolted from the stables, Chance Becket...and we both know it.*

Becket's demanded tame evening could be lived through now, knowing that the morning would bring the ride to Richmond Park.

CHAPTER TWELVE

THE RIDE TO RICHMOND Park was both uneventful and quite slow, thanks to the fact that Saul and Jacob followed behind the horses in the Becket traveling coach, a large wicker picnic basket shoved between the seats inside the vehicle.

It had to be a ludicrous sight, if anyone was watching: the Earl of Aylesford on his magnificent Andalusian, a beautiful young woman riding beside him...and the most mismatched, unlikely pair of duennas bringing up the rear.

Obviously, Chance Becket believed he could feel his sister safe as long as the servants trailed after them like puppies. Ethan supposed a man must believe what he needs to believe. This public courtship might or might not be necessary to explain Ethan's upcoming departure for Becket Hall, but as long as the minister said it was, and Chance Becket believed the minister, who was Ethan to complain?

He was quiet as he and Morgan rode out of London, for two reasons. One, he'd discovered he really didn't much care for seeing dawn from this side of it...and he could feel the heat emanating off Morgan, and wished to be clear of the city before giving her any reason to vent her obvious anger.

There was a third reason: a short, ugly crossbow by the name of Bessie. But he wouldn't let his mind linger overmuch on that head.

But that didn't mean he wasn't holding in some anger of his own, because he was fairly certain Chance Becket had said something—what, he didn't know—that had Morgan considering various ways to murder the man riding beside her.

How could Becket have slipped up? What had he said?

During their conversation yesterday in a coffeehouse at the bottom of Bond Street, Becket had told him he'd already sent off a note to his father, asking that the man find some reason to summon Morgan home to Becket Hall.

"To get her shed of me, of course. Did you think I wouldn't follow her?" Ethan had asked as they shared a bottle of wine.

Becket hadn't thought that, no. He'd felt sure Ethan would follow after her. "But ruining my sister's reputation—granted, with her help—wouldn't be quite so public at Becket Hall. Or quite so easy, surrounded by her brothers and father."

Ethan had conceded the man his point with a tip of his glass, followed by several long swallows of wine.

By the time they'd gotten to their second shared bottle, Ethan had learned that Becket believed his sister's interest to be fleeting, and that "there's no reason for permanent damage from a temporary aberration."

He'd thanked Becket for his concern, then declared for at least the fourth time that he planned to marry Morgan—indeed, had already decided to propose to her before they ever left London. If his heart was to be broken, so be it, but he would ask for Morgan's hand.

By the time most of the third bottle had been downed, they were calling each other Chance and Ethan, Chance had given his reluctant blessing, if not much in the way of encouragement, and the plan had been set.

Chance would write to his father again, informing him that Morgan would be arriving at Becket Hall within a few days, along with her hopeful suitor, the Earl of Aylesford. With him, Ethan would bring a second letter from Chance, explaining the plan for the rendezvous with the *Marianna.*

And the subject of Morgan and Ethan was then carefully dropped.

So what had Becket done? What had he said between last night and this morning? Why was Morgan so angry?

Ethan hazarded a look in her direction, one she returned for half a heartbeat before deliberately looking away from him. Perhaps he was reading too much into the thing. Perhaps Morgan, too, didn't much care for rising at dawn.

What Ethan couldn't know was that Morgan had been up hours before dawn, pacing her bedchamber, stopping only occasionally, to think about her brother's letter to their father, then begin pacing once more.

She'd found that damning communication entirely by accident. She couldn't sleep, so she'd written a letter to Elly, telling her sister what she would want to hear—that Morgan had been to the park for the Promenade, where her fine ensemble was admired by many; that Morgan had visited the theater, had worn the light green gown they'd planned for that event, and watched Kean himself deliver the Prologue; that Julia and Alice were well and happy. Morgan had then taken it downstairs to slip into the mail pouch on the table in the entryway.

She'd located the pouch with no problem, even though no footman remained in the foyer, but then noticed a folded and sealed letter that was not in the pouch. When she picked it up, she saw that there was no address on the outside, which meant to her that it would be hand-delivered in the morning, by one of Chance's staff.

She was still holding the letter, thinking her own thoughts, when Jacob had come into the foyer. He stopped in his tracks when he saw her.

"Morgie—Miss Morgan," he said, staring at the letter in her hands. "What are you…that is…fancy you up so early, just as if you wasn't a fine London lady now."

"Jacob?" Morgan had seen his intent gaze on the letter—and not on the fetching, rather low neckline of her dressing gown—and suddenly realized she held something important. "Where are you off to so early, hmm? All the way to Becket Hall to deliver this letter, perhaps? You'd bring me to London, and then desert me?"

"Oh, no, Miss Morgan," Jacob had said, his gaze finally finding her neckline, so that his face was rapidly turning beet-red. "I'm just fetching that letter there, to take to Billy."

Billy was one of the men who had come to England with them from the island. One of Ainsley Becket's most trusted companions, although he had come to London with Chance all those years ago. To protect him. To watch over him. To report to Ainsley. The Beckets had long ago learned to be very careful.

"Billy is traveling to Becket Hall?" she had prodded, beginning to fan herself with the letter, the slight breeze ruffling the lace at her bodice as she advanced toward Jacob…advanced *on* Jacob. "Why would he move his old bones to play messenger?"

"Oh, no, Morgie," Jacob had said, backing up with each step she took, his chest heaving in his agitation. "Billy stays here. There's someone else going. I'm just to fetch that…that what you're holding. Morgie, please, give it over."

"Certainly," she'd told him, drawing one edge of the folded sheets lightly along her cheek, down over her bare skin, to the neckline of her dressing gown. "Just as soon as I read and reseal it."

Jacob had protested, just as she knew he would, and she had gotten her way, just as he knew she would. Once the letter was resealed at Chance's desk, Jacob took it to Billy, who had probably told Jacob he was a fool who couldn't find his arse with both hands because he'd taken so long, and then sent the letter on its way and gone back to his bed. That was Billy's problem—the bandy-legged sailor was getting too old and soft to see what he once would have seen in an instant.

Leaving Morgan to her Pyrrhic victory as she slowly walked back upstairs to her bedchamber, sat down on the edge of her bed, removed her slippers and, one after the other, hurled them against the wall.

"Have you decided as yet?" Ethan asked her now as the roadway opened up before them, untraveled except by a few farm wagons heading toward London.

Morgan blinked twice and then turned to him. "Excuse me? I'm afraid I was…admiring the countryside."

"As you once said to me so sweetly—*liar.* If you'd changed your mind, Morgan, and didn't wish to ride out this morning—"

She felt herself melting as she looked at him, saw what could only be concern in his eyes. "Oh, Ethan, I'm sorry. It's just that Chance took it upon himself to come to my bedchamber this morning and warn me to behave myself today—as if I was some *child* he had to lecture. I'm afraid we had a terrible row, and now we aren't speaking to each other. But I shouldn't let that ruin our morning, should I?"

Ethan was tempted to say *liar* again, but he restrained himself, allowed her to think he believed her. "In that case, now that we've all twenty-five hundred acres of Richmond Park before us, I think a good, head-clearing gallop is in order, don't you?"

"Jacob and Saul won't be happy, but yes, that is why we came out here, isn't it?"

"I didn't think so," Ethan told her with a small smile. "But, then, I hadn't counted on our chaperones. Let me go back to speak with Jacob for a moment."

Morgan nodded, trying to control herself, get the memory of the letter out of her mind, and watching Ethan on Alejandro did a lot to assist her in that effort.

He had to have some plan to separate them from Jacob and Saul, some way for them to be alone. Twenty-five hundred acres, he'd said. Surely, in all of that land, there was a place where they could be private.

"Ready?" he asked as he rode back toward her, Alejandro clearly remaining at a walk only reluctantly. She realized that Ethan had removed his curly brimmed beaver, so that now the sunlight danced on his severely combed back blond hair.

Morgan looked toward the coach, to see Jacob sitting quite rigidly on the seat, his young face white with anger save for two spots of red on his cheeks. He was holding Ethan's hat, poor fellow, and hating every moment of it. She felt sorry for him, but not sorry enough to put a halt to their plans.

"Where?" That's all Morgan could say, because now Berengaria was turning in a full circle, as if dancing with the stallion.

Ethan pointed out over the lush green landscape, beyond several wide dips and swells, toward a stand of ancient oak trees topping the last visible hill. "To those trees. There are riding paths, but nothing wide enough for the coach to get up there. I told Jacob we'd have to meet him at the Star and Garter."

"Are we going to be late in joining them?" Morgan asked, patting the mare's neck, trying to keep her calm.

"Oh, very late, but a well-planned, unavoidable tardiness," Ethan said, winking at her. "Shall I give you a head start, madam?"

"You may go to the devil for that insult to my horse, sir—but we'll take it!"

Berengaria was slightly difficult to control at a

gallop at first, thanks to what Morgan considered to be the *blasted sidesaddle,* but she quickly reminded the mare who was in charge, and the ride became an absolute joy.

There was nothing in this world quite like the sound of hooves hitting the turf, harness jingling, the soft, fast puffs of the animal's breathing—all in a world gone infinitely small and immeasurably large at one and the same time.

Small, just the rider and her horse as one, moving together, their hearts beating in tandem, their breaths blending together.

And infinite, with all the world spread out in front of them, to be seen, to be traveled, even to be conquered.

Morgan loved to feel Berengaria's energy below her, only wishing for her own saddle, so that she could straddle the mare, feel all of Berengaria's strength against her thighs. She knew no other feeling that made her so aware, so joyous, so cognizant of being alive, than that rush of power and barely held control she felt when she was riding—free, unhampered, racing over ground barely touched by Berengaria's dainty feet, as near to flight as anyone could possibly wish.

And then Ethan was beside her, the Andalusian moving stride for stride with the mare, their heads pumping forward with each step, slicing the sweet-smelling air as the pounding of their hooves beat out a heartbeat of their own.

"God, but you're magnificent!" Ethan yelled to her as she smiled triumphantly at him, her delight dancing in her eyes. She was fearless, unafraid to take him on as an equal, to even best him, if she could.

"And you!" Morgan shouted, but the wind snatched her words, even as Ethan urged Alejandro forward, the Andalusian showing his dominance by moving away almost as if the straining Berengaria was standing still.

"Enough, sweetheart. It's not a defeat if you choose on your own to withdraw from the contest," Morgan cooed, bending close to the mare's ear. The animal eased its pace, either in answer to Morgan's command or, perhaps, so that Berengaria, like Morgan, could fully admire the sight of Ethan and the Andalusian as they flew across the green turf, conquering the long, slow rise to the trees as if it were flat ground.

Alejandro's long white mane could have been an angel's wing as it floated behind him, and the stallion's tail rode high, like a flag in a stiff breeze, as Ethan, now with both hands on the reins, bent low over Alejandro's neck, man and horse moving as one.

"Beautiful," Morgan breathed quietly as Berengaria slowed to a trot, her withers quivering from her earlier exertion. They reached the trees as Ethan was walking Alejandro in circles, cooling him before dismounting, coming to help Morgan to dismount.

She kept her hands on his shoulders, her breathing still a little rapid from her own exertion, and from excitement. "You have to let me ride him, Ethan. It would be like riding the wind."

"I would have said no, but now I've seen you ride, really ride. Although I don't know how Alejandro will take to a sidesaddle."

Morgan slipped her palms down Ethan's sleeves, then took one of his hands in hers. "Who said I want to ride him sidesaddle?"

Ethan raised one eyebrow as he looked down at her. "You ride astride at this Becket Hall of yours?"

Morgan's expression closed for a moment. "I do what I wish at Becket Hall, as everyone there well knows," she said, then quickly smiled. "Now, do show me these magnificent trees. Few trees grow nearly so high on the marsh before the wind knocks them sideways."

"In a moment," Ethan said, kissing her hand before tending to the horses. Alejandro wouldn't wander, but he tied him as well, far enough from Berengaria that the stallion wouldn't have it too easy if he decided to become amorous.

Taking Morgan's hand, Ethan led the way into the shadowed darkness beneath the ancient oaks, across deep black earth made so by decades of decaying leaves. They'd gone no more than twenty yards before they were effectively camouflaged from any prying eyes.

"Now, what's wrong? And this time, imp, the truth, please?" Ethan asked her, stopping in a small clearing where some dappled sunlight actually made it all the way to the ground.

"Nothing's wrong," Morgan said, knowing the time had come for truth. "I *enjoy* being treated like some sort of parcel, to be dispatched here, and then there, all at the convenience of men."

Ethan closed his eyes for a moment, shook his head slightly as he silently cursed Chance Becket. "Excuse me?"

"Don't pretend not to understand, Ethan," Morgan said, lightly tapping her short riding crop against her leg as she began to pace. "I read the letter."

Ethan spread his arms now, and nodded, wondering how long he could continue to play the innocent. "Of course. You read the letter. Thank you so much for clearing that up, imp. What in *blazes* are you talking about?"

"I'm talking about how Chance is sending me home. That's what I'm talking about. I'm *talking* about how you are to accompany me, to ask for my hand, but that Papa isn't to think anything of that, because you are anything but a *serious* man. I'm *talking* about how Chance has told my father—and thus my entire family—that I am suffering from a temporary infatuation with the earl, and Chance sincerely believes that spending uninterrupted time in the company of the ramshackle man will certainly cure one or both of us of that infatuation, so Papa should not worry, and then, next year, we'll try sending Morgan off to London for the Season experiment again, when she's older, more *stable. That's* what I'm *talking about!*"

"Jesus," Ethan muttered, pushing a hand through his hair, longing to push his fist through Chance Becket's face. It was even worse than he'd thought.

"Oh, don't apply to Him, Ethan. Worry about me. *Explain* to me. Are you really taking me to Becket Hall so that you can apply to my father for my hand? And don't you think you should apply to *me* first? I might not want to go. I might want to stay here."

Ethan raised his index finger, opened his mouth to speak...then shut it. Thought for a few moments before speaking again.

"Let me see if I have the straight of this, all right?" he asked her as she glared at him, possibly with wisps of smoke coming from her nostrils, as if she might charge him at any moment. "You're angry because I might want to marry you?"

"No! I'm *angry* because you think I want to marry you. Have we spoken of marriage, my lord? I don't recall the conversation. My God, we've only know each other a few days. Why would I marry you?"

Reminding this maddening woman that he had compromised her at least six ways from Sunday (since Sunday...), and had high hopes of doing so again (with her as his willing partner), Ethan thought, probably wouldn't be the thing to say at this moment.

"Because we've fallen in love with each other?" he suggested hopefully, finding himself suddenly very much in sympathy with the lovelorn Jacob, if this was how Morgan responded to any thoughts of affection.

Morgan laughed, and it wasn't a pretty sound, even to her own ears. "Oh, we've fallen in *something*, Ethan, but I'm not convinced it's love."

"You're not?" he said, recovering his composure, which he was quite unaccustomed to misplacing.

"No, Ethan, I'm not. And neither are you. I seriously doubt either one of us even knows what love is, frankly. Odette would tell me that you're a healthy young animal and I'm a healthy young animal, and it is only natural that we..." She felt her first flutterings of embarrassment after so many hours of simmering anger. "...that we feel a desire to mate."

Ethan's smile was slow and genuinely amused. "Mate, is it? Like the ram and the ewe, the stallion and the mare? How charming. And who in bloody blazes is Odette?"

"A very wise woman, apparently," Morgan said quietly. "Because you're not contradicting a thing I'm saying, are you?"

"Not a lot of it, no, I'm not," he told her honestly, because if there was ever a time for honesty, this had to be it. "You'd think a man of four and thirty would know the difference between love and desire, but I don't. I admit that. I only know, Morgan, that I've wanted you since I first saw you, and if that isn't love, it's damn well not indifference, either."

Morgan clasped her hands in front of her, to keep them from trembling. "Yes, I know. So why this sudden rush to marriage? Why can't we simply explore whatever is between us?"

"You're serious, aren't you?" Ethan asked, shaking his head. "Morgan, a gentleman does not compromise a young lady and then walk away. A gentleman marries that young lady. And, having spoken at some length with your extremely protective brother and listened carefully to what he said, a man would like to keep his head attached to his shoulders, as that makes it much more convenient to wear his hat. Am I making myself clear here?"

"No one has to know," Morgan said, refusing to see his point.

Ethan laughed. "Not know? Morgan, for the love of God, all I do is look at you, and I might as well climb to the top of Saint Paul's and shout it to the rooftops—I want this magnificent creature in my bed!"

Morgan turned her back to him. "You don't have to be quite so *detailed,* Ethan."

"Oh, I've only begun being detailed, imp. Because all you do is look at me, and the world knows you're more than ready to go to that bed. Your brother and his wife know it, and that's why you're being sent home, before we disgrace ourselves in public. My reputation doesn't matter, and is in tatters, anyway. But you, Morgan? You can still be salvaged. Send her home. Send him along with her. Let them be alone, but not *too* alone, not alone enough to cause trouble. She'll be tired of him in a week, and we won't need to marry her off to Jacob or some other unfortunate dupe before she whelps. Look at me, Morgan. Do you understand now? Look at me."

Morgan turned her tear-wet face to him. "Is he right, Ethan? Is my brother right? Will this…this…what we're feeling be over in a week?"

"I don't know, sweetings," Ethan told her, holding her gaze. "Is he? Your family knows you better than I do."

Morgan's head snapped back as if he'd slapped her. "Yes, they do, don't they," she said dully. "They know all about me. Maybe it's time you did, too."

Ethan took a folded handkerchief from his pocket and wiped at her tears. "You know, imp, I planned to bring you here this morning so that we could…be together. And, yes, so that I could propose marriage between us, so I could ask you to come to Becket Hall with me while I apply to your father for your hand. But I think we needed to talk this way, even if Chance has already said what I needed to say."

He dabbed at her nose with the handkerchief. "Now you will miss all of that, and with me planning a lovely speech, delivered as I go down on one knee at your feet. That will teach you to read letters not addressed to you, won't it?"

Morgan pulled a face. "He had no right to write those things about me. About us."

"He loves you. He worries about you." Ethan nearly added that there was another reason for this entire scheme, but he had the good sense not to further stir the muddy waters of Morgan's anger and confusion. Of his own confusion.

"I know he and Julia love me," Morgan said, beginning to fuss with Ethan's neck cloth. To keep her hands busy. To keep her eyes downcast. "But there's more. I think they're afraid."

"Of me?"

"No," she said, shaking her head. "Of me. Of what… of what I might be."

Ethan didn't say anything else, for he could see that Morgan was struggling with some inner demon, and to interrupt her now might be to send that demon back into hiding.

"Ainsley Becket isn't my father," Morgan said, grasping at a place to start. "Not my *real* father, although I've never known any but him. Ainsley bought me, you see, when I was only a few hours old and my mother carried me into the street and stopped him, offered me up for a few shillings. After all, having a screaming infant in the same room might lose her a few customers. Who wants to tumble a whore with a baby at her breast?"

Ethan had no words. He pulled Morgan close against his chest and simply held her, until she sighed deeply, then pushed herself away from him.

"They never say it, Ethan, none of them, but I know what they think. Is she her mother's child?"

"You can't know that, Morgan," Ethan said quietly.

"Can't I? It's what *I* think. I flirt, I tease—both come to me as naturally as breathing. I know what I look like, Ethan. I know, and I *use* it. How do you think I got Jacob to let me open Chance's letter?"

"You—?"

Morgan's heart was pounding now as she pointed at him, even as she began backing away from him. "Ha! You *thought* it, didn't you? Just for a moment, you *thought* it. My God, you thought—what did she do? I didn't *do* anything, Ethan, but be myself. And I'm not a nice person. Chance knows that. They all do. Oh, that's just Morgan, being Morgan. That's what they're saying now, Ethan. It's just Morgan being Morgan—she'll be just as interested in someone else next week. And what if they're right? You said it yourself—you don't know the difference between love and…love and lust. So how can I?"

"Morgan…"

She held up her hands, warning him not to touch her. "No. We're not finished yet. I'm not finished yet. I want you, Ethan. I want you so badly my teeth ache, and I'm not ashamed to admit that. And, if you still want me, then I don't give a damn about what I might feel next week, what you may not feel next week."

She drew in her breath on a sob, lifted her chin. "But if you propose marriage to me just to ease your conscience, Ethan Tanner, I will walk away right now, and never look back."

"Then there will be no more talk of marriage, I promise. And that's a bleeding shame, Morgan Becket, because you'd make a magnificent countess," Ethan told her, slowly closing the distance between them until he could slip his arms around her waist.

Morgan's involuntary cry was silenced by Ethan's mouth as they all but attacked each other—grasping, holding…grinding themselves together as the passion neither of them had ever denied concentrated on the here and now, scattering the next moment, the next days, the past and the future to the four winds.

They kissed and kissed, their mouths open, their tongues dueling…and it wasn't enough.

Ethan slipped his hands beneath the jacket of her riding habit and cupped her breasts. Squeezed. Stroked. And it wasn't enough.

Morgan let instinct take her, passion take her, as she pressed her lower body against his, felt a tightening, a sweet burning between her legs, gloried in his hardness straining against her hip.

And it wasn't enough.

"Sweet God…sweet Jesus," Ethan breathed against her ear as his passion, and her response to it, threatened to take him past rational thought.

Still holding her, Ethan sank to his knees, then laid her back on the deep carpet of last autumn's leaves, his hands almost immediately busy on the frog closings of her jacket, even as she raised her head, took small, nibbling bites of the skin just above his shirt points.

Chance Becket be damned. All of the Beckets be damned. All of society's conventions, society itself, be damned.

Morgan's hands were on Ethan's chest now, her fingers struggling with the buttons of his shirt, managing to open three of them before slipping inside, to burn her fingertips on his overheated skin.

She smiled in triumph when Ethan outwitted the last of the closings on her jacket, then she sucked in her breath as she felt him unlacing her shift, cried out in pleasure when she felt his hand close over one bared breast.

Ethan's breathing was labored, nearly painful as he lowered his head, took her nipple into his mouth even as she began a soft, sweet mewling in her throat.

And it wasn't enough....

Morgan bent her knees, bracing her booted feet against the ground as she raised her hips, her body seeking something she couldn't understand, but knew to be missing.

"Please," she whispered against his neck as he laid his palm low on her belly, pressed his heat against her, setting small fires inside her.

Anything. He'd do anything for her, everything to her. Take her places she'd never been, show her worlds she'd never known.

Make her his. Now and forever, his.

Ethan raised his head slightly as he reached down, found the hem of the generously wide, divided skirt of her riding habit.

He looked at her, his chest heaving, watched hers as it, too, rapidly rose and fell.

Encouraged by her reaction to him, he inched his hand past her high riding boot, to encounter the soft silk of her drawers.

Morgan wet her lips with her tongue, then swallowed hard over the thick knot of passion in her throat. "Ethan...yes..."

He closed his eyes for a moment, then slid his hand higher, along the soft skin of her thigh. Bent and kissed the valley between her breasts. Raised his head once more. Looked at her. Waited.

Morgan lifted her hips from the ground because it felt so right to do that. "Please..."

He first skimmed over her silk-covered belly, only slowly moving down, so that he could insinuate his thumb between her legs, keeping the pressure of his hand low on her, easing her hips back down to the ground as he told her with his touch that, no, he wouldn't leave, wouldn't stop, wouldn't desert her now.

Morgan looked up at Ethan as his expression became so intense, as his pupils widened, as his very skin seemed to tighten over his cheeks. He seemed so intense...and she understood that, as she, too, was feeling intense. And intent upon what he was doing to her beneath her skirt, overtop the thin barrier of silk that was all that separated skin from skin.

Ethan levered himself up so that he could now turn his hand, ease his fingers between her legs even as he used his thumb to hold the silk taut against her mound. He had no thought for himself, but only for her. Her pleasure.

Morgan felt the tightness of the thin silk against her sensitive skin, then gasped as Ethan touched her, somehow spreading the silk tightly over her while using one finger to stroke at her very center.

She kept her gaze concentrated on his face, but not without effort, for she longed to close her eyes, to grind the back of her head into the soft carpet of leaves, to lift her entire body by pressing her heels into the ground as his finger moved, moved faster, found a part of her she had never known existed.

Up. Up. Yearning, searching for something she couldn't find, but knew was there…just outside her grasp.

Ethan levered his upper body half over hers and bent to whisper in her ear. She was close now, the silk damp beneath his fingers, and he spread her as best he could as he kept up the friction of his finger against her center.

He couldn't take what he wanted, what he needed. Not yet. Not if he hoped to live with himself afterward.

But he could give her what she so longed to experience.

"Give over, Morgan. It only gets better, if you just give over." He moved against her faster, varying the pressure he applied, building the heat between her legs. "Trust me, let me take you there. Let me take you over. Like this, sweetings," he whispered before covering her mouth with his one more time, driving his tongue into her in the same rhythm as his fingers now moved over her.

He was everywhere. Invading her. The sensations filled her. urging her on.

Morgan arched her back, whimpering as her body grew warm, as her chest tightened…as her body began its own duel with Morgan's moving fingers; pulsing, pulsing…pulsing.

It was glorious, mind-shattering. A pleasure so great it was almost pain.

And then it was over.

And it wasn't enough….

"Ethan!" Morgan cried out as he held his stilled

hand over her. She grabbed at him in a near frenzy of need, pulling him on top of her, digging her fingernails into the fabric of his jacket, pressing quick, wild kisses against his neck, his cheek, still hungry for him, even hungrier than before.

"Morgan, go easy now," Ethan whispered, sliding his hand out from under her skirt so that he could hold her, gentle her, cradle her against him, will his own body back from the brink.

She had to hold him, go on holding him. He was her anchor, the only thing that could keep her from spinning off into the sky, still searching for more… more. "Oh, God—Ethan."

"Shh, it's all right, it's all right," he told her, stroking her back as he held her. "You'll be all right."

Morgan swallowed hard as her heart slowed its galloping pace, as her breathing evened out…as the hunger and the need settled into something less than terrifyingly intense.

Now she was content to cuddle, to relax inside his embrace, and she sighed, rested her head against his chest.

Ethan smiled ruefully up at the tall trees surrounding them. "Morgan, that's enough. You may be feeling sated and lazy, but I can assure I am anything but either of those things. Come on, time to put you back together and work on our excuses."

Morgan held on tighter. "I'm not ever getting up. I'm going to stay here until the both of us are covered in leaves and no one can find us, ever."

"Really. That's a pity, because I asked Jacob if he knew what was in the picnic basket, and he told me there was a lovely portion of Smithfield ham. So, as I'm a romantic fool only until my stomach puts up a protest—and remembering how much I like my head on my shoulders—we really do have to leave here."

"Spoilsport," Morgan grumbled, pushing herself away from him, then searching around on the ground for her shako hat, unmindful and uncaring that her breasts were still exposed to Ethan's gaze.

"For the love of—Morgan, you'll drive a man insane."

"Only you, Ethan," she said, grinning at him as she raised both hands over her head in order to position the hat at a fetching angle. "Only you."

"Well, then, you'll be happy to know you've been successful, for I don't know where my wits are, but I do know I no longer number them in my possessions, and most probably haven't since the day we met."

"Good," Morgan said, believing she might have accomplished something wonderful.

He took hold of her hands and pulled her to her feet, then tugged on the laces of her shift and tied them in a bow. He was feeling very proud of himself, of his restraint, but that didn't mean it didn't have limits. "There. Now maybe I can think again. Button your jacket, Morgan, and let me brush off your back. You're covered in leaves."

"Yes, I am, aren't I?" Morgan said, trying to look behind herself even as she slipped the knotted frogs into their braided holders. "But I'm sure you'll have a reasonable excuse for how I look—and yourself, of course."

"You depend too much on me," Ethan told her, brushing at her skirt, frowning at the darker patches where the damp of the ground had penetrated. "Another ensemble consigned to the dustbin, my dear. Ride out more often with me, and you'll soon have nothing to wear."

"One can only hope," Morgan said, drawing her fingers down his cheek, then pulling a leaf out of his hair. She smiled at him for a moment, then the smile disappeared. "I feel wonderful. But I want more, Ethan, and so do you. Half measures aren't for the likes of us. They only leave us wanting more."

Then she smiled, went up on tiptoe to kiss his cheek. She felt so free with him—not embarrassed, and most certainly not ashamed. If this made her wicked, she'd simply enjoy being wicked. "But you're still glorious."

Ethan watched her walk back through the trees, heading toward the horses. "Glorious? I'm a man in pain, imp," he said quietly, before following after her like the love-starved fool he had concluded he was well on his way to becoming, and not really minding at all. He did, however, worry about his total lack of restraint where Morgan was concerned. "That damn cylinder had better be ready on time, or we'll be standing a shocked and outraged London on its ear yet," he murmured into his neck cloth.

They rode in silence for a few minutes, until they were on one of the many riding paths, and then Ethan dismounted.

Morgan had already agreed that the story he'd made up out of whole cloth had its merits, but she wasn't too pleased with her part in the tale.

"I still say I should be the one that limps," she said

as they began to move once more, Ethan now walking ahead of Alejandro.

"No. It's enough that you fell off your horse—I don't need your brother seeing your limp and then thinking you could have as easily broken your neck. It might put him in the mood to snap mine. You fell, yes, but you're not injured."

"He won't believe I fell, you know. I'm a very good rider."

"True, imp," Ethan said, smiling back at her. "But that damn sidesaddle defeated you, correct? Besides, we practiced it that way, remember? Every time you limped, you giggled. Hardly a convincing performance."

Morgan giggled again now. Everything just seemed so delicious, now that she and Ethan had come to their understanding. "That's because it's funny. Why should we worry what Jacob and Saul think? It's not as if either one would cry rope on me to Chance in any case. They'd do anything for me, both of them."

Ethan kept walking. "Why, have you kissed Saul, too?"

She pulled a face at him. "No, I have not kissed Saul, too. I just let him see my ankles when I get in and out of the coach. Maybe a little more than my ankles. My knees. I don't understand why old men are so fascinated with knees. I think they're rather ugly, personally."

"I'll have to see yours before I can make a judgment."

Morgan frowned, realizing he'd been marvelously intimate with her, more than marvelously intimate with her…and yet he hadn't seen her knees. How strange.

"If I can't limp, can I at least walk? I feel silly, riding up here while you walk."

Ethan stopped in the middle of the riding path and turned to look at her as she sat on Berengaria's back. "Are you going to natter at me all the way to the Star and Garter?"

She shrugged. "Probably. How much farther?"

"Just around the next bend, if memory serves. We've been fortunate so far that this path is deserted. Alejandro, *limp.*"

Immediately the stallion's steady walk transformed into a nearly three-legged gait, his right hoof barely touching the ground as he favored it with each step.

"Very nice, very clever, but he doesn't look as if he's in pain. He almost looks as if he's dancing. He should look as if he's in pain."

"Nag, nag, nag. No, not you, Alejandro. Her. Alejandro, *be sad.*"

The horse bared its huge teeth in a head-tossing laugh.

"Very funny. I mean it, Alejandro. Be sad."

The stallion continued to limp, but now he lowered his head, his long mane nearly dragging on the ground, his tail hanging low.

Morgan clapped her gloved hands in appreciation. "That's wonderful. Such a smart boy. What else can he do? Jolly Roger knows some Spanish words, you know."

"How gratifying for him." Ethan looked back at her, his grin wicked. "Can your parrot fly?"

"Of course not, or he'd fly away. His wings are kept clipped. Why?"

"Because Alejandro can fly."

Morgan nudged Berengaria up on the path, so she was now riding alongside Ethan. "Oh, he can not."

"Ah, but he can. One day, if you're very, very good, and Alejandro forgives you for doubting him, perhaps he'll show you."

"I'll hold you both to that," Morgan said, then looked down the path to see that they were very near the Star and Garter. "Look, there's the coach. Oh, and there's Jacob, pacing like an old woman."

"And with that pistol stuck in his breeches. Yes, I see him. Now remember. You fell when your mare stepped in a rabbit hole, I raced to your side, you're fine, but Alejandro stepped into the same hole, and he was injured when he fell, coming up lame, which is why we're so late. Agreed?"

"You should write stories, Ethan. Nobody would believe them, but they might be fun to read."

"I'll remember that. It will give me something to occupy my time once I reach my old age. If I reach it, that is."

"Meaning?" Morgan asked as Jacob came stomping down the path toward them, looking very much like a vicar about to deliver a sermon on hell and brimstone.

"Meaning, imp, the more I'm with you, the more I wonder if I'll be allowed to reach an old age. Hell, as I think about the thing, reaching next week might well be a struggle."

"I—" Morgan began on a laugh, then ended, "I really do enjoy you, Ethan Tanner." Which was much more prudent than saying *I really do love you, Ethan Tanner.* And why should she say any such thing in the first place?

Morgan sighed to herself as Ethan began telling his

tall tale to Jacob, wondering why what her mind thought so reasonable her heart was finding increasingly unable to understand....

CHAPTER THIRTEEN

"SHE KNOWS," Ethan said shortly, slamming down his curly brimmed beaver before leaning both palms on Chance Becket's desk at the War Office and glaring at him. "Christ, man, and you work here? The way you keep secrets, I'm surprised we aren't all speaking French by now."

Chance remained calm, already understanding who *she* was, and knowing it never paid to overreact to anything that *she* might do. After all, at the bottom of it, Morgan was a Becket and, wild as she might sometimes be, obstinate as she might often be, she was never a fool. "What does she know?"

Ethan pushed away from the desk, subsiding into one of the chairs that faced it, but still glaring, because it felt good to glare. "I don't know. Some of it? All of it? *Enough.* What in blazes did you write in your little missive home to Papa?"

"She—bloody hell, I left it on the table in the foyer because the maids were still fussing about in my study." Chance looked at Ethan. "She found the letter and read it? Never mind answering. If she found it, she read it. Although I'm surprised you're still in one piece. Amazed, frankly, that *I* am. What did she tell you?"

Ethan shook his head. "Has it occurred to you, Chance, that the two of us, grown men, are sitting here, mutually afraid of one small female?"

"Oh, not afraid. Not really."

"Not really, you say? Then pick another word, why don't you," Ethan said, pointing to the drinks table as he stood up, then returning Chance's nod before pouring them both glasses of wine.

"Careful. Cautious. Strong, yet allowing enough leeway as to not bring disaster down on all our heads—it's difficult to narrow everything down to one word."

"So we'll stick with *afraid,* why don't we?" Ethan suggested, handing Chance a glass. "Because, my new friend, I'm afraid you've bungled this one badly, and I'm paying the price. We may *all* be paying the price."

Chance took a sip of wine, looked at Ethan, then decided to down the entire contents of the glass. "Meaning?"

"Meaning that she may have taken exception to being shipped to Becket Hall without being asked, her Season over before it's really begun. Meaning that the idea that she might be infatuated with me—*ramshackle* as I am—didn't anger her half so much as learning that you think she won't remember my name next week."

Chance looked at his empty glass, wishing it full again. "Sorry about the ramshackle."

"Thank you for that, at least," Ethan said, putting down his own empty glass and picking up his hat. "You'll be happy to know that your sister does not wish to marry me and is, in fact, only agreeing to allow me to accompany her to Becket Hall as long as I *refrain* from asking her to marry me. She was very clear on that head. Excruciatingly clear."

Chance nodded, not at all ashamed to feel relief flooding him. "That sounds like Morgan. Never wants to do anything anyone wants her to do. Julia and I have discussed that, as a matter of fact."

Ethan took his gloves out of his hat and began pulling them on. "Then this news must be gratifying to you both. Thankfully, she's agreed to return to Becket Hall, with me tagging along, the hopeful suitor, and I suppose I can only be grateful you didn't mention the *Marianna* in your letter. You didn't, did you?"

"No, no, I've got that here," Chance said, pulling out a drawer in his desk and extracting the sealed letter. "You may as well take it now. Read it if you feel the need, but it only introduces you to my father and asks him to assist you in any way possible. I'll leave it up to you to decide how much you want to tell him."

"You're convinced he'll be willing to help?"

Chance nearly said, *and extremely capable of helping,* but stopped himself in time. "He'll be delighted, I know, as he follows the newspapers quite closely. You will probably have to listen to his opinions on the war while you're there, but don't delude yourself into thinking that living in the back of beyond means your soon-to-be host doesn't know more and see more than most anyone here in London."

Ethan inclined his head in acknowledgment of that bit of information, then said, "I've spent a few hours reading about Romney Marsh. Interesting place, for a marshland with shifting shorelines and more sheep than people. We had one close-run call at Dymchurch already, and Becket Hall isn't that far away. Do you think the *Marianna* will have any difficulties with the Waterguard because of the amount of smuggling that supposedly goes on up and down that area of the coast? I imagine they patrol quite often."

Chance kept his gaze steady on the Earl of Aylesford. "Because French spies have been known to travel back and forth to France on smuggling runs, we here at the War Office, and in the Royal Naval Office, are very much involved in protecting the coastline. I can tell you that we've had no reports of any problems with smugglers in the vicinity of Becket Hall for well over a year. So, no, I don't foresee any difficulties for the *Marianna.* She'll merely be stopping there for a brief visit with Ainsley Becket, dropping anchor beside my father's sloop, the *Respite,* and then heading out of the Channel, into the open sea."

"Well, then, you say I shouldn't worry, so I won't. Thank you."

"Yes. I'm sure the messenger we dispatched on horseback yesterday has already reached the *Marianna,* which is undoubtedly already back at sea, skirting the coast at a safe distance between our shores and France. The ship will put in alongside the *Respite* sometime after dark on Sunday night."

Ethan kept his own expression neutral, even as something—something he could not put a name to—stirred a deeper interest in Becket Hall, and, most especially, the family that lived there. This unusual family, this diverse family.

"Then it's settled, but only on that end. We're running out of time, you know. If we end by riding hell-bent for leather to the coast because we're out of time, Chance, it isn't only Morgan who'll be asking questions. We must leave tomorrow, Friday at the latest, breaking the travel into two days. Have you heard anything about the preparation of the communication packet?"

Chance shook his head. "That's above me, I'm afraid. I've only been told to smooth the way for the rendezvous itself. After all, we can't keep reassigning any Waterguard officer with a brain in his head. Hopefully, this will be the last time we need to use your friend."

"Or, in other words, our last chance to avoid another war," Ethan said, sliding the letter inside his jacket. "Hopefully, we leave in the morning for Becket Hall, but there's no reason for Morgan not to have one more evening in society. There's a ball tonight at Lady Beresford's, and I've already arranged for the three of you Beckets to attend as my guests. Until then?"

"Yes, yes, thank you," Chance said, as Ethan headed for the doorway, wondering if Julia would feel up to attending, as she'd been kneeling with her head over the chamberpot this morning as he'd left for the War Office, frantically waving him out of the room.

Having accomplished all that he felt he needed to do, Ethan was nearing the staircase when he heard his name called. He turned to see the minister himself hailing him.

"The communication is ready?" Ethan asked, retracing his steps.

"No, curse it, not yet. Nearly, but we keep coming back to this impressment nonsense. How can we be impressing our own citizens? Ludicrous, especially as those sailors are assisting the enemy. Trading with France, you understand."

"Oh, I understand, my lord. But, then, it's not me our government has to convince. Nor do I have to *impress* on you how dangerous is the position of my contact, who has no great reason to be sailing in the Channel, and whose ship and presence has to be raising questions from anyone with even a small measure of curiosity."

"Yes, yes, you've made yourself very clear on that, but the new time and place are already set, nothing we can do about that now, eh? All we're waiting on is one small change in the language of a single paragraph, and his royal highness' signature. Tell you what—the cylinder will be delivered to Upper Brook Street by nine tomorrow morning. Becket still sees no problem in having you escort his sister to the family home?"

Ethan grinned. "No, sir, none. Amazing, isn't it?"

The minister looked hard at Ethan for a moment, then took hold of his sleeve and pulled him into a small alcove in the marble-lined hallway. "There's something else I'd like you to do, Aylesford, as long as you'll be in the vicinity. You will be staying at Becket Hall for at least a few days, correct? Wooing the girl?"

"Unless they boot me out on my ear, yes, I suppose so," Ethan answered, wondering where this conversation was heading.

"Good, good. I thought so. Behave yourself, then, stay as long as possible."

Ethan allowed his left eyebrow to climb his forehead. "Matchmaking, my lord? That's so unlike you."

"*Faugh!* That's Becket's problem, thank God—and if they're willing to overlook the obvious in order to gain their gel a title and a fortune, that's their never-mind, not mine."

"Isn't it strange? I always come away from meetings with you, my lord, feeling so very *good* about myself."

"What? Must you keep interrupting? I've asked this before, of Becket himself, over a year past now, I believe, and now I'll ask it of you. Nobody would suspect you of anything remotely serious, now would they?"

"I'm becoming both more flattered and more intrigued by the moment. Please, do go on."

"I'm attempting to do that, Aylesford, but it isn't easy, asking a favor from the likes of you."

"Oh, better and better. I really should be keeping a list somewhere, of all the accolades you insist upon heaping on my head."

The minister's face was flushing an angry red, from his considerable jowls to his badly receding hairline. "Just make it a point to keep your eyes and ears open, that's all I'm asking."

"Certainly, sir. I will be all attention. In aid of what, precisely?"

"Watching for signs of smuggling, of course. As I said—I think I said—Becket did some snooping for us in the general area last year, and a certain...*violence* that had been reported to us has not reoccurred. Nasty business—very nasty, and potentially embarrassing—but over now. According to Becket, who speaks with his family on our behalf, there are no longer any problems. But lately there have been rumors that have reached our ears."

"Rumors. Really. Of what?"

"Rumors that smuggling is still going on in the area, of course. And where there are free traders, there are often spies."

Ethan laughed softly. "And you want *me* to poke about, looking for these spies, these smugglers? Oh, I don't think so, my lord. I wouldn't have the faintest idea how to begin. Send Becket back there, as it sounds as if he was successful last year."

The minister shook his head. "No, can't do that. He's married now, for one, and the rumors...well, they seem to possibly implicate—ah, there's my clerk, waving to me. Perhaps his royal highness can see me now. Never mind what I said, Aylesford, I certainly couldn't have meant anything. Simply too much work, too many worries, too little sleep these past days. Don't know why I thought you'd be of any use. The communiqué will be delivered to Upper Brook Street in the morning."

He gave Ethan a hearty slap on the shoulder. "Don't fail us!"

Ethan stepped back, bowed, then watched the minister hurry away. He stood where he was, mentally reviewing both his conversation with Becket and this last one, with the minister. Becket had said that smuggling was not a *problem.* The minister had said that Becket had told him smuggling was not a *problem.*

But Becket hadn't said, to either man, that smuggling did not still *occur* in the vicinity of Becket Hall. A matter of slicing up words?

But the minister had also mentioned rumors.

"Rumors of smuggling still going on, obviously.

Rumors implicating…*whom,* my lord?" Ethan asked the air before turning once more for the staircase. "Bloody hell. Don't I already have enough problems?"

CHAPTER FOURTEEN

"...NINETY-EIGHT, ninety-nine, *one hundred!* I'm coming to find you, you little dickens!" Morgan dropped her hands from her eyes and turned about in the drawing room of the Upper Brook Street house...to see Ethan leaning against the archway, his arms crossed on his chest, an unholy grin on his face.

"What, may I ask, are you doing?"

"You obviously had no brothers or sisters, or you'd know," she said, kneeling on one of the couches, then quickly leaning over the back of it. "No, not there."

She looked at Ethan as she walked over to poke behind the draperies on either side of the large windows facing the street. "Not here, either. Clearly they're trying harder this time, the buggers."

Ethan heard a quick, girlish giggle from somewhere behind him, in the foyer, and prudently moved farther into the drawing room. "*Clearly,* there is a game afoot," he said as Morgan flung open the glass doors separating the drawing room and dining room, then disappeared inside.

"Yes, and you can't help me look," she told him, bending to peek under the large, cherrywood table. "And what are you doing here, anyway?"

"Being terribly in the way, obviously," he replied, wondering if she would be angry or pleased if he told her she looked absolutely delicious to him, dressed as she was in a simple gown, her long hair loosely pulled back at her nape with a pale blue bow, the thick, straight ebony length of that hair cascading down her back. "But, in point of fact, my mother is outside, in her coach."

"Your mother?" Morgan, who had been down on her knees, peering into a dark cabinet, raised her head quickly, bumping it on the wood. "Ouch!" She got to her feet. "Why didn't you bring her in? Why is she here? I didn't know your mother came to town. I didn't think she did."

She rubbed the top of her head. "Oh, that hurts."

Ethan took her face between his hands, then bent to place a kiss on the spot she'd been rubbing. "There. All better now. My mother came to town yesterday, to select fabric for costumes, which is the only reason she ever comes to town. She and Algernon will be performing *A Midsummer Night's Dream* next, you know. Our extremely large and ungainly cook will be playing Nick Bottom, and I'm nearly heartbroken to possibly miss his moment upon the stage."

Morgan gave up her search for a moment. "Nick Bottom? He's the weaver who plays Pyramus. Puck turns his head into that of an ass. Doesn't your mother *like* your cook?"

"You know the play?"

She pulled a face at him. "Don't sound so surprised, Ethan. Of course I know the play. 'Lord, what fools these mortals be!' Now please go fetch your mother in here. Leaving her outside in her coach. Shame on you."

Ethan shook his head. "She won't come. *Maman* doesn't care for London, and only stopped to see you as she races back to the safety of her castle and her comfortable, make-believe world. So," he said, indicating the doorway to the foyer, "if you wouldn't mind?"

"Of course I don't mind," she said, already on her way to the door.

Ethan stopped her, snagging her arm at the elbow as he pulled her close, to whisper in her ear. "Haven't you forgotten something. Some *one* something?"

Morgan slapped a hand to her forehead. "Alice. I've forgotten Alice. Oh, the poor thing, she's probably all cramped and miserable, stuck behind a chair somewhere. Quickly, help me find her."

"It's a large house, imp. Did you put any limits on the game?"

Morgan nodded, heading for the foyer once more. "Only on this floor, because Julia isn't feeling well. I've been entertaining Alice since we came back from—" She looked up at him, smiling. "From our lovely ride this morning in Richmond Park, my lord. How is Alejandro faring?"

Ethan frowned, since they both knew that Alejandro fared very well, but then Morgan made a great business out of letting her arms hang loose at her sides as she took three faintly clumsy steps, then pulled an imaginary pistol from her imaginary waistband.

Jacob. He was here?

"Alejandro's much better, thanks to the poultice one of my grooms made up for him, thank you. I am only gratified that you were served no injury, Miss Becket." Then he mouthed the word: *Here?*

Morgan nodded furiously, then grinned.

"And you're playing hide-and-seek with your niece?"

And Jacob, Morgan mouthed silently, trying not to giggle when Ethan's eyes opened very wide.

"I don't wish to keep your mother waiting, my lord," Morgan added out loud, looking around the drawing room once more, certain she'd checked everywhere. "Still, I probably do need to first find Alice."

Ethan mentally weighed the right and the wrong of the thing, then pointed to the foyer.

"I know," Morgan said loudly, "I haven't checked the entryway, have I?"

Ethan made her an elegant leg, the dramatic flourish of his arm indicating that she should precede him into the foyer, and then he followed, just in time to see her peer behind a huge urn and cry out, "Aha! Found you!"

As he looked on, Jacob stood up and moved out from behind the urn, his hands on the shoulders of a small, blond-haired girl of about six.

"You took forever to find us, Morgie," the little girl said in some triumph. "Jacob said it would take you forever because this was just the best hidey-hole ever, didn't you, Jacob?"

Red-faced with embarrassment, Jacob dared a quick, angry look at Ethan before saying, "I'm guessing the game is over, sweet Alice. Miss Morgan's got other things to do now."

"You called her Morgie before," Alice piped, taking hold of Jacob's hand. "You did, so I am, too. And I think it's very bad of you, Morgie, to stop our game."

Morgan went down on her knees in front of the girl.

"I'm sorry, sweetings. But if Jacob takes you down to the kitchens for some jam and bread, would that make you happy again?"

"Can Buttercup come, too?"

"I'll fetch her," Jacob said dully, heading for the drawing room, shooting another chilling glance at Ethan. He was back in moments, carrying a large, pink, stuffed rabbit and looking as if he would rather be roasting chestnuts in hell than be where he was at this moment. "Come along now, Miss Alice."

Ethan watched the two of them head down the hallway, toward the private areas of the narrow house. "How on earth did you talk him into playing hide-and-seek, *Morgie?*"

Morgan bit her bottom lip for a moment, then smiled at him. "On her own, Alice didn't really know how to hide very well, so I asked Jacob to help."

"Be careful what you ask that boy to do, Morgan," Ethan said as one of the footmen held open the door for them. "You may think you have that lovesick fool wrapped around your finger—but one day you may push him too hard."

"Jacob? No. Jacob would never hurt me. We were just playing a game."

"It wasn't you I was referring to," Ethan said sternly, "and you're getting too old for games."

Morgan stopped short on the second marble step and looked up at him for a few moments. "I didn't mean— I've *never* meant to—"

"I know, and Jacob probably does as well," he told her, lifting her hand to his lips. "Now, smile, and come say hello to *Maman.*"

Morgan shook off her sudden, unexpected feelings of guilt and lifted her skirts when a groom opened the door to a huge, luxurious traveling coach. "Countess!" she exclaimed as she stepped up inside the coach and sat herself down on the rear-facing seat, bravely ignoring the enormous ass's head on the squabs beside her. "How good to see you again."

The countess was dressed much more conventionally today, but her smile was just as muzzily delightful. "Ethan explained? I don't show myself in Mayfair if I can help it. I simply sneak in on mice's feet, and then quickly tiptoe back out again. Ever since..." she leaned closer, to whisper, "*the incident.*"

"*Maman,* I thought you were here to invite Miss Becket to come visit you next month."

"Yes, yes, Ethan, I remember," she said, making shooing motions with her hands. "Now go away for a moment. I don't eavesdrop on you."

"Yes, Ethan, she doesn't eavesdrop on you," Morgan said, longing to kiss the older woman's cheek, give her a tight hug. "Go away."

Ethan looked at his mother, knowing she wouldn't understand an unspoken warning, then closed the door to the coach, already pulling a thin cheroot out of his waistcoat. This could be a long wait.

Inside the coach, Morgan had already asked the countess to explain the *incident.*

"It was quite wonderful, actually, once you got past the horror of the thing. I was shopping in Bond Street—this was several years ago—with Ethan accompanying me. A horrible man, who shall remain nameless, approached us on the street and said something nasty to

The Reader Service — Here's How It Works:

Accepting your 2 free books and gift places you under no obligation to buy anything. You may keep the books and gift and return the shipping statement marked "cancel." If you do not cancel, about a month later we'll send you 3 additional books and bill you just $5.24 each in the U.S., or $5.74 each in Canada, plus 25¢ shipping & handling per book and applicable taxes if any.* That's the complete price, and — compared to cover prices of $5.99 or more each in the U.S. and $6.99 or more each in Canada — it's quite a bargain! You may cancel at any time, but if you choose to continue, every month we'll send you 3 more books, which you may either purchase at the discount price...or return to us and cancel your subscription.

*Terms and prices subject to change without notice. Sales tax applicable in N.Y. Canadian residents will be charged applicable provincial taxes and GST.

his companion, loudly enough for us to hear every word. Something that had very much to do with my late husband and how I had tricked him into marriage in order to steal the fortune I was, obviously, spending hand-over-fist now that he was underground."

The countess sighed, but Morgan felt sure she could see the hint of a smile teasing the corners of her mouth. "I will say, it isn't often one sees a duke on his backside in the gutter. And it was a rather large puddle, too."

"Ethan knocked him down?"

"Oh. Oh, yes. Definitely. One moment the man was standing there, *grinning* at his companion, and the next, my bandboxes were scattered everywhere and Ethan was standing over the man, ordering him to take back his words. I've rarely come to town since then, and never to Bond Street. I have to protect my son, you understand."

"It sounds as if he does a very good job of protecting *you.* And the duke—that is, the man didn't call him out?"

"No, of course not. He may have been a boor, but he wasn't a fool, and swore to anyone who dared ask that he'd tripped—or so Ethan told me later. Ethan has quite a reputation, you understand. With both the sword and the pistol. I shouldn't call him out, I know. Now, since Ethan will be sticking his head back in here at any moment to inform me that his prized Friesians can't be kept standing much longer—may I have your promise to visit me next month? I've yet to set the exact day for our performance, I'm afraid."

"I would be delighted, ma'am," Morgan told her

sincerely. "I am returning to Becket Hall tomorrow for a visit, but if you were to write to me once you've settled on a date, I will most definitely be there."

The countess frowned. "You aren't staying for the Season? Does Ethan know?"

"Yes, ma'am," Morgan said, wondering how much she should say. But, then, Ethan had been the one to leave her alone with his mother. "Your son will be traveling with me. I'm looking forward to showing him Romney Marsh, as he's never traveled there."

"Never… But, isn't Dymchurch somewhere in the marsh? Yes, I'm sure it is. He has traveled there or near there at least two or three times in the past year alone, I'm sure of it. I wouldn't know why he'd say anything like that."

"No, I wouldn't, either," Morgan murmured quietly just as the door swung open and Ethan stuck his head inside to, as she'd predicted, remind his mother that his team had been left standing long enough.

"Ethan," his mother said, placing a hand on his arm. "It's Dymchurch, isn't it? Where you've been visiting this past year?"

Ethan covered his mother's hand with his own, his smile indulgent, even as his heart skipped a single beat. "Dymchurch? No, *Maman,* you must have confused the name. I'm ashamed to admit I haven't stepped inside any church in a very long time, dim or otherwise. And, for your sins, *Maman,* neither have you."

The countess blushed beneath her fetching straw bonnet. "Now you're making me sound the heathen," she complained, obviously diverted.

But Morgan was not. Dymchurch was no more than

a long stone toss from Becket Hall. Also directly on the coast. Also very much in Romney Marsh. Yet he'd told her he'd never been there, had joked about once traveling to Camber for a funeral, but that was all.

He'd lied to her.

Why?

What else had been a lie?

Suddenly the reason for their trip to Becket Hall seemed not as clear-cut as it had when she'd read Chance's letter to their father.

Morgan had been a Becket longer than she'd been a woman madly attracted to a man, and a lifetime of loyalty and necessary secrecy weighed more than desire, had to weigh more than anything else in this world. If there was a choice to be made, there could be no question how she would choose. None.

But she hadn't expected, could not have known, that this obvious choice would hurt so much....

Keeping her smile bright and her tone light, Morgan kissed the countess goodbye, and then stood on the flagway next to Ethan as the coach rolled away from the curb, into the late afternoon traffic.

"She wants me to be her guest at Tanner's Roost, to see her performance of *Midsummer Night's Dream,*" she told Ethan as they reentered the house.

"And could you think fast enough to come up with a believable excuse?" Ethan asked her, following her into the drawing room.

Morgan smiled, shook her head. "No, I accepted with my thanks. Do you mind?"

"Not at all," he said, closing the double doors to the foyer before crossing to Morgan, taking her hands in his. "Are you all right? After this morning, I mean. I must be out of my mind to have—"

She pressed her fingertips against his mouth for a moment. "Don't apologize, Ethan. Don't ruin it. Now, don't you want to kiss me?"

"Not in your brother's house, no," Ethan answered honestly. "We're beyond mere kisses, Morgan, yet still not where we might go. The next time I kiss you, I don't think I'll be able to stop until we've explored all that there is between us."

Morgan stepped closer to him. "Afraid you'll have no choice but to throw me down here on this fine carpet, and have your wicked way with me?"

"Quite the reverse, imp," he said, lifting her hands to his mouth, one after the other. "I'm afraid you'll throw *me* down onto this fine carpet and have your wicked way with me."

There was a new game being played out in the drawing room in Upper Brook Street.

A dangerous game of make-believe.

Tease her, make her forget what she heard.

Tease him, pretend you believe what he said.

She danced away from him, picking up the ivory-sticked fan Alice had been playing with earlier, and opening it, waving it beneath her chin. "La, sir, I fear I don't understand your meaning."

"The devil you don't," Ethan said, shaking his head. "I've got a few matters of business to settle before we start off in the morning to charm your family into believing I'm a harmless fellow, so I'll take my leave now, with your kind permission."

"Chance wants us to spend one night on the road, to

give his letter time to reach Becket Hall, and for Papa to send outriders to meet us. Perhaps also to give my brothers time to clean and load their pistols before they're introduced to my hopeful suitor. Did he tell you that?"

"He did," Ethan answered, opening the doors to the foyer once more. "He even suggested an inn to stop for the night and wait for the outriders. He didn't add that Saul and Bessie would be sleeping outside the door of your bedchamber, but I heard the words, anyway."

Morgan's laugh was clear and pure, even as she felt herself going dead inside. "It's a shame we can't make the journey in one day, but it would mean setting a fairly bruising pace, and driving across the marsh in the dark. I can't wait to show you Romney Marsh. You'll see that not everyone lives in a castle in the middle of a forest."

Ethan had his back to her when she said the words, accepting his curly brimmed beaver and gloves from a footman. He turned to her, searched her face for any hint of suspicion, and found none. "I look forward to the experience." Then he stepped closer, whispered into her ear, "I look forward to every experience with you."

It had been only a little lie…if the countess hadn't been entirely mistaken, so that it was no lie at all. And yet now, Morgan felt a quick, hot surge of anger, of betrayal, whip through her. She couldn't play the game a moment longer. "Is that so, my lord? While I, on the other hand, look forward to—"

"Miss Morgan?"

Morgan whirled on her childhood friend. *"What?"*

"Excuse me, Miss Morgan," Jacob said, his eyes downcast, "but Miss Alice is asking for you."

Morgan wanted to kiss Jacob for the interruption. She'd almost made a horrible mistake, given in to the impulse to call Ethan a liar. "Oh, yes, of course. Thank you, Jacob." She turned to smile brightly at Ethan. "I promised to read to her before I have to begin dressing for this evening. So, if you'll excuse me, my lord?"

"I had been about to leave anyway, Miss Becket," Ethan reminded her, longing to touch her, longing to hold her, longing to get back whatever the hell had gone missing in the past few minutes. Longing to tell her anything she wanted to know. "But you were saying?"

"Saying?" She shrugged her shoulders. "No, I don't think so, my lord. And it certainly couldn't have been anything important, not if I've already forgotten."

She offered him her hand, he bowed over it, and was gone after a softly murmured, "Until tonight."

"Jacob," she said, still looking at the door that had just closed on Ethan's back. Part of her wanted to run after him; part of her wanted never to see him again. All of her hurt. Hurt badly. "We watch him like a hawk watches a hare."

She turned to look at her friend, her jaw set. "Understand?"

"Just like you say, Morgie," Jacob told her, caught between confusion and a joy he couldn't conceal. "Like two hawks, we'll watch him. You can count on me."

CHAPTER FIFTEEN

CHANCE APPROACHED his wife from behind, leaning over the back of the couch to sneak a kiss from her. "Umm, you taste good. Smell good, too. Peaches."

Julia used the small knife to slice more of the succulent fruit from the peach in her hand, and held it up to her husband. "Only one piece for you, I'm afraid. I'm ravenous."

Chance came around the couch to sit down beside her, noting the pair of peach pits already in the small bowl in his wife's lap. "Obviously. And yet, just this morning, I distinctly heard you say you'd never eat again."

Julia spoke around a mouthful of peach. "I was wrong. And I simply had to have peaches. They cost the earth, by the way, so be prepared to see the household budget shattered."

"I think the budget can handle a few peaches. Even a plum or two, if you're so inclined. Now come here, sweetings. There's a bit of juice on your lip and I—"

"Chance!"

He closed his eyes, his lips a scant inch from his wife's. "Strange how it never before occurred to me to have a lock put on the morning room doors," he said, then turned to look at his sister. "You bellowed, Morgan?"

Morgan crossed the carpet and plopped herself down in a chair facing the couch. "I didn't bellow. I just wanted to be sure I had your attention. It's about my trip home," she told him, crossing one leg over the other, ignoring Julia's quiet tsk-tsk at this obvious breach of ladylike posture.

"What about the trip home? You've already agreed to go back to Becket Hall for a visit. With your *beau,* no less," Chance said, which earned him a sharp dig in the waist from his beloved's elbow.

"That was your idea, not mine, remember? I was never asked, I was *told,*" Morgan pointed out, reaching to take a peach from the bowl on the table between them. "Oh, and by the way, no matter what Ethan said to get you to agree to send me back, he is *not* going there to ask for my hand in marriage. I've already warned him not to do that."

Julia felt fairly certain her eyes had begun to pop out of her head. "But...but that's the entire purpose of the trip, even though you're supposed to pretend you aren't aware of that fact, then be suitably surprised. Surely Chance explained this to you. He told his lordship he can't ask him. He has to ask your papa, Morgan. That's the way it's done."

"If it's to be done, yes, I suppose so," Morgan admitted around a healthy bite of peach. "Which it's not. Going to be done, that is."

Chance and Julia exchanged looks.

"You're no longer seeing his lordship?" Julia then asked, frowning.

"Oh, I'm still seeing him. I'm going to be watching him very closely. He's up to something. I thought this was all happening much too fast, and you'd agreed much too easily, brother mine."

Chance spared a moment to wish his sister was a featherbrained ninny interested only in clothing and balls and finding a rich husband. "Really? Up to something? And what would that be?"

Morgan looked at the half-eaten peach, wondering why she'd thought she was hungry. "I don't know. I just know he wants to get to Becket Hall, and that I may be a part of his plans, but I'm definitely not all of the plan. I only know that I very much resent being *used.*"

Julia put her hand on Chance's leg, to stop him from speaking. "Are you saying he has only pretended to be…interested in you?"

"Oh, no," Morgan said, because she was basically honest, if not always modest. "He's wild for me. I'm wild for him, for that matter. Nothing's changed there."

Julia was confused. "Then why wouldn't you marry the man, if he wants to marry you?"

Morgan wished she had a ready answer for that question, but she didn't. After all, how could she say, in her brother's presence, that she wasn't sure she knew the difference between love and lust? Or much cared, when she got right down to the thing. She and Ethan wanted each other. Why wasn't that enough, without all this business of rushing to the altar? Why did wanting the one always seem to mean accepting the other? She'd make a horrible wife. Didn't they all know that?

"That's not the point, Julia," she said quickly. "He lied to me just now. Well, he lied to me when we first met, but I only found out about that lie now. I don't know why he did, but he did, and I'm going to discover why. Otherwise, he can't go to Becket Hall, and if he doesn't go, I'm not going. If I've learned one thing in this life, it's that the family must come first to all of us."

"Very commendable, Morgan," Chance said, at a loss for anything else to say.

"Yes, I know. But then it occurred to me that you feel the same way, Chance, and yet you seem all hot to get Ethan to Becket Hall, don't you? So maybe you know something I don't know, but should."

Julia looked at her husband, who was in the process of rubbing at his temple. "Headache, darling?" she asked, unable to hold back a smile. She'd warned him Morgan was too intelligent to simply be shipped off willy-nilly without asking a few pertinent questions. Even a lovesick Morgan was too intelligent for that.

Chance sighed, then tried to be reasonable. "Morgan…look. You're leaving tomorrow morning. It's all arranged. I can't have the two of you wandering around London looking for places to make public spectacles of yourselves. Or did you really think I believed that nonsense about you falling off Berengaria? You haven't taken a tumble in ten years."

He thought, but did not add: *It's an entirely different kind of* tumble *I'm worried about here.*

Morgan leaned forward in her chair. "You're not listening, Chance. He *lied* to me. He told me he's never been to Romney Marsh."

Chance blinked. "What?"

"I said, he told me he's never been to Romney Marsh. But, when his mother was here earlier, she said he has been, and then he tried to pretend she was mistaken, but he didn't fool me. He *lied.* It was so obvious. He looked as if he wanted to stuff a rag in his mother's mouth, to shut her up. I pretended not to notice, but I think he noticed that I noticed."

"I believe I may have just caught your headache, darling," Julia told Chance. "When was his lordship's mother here? I wasn't told anyone had come to visit."

"She wasn't exactly here," Morgan explained automatically. "She stayed outside in her coach."

"Why would she do that?"

Morgan rolled her eyes. "Does it matter? She had the head of an ass in the coach with her—maybe she didn't want to leave it alone."

Now Julia blinked. "Excuse me?"

"Wait," Chance said, feeling the conversation taking a path not necessary to get them wherever in hell they were going. "Morgan? Does it matter that his lordship's mother stayed in her coach?"

"No," Morgan said, happy to be off the subject. "What does matter is that Ethan lied to me and there was no reason for it. At least not one I can think of offhand. But a lie is a lie, and I don't like them. And, as I already said, my next thought, naturally, was to think of you, brother dear. You've been entirely too happy to send me off with Ethan. You know something, don't you?"

Chance was torn. If he didn't tell Morgan the truth, Aylesford's lie could very possibly put an end to this intense infatuation that was, frankly, almost embarrassing to watch. He couldn't consider that to be a bad thing.

But if he didn't tell her the truth, yet insisted they

travel to Becket Hall, she'd be watching Aylesford's every move, and that could ruin everything.

So he'd tell her. Except if he told her, she'd be more infatuated than before—women adore heroes, even if Ethan Tanner wasn't much more than a glorified messenger.

And if he told her the truth, she'd still follow after him everywhere he went while at Becket Hall, just so she wouldn't miss anything.

"Damned no matter what I say," Chance muttered under his breath, then realized that both his wife and his sister were looking at him strangely.

"You said something, darling?" Julia asked.

"I asked if I could borrow that fruit knife, and slit my throat with it," Chance said, then stood up, looked sternly at his sister. "Morgan, what I'm about to tell you is not to be repeated—or acted upon by you. You understand? Lives may very well depend on your discretion, which is enough to have me reaching for that knife."

"Lives depend on—*Ethan?* So you knew about this? About his lie?"

"Not his lie. Not precisely that. But, yes, I know something."

"I knew it! There's some sort of *plot* here, something that has to do with Romney Marsh? With Becket Hall? *That's* why you were so quick to send me off with him? Oh, that's rotten, Chance. You're both rotten. Plotting together, the two of you? I didn't think you even *liked* Ethan."

"You're jumping to conclusions, Morgan," Chance told her. "This is the king's business. It has nothing to do with whether or not I like his lordship. And who said I didn't like him?"

Morgan shrugged, momentarily diverted, then quickly got back on point, her mind racing. "This sudden trip to Becket Hall is a ruse, isn't it? I knew Ethan couldn't be as useless as he pretends to be. He's much too smart to be useless, insists too often that he's useless. Don't tell me he's looking for smugglers, too. Didn't we have enough of that last year? Is the Red Men Gang showing itself again? Is that it? But what would Ethan have to do with any of that?"

"Not smugglers, Morgan," Chance told her, sitting down once more. "And, before I tell you, you have to swear to me that you won't say anything. Not to Ethan, not to Eleanor or the others, not to anyone. You won't say anything and, more importantly, you won't *do* anything. Do I have your word?"

He waited the space of five heartbeats. "Morgan?"

She stood up, shaking her head. "No. I can't do that, Chance. I can't promise. Not when I don't know what I'm promising."

"Oh, for the love of Christ…"

"She's right, darling," Julia said, patting his thigh. "I think you have to first tell her, then ask for her promise. It's only fair."

"Fair? You can say *Morgan* and *fair* in the same sentence?"

Morgan held out her hands, motioning for silence. "Just tell me one thing. Did Ethan meet me by chance or by design?"

Her brother looked at her, saw the first bit of nervousness in his sister's eyes. "Your meeting was purely by accident, and well before…before anything else. Becket Hall was an afterthought."

Morgan smiled. "Thank you, Chance. That answers most everything. The rest I'll get from Ethan on our way to Becket Hall, so that you aren't betraying a trust."

"What makes you think *he'll* betray a trust? How do you know he'll tell you anything?" Chance called after her as she headed out of the room.

Morgan turned, grinned at him. "Oh, brother mine, you don't really want me to answer that, do you?"

"She's got you there, darling," Julia said, handing him a peach. "I think I'm sorry we're not traveling with them tomorrow. His lordship doesn't know it yet, but he's in for quite a journey."

"I'm going to pretend I didn't hear that," Chance said, then took a large bite out of the peach.

"That's fine," Julia said calmly. "But please don't pretend not to hear this—when were you going to tell *me* what's going on, hmm?"

"Bloody hell…"

CHAPTER SIXTEEN

MORGAN STROLLED into Lady Beresford's ballroom on Ethan's arm, still smiling as she thought about Lord Beresford's appreciative stare (if the man wasn't an earl, she would have thought he had leered) as they'd gone through the receiving line at the top of the stairs. When she'd curtsied, he'd nearly fallen on her, he was so intrigued by the neckline of her gown.

Her mirror had already told her she looked well in the ivory silk. The neckline was very French, or so the modiste Chance had sent to Becket Hall had told her, and extremely modern, cut nearly straight, with the short, tight, off-the-shoulder sleeves a part of the same bias-cut material.

She'd have some difficulty raising her arms very high, but the modiste had pooh-poohed that, saying that women have always had to sacrifice comfort for fashion.

One price Morgan had refused to pay had been that of a corset, which she'd flatly refused to wear with any of her gowns, much to her sister Eleanor's distress. "You're possibly a bit too *lush,* Morgan, to not be bound in some way."

Well, Lord Beresford didn't seem to mind that she

was "too lush," and neither did any of the gentlemen who'd stood on the stairs behind and in front of her as they'd waited for the receiving line to inch its way up to the host and hostess.

In fact, Chance had asked her—twice—if she was sure she wasn't chilly, and might want to consider wrapping her shawl around her shoulders.

And each time, Ethan had laughed.

She adored him for laughing, for being pleased with the attention she was drawing from all sides. His pride was as obvious as was Chance's brotherly dismay.

And when, in the midst of the crush of people, Ethan had found a way to surreptitiously stroke a hand down her backside, his touch lingering as he lightly cupped her, she'd thrown back her head and laughed out loud, drawing even more attention—a combination of smiles, and frowns, and one low whistle from a gentleman standing three stairs above them.

Chance had glowered. Ethan had lifted her hand, pressing a kiss into her gloved palm. A gesture of ownership, she was sure, but one she'd allowed him, for the moment.

The ballroom they'd finally entered was a fairyland of pink tulle and sparkling candles that made the large room nearly as bright as day. Which was also wonderful, because all that candlelight seemed to be captured, then reflected, magnified, on the thousands of clever, tiny silver disks that had been hand-sewn into an all-over pattern of palest-yellow roses that fell from Morgan's high-waisted bodice to the scalloped hem of her demi-train.

She'd needed no jewelry, and therefore wore none,

choosing instead only a thin, yellow satin ribbon tied midway up her neck.

"Some women glow, Morgan," Ethan whispered to her as they stood—posed, actually—just inside the ballroom as their names were announced by a liveried footman. "You sparkle, like sunlight dancing on the water. And your hair is driving me insane. I keep longing to touch it. To touch you."

Morgan kept smiling, kept her gaze wandering over the room. "You've been touching me, Ethan. With your eyes, for all of the time it took your coach to get us through the traffic."

"When I wasn't contemplating booting your brother and his wife out onto the cobblestones and ordering my coachman to take us to Grosvenor Square, yes. But you know that, don't you, minx, just as you know your poor brother is about to have a small apoplexy as he stares down your most ardent admirers. I think I'd best find him a drink. Go with your sister-in-law, and try not to get into too much trouble until I'm back, all right?"

Julia had overheard Ethan's last words, and agreed with him. She took charge, leading Morgan down the very center of the parquet ballroom floor, as she, too, had noticed all the attention, the looks, the whispers. Shame on her, but she *was* enjoying herself as she watched Morgan become an instant Sensation, just by being Morgan.

"It's rather fun, isn't it, Julia, teasing society." Morgan lifted one gloved hand to deliberately stroke the thick lock of hair that fell from her slightly off center part to caress the side of her face, curve in slightly as it just managed to touch the swell of her right breast. Louise had piled the rest of "this mass of hair!" on top of Morgan's head, wrapping it rather than curling it, then saying she'd done the best she could and she was going to have a small lie-down once everyone was gone.

But Morgan hadn't fully realized to what extent she would look so unlike the other supposed debutantes in attendance this evening. Julia, as one of the matrons, was clad in a lovely clear blue, and there were other ladies in attendance wearing a full rainbow of colors.

But the debutantes were all in white or ivory. Rather like pale, hopeful brides, Morgan thought, smiling to herself, because she knew she might look like many things, but bridelike most probably wasn't one of them. Neither was *virginal,* even if that was still technically the truth. Her brother Spencer, always happy to say whatever was on his mind, had once told her she couldn't look innocent in a nun's wimple.

"I see that smile, Morgan," Julia said, leading her toward the side of the ballroom, then sitting down beside her on one of the uncomfortable chairs lining the wall. "You've taken stock, and now you think you are the most attractive, interesting young lady in the room, don't you?"

"The blonde over there, beside the woman in black, is quite beautiful," Morgan said, doing her very best not to let her smile grow any wider. "There's the small redhead we passed on our way over here. She made me feel like a large, ungainly giant. But yes, Julia, I think I can safely say I am one of the more attractive debutantes here tonight. Certainly my gown is one of the most spectacular. It makes no sense to pretend otherwise, because that would just be false modesty."

Julia sighed. "And Lord only knows no one has ever been able to accuse you of that particular sin. You've got at least three dozen hopeful mamas sending dagger glances at both of us, by the way. I imagine his lordship is being hounded for your name, and your poor brother is fully occupied trying not to punch anyone."

Morgan shrugged. "I can't help who I am, Julia. And, since I can't help it, why should I deny myself some enjoyment? I *like* being looked at, admired. I…I like the power it gives me."

"Power? I never…hmm. I never considered that, but I suppose power is a perk of the sort of beauty you present. But why would you want power?"

"Because men have it," Morgan said simply, turning to smile at her. "Power, freedom. I'm not you, Julia, earnest and steadfast, and I'm certainly not Elly, although she does quietly rule, doesn't she, in her frailty, in her subdued way? I think my blood runs hotter somehow. I need more. I need to *feel* more. I need to be in charge of my own destiny."

Julia opened her mouth to inform Morgan that her sister Eleanor was far from frail of spirit, then thought better of it. "Oh, Morgan. Is life really such a struggle for you?"

Morgan smiled. "A struggle? Of course not. As long as I'm in charge."

"Is that why you won't consider marriage to his lordship? Because then you might lose control, have to give some of yourself over to him?"

"No," Morgan answered quickly, perhaps too quickly. "That is…I don't think so."

Julia covered Morgan's hands with her own. "Sweetheart, loving a man who loves you is not ceding control of anything. It's giving, and taking, and sharing. Love, marriage—neither is a contest of wills, and there aren't any winners, any losers. When you can look at a man, let him see you for all that is good in you, all that may not be quite so wonderful, let him really *see* you, the *real* you, let him *know* you, and he does the same with you? I…well, I guess what I'm saying, Morgan, is that, in love, surrender is the real victory."

Morgan realized she was blinking back sudden tears, which certainly hadn't been a part of her plan for this evening.

"I wish I could be you, Julia. Chance is so lucky. I'm afraid any man I married would be wishing me gone within a week."

"Even his lordship?" Julia asked, indicating with a slight tip of her head that Ethan and Chance were approaching, each of them carrying two glasses. "I somehow don't think he would feel that way. You two are so alike, it's frightening."

Morgan looked at Ethan, splendid in his evening clothes, and slowly smiled. "He gives me a good fight, I'll say that for him," she said, feeling the now familiar curl of desire deep in her stomach.

Julia sighed, shaking her head. "Oh, Morgan, Morgan. A good fight? Is that what you call it, how you think about it? You look so grown-up, but you still have so much to learn about men, about life. You have no idea how involved your heart is with this man, do you?"

"No, Julia," she said, suddenly more serious than she'd ever been in her eighteen years, "I don't. I really, truly do not know. He scares me. I scare myself. I've never felt like this, Julia, and I don't know what I'm feeling. And as Jacko would say, that's a bleedin' pity, isn't it?"

Morgan watched as Ethan was stopped by a pair of young gentlemen, both of whom were asking him questions at the same time. He smiled at them indulgently, then said something that had them both looking as if they might begin weeping buckets, right in the middle of the dance floor. Then Chance added something of his own to the conversation and the pair of young sprigs slammed their evening-slippered feet together, bowed and retreated.

Clearly the young gentlemen had been warned off and, just as clearly, word would travel quickly throughout the ballroom that Miss Morgan Becket was "spoken for."

"They had no right to do that," Morgan said, trying to raise some anger inside her, but failing miserably. "Ah, well, nobody wants Chance to have an apoplexy, do we, now that he's about to become a papa again. But I truly pity Alice, if he's going to be such a protective bear about her when the time comes for her to have a Season."

Julia allowed the redirection of what had been an unexpectedly serious conversation. "Fortunately, we still have a few years before he has to begin pacing the floor with that problem. Finally! I'm so thirsty," she added as Chance and Ethan reached them.

"It's lemonade, dearest," Chance told her, "and none too cold, either. Same for you, Morgan."

"While you two swallow down what is probably well-chilled wine," Morgan said as she accepted the glass Ethan held out to her. Then she turned to Julia. "Power. Being in charge, making decisions for us, merely because they wear breeches and fight wars. See what I mean?"

Julia took a sip of warm, watery lemonade and grimaced. "Yes, I begin to understand your point, Morgan." She patted the empty seat beside her. "Husband? I think we need to talk."

Morgan laughed and got to her feet, handing her glass back to Ethan. "Here, dispose of this, and we'll take a turn around the room. I don't think we want any part of what these two will be saying to each other for the next few minutes."

Ethan inclined his head slightly, looked at the offending glass of lemonade, then handed both it and his own wineglass to a young man who had been standing not three feet away, openly goggling at Morgan (or her décolletage). "Miss Becket has just informed me that she would be eternally in your debt if you were to see to the refilling of these glasses, Bickford."

Morgan covered a smile with her gloved hand as the towheaded youth all but ran off. "That wasn't nice. Especially since we won't even be here when he gets back."

"True," Ethan said, offering her his arm. "But better to learn young that there are bound to be disappointments in this life."

Ah, here was her opening, rather earlier in the evening than she'd planned, but still she rushed to take it. "Along with discovering that there also are those who will shamelessly and without compunction utter whacking great fibs, even to those they declare they admire."

"Ouch. I think that one might have actually drawn blood, imp." Ethan hadn't needed more than that single statement to know that he'd been correct to believe he hadn't successfully denied his mother's innocent *sharing* of information. "What do you say to a stroll in the gardens? I hear Lady Beresford paid a small fortune to steal Viscount Wallingford's head gardener."

"Then this should be an edifying and even informative interlude, shouldn't it? Seeing the flowers by moonlight, that is."

Ethan guided her across the dance floor just as couples were streaming onto it for the first set of the evening, and within moments the two of them were outside, standing on the long stone balcony that ran the length of the ballroom.

The tension between them, which had risen so quickly and unexpectedly, was nearly visible—almost sparkling in the moonlight, as was her glorious gown.

He thought, quickly and fervently, of pulling Morgan into the shadows and thoroughly kissing her full, currently pouting lips. But he had a healthy sense of self-preservation, and fought down the urge.

What truly amazed him was that he was ready, even eager, to explain his actions, something he had never chosen to do before, with anyone, even his own mother.

"This is about Dymchurch, isn't it?" he asked, looking at Morgan's straight spine as she stood at the stone railing, peering out over the flambeaux-lit gardens.

"Haven't been in one in years, dim or otherwise," Morgan said, turning to look at him. "I know you didn't have much warning, very little time to perfect your fib, but that was truly pathetic, Ethan."

He guided her toward a short flight of steps that led down into the gardens, not speaking again until they had passed two other couples strolling the paths, and reached an area where the flambeaux cast more shadows than light.

"Now, about my pathetic lie..." he began, standing close to her, lightly rubbing his palms on her bare upper arms.

"Miserable and pathetic. But I don't care that you lied," Morgan told him, reaching out to finger the lapels in his neck cloth. She couldn't be near him without touching him. "I just need the truth now. Why are we going to Becket Hall tomorrow?"

Ethan raised one eyebrow. "Straight to the heart of the matter, I see. You don't want me to grovel for a bit? Shower you with excuses? Admit that I lie even when the truth, as far as I knew at the time, would have been perfectly harmless? That I'm a bad, bad man, that deception comes to me quite naturally?"

Morgan smiled up at him, knowing she no longer had to say the words *like recognizes like* for him to hear them. "Oh, I know all of that, although the groveling might have been interesting, for a few moments. You lied because whatever you do when you travel to Dymchurch—two or three times in the past year, your mother said, as I recall—is a deep, dark secret. So, with the lie behind us, all that's left is the secret."

"I adore the way your mind works, imp," Ethan told her, bending to place a kiss behind her ear. Then whispered, "But I can't tell you."

Morgan had expected some resistance, had even planned for it. "Very well. Chance wasn't much more forthcoming earlier today, although he did hint that lives depend on what happens when we get to Becket Hall."

Ethan was genuinely surprised, but then realized that even a brother would recognize a losing battle when Morgan brought one to him. "He said that?"

She rolled her eyes in exasperation. "*I,* Ethan Tanner, don't lie. I may choose not to lay my entire life bare to you, or anyone, but I don't lie. *Yes,* Ethan, that's exactly what he said, and I believe him. I have to, because it's the only thing that makes sense, makes me understand why Chance seemed so eager to have us both out of London. You're on some sort of mission from the War Office, I imagine, just as Chance—well, never mind about that."

"My mission, as you call it, is not the only reason he wants us gone. In fact, my needs simply happened to dovetail nicely with plans he'd already made—yes, without your knowledge. He thinks we're on the verge of making spectacles of ourselves in public and, in that, he very well could be right."

Ethan lightly ran the tip of one finger over her full bottom lip, his voice lowered to a rather hoarse whisper. "Or don't you want me as much as I want you? Right now. Right here."

Morgan's smile began slowly, then grew wide. "See? Isn't the truth wonderful? Even freeing?" She pressed her palms against his chest, leaned in closer.

"I'm still not going to tell you, Morgan," he said, pretending a humor he didn't feel. What he felt was his blood pumping, his body stirring while he watched the smooth rise and fall of her breasts and her sweet breath teased his senses. "It's enough that I tell you I will confide everything to your father, and that Becket Hall will not be in any danger from anything I might do while I'm there."

"I'm no longer worried about that. Chance wouldn't allow you within ten miles of Becket Hall if he thought otherwise. Is it a spy who will tell you about Napoleon? Are you meeting a spy? Is that it? Are you taking something to him, or receiving something from him?"

"Morgan, stop."

She shrugged, dropped her hands to her sides. "Very well. But I do think it very unfair of you and Chance to let me conclude that you wanted us to go to Becket Hall so that you could ask my father for my hand in marriage. What if I'd told Papa you were going to ask him, and told him that I loved you desperately, so that he should please, please say yes? You don't know my father, Ethan, or my other brothers. If they thought, even for a moment, that you were taking advantage of my girlish heart? Why, I shudder to think of the consequences for you."

"But, Morgan, if you had gone to your father, said those things to him, and he had questioned me, I would have immediately declared my hope of marrying you, so that you could make me the happiest of men. That is, after all, what I've already planned to do."

Morgan stamped her slippered foot on the ground, to lend emphasis to her next words: "That is *not* the answer. You already know I won't marry you and—"

"Yet," Ethan interrupted, just as she was about to

fumble in her exasperation. "You haven't agreed to marry me *yet*. But I have high hopes that, over time, you will find me irresistible and your arguments against marriage weak. Oh, wait. You find me irresistible *now*."

He frowned, sighed. "That must be quite a dilemma for you, Miss Becket, as you so desperately hold on to your convoluted, and quite wrong, thinking. You may worry as to precisely who you are, but I do not. You're Morgan, and that's more than enough for me. Too much for most men, I'll grant you that, but not too much for me. Although I will say my bravery astounds even myself."

Morgan folded her arms beneath her breasts, blowing out a breath in exasperation. "You're impossible. No wonder no one likes you."

Ethan's explosion of laughter sent an unsuspecting bird winging into the sky above his head. "Not used to not being able to get your own way, are you, imp? Not by cajoling, or threatening, or..." he trailed a single fingertip down her bare skin, easing it beneath her gown, into the cleft between her breasts "...teasing."

He hooked his finger against the taut silk, slowly pulling her toward him. "But, then, being the terrible man I am, if you decided to do more than tease, I might tell you what you want to know."

The moment he said the words, even before Morgan's complexion went deathly pale, her features settling into a mask of pain, Ethan knew that he, with an entire world of words to choose from, had said exactly the worst thing possible. "Morgan, I'm so sorry, I—"

"No. Don't apologize," she said, putting her hand on

his, holding it where it lay. "Not when you're right. But you can keep your secrets now, Ethan, just as you can keep your proposals. If you want me, take me, and if I want you, I'll do the same. That's the way we began, and that's all we really have. Everything else is a needless complication."

"No, damn it, it's not," Ethan said, still wishing back his painful words. "I've done everything wrong, from the very beginning, from the first moment we met."

"You thought I was someone's mistress that day," Morgan said, nodding her head. "I realized that. But I didn't care."

He lowered his voice. "But you care now?"

Morgan looked toward the ground, avoided his gaze. "I never thought I was any more than I was. Fine feathers don't make fine birds." She looked up at him. "But I didn't hate myself for who I am, what I am, until just now. Until you made me feel so...dirty. I would have...would have made love with you tonight, just to find out your secret, your mission, or whatever it is. I would have done that, I *planned* to do that. My mother was smarter. At least she never spread her legs except for money."

"You are *not* your mother."

"I'm her child," Morgan said, forcing a smile onto her face. "Spencer says I'm *earthy*, whatever that means. They tried, they all did, to make me into a lady, but nothing has stuck, has it? I saw you, and all I knew was that I wanted you, had to have you. That you knew the secret that would make me come alive, help me find what I've been looking for without even knowing I was looking."

Ethan stroked the back of his hand down her cheek,

longing to hold her. "I don't know another woman, another person, who would be so honest."

"Then why did everything have to get so complicated?"

"There's nothing complicated about the way we react to each other, Morgan," he told her quietly. "Two healthy animals, remember? Still, it was up to me—older, supposedly wiser—to also remember the rules. Convention demands we marry—the earl, the daughter of a fine house. And one thing more, as long as we're wasting the moonlight by standing here confessing to each other."

Morgan looked at him in question, concerned for the pain in his eyes, more concerned for him than she was for herself.

"I knew, Morgan Becket, from the first moment I looked at you, that if any other man touched you I'd have to kill him. I had to be the first, the first to hold you as you experienced the full blooming of the passion I sensed in you. After that? Damn me, as I damn me, because I didn't think beyond that moment, the moment I'd hear your soft moans as I took you to the brink, and beyond. As you took me with you."

His smile was rueful. "I'm new to this, but how's that for honesty, Morgan?"

It took her some moments to find her own voice. "I never thought beyond that moment either, Ethan. We...we're a fine pair of fools, aren't we?" she whispered, blinking back tears. "And now look at us, tangled in all sorts of webs. What do we do now?"

Ethan felt certain that any more talk of marriage, or of his mission in Romney Marsh, would only serve to destroy the small progress they both seemed to have made in their blunt exchange of honesty.

"Why, Miss Becket," he said, holding out his arm to her, "I believe we go back inside before your brother mounts a search party—an armed search party—and we enjoy the ball."

Morgan's heart skipped a beat. The worst was over, at least for now. "Enjoy each other, enjoy the moment?"

"If that's all we have, yes. Tomorrow's another day, and our thorny problems will wait for the sunrise. But," he said, bending to whisper in her ear once more, "everything's simpler by moonlight. Let's go enjoy the ball."

"I know how to waltz, you know," Morgan told him, willing back the lingering threat of tears as she took his arm and smiled up at him. "Eleanor tells me the waltz is frowned upon in London, although most of Europe has been dancing the thing for years. Such a shame, don't you think? It's a beautiful dance. I so long to dance the waltz."

He'd talk about any subject she might choose. He'd do anything she wanted, give her his soul if she asked for it. But a waltz? All she asked for was a waltz? "When I was last on the Continent I had occasion to dance the waltz, yes. But you're right. It's not accepted here. Entirely too *fast,* you understand."

"Too fast for whom, my lord?" Morgan asked him, as suddenly all she wanted to do was stand London on its ear and then turn her back on it, never to return. "Certainly not us."

Ethan lost his smile. "Morgan, you're not serious, are you?"

She shrugged, her heart lifting with each step they took in the direction of the ballroom. "Isn't it you who told me you regularly outrage the ton? How long has it been since the last outrage?"

"Oh, a good year, at the least."

"Chance and Julia, poor things, would be mortified, of course."

"That's true enough."

"But they won't be surprised."

"Also true. I imagine it will cost me a small fortune to bribe Lady Beresford's fiddlers."

"I admit to not knowing you very long, but I don't imagine you as someone who pinches pennies."

Ethan stopped at the bottom of the stone steps to the balcony, rested his hands on her bare shoulders. "You want this. You really want this? You want to outrage the ton?"

"Not as much as I would have earlier this evening, but I do love to waltz and I think my gown would look wonderful as you swirled me round and round," she answered truthfully…always truthfully. "Am I using my…my *charms* to get what I want from you?"

"Honestly?" Ethan answered with a slow grin. "It may have begun that way, but I have made it a practice never to do anything I don't want to do. I suppose I'll have to think about this once I take you back to your brother. But are you certain you still don't want to *charm me,* just a little? I'm not adverse to the idea, you know."

She shook her head. "No, I won't do it. I'm reformed, as of right now. Not with you, not with Jacob, not with anyone. It was a childish thing to do, and too easy to be considered a real victory, if you must know. Well, until you."

"I'd hate to think I've entirely cured you of the practice, as I rather enjoy it."

"Really? In that case…" Morgan said, then went up on tiptoe, to press a short, hard kiss on his mouth, ending the kiss with a quick flick of her tongue against his lips. "Feeling charmed now, Ethan?"

"Teased would be more the word," he said, savoring the swift, yet memorable touch of her breasts against his chest. "And, yes, I could grow used to it."

"Then I may have to rethink my new resolution," Morgan told him as they climbed the steps and r'entered the ballroom. "Oh, Lord, would you look at that? There's that poor boy, holding our glasses and looking crestfallen. Shame on us, Ethan."

"I imagine if you offered him a dance, the fool wouldn't feel it necessary to go home and hang himself."

Morgan laughed up at Ethan. "People don't *die* from being flirted with, Ethan. But you're right, I'll go dance with him. Bickford, wasn't it?"

Ethan watched as Morgan skirted the perimeter of the large room, coming up behind Bickford, who visibly jumped when she spoke to him. Watching the boy's face turn a painful red, Ethan smiled almost indulgently as Bickford looked around frantically, then dumped both glasses into a potted palm before he led Morgan out onto the floor, where they joined in a set already forming for the next dance.

"I thought you years too old for her at the beginning, you know," Chance said from just behind Ethan, who then turned to look at Morgan's brother. "But I've changed my mind. Not that you'll ever control her, for no one will, but at least she won't be able to control you. If she could, she'd be bored with you in a month."

"You make it sound as if you've studied Morgan like some bug under a glass. I don't like that," Ethan answered tightly. "She told me you've all tried to clip her wings. I don't like that, either. If being older means being wise enough to know that would be to destroy everything that's so uniquely wonderful about her? Then yes, I am the man for her. God knows she's the only woman for me."

Chance inclined his head slightly, acknowledging the words, the sting in those words. "We may have bungled things with Morgan," he admitted. "She was always a…difficult child to reach. One of the younger ones, in a very large group."

Ethan was all attention, eager to learn anything he could about Morgan. "Eight of you, is that correct?"

"Four boys, four girls. I believe Morgan was about four years old when we came to England. Elly was frail, and needed extra attention for quite some time. Fanny always had Rian to protect her, and Cassandra, of course, is rather special to Ainsley—to our father. Morgan…" He hesitated, gathering his thoughts, pushing down his own guilt, for he had deserted the family nearly the moment they'd reached England. "Morgan was quite often left to her own devices, I guess you'd say. Not that she tolerated being overlooked. She ran wild, mostly, but she also found…ways to get the attention she craved. But there's no harm in her, Aylesford. Always remember that."

Ethan looked out over the dance floor, to see that Morgan and Bickford had come together in a movement of the dance. She was smiling at him as if he was the only man in the world, and the boy nearly came to grief, tripping over his own feet. "No," he agreed with a smile. "She means no harm. That's the difference between us. I always did."

He turned to Chance. "She wants to waltz. Here. Tonight."

Chance winced, closing his eyes. "She would. Ainsley warned me about that. What are you going to do about it?"

Ethan answered slowly. "I don't know. I don't doubt her motives, but I do doubt my own, even as I'd like to believe I'm finally through with getting some of my own back for the way society has treated my mother. I'm sure you know the story."

Chance nodded, then considered Ethan's words. "Morgan and the ton don't make for a good fit, do they? Once she's back at Becket Hall, I doubt she'll want to return to London very often, if at all. It isn't *real* enough for her."

Now both men were looking at her. "I've no great love for polite society myself," Ethan pointed out quietly. "Morgan's horse mad, and I admit to the same failing. She'd be quite content mucking about in my stables, I believe, as am I. Once or twice a year would probably be often enough for us to come to town, frighten the natives."

He turned to Chance, smiling broadly at his own small joke. "We really do have more in common than you and your lady wife might believe. We could be happy. I know we'd be happy."

"You don't have to convince me, Aylesford. My wife has already done that. It's Morgan who presents the problem, the way I hear it. But I believe you're sincere. God only knows why, but I do. Which leads us back to this idea of a waltz, doesn't it?"

Ethan still didn't know what to answer, and was kept from answering in any case by the interruption of his aunt, who had come up to him and was looking at him as if deciding which of his cheeks to slap. "Aunt? I didn't see you here. Hiding Fenton under your skirts, or is he off losing my money at the card tables?"

"Don't you dare," the matron told him, waving her closed fan inches from his chin. "Do you have any idea how you embarrassed me the other day in the park?"

"I've a fairly good suspicion of that, yes," Ethan answered, smiling at Chance, who looked to be enjoying himself. Good man, Chance Becket. Too serious at times, but a good man.

"Don't be smart," Mrs. Tirrel ordered, tapping the fan sticks against Ethan's chest. "I hate when you're being smart."

"Accustomed as you are to your son's stunning lack of intelligence, I'm sure you do. Yes, I can see your problem. I'm only surprised you do, madam."

Chance actually flinched before shaking his head and covering his laugh with a cough.

"I'm ashamed to be your relative," Mrs. Tirrel said, seemingly having run out of anything else to say, and falling back on her favorite insult.

"How wonderful, Aunt. With any luck, you'll disown me. But, since that can't be accomplished this evening, it would please me very much if you'd just *go away.*"

"I have every intention of leaving you standing here, and cutting you in future, Ethan Tanner. But I am here for a reason, and that reason is to tell you that your… that the *female* you are foisting on us is totally unacceptable. You are the earl, you have responsibilities, not that your father ever understood that. But that girl? Flaunting herself in that gown. And that hair! She looks like a washerwoman, just tying up all that vulgar dark hair—not a wave, not a curl. And no funds for jewels, obviously. Your mistresses wear better. Why, she looks positively *foreign.*"

"Exotic," Ethan corrected, speaking through clenched teeth. "The word you were searching for is *exotic.* And, yes, she is. Marvelously, wonderfully exotic. Oh, and we hope for at least a half-dozen children. You'll break the news to Fenton, won't you, that the earldom will soon be completely out of his reach? And have him listen closely as he heads for his next gaming hall, so he'll hear the distinct warning *snap* of the closing of my purse."

Mrs. Tirrel stood there for a few moments, blinking, sputtering, and then—to Chance's complete and utter amazement—said, "Why, of course I shall tell Fenton your happy news, Nephew. My felicitations on your upcoming marriage. I…I knew if I but nudged you enough, you'd tell me what seemed so *obvious* to me the moment I saw that lovely young lady enter on your arm. Why, I—"

"Aunt," Ethan said quietly, pinching the bridge of his nose between forefinger and thumb. "Go away. Now."

"But—"

"The allowance will continue. But only if neither

you nor Fenton enters my line of vision for the next, oh, five years should do it. Understood?"

Chance watched the woman scurry off as if someone had lit a fire beneath her feet. "I think it's safe to say she understands. So, my friend, how much do you think it might cost the two of us to convince the fiddlers to saw out a waltz, hmm?"

Ethan, who had been watching Morgan again, his aunt's appearance already forgotten, turned to smile at Chance Becket. "Morgan and I may be deserting society, but you'll still be here, still at the War Office. Would your wife approve? We'll be asked to leave the premises, you know, and then shunned for quite some time. Rightfully so, I would point out to you, although Maude—Lady Beresford—won't really mind."

"My wife is pregnant. I don't think we'll be tempted to move in society for quite some time. And Morgan has earned this treat, don't you think?"

"We have been rather manipulating her, haven't we, using her to cover my trip to the coast?"

"Nobody uses Morgan, Ethan. Not for long, and never twice. Ten pounds?"

"Fifty, I think, as there are five of them up on the dais. I'm feeling generous this evening. Go prepare your wife."

CHAPTER SEVENTEEN

MORGAN HADN'T LET Louise fold away the gown, but had just shooed out the maid, then held the garment up in front of her as she began to glide around the bedchamber in her bare feet, humming the tune she'd never forget.

They'd watched the other dancers, then gone down to supper, to share a plate Ethan had piled high with slices of fruit and meat. He'd introduced Morgan to several people and she'd promptly forgotten all of their names and titles, because she saw no reason to commit them to memory.

Three matrons had asked her for the direction of her modiste, and another had gushed most embarrassingly over Morgan's "simply remarkable" hairstyle, and that had been nice.

But nothing had been better than what happened once they'd returned to the ballroom.

Ethan had given her no hint that he'd actually arranged for the playing of the lovely Viennese melody, but when it had begun, and the dancers all seemed to freeze in place, looking confused, he had taken her by the hand and led her past them, to the very center of the floor, holding her at arm's length, walking the two of them in a slow circle directly beneath the largest chandelier in the ballroom.

Nobody had spoken. She doubted that many of the people watching them had even breathed. There was nothing but the music and the man in front of her. The circle he'd drawn with their bodies had carved out their own small world in the midst of a multitude.

He'd released her hand then, and bowed most elegantly, and she'd curtsied to him deeply before slipping two fingers through the silken loop halfway down her gown's flared skirt. She'd then stepped into his outstretched arms, to be quickly, breathlessly whirled into the magic.

She'd held her chin high, and he'd leaned slightly away from her, still keeping her safely within the circle of his arms as their gazes met, locked.

This was nothing like the dance as she'd learned it under Monsieur Aubert's reluctant tutorage.

Morgan's gloved hands had seemed to burn pleasurably, one on Ethan's forearm, the other held high in his grasp as he gently maneuvered her backward, then forward, before stepping into yet another turn. And another. And another.

She'd thrown back her head and laughed in utter freedom, utter enjoyment, feeling as if she and Ethan were creating their own breeze as he deftly danced her around the room, everyone stepping back, moving out of their way.

"I'm flying," she'd told Ethan breathlessly.

And he'd replied, "You're beautiful."

The floor was theirs. The music was theirs. The magic was theirs.

And then, much to her surprise, Morgan saw that Chance and Julia had joined them on the dance floor.

"In for a penny," Julia had told her as she and Chance whirled by them, and Morgan realized that Julia was a most beautiful woman...something Chance obviously knew, as he was looking at her like a besotted bridegroom.

"Uh-oh," Ethan had warned, much too soon. "I do believe Lady Beresford is attempting to engage my attention, thankfully not by tossing a chair in our general direction."

"Ignore her," Morgan had told him, and he had done just that, so that the music, that lovely music, hadn't stopped until Lady Beresford redirected her anger toward the musicians.

Morgan came to a halt now, in front of the long mirror in her bedchamber, holding out the skirt of her gown, swaying from side to side as she grinned, remembering what had happened next, when they'd reached the small antechamber just outside the ballroom (only after Ethan had bowed to their "audience," and Morgan had curtsied once more).

Lady Beresford had come up to them, breathless, just as Ethan was settling Morgan's spangled, transparent shawl over her shoulders. "Get out! Get out, get out, you *horrid* man. And take this...this creature with you, whoever she is!"

"Why, Maude," Ethan had said affably, "you know who this is. You were introduced earlier. Miss Morgan Becket, of the Romney Marsh Beckets, of course. This fine gentleman," he'd added, indicating Chance with a slight inclination of his head, "is Mr. Chance Becket, and—"

"I don't care who they are, Ethan! To make such spectacles of yourselves with that horrid dance! You're horrid people!"

"Oh, come on, Maude, admit it." Ethan had pressed on as Morgan pushed the side of her fist against her mouth to stifle her giggles. "You'd love to dance the waltz. Besides, your ball will be the talk of Mayfair this Season, and that can't possibly be a bad thing, hmm?"

"You're incorrigible," Lady Beresford had said then, but Morgan could tell she was weakening. No wonder Ethan was able to be so naughty—women adored him. "I will expect a rather enormous bouquet of my favorite yellow roses delivered tomorrow morning, accompanied by your effusive apology. A poem, in fact, wouldn't come amiss."

Ethan had bowed to her, assuring her ladyship she would not be disappointed.

"Oh, you never disappoint, Aylesford. Why do you think I keep inviting you? The waltz will be accepted in London at some point—the younger ones will demand it. But not tonight! Now, if you'll kindly pretend for my guests that I have just succeeded in tearing a large verbal strip off your shameless hide, and promise you'll come to Beresford in the fall to dance the waltz with me, I shall forgive you."

"Done and done, dearest Maude. Shall I drop to my knees, kiss the hem of your gown, weep copiously?"

"No, that would be suspect. Just don't grin at my back as I walk away, you jackanapes."

And then Lady Beresford had drawn up her pudgy

self, huffed a time or two, and turned back to the ballroom, leaving all four "horrid people" to hold each other up as they laughed like loons all the way to the flagway, and Ethan's waiting coach.

Why, they'd laughed all the way back to Upper Brook Street, just like four very good friends. And that, Morgan was amazed to realize, had turned out to have been the best part of all.

She backed away from the mirror, moving into the dance again, once more humming the tune, her eyes closed as she held on to the gown and her memories, whirling round and round the bedchamber. It was late, but she couldn't sleep. How could anyone sleep after a night like this?

Round and round...dipping, turning...nearly able to feel Ethan's arms around her. Round and round and—

"Jacob!" Morgan exclaimed, the gown slipping out of her hands as she grabbed on to his shoulders after colliding with him, nearly losing her balance. "What in blazes are you doing here? Is something wrong?"

Jacob's mouth had dropped open, his eyes fairly bugging out of his head, and Morgan belatedly realized that she stood before him in her thin lawn chemise, which barely covered her breasts.

She dropped her hands and lifted her chin, glared at him. "You will of course inform me when you've had your fill of looking, Jacob. And then you will tell me why you are in my bedchamber, and why you reek of ale."

Her childhood friend narrowed his eyes, not looking away. "You said to watch him. Like a hawk, you said. Why, Morgie? So I can see him touching you, kissing you?"

"You were hiding somewhere?" Morgan asked, remembering the short interlude Chance and Julia had allowed her and Ethan in the drawing room once they had arrived home from the ball. "Where, Jacob? Where did you hide? You should tell young Alice. She'd love to find a better hiding place."

He ignored her sharp answer, even as he couldn't ignore the stirring in his loins. She hadn't moved to cover herself. Why? Because she wanted to embarrass him? Or was she nothing more than a strumpet who would tease anyone, let anyone touch her?

Anyone save him.

But he could only repeat what he'd already stated: "You said we were to watch him. You said it."

Morgan sighed, nodded her head. "I did, didn't I, Jacob? I'm sorry. I was angry when I said that, and confused. But I was mistaken, and the earl is harmless. Really."

"Why, Morgie?" Jacob shoved his fingers through his hair. His ears buzzed. His blood was becoming hot. "Because he kisses you? Because he touches you? Because he's an earl?"

For the first time since her initial shock at seeing him in her bedchamber, Morgan felt nervous, and somewhat ashamed. She rushed into speech. "No, Jacob, it's nothing like that. Chance approves of him."

"But you said—"

Morgan rolled her eyes. Jacob was clearly drunk. "Yes, I said, but now I'm *un*-saying what I said. He's traveling to Becket Hall with us tomorrow. Now go away, Jacob. Or do you think I can't smell the drink on you? Shame on you."

Jacob moved his jaw back and forth, breathing deeply through his nose. Looking about as dangerous as a puppy, poor thing, and Morgan almost said as much. Except she'd promised herself she was done with teasing, with flirting with innocents like Jacob just to get her own way.

She bent down and picked up her gown, holding it against her breasts.

"You said…you said…" Jacob continued, pointing a finger at her, wishing his head was clearer. "Outsiders aren't welcome at Becket Hall. You said that. Everyone says that. They're dangerous."

Morgan still hoped to reason with him. "Julia was an outsider, Jacob. But she's one of us now."

"That's different," Jacob declared, his voice growing louder. "She's a woman."

"Oh really," Morgan said, trying not to laugh, for that had to be the most ridiculous statement she'd ever heard. "How is it different for women, Jacob?"

She was so beautiful. Jacob ached for her. "I don't know. It just is. They just are. *Stop asking me questions.*"

Morgan was feeling more and more uneasy the longer Jacob remained in her bedchamber. He was so different tonight, so vehement. *Unmanageable.*

"All right, Jacob. I'll accept that. But you have to accept that the Earl of Aylesford presents no danger to anyone at Becket Hall."

Jacob narrowed his eyes, remembering his anger. "You're only saying that because you're sweet on him."

"Ah, Jacob…" Morgan put her hand on his shoulder. "Yes. Yes, I am. I'm…sweet on him."

Jacob reached up, grabbed her hand from his shoulder, flung her away from him with some force. "You see? Women!"

Morgan squared her shoulders, narrowed her gaze. "I think you would be smart to leave, Jacob, and we won't speak of any of this again."

"No! No, I'm telling you. Mrs. Chance Becket is all right because she's Mrs. Chance. She'd never hurt him. It's a female's nature. You'd do the same with the earl, no matter what, never seeing any danger. It's a female's nature."

"Ah, marvelous. Jacob Whiting, the drunken philosopher." Morgan turned her back on him. She'd go to the bed, pick up her dressing gown, but that would tell him she was concerned for her appearance in front of him, and she wanted him to believe she saw him as her childhood friend—safe, and no threat to her.

"I don't know what that means—philosopher. Tell me what that means."

"I don't have time for that right now, Jacob, and you're going to have a horrible headache tomorrow morning. I'll simply agree with you. I worried about the earl earlier, I've admitted that. But *both* Chance and I are now convinced that we have nothing to fear, nothing to worry about as far as the earl is concerned. Becket Hall is in no danger. I apologize yet again for worrying you, but I won't continue to apologize—or argue with you. I know you understand that. *Good night,* Jacob."

She was in the act of reaching for her dressing gown when Jacob grabbed her upper arm, spun her around to face him. She felt his fingers digging hard into her flesh, but refused to wince. Inches away from him, she smelled the sourness of his breath, felt repulsed by this lad who'd never before been more than her faithful friend…her faithful puppy dog.

"Why him, Morgie? Why him? Why not me? You're too good for the likes of Jacob Whiting now, with all your fancy London clothes and parties? I've done everything you ever wanted, Morgie. I know why you kiss my cheek, why you tease me. You want what you want. You shouldn't be doing that, Morgie. I'm a man grown, and I want what I want." His fingers squeezed even tighter, and he shook her. *"Look at me."*

Morgan stared up into Jacob's eyes. Jacob's once kind, trusting, simple eyes. "We…we were children. And I was wrong. Mean, selfish. I'm sorry, Jacob. I'm more sorry than you can ever know, and I've realized my mistake. I hurt you, and I know that now. But, please, this has to stop. You have to leave."

He shook his head. He was touching her. He wanted to go on touching her. Just once. Just this once, it would be Jacob Whiting holding her. Just this once. "No. Not yet. I'm owed, Morgie. I'm *owed,* and I'll take what you give him."

Morgan's eyes went wide as Jacob slammed his mouth against hers in a rough, clumsy, even pathetic kiss that tasted of ale and desperation.

His hands were on her breasts, squeezing her painfully through the thin fabric of her chemise, even as he pushed himself against her thighs.

Morgan closed her eyes, but not before a single tear escaped, to run down her cheek. She didn't move, didn't struggle, but accepted the assault as a punishment long overdue.

One last time, her mother's child.

Jacob's work-callused fingers struggled for a few seconds with the ribbon that held her chemise closed, then he grabbed the neckline in his fist and ripped the thin fabric to her waist in one violent movement.

He stepped back slightly, breathing heavily, his mind at last coming back from the dark place that had captured it, and looked at what he had done.

Realized what he had done.

Morgan stood before him, her arms at her sides, her hands drawn into fists. Her breasts were completely exposed to him, and he could see angry red marks where he had touched her.

He'd hurt her. God, he'd hurt her! His Morgie. How could he have…? How could he…?

"Aw, Morgie…"

Morgan saw his confusion, the almost comical bafflement in his eyes. And then she saw the pain. Pain she never wanted to see in anyone else's eyes, ever again. Pain she'd put in Jacob's eyes. Without a word, she turned, picked up her dressing gown and held it in front of her breasts.

Jacob spread his arms wide, staggering where he stood. "What have I done? Look…look what I've done! Morgie…"

"It's all right, Jacob," she said quietly. "I'm all right. This wasn't your fault. It was mine, and I know that. Just as I knew you'd never really hurt me."

Jacob lifted his hands to his cheeks, roughly pushed his fingers through his hair as he bent his head, laced them hard against the back of his neck. He should be struck blind. He should be struck dead. Odette should put a curse on him. Maybe she had….

"I'm sorry. I'm sorry. I'm sorry."

"So am I, Jacob," Morgan said, her playmate gone, her friend gone. Her childhood, gone.

Jacob's chest heaved with each tortured breath as he finally dared to look at her. "I love you, Morgie. I've always loved you."

Morgan squeezed her eyes closed, her fingers pressed hard to her mouth to keep the sobs from escaping. "I love you, too, Jacob," she told him in a whisper, watching as he turned and walked from her bedchamber, his steps slow, like those of a very old man.

Only after the door closed behind him did she sink to her knees on the crumpled gown she had worn with such happiness, wrapping her arms about herself as she slowly rocked back and forth, back and forth. "I'm so, so sorry…."

CHAPTER EIGHTEEN

ETHAN PULLED HIS WATCH from the pocket of his waistcoat and glared at it as he stood on the flagway outside the Becket home in Upper Brook Street. Half-past nine.

He'd been inside, earlier, to find that not only was Morgan not ready to leave, but the cylinder had yet to arrive. He and Chance had spoken for some minutes, and then Ethan had come back outside, to tell his coachman to walk the team around the block to keep them from becoming chilled in the early morning air, leaving Alejandro tied to the hitching post.

He was on his way back inside when he heard his name called, and turned to see Lady Judith Quinnen and her maid stepping out from the next house down the street.

Returning to the flagway, Ethan tipped his hat, bowed to the young woman whose beauty had done nothing to blind the gentlemen of the ton to her acidic tongue and starchy ways these three seasons past. "A good morning to you, my lady," he said, wishing her on the other side of the globe. "You're out and about early."

"I am always out and about early, Lord Aylesford, which you might know, if you'd ever moved yourself to rise before noon, which I sincerely doubted until this morning. I much enjoy the park without its usual crush of cits and hopeful social climbers clogging the paths, ogling their betters."

She lifted her parasol higher on her shoulder, looking at him with her pale blue, unblinking eyes. "Such as that unfortunately flamboyant creature you teased into helping you make a spectacle of yourself last evening."

"You'd be referring to Miss Morgan Becket, sister of your neighbor, as circumstance would have it." Ethan pulled a thin cheroot from an inside pocket, just to watch some sort of emotion crowd into those too-placid eyes, even if it was horror at the thought he might actually *light* it in her presence.

Lady Judith shrugged a single shoulder, ignoring the cheroot. "Whoever she is. I'm sure I'm not in the least interested in such an obvious heathen."

Ethan smiled around the cheroot he now held in his teeth. "Ah, but my dear lady, haven't you heard? Heathens are all the crack these days. So sad you're so deadly dull, isn't it? But don't despair, it's only your third Season. Perhaps next year will be your year. Although you are getting a little long in the tooth, aren't you?"

"I never liked you, Aylesford," she said coldly.

Ethan tipped his curly brimmed beaver in acknowledgment of her insult. "See me as figuratively at your feet in gratitude, madam. And now, good day to you. I know you'll want to rush off, to beat the cits."

He struck a stick match against the rough side of one of the marble steps, smiling as he lit the cheroot while watching Lady Judith flounce off toward the park, her elderly maid all but skipping to keep up with her. Oh, yes, he was a bad man. A bad, bad man…

"Umm, that smells good. Papa smokes one every night after dinner, out on the terrace, and I adore the smell. Although I did become deathly sick when I stole one and tried it for myself. Who was that you've just insulted in my defense?"

Ethan turned to look up the steps, and saw Morgan standing in the doorway, a hatbox in her hand. "Does it matter?" he asked, tossing the cheroot in the direction of the gutter. "And I'd adore seeing you try another cheroot someday."

He held out his hand to her and she extended her own as she walked down the steps to him. "I'll remember that. And I'm sorry I'm so late. I…I'm afraid I didn't get to sleep until it was nearly dawn."

"Thinking about last night?" he asked, bending over her hand, longing to pull her fully into his arms. She was beautiful this morning, but perhaps a little pale, and her smile wasn't as bright. "Did you have second thoughts about our little…exhibition?"

She shook her head, realizing that their waltz seemed long ago—a lifetime ago. "No, not at all. I see Alejandro, but where is your coach? My baggage is already packed in my own traveling coach, save for this," she said, holding up the bandbox, "but I doubt there's room for either of us. Oh, and Louise, of course. My maid."

Ethan took the object from her, raising his eyebrows as he felt the weight of it. "She'd be in here?" he asked, hefting the box.

Morgan smiled for the first time since the previous

evening. "Oh, yes, certainly. Cut into several pieces, naturally, so she'd fit. In truth, that's why I'm so tardy. She had very long legs."

"I love these occasional glimpses into the way your mind works, imp, even if they sometimes frighten me. Ah, and here's my coach, back again."

Morgan looked up at the still open doorway. "And here's Louise—walking quite well, all things considered."

The maid stopped when she reached the flagway, her head bowed as she dipped both knees in a quick, bobbing curtsy.

Ethan pointed to the woman as she climbed into the coach. "She really travels in with us?"

Ah, Morgan's second smile of the morning. Ethan was so good for her. Soon she'd be her old self again, even if, so far, her cheerfulness was taking enormous effort to achieve. "I distinctly remember someone telling me, only a few days ago, that a proper female should not travel without her chaperone."

Ethan discreetly scratched at his temple as he leaned down to whisper in her ear. "You pick the damnedest times to be proper, imp. I was looking forward to our privacy inside the coach."

"I know," Morgan told him, also whispering. "Which is why Saul will be meeting us just as we reach the turnpike, so that he can take Louise up with him and turn Berengaria over to me. But one must make concessions to one's pregnant sister-in-law. She's delicate, you understand."

Ethan lightly flicked a finger against the side of Morgan's nose. "In that case, I applaud your use of troops, General," he said, grinning. "How does Jacob feel about this arrangement?"

"Jacob?" Morgan's stomach gave a small, sickly flip. "Why would you ask about Jacob?"

"I don't know," Ethan told her, confused by her question, and by the tone she'd used to ask it. "I think of him rather as a loyal hound, I suppose. One who bites if he feels his mistress is in any danger."

"Jacob will be fine," Morgan said, thankful to hear Chance's voice behind her, calling to Ethan.

"Excuse me, my dear," he said, and left her on the flagway, where she was grateful to be alone so that she could force her raw nerves back under control.

He returned in a moment, carrying a small leather satchel he quickly handed up to his coachman.

"Morgan? If you're ready, I think your brother would like to say goodbye to you once more."

She pointed toward the coach. "What was—no, never mind." She lifted the divided skirt of her deep burgundy riding habit as she climbed the few short steps to the doorway, then flung herself into her brother's arms, holding him tightly as she pressed her cheek against his chest.

"Here, here," Chance said, surprised as well as pleased. "You're not passing out of our lives forever, you know. Julia swears she can't feel so sickly every morning forever, and we'll be traveling down to Becket Hall before you know it."

"I'm so sorry, Chance," Morgan said against his chest.

"Sorry?" He carefully wrapped his arms around his sister, who had, in his memory at least, never hugged anyone. He was certain she'd most definitely never apologized to anyone, for anything. "Julia and I knew what we were doing last night, and we enjoyed ourselves. There's no reason to apologize."

Morgan sniffed back tears and looked up at her brother, who was standing on the step above her. "Not that. Oh, perhaps that. But not that, really. I'm sorry for…for *everything*. I haven't been an easy sister."

"That's true enough, if I think about the events of last year. You're referring to the night you waited for me outside of Julia's bedchamber?"

"Yes, for that." Morgan sniffed, amazed at herself, how easily tears were coming to her. She, who rarely ever cried. "And for riding out with…you know… without any of you knowing. And…and for everything else."

Chance drew his handkerchief from his pocket and dabbed at Morgan's tear-wet cheeks. "Are you by any chance confessing to being the one who *borrowed* one of my best pistols, shot out one of the windows in Ainsley's study and then put the pistol back, hoping no one would know?"

Morgan's smile was watery, but it was a smile, and Chance began to relax, because his sister had been acting very strangely.

"No, that was Fanny and Rian. But I probably did everything else. Do you forgive me?"

"Morgan, are you all right?"

She gave a weak laugh. "No, Chance, I don't think I am. But I'm going to be, I promise."

"And his lordship? Are you still of the same mind about not accepting his proposal?"

"I don't know," Morgan answered honestly. "But I do think I'm a better person today than I was just a little while ago. Maybe even since yesterday."

Chance put a crooked finger beneath her chin, lifted her face toward his. "Morgan, you're a very good person, and you always were. I don't know what's going on inside that head of yours, but please, don't change too drastically. I would miss Morgan Becket very much."

She kissed his cheek, gave him one last hug, and then turned and ran for the coach, bypassing Ethan's offer to assist her as she quickly mounted into the vehicle.

Moments later, after putting up the step, Ethan joined her, closing the door behind him before settling back on the front-facing seat. "Forgive me for asking the obvious," he said, handing her his handkerchief so she could wipe at her eyes, "but are you quite all right? Are you sorry to be leaving London so soon?"

"Oh no, Ethan, I'm delighted to be leaving London," she told him sincerely. "Almost, I imagine, as delighted as London is that I'm leaving."

"I see," he said, grinning as she rather lustily blew her nose. He looked very pointedly at the maid, who sat facing them, and she lowered her gaze to her lace-mitted fingers. "And you're delighted to be with me?"

Miserable as she was, feeling as determined as she was to be a better person, Morgan knew there were some mountains that could never be climbed, some foes that would never be defeated. One of those foes to her determination to reform her behavior was her dislike for secrets, unless they were hers.

And Chance had said he didn't want her to change *too* much.

"Not as delighted as I'd be if you told me what was in that satchel you handed up to your coachman. Chance had a visitor in his study earlier, and that visitor hadn't arrived via the front door, or I would have known. A clandestine visitor, a satchel traveling with us to Becket Hall? Yes, I'd definitely be delighted to know what is in that satchel."

"Easily answered, my dear. That was my valet you saw. Being so cramped for space, and knowing of the Becket family's expertise in the matter, I had your brother cut him up and stuff him in the satchel. The way you did with your maid and bandbox, correct?"

There was a quick, startled gasp from the other side of the coach, and Morgan shot Ethan a "now look what you've done" glare, then climbed across the coach to sit beside Louise. "His lordship was only funning, Louise. You're here, aren't you? Inside this coach, not a bandbox, and with all of you in one piece."

"And with working ears, too," Ethan said, settling back more comfortably against the squabs. "But you're going suddenly deaf now, Louise, aren't you?"

The maid's head bobbed up and down quickly, nervously. "Can't hear a thing, milord. Don't see nothing, neither."

Morgan maneuvered herself back across the coach, giving Ethan a playful punch in the midsection before sitting down close beside him. "You're as mean as I am," she whispered to him.

"Yes, no wonder we rub along together so well," Ethan said, raising the hand that had just punched him, and kissing the bare skin above Morgan's glove. "Questions, and answers, are for later, imp, save this one. Where do we meet your coach?"

"I'm not sure. Just outside of London proper, I believe. Saul knows the way, in any case."

"We may encounter my outriders in the much same area," Morgan said, having dispatched three footmen directly from the stable behind Grosvenor Square. "This conveniently crested coach, yours, my traveling coach...we're quite the entourage. I imagine the entire world and his wife will know the Earl of Aylesford is decamping to visit the family of that delicious woman he waltzed with last evening. You can't turn me down now, Morgan. I'd have to leave the country."

Morgan knew her grin to be positively wicked. "Poor man. Wherever will you go? The Continent is barely safe at the moment."

There was a quick, and just as quickly stifled, giggle from the other side of the coach, followed by a quiet, "Sorry, milord."

Morgan's eyes were dancing with glee as Ethan shot her a most terrible look. "I'd have an answer to that, imp, but as I have been so recently reminded, I'm not at my best before noon."

He then stretched his long legs out on the facing seat, beside a newly startled Louise, slid down low on his spine and tipped his hat to shade his eyes. "Wake me, please, when we reach the inestimable Saul."

CHAPTER NINETEEN

ETHAN LIFTED THE BRIM of his hat, blinking at the sunlight slanting in the side window, feeling slightly abashed that he had actually fallen asleep. Until, that was, he realized Morgan was also sleeping, curled against his chest, his arm having somehow made its way across her shoulders.

He smiled, as this was a rather delightful circumstance, before remembering the maid's presence. He looked across the space dividing them and, yes, there she most certainly was, bright-eyed and apple-cheeked, and still very much in the way.

But the coach had stopped, which Ethan could only consider a good sign, and when a moment later the equally bright-eyed and apple-cheeked face of one of his grooms appeared at the off window, his spirits rose even higher.

Careful not to disturb Morgan, who seemed to be sleeping the sleep of either the innocent or the dead, he quietly lowered the window. "Well met, Harold. I take it we're at the tollhouse outside Dartford?"

"Yes, milord, just as you told us ta be. There's another coach here, waiting on yer. Coachie's all right, but the other one ain't the chatterin' sort, if yer take m' meanin', milord. Coachie has him tied to the box, so he won't go tumblin' off, and he's lookin' a mite green."

"Really," Ethan said, assuming Harold meant the inestimable Jacob. The boy hadn't seemed the sort to try to drown himself in a bottle. "The worse for drink, is he?"

"He's not the better for it, milord, I'll say that. Offered him a hair from the dog what bit him, but he just went greener, and cast up his accounts all over the side of the coach. Happens to those country lads when they comes to town, not used to nothin' save their mama's milk, eh? You'll be wantin' Alejandro now?"

"Yes, Harold, thank you. And Miss Becket's mount as well, if you please. Are they serving, inside the tollhouse?"

"Scones and tea, milord. I asked. Ordered some up for you and the lady, I did, not ten minutes past, figurin' yer'd be comin' along about now."

"Good man. As I believe I've heard it said about you, Harold, you'll go far."

"I'm tryin', milord. Lookin' for butler's keys, someday," Harold said cheekily, and ran off, probably to do something else he felt would impress his employer all hollow.

"Jacob's sick?"

Ethan turned to Morgan, to see that she was awake and in the process of sitting up straight once more, adjusting her shako hat on her head. "Inebriated, imp, although I believe he's now on the other, much less pleasant side of the experience. I suppose you want to see him?"

Morgan concentrated on retrieving her gloves, which had slipped to the floor of the coach at some point. "No, not really. I shouldn't want to embarrass him. I'm sure Saul is taking very good care of him. Where are we? Did you say Dartford?"

"Yes, I did, but we're only on the outskirts. Dartford, as well-positioned as it is, and as well-traveled as its turnpike may be, is not a place most wish to visit for any longer than it takes to traverse from one end to the other by coach. The finer arts of sanitation still seem to elude the citizens' collective grasp."

Morgan wrinkled her nose. "Then we will most certainly not tarry. Did we pass through here on the way to London?"

"No, there was no need, not when we were traveling from Tanner's Roost. Now, come along—no, not you, Louise, thank you—and we'll have some refreshments while everything and—" he looked at Louise one last time "—every*one* is resettled."

Louise must have spent the past few hours considering her Duty To Her Employer, for she nervously cleared her throat, then said, "I am to stay with Miss Morgan, milord."

"Miss Morgan," Ethan explained as he would to a child, "will be riding with me ahead of the coach until we reach the inn at Headcorn. So, unless you ride, Louise, or are able to run exceedingly fast…?"

The door to the coach opened and a hand reached inside to pull down the step…and Louise was gone before Morgan could betray herself with a giggle. "Lady Beresford was right. You're incorrigible."

"And more eager than you obviously know to be alone with you somehow tonight," he told her. "But this shall have to satisfy me for now, I suppose."

He tipped up her chin and lightly pressed his lips against hers. It was a chaste kiss, just as he'd planned it…until Morgan wrapped her arms tightly around him, grinding her mouth to his before breaking the kiss, pressing her cheek against his.

"Hold me a moment, Ethan," she whispered, and he heard pain in her voice. Pain she didn't explain and that he could not fathom. He remembered how she had held on to her brother earlier, and now it seemed to be his turn to hold her. To comfort her?

"Morgan, what's wrong?" He played light kisses against the side of her neck. "Something's happened, hasn't it?"

Morgan hated herself for allowing Ethan's touch to set off all her pent-up emotions, emotions that had haunted her for all of last night after Jacob had left her bedchamber.

She wanted to be strong. She wanted to forget what had happened between herself and Jacob. She'd spent a good hour on the floor, weeping, mourning the loss of what had truly been her best friend, perhaps her only real friend.

And she couldn't tell anyone what had happened. Most especially not Ethan.

She had to stop being such a watering spot, such a weak ninny, and get herself back under control. She had to!

Ethan eased her away from him, and she allowed him to, even as she longed to hold on to him. "Is it all too much, Morgan? Have I pressed too hard? Asked too much, too soon? Because it doesn't have to be that way, sweetheart. It shouldn't be that way, in any case. I won't press you for any more…intimacies."

He was backing away from her? *Now?* Now, when she needed him more than ever? When she needed his touch, and not only so that she could forget Jacob's?

Was that selfish? Yes, it was. But then, she'd always been selfish. It had always been what Morgan wanted, always what Morgan believed she needed….

Ethan was older. An earl. Sophisticated, intelligent. But still a man, and how much of what he thought he felt for her was a result of her teasing, her outrageous behavior? And she *was* powerful. She'd perfected those powers over the years. With poor innocent foils like Jacob Whiting.

She was who she was—perhaps even worse now, now that she had looked at herself, really seen herself—and Ethan could offer her any *out* in the world and she would not take it. She'd begun this journey, and now she would continue until the end, whatever that might be, wherever that journey may lead.

Why, she had already all but asked Ethan to seduce her. She'd given him all the signs that she would be receptive to his every advance. And she *had* been receptive, even the instigator.

She was shameless.

Because you want him, a voice inside her head told her, taunted her. *He stands before you. Your dangerous man. This isn't a game, this isn't silly practice with a callow youth. This is real. This is your equal. Together, you either rule your world, or you completely destroy it. But you can never deny it. And you can't turn away….*

Morgan spoke to that voice as much as she did to Ethan when she said, "We started down this path the day we met, Ethan. Walk it or run it, we'll end at the same place. That's our only choice."

"There are always choices, Morgan," Ethan told her, becoming more worried for her by the moment.

"No," she said quietly. "Not this time. We have to see where the path ends."

"I hope I already know where it ends. With you and me together. On your terms, on my terms, with the blessings of your family and church, or damned by everyone. That doesn't matter. It should, I suppose, but it doesn't."

Morgan touched his cheek with the back of her hand, that hand only trembling slightly as she ran it down his jawline and throat. "I didn't eat breakfast, Ethan. I'm very hungry." She slid her index finger up and over his chin, tugged down his bottom lip, slipped her finger between his teeth. "Are you hungry?"

Ethan knew not to push at her; she was too fragile at the moment. He'd follow where she led, move only at the pace she set. For now.

He nipped at the sensitive tip of her finger, then took hold of her hand and placed a kiss in her palm as they looked deeply into each other's eyes.

"You already know the answer to that question, imp. But it's time we satisfied another hunger with some tea and scones, and then be on our way. As for anything else, we can leave that discussion for later."

Within the hour, the small train had left Dartford behind them, Ethan and Morgan riding out ahead of his coach, followed by his traveling coach, then the Becket coach carrying Saul, Jacob and a nervous Louise, and then three Aylesford grooms whose main job, it would seem, was to chew the dust raised by the three coaches. If a band of highwaymen were to appear, it was doubtful the outriders would even see their approach.

The sunlight, the fresh air, just being on Berengaria's back had done wonders for Morgan, who had been happy to leave her melancholy behind her, unaccustomed as she was to lugging it around with her like rocks in a sack.

"When can we give them a run?" she asked Ethan when the crush of traffic that had seemed to decide to collect in Dartford and its outskirts at last gave way to the occasional coach or farm wagon.

"Not on the roadway," Ethan told her, pleased to see her smile, and the hint of mischief back in her eyes. "Another mile, and there's a fine field surrounded by a narrow dirt path. Until then, may I suggest we simply ride at a sedate pace and enjoy the scenery…and each other."

"At one and the same time? Is that possible?" Morgan asked him, thrilled when he laughed. "Oh, very well. Would you like me to sing for you?"

"You sing?"

"Not well, no. Do you?"

"I do. Extraordinarily well, as a matter of fact."

"Really? I'll have to tell Eleanor. I'm sure she'd be more than happy to accompany you on the new piano Papa had shipped to Becket Hall last year from…well, from somewhere. Do you play?"

"Only with you. Hopefully." Ethan smiled at her, pretending not to understand that Miss Eleanor Becket's piano, if it had been "shipped here" in the past few years, had a very good chance of having reached England's shores on a smuggler's craft.

"I don't play, either," Morgan said without regret. "But I shoot very well. And I can fence."

"Fence. With real weapons? Who would be insane enough to teach you a skill like that?"

"Jacko, my father's very good friend. You'll meet him at Becket Hall. Steel your hand for a crushing before you offer it to him. Jacko likes to believe he's still the strongest man at Becket Hall and in the village."

"But he's not?"

"That would be difficult to say, as no one ever seems eager to test him. I imagine he's looking forward to meeting you."

"You're enjoying yourself at my expense, aren't you, imp? Very well. Jacko, you said. I'll remember the name. Is there anyone else I should be…aware of?"

Morgan's smile faded. "Odette. You probably should be aware of her, even if you never see her, as she doesn't mingle much with the family. We go to her, not the other way around."

"Ah, a mysterious lady. I believe you may have mentioned her name at one time. Tell me more."

Morgan wished she'd never begun this conversation, but Ethan was going to be at Becket Hall. He had to know about Odette; it seemed only fair. But that didn't mean he had to know about the island, about anything else. Even though she longed to tell him. Oh, how she longed to tell him, tell him everything.

Just as Jacob had said she would do. *It's a female's nature….*

"More about Odette?" Morgan murmured. "She's been with us forever, I think."

"So she's a nurse, a nanny?"

That made her laugh. "Odette? No, and I wouldn't let her hear you say that, were I you. She's a priestess. A very powerful priestess. Have you ever heard of voodoo?"

Ethan was beginning to realize just how little he actually knew about Morgan, about all the Beckets. "I have, as a matter of fact. There was a voodoo priest who set himself up in Piccadilly a few years ago, as I recall. Gentlemen of the ton were flocking to him as he promised he could make them—well, never mind that. He was eventually thrown into prison for, shall we say, nonperformance. Does your priestess promise miracles?"

Morgan's mind immediately flashed back to her mostly dim happy memories of the island, and the more vivid if confused memories of what had happened that last day before, as she'd heard Courtland say, they'd all died and come to England. "There are no miracles, Ethan, you know that. But she's still very powerful in some things. Is this the field?" Ethan looked to his left, surprised to see how far they'd come.

He'd been involved in watching Morgan's face, and wondering how someone so young could seem to be hiding so many secrets. It wasn't that she was not honest; she seemed honest to a fault. It was that she told him things, yet left so many things unsaid. Very carefully unsaid.

What did he really know about her? That he wanted her? Was that enough?

"Yes, that's the field. If we keep to the perimeter, we can ride all the way around it without falling afoul of the owner."

"We wouldn't want to do that, would we?" Morgan said, settling herself more firmly on the sidesaddle. "It's a fairly narrow pathway."

"Yes, it is. Are you ready to—?" He held Alejandro back as Morgan turned Berengaria's head and dug her heel into the mare's flank. "My friend, we males are destined always to follow, I fear. But we manage, don't we?"

The ride around the field was accomplished much too soon for Morgan's satisfaction, but when she returned to the roadway it was to see that the coaches still were not visible behind them.

"We could go around again, with you in the lead this time," she told Ethan, and then laughed, because he was wiping at the sleeves of his hacking jacket, trying to rid it of the dust kicked up by Berengaria's hooves. "Um… on second thought…"

"I'm so happy to amuse you, imp," Ethan said, taking off his hat and beating it against his thigh, sending up clouds of light brown dust. "Don't laugh, Morgan. This could be bits of Alexander, you know."

She rode back to him, Berengaria dancing in place as she brushed at the back of his hacking jacket. "'To what base uses we may return, Horatio! Why may not imagination trace the noble dust of Alexander—'"

"'—till he find it stopping a bunghole?'" Ethan finished along with her, then smiled in appreciation. "Not one of Shakespeare's best known quips. My compliments, madam."

"A compliment wasn't exactly what I received when I asked Papa to define bunghole," she told him, smiling at the memory.

"No, I imagine not. How old were you at the time?"

"Nine or ten, I suppose. Why?"

"Because I don't know that many young ladies who quote Shakespeare, that's why. My compliments again, madam."

She turned Berengaria and they were once more moving along the main road at a companionable canter. "I'll accept your compliments and mention that your surprise is evident as well. Why shouldn't I be able to quote Shakespeare? There is an enormous library at Becket Hall, and more long dark winter nights than you can imagine."

"So that you've read the complete works of Shakespeare? Amazing."

Morgan raised her chin, attempted to look at him down her nose, as if highly offended. "'As the old hermit of Prague, that never saw pen and ink, very wittily said to a niece of King Gorboduc, "That that is, is."'"

"I beg your pardon?"

"As well you should, my lord. *Twelfth Night.* Act Four, I believe. What is…is."

"Ah, the woman is throwing down the gauntlet. Very well," Ethan said, more than happy to rise to her challenge. "'Yond Cassius has a lean and hungry look….'" He bowed in his saddle, a sweep of his arm indicating that she should speak the next line.

Morgan grinned. "'He thinks too much. Such men are dangerous.' From *Julius Caesar.* First act. But enough of the easy ones. Everyone knows Shakespeare."

"*Everyone,* Morgan? By everyone, you must mean

all of you Beckets. Certainly not the majority of my acquaintance. Most definitely not the ladies. So, imp, you shoot, you fence, you ride astride when not in town, and you quote Shakespeare. Is there anything you can't do? Because I begin to feel woefully inadequate in comparison."

"Ah, but you sing. You said so. Beautifully, I think you said. We'll have to make you sing for your supper."

"You wouldn't dare."

"No, I suppose not. Besides, I doubt you'd obey. You'd just pack up and leave, and I wouldn't like that."

Again, in the midst of banter, she had gone serious.

"Morgan, we've only known each other a few days, but I think I know you well enough to ask this—what's wrong? What happened between the time I left you last night—rather thoroughly kissed, as I remember the thing—and this morning? Because something did. You're as nervous, as my mother would say, as a long-tailed cat around a rocking chair. I promise you, I would never do anything you don't want me to do, all right?"

Morgan looked at the scenery without seeing it. "You mean tonight, at the inn." She nodded. "I know that, and we've already discussed it. I'm more than happy with our plans. But thank you."

Ethan heard himself say, "You're welcome," and immediately felt the fool.

They lapsed into silence, giving him time to think back over the events of the previous evening, compare them to Morgan's mercurial behavior today. She was trying, quite diligently, to appear as if nothing was wrong, that she was the same Morgan who had melted in his arms.

Was it the prospect of leaving London? Of returning to Becket Hall?

He'd think she felt slighted by him for not telling her about the satchel, about the whole damn silly business he was honor-bound to perform once they got to Becket Hall—but that couldn't be the problem. She'd accepted that he couldn't tell her more than she already knew.

Hadn't she?

Besides, she wasn't angry. If Morgan were angry, he felt sure, he'd know exactly why, because she'd tell him.

This was different. If he had to put a single word to describing how he believed Morgan was acting today, that word would be *wounded.*

"We'll be in Headcorn within the hour," he said when the silence became uncomfortable.

"You do know that Papa will be sending outriders from Becket Hall to Headcorn, to escort us the rest of the way tomorrow. What if they've already arrived?"

"Why then, I imagine I shall have to be very, very careful later this evening."

The smile Morgan shot him was, he believed, her first real one of the day….

CHAPTER TWENTY

JACOB COULDN'T STAY in the common room of the inn, not with Saul trying to goad him into drinking a mug of ale, telling him he wasn't really a man grown until he'd been drunk as a lord for three days running, and Jacob was two days short.

Everyone in the common room, strangers to him, had laughed, had joined in the teasing. One of his lordship's outriders had even offered to buy the barmaid for him for an hour— "Take ye at least that long get your courage up, let alone raisin' up anythin' else," he'd said, and everyone had laughed again.

Everyone treated him like a puling infant. A dumb, stupid baby. He was a man grown, all of twenty years old, and nobody saw that, nobody cared.

Morgie cared, or used to. She'd never laughed at him. She was his friend. And now he'd ruined that, too.

He tried so hard, and still he could do nothing right. He should go to war, that's what he should do. Come back with scars and one of Napoleon's golden eagles. *Then* he'd be a man. Or he could die, be a hero. But he couldn't go back to Becket Hall. Not now, not after what had happened. He just couldn't. Not with Morgie lost to him…

His hands stuck deep in his pockets, Jacob walked with his head down in the dark, toeing a stone ahead of him as he slowly made his way toward the stables, where he could be alone, maybe get kicked in the head by one of the horses, and put out of his misery.

So intent was he on his misery that he nearly jumped when the scrape of a stick match against stone was followed by a small, yellow flare of fire.

He peered into the darkness just at the corner of the stables, ready to curse whoever was hiding in the shadows, scaring him like that…and saw a pair of hands cupped around the flame, the first hint of smoke as the person lit a cheroot.

But when the man lifted his head, and looked at him from beneath the brim of his hat, Jacob's words stuck in his throat.

"Hello, Jacob," Ethan said quietly, pushing himself away from the wall, the lit cheroot between his teeth. "Feeling more the thing tonight, are you?"

"I…I…" Jacob nodded furiously, bringing the fading remnants of his daylong headache back for another airing. "Something I can do for you, milord?"

"Oh, yes, Jacob, I believe there is something you can do for me. Or, rather, something you can tell me. Is there something you want to tell me, Jacob?"

It had been a guess, no more, but Ethan had put together Morgan's unhappiness and Jacob's descent into a bottle, and come up with the idea that something had happened between the two of them. Something decidedly unwonderful.

Now, looking at the boy, at the guilt and pain so evident in his eyes, Ethan drew deep on the cheroot, blew out a stream of blue smoke, then asked, "You and Miss Becket argued?"

"I...that is...she told you?"

"No, Jacob, she didn't. Your Morgie would never say a bad word about you. But she's unhappy, Jacob. Miserably unhappy, and you're about to tell me why."

Jacob pushed his hands through his hair, his chest heaving as his breathing turned rapid and painful. "It's my fault. Everything's my fault. I saw you. I saw you kissing her. Touching her."

"Did you now," Ethan said smoothly, remembering his moments alone with Morgan last night, in the drawing room. It would appear that Jacob had found at least one very good hidey-hole there. "And you didn't like what you saw?"

Jacob looked at the earl, his expression tortured, tears on his cheeks. "Why? Why you? *I'm* the one knows her, *I'm* the one she should be... Is she all right? Is Morgie all right?"

Ethan was liking this less and less. "What did you do, Jacob? Once I was gone, and your Morgie was alone—what did you do? Did you go to her? Did you go to her bedchamber, Jacob? *Did you?*"

"She had to tell me," Jacob tried to explain, wiping at his wet cheeks, rubbing his hand beneath his dripping nose. "She said to watch you. She *told* me! Watch him like a hawk, Jacob. Can't let anybody know, you know. Nobody's business, and dangerous. Nothing about the island, nothing about the Ghost. Can't let strangers in, can't let them see. *Watch him,* Jacob. That's what she said. And then she let you *touch* her. I saw you touch her. But what about *me?*"

Ethan remained very still, and the boy rewarded him by rambling on in his agony, speaking to himself, his eyes tightly closed, his head down.

"Tells *me,* and then she says no, I was wrong, Jacob, don't worry, Jacob. Because he kissed her. She'd forget all of us, just to kiss him. She'll tell him. She'll tell him *everything.* Females do that. And we'll hang. Don't do it, Morgie. Stay with me, Morgie. Don't let him in. *Why can't it be me?*"

Ethan stored away everything Jacob had said about islands, and ghosts, and even hangings, concentrating on the one thing that mattered. The only thing that mattered. "Did you touch her, Jacob? Jacob, answer me. Did you touch her? *Did you hurt her?*"

Jacob looked up at Ethan, his hands clapped hard to the sides of his head, his face a mask of pain and self-loathing. "Oh God. Oh God, oh sweet Christ. I didn't mean to hurt her…I didn't mean to…."

Ethan wanted to kill the lad where he stood, his anger was so hot, so wild.

But Morgan loved this boy, this sad, confused boy. Even now, she was protecting him, probably even blaming herself, if Ethan knew her at all, and he believed he was beginning to know her very well. Jacob's sin, with Morgan taking on the blame for that sin.

One question. He had one more question. And, depending on his answer, the boy would live or die.

"Did you rape her, Jacob?"

"No!" He shook his head violently. "No, no. Not that. I stopped, I stopped! It was wrong, I knew it was wrong. And she just *stood there!* She didn't yell, didn't

try to stop me. She just stood there! And...and then she told me she loved me. She said she was sorry. *She* was sorry. What did *she* do? It was *me!*"

Ethan cursed under his breath. Yes, he knew Morgan well.

Jacob wiped at his face again, and looked to Ethan as if he had answers. "I don't know what to do now. What do I do now?"

"You find a way to live with your mistakes, that's what you do. That's what we all do," Ethan told him. "And, if you're lucky, someday you may even get to make up for them. You're a fortunate man, Jacob. Miss Becket cares for you, cares for you deeply. Give her reason to continue caring for you. That's all you can do."

Ethan took one last pull on the cheroot, then ground it beneath his boot. "And I wouldn't worry overmuch about Miss Becket giving away secrets, when they roll off your tongue so easily. Get yourself back to Becket Hall, you and your mouth, and stay there until you learn to control both it and yourself. Oh, and not another word about any of this to Miss Becket, understand? You've said and done more than enough."

Jacob sniffed. "You should kill me," he said, putting a hand on Ethan's sleeve. "I need to be killed. Morgie shouldn't be the only one hurt."

"Is that a request, Jacob?" Ethan asked as the younger man dropped his hand. "You feel the need to suffer?"

Jacob nodded, lifting his chin. "It isn't right that I shouldn't."

Ethan rubbed at the bridge of his nose for a

moment, thinking about this, then smiled. "You know something, Jacob? You're right. Boys are scolded. Men are knocked down."

And then he hit him flush on the jaw, and Jacob flew back onto his backside in the dirt. He lay there for a few moments before he sat up, shook his head, then reached into his mouth, taking out a bloody bottom tooth the punch had knocked loose.

And then the boy smiled. He actually smiled. "Thank you, milord."

Ethan rubbed his right fist, felt the scrape on his knuckle where it had come into contact with Jacob's teeth. "No, thank you, Jacob. I think we both feel better now. Now make yourself scarce, before I want to feel better again."

CHAPTER TWENTY-ONE

LOUISE SNORED with an enthusiasm that made Morgan smile as she slid out of the high tester bed, her feet searching on the carpet for her slippers.

She stood up, pulling her dressing gown with her, and slowly pushed her arms into the sleeves, tied the ribbon at her neck.

It was dark in the bedchamber she'd been assigned, but the moonlight shining through the threadbare drapes revealed the few bits of furniture that lined the walls of this room beneath the eaves. There were only two guest chambers on this floor, hers and Ethan's.

Which should work out well.

Louise's pallet bed had been placed in front of the door—on Chance's orders, Louise had told her as she'd apologized profusely. But that didn't matter. Chance should have realized that it didn't matter. And he probably did, Morgan thought now, smiling.

She tiptoed to the casement window she'd unlocked earlier. She had also rubbed its hinges with bacon fat she'd taken from the kitchens in Upper Brook Street and hidden in her bandbox, among other things she thought she might need: two sheets she'd cut into long strips and knotted together, a tinderbox, candles and a heavy pewter holder, and one of Chance's dueling pistols. Just in case.

Chance had been wrong about who had taken his dueling pistol all those years ago and shot out Papa's study window, but he would know who had *borrowed* his pistol this time.

Still, if she had to use sheets to escape her bedchamber, a woman should not be traipsing about in the dark of night in her dressing gown without some sort of protection, now should she?

Ethan had said he'd come to her tonight. They'd both been waiting for this night since the moment they'd first met. But if he had decided it would be too dangerous, if he had decided to be a gentleman…? Well, she'd just have to convince him otherwise, wouldn't she?

And he had not come to her chamber. She'd waited until the moon was high in the sky, and he had not come.

So she would go to him.

Taking one last look at the sleeping maid, who probably wouldn't wake if the French invaded and began firing cannon at the inn, Morgan climbed onto the chair she'd earlier placed in front of the window, then held her breath as she pushed open the casement and looked out over the fairly flat roof.

And smelled smoke.

She poked her head out of the window and looked to her right, to see Ethan lying back against the shingles in his breeches and shirtsleeves, his knees bent, his arms behind his head.

He turned to her and spoke around the slim cheroot

clamped between his teeth. "Hello, imp. Lovely evening, isn't it? I was sure you'd figure some way around the inestimable Louise."

Morgan rolled her eyes. "Why are you out there?" she whispered fiercely. "Why didn't you knock on the window, or something?"

"I trusted your judgment as to the timing," he said, tossing the cheroot high into the air, so that it landed in the dirt inn yard, clear of the building. "Care to join me? It's a beautiful night."

"I must be insane," Morgan muttered, hiking up the skirts of her nightrail and dressing gown, then levering one bared leg and her upper body out the window at the same time, which wasn't exactly graceful, but was hands-down better, she'd decided, than crawling out on her belly.

Ethan sat up and reached for her, helping her fully onto the gently sloping roof, and then they both were lying on their backs, side by side, looking up at the stars. "Comfortable?"

"Not really, no," Morgan said, turning her head to look past him. "That's your window?"

Ethan grinned at her. "It is. I've just been contemplating what would happen if a stiff breeze were to come from nowhere, slamming it shut with me still out here."

"You didn't remove the lock?" Morgan asked, incredulous. "I removed the lock from my window hours ago."

Ethan believed he might one day be unsurprised by Morgan, but he was fairly certain it wouldn't be any day soon. "And how did you achieve that, may I ask?"

"With my knife, of course. You seriously mean you didn't think of that?"

"You have a knife?"

"I have a knife."

"With you now?"

Morgan thought of the pistol she'd left inside, on the chair. "Not here, silly. Back there. With my pistol."

"Only you would bring a knife and a pistol to a romantic assignation." Ethan chuckled softly. He took hold of her hand, pulled them both up onto their knees. "And the woman wonders why I waited for her to come to me rather than the other way round. A gentleman caller could get his head blown off."

"You're laughing at me," Morgan said as, bent at the waist and holding hands, they made their way to his open window. "Wasn't it you who said we might encounter some problems tonight, that we should be prepared?"

Ethan slipped inside his room and, his hands now around her waist, lifted her down beside him. "Prepared, yes. Prepared to cancel our plans. I never realized you'd take my words as a warning to arm yourself, imp. Although your determination flatters me. Are you so anxious to be ruined?"

Morgan placed her palms against his bare chest, where his buttons had fallen open, then slid them up and onto his shoulders. "Are you so anxious to ruin me?"

With the help of the moonlight, he looked deep into her eyes, and saw no lingering shadows. She'd faced her demons and conquered them, or had hidden them away. She certainly gave no hint that she wanted to talk with him about Jacob, about her strange mood earlier today.

He had to try. One last time. And he'd try with honesty, speaking from the heart he suddenly realized was in real jeopardy.

"We will marry," he told her quietly, reaching up to untie the satin ribbon at her throat. "We have to. I can't imagine my life without you in it."

Morgan's smile was small and somewhat sad. "Very pretty. Was that to soothe your conscience, Ethan? I'm not asking for anything more than what we'll have here tonight. What we've been moving toward from the beginning. Please, just give me tonight. Give us both tonight."

He wanted her, wanted her so badly. But she spoke as if this was their ending, not their beginning. He needed all of her, and he needed her forever. Even when he'd tried to tell himself that what he'd felt for her was based on their obvious physical attraction to each other, he'd known there was more. Much more.

Once he'd possessed her, buried himself inside her and taken them both to the heights, could he let her go?

Not as the earl, not as a gentleman, not as someone bound by the strictures of society…but as a man. Could the man in him ever let her go? *Never.*

So he said what had to be said, even if that meant he'd never have her. He didn't know what the words he would say meant, but he knew that she would.

"Is it the island, Morgan? Is it the ghost? Is it that once you're back at Becket Hall, safe in Romney Marsh, I can't be allowed in, can't be trusted? Will you let me love you, even love me in return, and then send me away? Can you do that? You'd give me your body, and still not trust me?"

Morgan had begun backing away from him as he

spoke, and when her legs encountered the seat of a chair, she collapsed into it, still staring at him. "You… Chance?" She shook her head. "No, not Chance." Her eyes opened wide. "*Jacob.* Oh, Jacob, what did you do now? Hadn't you done enough?"

Ethan turned to close the casement beside him, then looked at her. "Only those few words, Morgan, that's all he said. The island. A ghost. The need to keep outsiders away. The chance you may all hang. I don't understand any of it, Morgan, although I believe I could make a few educated guesses. I only know that whatever it is you're all hiding at Becket Hall, you don't trust me enough to believe you can tell me. It isn't that you don't want to marry me, Morgan. I doubt you plan to marry any man, because you can't let any man too close. So you're using me, which is fairly lowering, imp. Using me to satisfy some curiosity I've raised in you. What would it be like to know a man? Know this man? So different from the men she's known."

"No," Morgan said, slowly shaking her head. She could see pain in Ethan's eyes. What was wrong with her? Was she destined to hurt every man who cared for her? "No, you're twisting everything. It's not like that. It was never just that."

"I know, Morgan," Ethan said, going to his knees in front of her. "Like recognizes like. Your mother's child. Nothing about you is simple, darling. You're a puzzle I can't unlock, that you can't seem to unlock, either. So what do I do? Do I take what I want, knowing this is all you're willing to give, all you're not afraid to give?"

He got to his feet, figuratively throwing down his last card, hoping it was the trump card. "I don't think so, Morgan. Much as I want you, ache for you, I don't believe I could live with that half measure. I might have thought I could, those first few days, but not now. Now, Morgan, it's all or it's nothing."

She looked up at him, tears standing in her eyes, and some trick of the moonlight seemed to bathe his entire body in a red glow rimmed with yellow…the same aura she had seen around him that first day, as he stood in the bright sunlight.

Her dangerous man.

Did she trust him? Could she trust her own instincts?

Could she let him go?

"I…I can't tell you all about the island," she began slowly, "because I was still very young when we left it, came here. But Papa…Ainsley and Chance and the others, they…did some things." She looked away, closed her eyes. "We had to live, and that's how we lived. And then something horrible happened, and we had to leave. We all had to…to die, and come here. Be the Beckets."

Ethan knelt in front of her once more. He thought for a moment about Chance Becket. Outwardly, a London gentleman…but there had been more to him—he'd sensed that, too. A leashed wildness, an intensity not often found in London gentlemen. Ethan could picture the man on the deck of a ship, shouting out orders. "I think I'm beginning to understand. They were pirates? Privateers?"

Morgan bit her lips between her teeth, and nodded. "Papa took care of us, all of us, and then we had to leave, and we came here, and Papa ordered the ships dismantled, and now we stay here. We're safe here.

Nobody knows." She looked at him, straight into his eyes. "Nobody."

"Because they'd all hang for their crimes against the Crown," Ethan said, tight-lipped. "Then why come here? Why not America?"

She crossed her arms over her breasts, began to rock. It was such a long story, with so many twists and turns. "It was safer to hide here, where our enemy wouldn't think to look. Ethan—it would take me days to explain, to make you understand. But this is my *family.* I've just trusted you with my family. Jacob was right. You can't trust a female when she wants a man. And now my family's safety is in your hands. What does that make me, Ethan? The world's greatest fool?"

He pulled her into his arms. "Hush, darling," he breathed against her ear as she wrapped her arms around him, as he lifted her high and walked to the turned-down bed. "It's all right, everything's all right. I shouldn't have pushed. I'm sorry. We won't talk anymore about any of this. None of it. We're here, just as we knew we would be, were meant to be. Tonight is our beginning, not our ending."

She looked up at him as he joined her on the bed. "There's so much you don't know. And if they don't accept you—"

He smiled slowly as he finished untying the ribbon on her dressing gown. She was so beautiful in the candlelight, and he knew he'd been waiting all of his life for this moment. "Ah, but I'm such a likable fellow. After all, you like me." He placed a soft kiss on her mouth. "Chance likes me." He kissed her bared shoulder. "His lady wife tolerates me."

He pushed down the sleeve of her dressing gown, to continue his line of kisses, and then stopped. Looked. Saw the bruise on her upper arm. The purplish imprint of four fingers and thumb, circling her tender skin.

Jacob.

He should have hit him harder.

Without saying a word, Ethan kissed the center of the bruise, then levered himself up so that he could look down into Morgan's face.

"It's all right," she told him quietly. "It was a mistake…an accident. He didn't mean it. Please."

"Don't blame yourself," Ethan said, stroking her cheek. "He lost you, and he knew it. Just as he knew he never really had you, could never have you. That's not your fault, Morgan. You were his dream, he wasn't yours."

Morgan let out a relieved breath. "I would have told you, but I was afraid you'd—do something."

Ethan smiled. "Oh, I did do something, Morgan. Jacob needed someone to do something."

"I don't understand."

"You can forgive a man his stupidity, but that doesn't mean he doesn't need to feel some sort of punishment." Ethan slowly worked her other arm free of its sleeve. "I obliged him."

"Oh," Morgan said, feeling her worries about Jacob falling from her even as her dressing gown disappeared. "I suppose this is something you'll tell me that men understand, and women don't?"

"Something like that. Tell me, have you noticed that I'm undressing you?"

"I've noticed that you're not kissing me," Morgan said,

feeling confident and daring and more than a little interested in whatever might come next. How free she felt, with just a small part of her secret now shared with this man.

Ethan grinned. "Not very virginal of you to point that out, darling."

"Really? I think I am entirely too virginal, my lord." She slid her hands inside his opened shirt. "But I believe you might be able to rectify that problem?"

They kissed, openmouthed, their tongues immediately dueling, their passions, banked and waiting, bursting immediately into flame.

He drank from her and she from him, each kiss new, each kiss different, each kiss leading to the next.

Clothing was superfluous, so it was quickly gone, and they pressed their naked bodies together as heavy, drugging kisses continued, both of them consumed with wanting, yet reluctant to leave one pleasure for another.

Morgan held him tightly, her hands pressed firmly against his back, her nails digging into his skin, dragging up and down, pulling him closer, hard against her. She buried her fingers in the hair at the back of his head, swept her other hand low, over the muscled tightness of his buttocks. She skimmed the base of his spine, traced the small dip there and smiled against his mouth when he groaned low in his throat.

Ethan felt himself straining toward completion and knew he'd never forgive himself if he didn't slow down, if he gave all control over to his body.

Breaking their kiss, he began moving the length of her slim throat, pressing his lips against her soft flesh, tasting her as he dragged his tongue in the valley between her full, firm breasts.

He reached up for her hand, pulled it down and cupped it around the bottom of her breast, holding his own hand over hers as he lifted her, brought his mouth over her nipple and began to suckle.

"Ethan…"

His tongue danced across her nipple, flicking faster, faster, and Morgan, the sensual animal he knew her to be, pushed her breast up to him, offering herself totally, completely.

Much as he wanted to go slow, his need for her wouldn't let him. He took his hand from hers, skimming his fingers down over her rib cage, past the swell of her hip. Felt the quiver of her flat belly as his touch set off a response that also served to raise her hips up to him.

She knew. She knew where he was going, what he would do. And with no barriers this time, nothing to keep either of them from that most intimate touch.

Morgan bent her knees, digging her heels into the soft mattress…then held her breath, waited for his touch. Ached for his touch.

"Oh, God…"

She was wet, ready, and Ethan spread her so that he could stroke, stroke, and then dip carefully into her and stroke again. He felt the small, hard swelling of her and spread her even wider.

Her thighs fell open as he slid his leg over hers, her small, soft cries urging him on as his tongue and his finger kept time, his double assault also doubling the intensity of Morgan's need, an intensity that showed itself in the way she moved against his hand as she pleaded, "Please…please…"

Now. Ethan heard his own silent cry as he levered himself over her, moving his kiss from her breast to her mouth, but keeping his hand moving, moving…while he settled himself between her legs.

One swift, strong thrust, and he was inside her, the last barrier breached, and Morgan was clinging to him, her fingers splayed on his back even as she lifted her legs onto his buttocks, allowing him to nestle completely into her.

She was wildfire, she was quicksilver, she was animal heat and Eve's handmaiden. She was everything in the world, nothing that had ever been before, and she made him want to be the world to her, as well.

He would die for her, he would kill for her. He would keep her secrets, dry her tears, share her laughter.

He would love her until he died, and beyond.

He stilled his finger against her when he felt her begin to move, pulse out her pleasure, and when she pushed back her head with a cry of wonder, he buried his mouth against her throat and drove into her one last time, the force of his own fulfillment shattering his every nerve, so that he collapsed against her, perspiration sheening his body.

Morgan lay very still for a few moments, nearly overcome with emotion, before she took Ethan's head between her hands and began showering kisses over his face, his eyes, his mouth.

As her pounding heart at last began to slow, she kissed him one last time, then pressed her cheek against his shoulder and sighed deeply.

No words. There was no need for any more words.

Ethan smiled as he slid his arms around her back, holding her close as he turned onto his side, still inside her, loath to leave her.

Morgan wrapped her arm around him as she settled into the hollow of his shoulder, and was asleep in moments, leaving Ethan to lie there with her in the spill of moonlight, stroking her dark hair back from her face, occasionally kissing her forehead, and feeling sorry for every man in the world who wasn't him....

CHAPTER TWENTY-TWO

MORGAN CARRIED HER bandbox outside the next morning, once again not wanting Louise's prying eyes to see its contents. Of course, if the woman had wakened just ten minutes earlier, she would have had an even worse surprise—seeing her mistress climbing in through the window.

Smiling, feeling wonderful—*alive!*—Morgan waved hello to the half-dozen outriders who had shown up sometime during the night and were now milling around as only men can do, looking busy while doing nothing.

They would reach Becket Hall before dusk, especially if she could talk Ethan into splitting the outriders, taking only his three along as the two of them rode across Romney Marsh, the coaches left to follow.

She couldn't wait to show Ethan the marsh, *her* marsh. They'd ride straight to the Channel, straight past Becket Hall, and they'd introduce Alejandro to the sea.

Anything she could do to delay the moment when Ethan and her papa met, the moment the family would stand between them, judging Ethan, gauging him.

Would they see just the London gentleman? Or

would they see what she saw? The man. The man who was so much, and didn't even realize how much more he could be? Her other half…the half that made her whole.

She walked around to the rear of the stables, knowing the horses hadn't yet been brought out and placed between the braces, for she'd poked her head into the small common room and seen Saul still shoveling eggs and country ham into his mouth.

Jacob hadn't been there, and she was in no great hurry to see him, so she didn't hunt him out to ask him to put her usual saddle on Berengaria. She'd unearth it from the boot of the traveling coach and do so herself.

And when she mounted Berengaria, Ethan would smile. Not scold, not argue, not even raise an eyebrow to slightly mock her, act as if he was *indulging* her rather than treating her as his equal—his equal in all things. He accepted who she was, without reservation, without question. He gave without question.

He'd only asked for all of her in return, and she was finding out that all of her was what she wanted to give him.

Morgan smiled in the bright sunlight, knowing it was Ethan who had taken away all her shadows.

Swinging the heavy bandbox, humming quietly as she walked, very aware of her body in a way she'd never been before, and picturing Ethan and herself flying over the soft marsh ground, the wind in their faces, the smell of the sea coming to them, Morgan turned the corner of the stables. She took a few more steps before something bothered her, stopped her.

Where was the guard?

Even at a small country inn such as this one, chosen by Ainsley Becket precisely because it was so small, and away from the more heavily traveled, more direct roads, coaches weren't left unattended, not for a minute. Especially when they were fully loaded and ready to move.

"This is what happens when there are too many men about," she grumbled to herself. "Each thinks the other is doing the job, and none of them are doing more than standing about, bragging and spitting."

She turned to retrace her steps, then realized she still held the bandbox. She'd put it in Ethan's coach, *then* go tear a strip off somebody's hide for being so careless.

But as she passed the first coach somebody grabbed her arm and pulled her between the vehicles, causing the bandbox to fall from her grasp, and she looked up to see a well-dressed stranger glaring at her as if she were an inconvenience he didn't need at the moment.

"Who are—*let me go*!"

The man said nothing, only dragging her with him as he peered out from between the coaches before pulling her along to the third one. Ethan's crested coach.

She didn't make it easy for him, but she was no match for the man, either, which infuriated Morgan to the point where her safety became only a secondary consideration.

She struck out at him with her fist, aiming for and hitting his exposed Adam's apple, and the man howled, cursed, then punched her. His blow glanced off her chin because she'd been expecting nothing less of the man, but still connected with enough force that, when he let go of her arm, she fell to the ground.

"Ethan!" she yelled as loudly as she could, scrambling to her feet once more as the man climbed up into the boot, then just as quickly jumped down to the ground again, to yank open the far door of the coach.

"Thief! Thief!" Morgan shouted, picking up a large stone from the ground next to her and throwing it at the man's back as he stepped away from the coach, Ethan's satchel in one hand, a pistol in the other.

"Too pretty to die, but so unfortunately *loud.* Be silent, *chérie,*" he said, grinning down at her, aiming the pistol at her as she once more prepared to go on the attack. "I leave you now. A thousand pardons for the inconvenience, *ma chou.*"

"Get away from her! Bastard!"

Both Morgan and the Frenchman turned to see Jacob running toward them, struggling to pull the pistol from his waistband.

"Jacob—no!" Morgan cried, but it was too late.

While he still fought to free his weapon, Morgan heard the bark of the other man's pistol, and flinched as if expecting the ball to enter her body.

But it was Jacob who fell.

"Jacob!"

Morgan rushed to him, falling onto the ground beside him even as the man who'd shot him stepped over Jacob's legs. "The puppy dies for you, *mam'selle.* So unnecessary. And now I must leave you."

"The devil you will!" Morgan pulled Jacob's pistol from his waistband and held it in front of her, cocked it. "Stand where you are, you French bastard!"

Jacob moaned, distracting Morgan's attention for a

moment, as she'd been sure he was dead, and the Frenchman made a move toward her, toward the pistol.

It was the last move he made, unless anyone chose to count his fall to the ground, a small, ugly red hole precisely between his eyes.

Morgan looked at the man dispassionately, then threw the pistol from her and bent to Jacob once more. There was a wet, red stain on his shirt, and it was spreading rapidly.

"Oh God," she said, pressing her hands against his shoulder. "Please God, please God, *please.* Jacob!"

She felt hands on her shoulders, and shook them off.

"Morgan," Ethan said, his gaze on the man who lay dead on the ground, blue eyes open as he looked up at the sky and saw hell. "Morgan, you have to let us help Jacob."

"No." She shook her head violently. "So much blood." She pressed her hands harder. "I have to stop the bleeding."

But Ethan ignored her protest and slid his arms around her waist, bodily lifting her up and away from Jacob so that the men from Becket Hall could pick him up, carry the boy into the common room.

Three of them stayed with the coaches, weapons drawn, as if expecting a new attack.

"Jacob!" Morgan struggled to be free of Ethan's hold, and when he wouldn't release her, but only turned her around so that he could hold her close to him, she beat against his chest. His white shirt, her bloody fists.

"It's all right, Morgan," Ethan told her over and over, looking past her to one of the men, who was shaking his head at the hysteria of women, he supposed.

"I have to go to him!"

Ethan pulled her nearer, to whisper in her ear. "No, you have to stay here. Come on, Morgan, behave, stop hitting me. We have an audience, and I think they might be expecting me to control you rather than kiss you."

He looked past her again, to the men of Becket Hall, and added more loudly, "Jacob's fine. He'll have a lovely sling, and a scar he can brag about to the ladies. It's all right, darling, it's all right."

"How can you know that?" Morgan asked, the fight suddenly leaving her. She felt weak all over, a part of her wondering how she managed to stand upright.

"The wound's too high for real trouble, that's how I know. And Jacob's quite the hero, isn't he? That was one hell of a shot from the boy. Took a steady hand and a fair amount of bravery."

The men watching and listening nodded in agreement, two of the three looking fairly incredulous, but still nodding. Jacob was a hero.

Morgan blinked up at Ethan, then remembered. She'd acted, not thought, all of her attention concentrated on Jacob…and then on the man who'd shot him. She barely remembered yanking Jacob's pistol from his waistband and raising it…firing it.

She turned her head, saw the Frenchman sprawled face-up on the ground, the satchel still beside him.

It had been an easy shot; the man hadn't been more than four feet from her. She'd aimed, she'd squeezed the trigger. And a man was dead.

And that was just fine with her. Jacob was a hero. Jacob was a *man;* they'd all see him as a man now.

She'd taken so much from him, she could give him this. He deserved it.

"Jacob," she said quietly as she watched Ethan pick up the satchel. "He'll...he'll really be all right?"

"Morgan..." Ethan soothed her quietly, putting his arm around her as they walked toward the inn. "I saw what happened. Not all of it, but the end. I wasn't sure you'd want anyone else to know, you understand? But I know, and I'm more proud of you, and worried for you, than you probably know. Did I say the right thing?"

She leaned her head against his shoulder. "You said exactly the right thing. Jacob's a hero. And I'm fine. My jaw's a little sore from the Frog's sloppy punch, but that's nothing. But nobody else will be fine when I find out who was supposed to be guarding that damn satchel of yours."

For the first time since he'd heard Morgan yell his name, and he'd begun running toward the coaches, Ethan began to relax. "My God, imp, you're unbelievable."

She smiled up at him, reaction taking a firmer hold on her, so that he could feel her trembling against him. "Yes, I know."

He pulled her tighter. "You're also incorrigible."

"Yes, I know."

"And I love you so very much."

"Yes, I—" She looked up at him, her eyes wide. And then she smiled.

She was still smiling, walking slowly and frequently stopping to look back at Ethan, after Louise appeared out of nowhere, clucking like a hen with one chick, to lead her away even as she called for hot water and a tub to be brought to Miss Becket's room immediately.

Ethan didn't move until she was out of sight, then gave a small head signal to Harold, who always seemed to be present when he was needed. The groom called to his two mates, who all followed Ethan back to the coaches.

They had a Frenchman to bury....

CHAPTER TWENTY-THREE

"ARE YOU GOING TO TELL ME what's in that thing and why a Frenchman would dare to come here in order to steal it?" Morgan asked as they headed out of the inn yard in Ethan's coach, the satchel on the facing seat.

Rather than answering, which he was still loath to do, Ethan noticed a gold chain peeking out above the neckline of Morgan's riding habit and tugged on it. "Perhaps. If you'll tell me what this is. A locket? A keepsake? I don't remember you wearing jewelry before now."

Morgan opened the top button on her jacket so that she could pull out the chain and what it held. "It's my *gad,*" she said, "a gift from Odette, and one I'd best be wearing when I see her. Strangely, it didn't seem to go well with my silks and satins."

He took the thing in his hand, frowned at it. "All right. My question still stands. What in blazes is this?"

"My *gad.* My protection—" she lowered her voice and looked at him mischievously "—against all manner of evil influences. Voodoo, Ethan, voodoo." Then she sat back, smiled. "It's an alligator tooth soaked in a conglomeration of things that would both shock and dismay you were I to tell you about them. Odette believes very firmly that our *gads* are what keep us all safe."

"And you believe her?"

Morgan shrugged. "The last thing I did before leaving my chamber this morning was to put this chain over my head. Jacob was wearing his—I saw it when I went to see him after the surgeon left. I've learned not to ask too many questions when Odette is involved. Now, are you going to tell me what I nearly died for, or not?"

Ethan reached for the satchel, working open the leather straps and lifting out the slim, heavily engraved, two-foot-long silver cylinder, which he handed to Morgan. "Not what you were expecting, I'd imagine?"

Morgan ran her fingers over the engravings, frowning when she encountered what looked to be a repair where the cylinder had been cut open at some point, then sealed again. "Do the engravings mean anything? They're pretty, but it's difficult to believe they're significant."

"It's what's inside that's important," Ethan said, retrieving the cylinder, slowly turning it until he found the mark pressed into it. "My friend thought it amusing to use this. To remind the English government of the man who made it. See here?"

Morgan squinted. "What is that?"

"That, my dear, or so I'm told, is the mark of a certain silversmith, one Paul Revere. The man's dead now, but there are many in our government who remember the name."

Morgan shook her head. "I suppose we can discuss that later and you can tell me more. But for now, what's inside that cylinder, and what are you doing with it? Chance knows, so it's only fair that I do, too."

"Ah, that's a novel thought—that the world might be fair."

"Don't interrupt with logic, please. Why must you take this thing to Becket Hall? Or isn't that where you're taking it? Are you leaving me, riding to Dymchurch? And before you answer me, remember that I've already told you a secret."

"Not that you'll hold that over my head, or anything similarly female," Ethan said, replacing the cylinder and closing the leather straps once more. "Very well. After all, it's only the king's secret I'm telling. Nothing important. Although I'd probably lose my head for telling it—but you shouldn't worry *your* head about that."

"I won't," Morgan said, trying not to smile. "Now, tell me."

"So nice to know you care, imp. Very well. There are some in our government who believe a war with the United States can be averted if calmer heads are allowed to rule."

Morgan frowned, completely confused. "This isn't about Napoleon? But that…that *man,* he was French. *America?* Papa talks about that at the dinner table all the time. It's all very troubling to him. England doesn't need another war, but he sees war as inevitable and, partial as he is to England, he also very much admires America. Go on."

Morgan smiled. "How wonderful not to have to explain every detail. I really look forward to meeting your father. In any event, some in our government, some in the American government, have been…corresponding this past year, hoping to find a middle ground that gives both sides some satisfaction—"

"Thus averting a war," Morgan finished for him. "And you? What part do you play in all of this?"

"I'm no more than the lowly messenger," Ethan told her as the coach rocked on increasingly rough roads through the early afternoon, their departure having been delayed until Jacob's wound was tended. "A supposed trading ship slips into a small harbor, the cylinder is delivered to the War Office, opened, its contents read. There is a response written, the cylinder is closed, and I return it to wherever I'm told, then go back to my useless life until I'm summoned again."

Morgan was slightly crestfallen. "That's all? Wait. You said your *friend.* Is that why you—no, I still don't understand."

So Ethan explained how and why he'd become involved, ending with, "But I don't think she worried about more than someone intercepting a message and changing it to one that was more in keeping with whatever the more bloodthirsty of our government may want. In other words, she trusted her messenger to deliver her messages to London, but trusted me to safely transport any reply back to her."

Morgan nodded. "She didn't want to put her own messenger in danger, in case he was followed once he was in London. He would slip into the city easily enough, but possibly not leave quite so alone as he arrived. Yes, I understand that. And if you're the messenger she wants to bring back a response from the king, it could only mean she trusts you implicitly." Morgan kissed his cheek. "And you call yourself useless. Shame on you."

"Yes, thank you," Ethan said, slightly abashed. "However, I don't think she realized that the French would have begun to take an interest, although *we* should have. The *Marianna*'s been in these waters too often not to have someone take notice."

"Marianna. Is that your friend's name?"

"Yes, both my friend and the ship. An old friend, Morgan," Ethan explained. "An old friend married to an old friend. They emigrated to Virginia to begin a shipping company."

"Go on," Morgan said, deliberately teasing him. "She's married and…?"

"Widowed, sadly. Richard was aboard one of his newest ships, flying the American flag, naturally, when it was stopped and boarded by our navy. They were looking for English sailors to press into service, and Richard objected to being taken. A fight broke out, as I understand it, and he was killed. Now Marianna has devoted herself to avoiding any more bloodshed."

"But why? I don't understand that. I'd want war. I'd want to *make* war myself."

"Yes, imp, I'm convinced you would. I'll try very hard never to get myself killed, if only to save the world from your wrath."

Morgan sniffed, then sat quietly for a few moments, thinking about everything Ethan had said. "So. You meet this Marianna woman. Where? You didn't tell me where."

"This time? This most probably last time? The *Marianna* will be anchored off Becket Hall on Sunday night. At least that was the plan as Chance helped to work it out with the minister at the War Office. At my suggestion, since I'd found this sudden need to see Becket Hall."

"Because you were curious," Morgan said.

"Because I wanted to ask you father for your hand in marriage," Ethan corrected. "You still don't really believe that, do you?"

"I'm beginning to," she said, not realizing she'd reached up a hand to press it against the *gad* once more hidden beneath her jacket. "And everything was going according to your plan—yours and Chance's plan—until that Frenchman showed up at the inn, correct? I think I understand why he wanted the cylinder. The French would welcome England's troops and ships being divided between fighting fronts, wouldn't they? They've somehow learned about the messages, and wanted to disrupt them, possibly even substitute their own message, one that would be highly provocative."

"Yes," Ethan said, sure he could look into Morgan's eyes and all but see her brain working. God, she delighted him! "Perhaps something on the order of 'Die, you filthy pig Americans,' and then signing Prinny's name."

Morgan glared at him. "Very funny, Ethan. Don't interrupt. They know you're the messenger. They followed you—someone followed you. And, if they're following you, they're probably also watching the *Marianna*. If they haven't already captured her. No matter how they stop the messages, they simply need them stopped. You have thought of that, haven't you?"

Now it was Ethan's turn to kiss her cheek, for she was truly an amazing woman, with a mind that worked quickly, efficiently, on a problem most of his male acquaintances wouldn't grasp in a fortnight of explanations.

"I have, General Becket, yes. But there's not a damned thing I can do now but wait at Becket Hall, watching for the ship. This message means nothing, I know that. Our government refuses to budge on the idea of what the Americas call impressment. Marianna's been risking her own ship, her own crew, her own life, only to delay the inevitable. The majority of Madison's government, and ours, is set on war."

"And Chance knows all of this, because of his position at the War Office. He's told my father about the *Marianna*?"

"I carry a letter from him, yes. Your brother believes your father could prove useful, if we need him."

Morgan smiled, relaxing as much as it was possible to relax, knowing the danger they were in if Becket Hall drew the attention of the French. For most of the previous summer, a French ship had patrolled just outside the range of English guns, deliberately serving as a reminder of just how close danger could come at any time. Attracting the attention of the French to Becket Hall in particular would mean attracting the Waterguard as well, and the Black Ghost Gang would see their smuggling runs come to an abrupt halt because of an overcrowded sea.

And that was another secret she'd have to remember to share with Ethan someday. But not now. She had to concentrate on their current problem.

"All the *Marianna* has to do is to drop anchor at Becket Hall. If she can do that, Papa and Courtland and Jacko will take care of the rest."

"Really," Ethan said, smiling at the fairly smug tone of her voice. "You've so little confidence in my ability to handle the situation?"

"Don't be silly. But there's safety in numbers—everyone knows that."

"You're that formidable a family, are you?"

She slipped her arm through his, leaned against his shoulder. "Worried?"

"Terrified," he said, kissing her upturned face. "But my quavering knees aside, the more I think about the thing, the more sure I am the Frenchman was acting alone. In any case, the inn yard was the last chance anyone had to get the cylinder, now that your father's men have joined us. So, if you want to ride now, I wouldn't say no. The cylinder, however, stays here."

"With my outriders."

"If you don't mind, yes. If those six frighten me, any Frenchman who sees them will be long gone by now."

"Will I meet this Marianna you used to know but who married someone else?" Morgan asked as Ethan shifted to the other seat, then opened the small door to call up to his coachman.

Ethan turned to look at her, not surprised that Morgan had returned to the subject of Marianna. "She was a long time ago, imp. Another lifetime, and she chose the better man."

"Her Richard was undoubtedly a good man. But I will meet her? She's coming to Becket Hall, isn't she?"

"I don't know if there will be time for visits, imp," Ethan said as the coach slowed, then stopped, and he helped Morgan down in the middle of what looked to be a vast, flat land populated only by sheep. "That depends on the tides, I imagine. And the possibility of pursuit. Where are we?"

Morgan cast her gaze left and right, then lifted her head and sniffed the air. "Closer to home than you might think," she said, then pointed to the east. "With the land this flat, we travel by church spires, which is why they're built so tall. Outsiders think we're very religious, which many of us might be. But for many more, those spires show the way for free traders on even the darkest night. I believe that's Smarden's spire, over there. You can barely see it, but if you squint..."

"Free traders. Smugglers," Ethan said as Harold rode toward him, leading Alejandro and Berengaria. "Should I ask how you know about such goings-on?"

Morgan turned to him, grinning. "No, you probably shouldn't."

"I didn't think so," Ethan said, walking with her toward the horses, only to have Harold noisily clear his throat. "Yes, Harold?"

"That's the wrong saddle on the mare, milord," he said, bending down to whisper the words. "One of those hulkin' beasts what joined up with us put it on by mistake, but I didn't think it was my place to say so. Shall I fetch the lady's sidesaddle?"

"No, Harold, the mare's fine, the saddle's fine. We're still in England, but entering a new country in many ways, and the rules here are...different."

"Sir?"

"I know, Harold. I don't understand all of it yet, either. But we'll muddle through." Ethan watched as one of the outriders cupped his hands for Morgan, and she vaulted smoothly onto Berengaria's back. She looked magnificent. "Yes, we'll muddle through...."

CHAPTER TWENTY-FOUR

MORGAN RACED THROUGH her toilette, still unaccustomed to having a maid to help her or, in the case of the constantly fussing Louise, hinder her.

"Really, Louise," she said as she tapped her foot and looked into the mirror over the dressing table, "my hair is fine the way it is, and it's always like this."

"It shouldn't be, Miss Becket. Let me try one more time, please. Ladies who have made their come-out wear their hair up, everyone knows that. You've just so *much* hair, and all of it so slippery and straight. If you'd only let me warm the curling stick..."

Morgan almost relented. Almost. But Ethan could already be downstairs, surrounded by her family. And, she thought, smiling slightly, he wasn't even armed.

"I can't, Louise," she said, getting to her feet, using a quick shake of her head to toss her long hair back over her shoulders. "Either we tie it all up with a bow, or I go downstairs like this. We're not in London, Louise. Nobody cares."

Louise made a short *humph* sound and relented, picking up a length of blue ribbon and motioning for Morgan to turn around. "I'll be happy to go back to civilization, you know."

"And I'll be delighted to—oh, Louise, I'm sorry. I love pretty things, I really do. But I'm home now, and my family is waiting downstairs."

Louise fussed with the edges of the bow she'd tied at Morgan's nape, then stood back to admire her work. "His lordship is waiting downstairs, Miss Morgan, that's what you mean. You should keep him waiting."

"Yes, so Mrs. Julia has already told me," Morgan said, shaking out the skirts of her ivory silk gown accented with deep blue embroidery at the neckline, sleeves and hem. It was one of her favorites. "There. How do I look?"

"Like butter wouldn't melt in your mouth, and much better than you should do after the day you've had," Louise said, putting a hand to the small of her back as she all but tottered to a chair and sat down. "Blood, and dead men, sleeping on pallets hard as stone. Bad roads and nothing but grass and sheep to look at to pass the hours. Never seen the sea before, and never want to again."

Morgan acted on impulse and leaned over to kiss the older woman's cheek. "I'll ask someone to bring up some tea and cakes, all right? And then you can go off to bed. I won't need you anymore tonight, I promise."

Louise opened her mouth to respond, then quickly decided that a person stuck between the deadly sea and a desolate land should know better than to say, "No, *he'll* be helping you off with that gown, won't he?" and simply smiled and nodded as Morgan left the bedchamber.

Morgan raced to the head of the stairs, to be joined there by Cassandra, her youngest sister, who had more than likely been lying in wait for her.

"I saw him, Fanny and me both, when he came upstairs," Callie said, her eyes wide. "Quite the London gentleman, Fanny says. His clothes are wonderfully fancy. None of the boys dress like that, except maybe Chance, and then only when he first arrives from London. Very fancy! Courtland dresses as if he expects to fall in a puddle at any moment, and wants to make sure it wouldn't matter. Is your fancy man really going to marry you and take you away? Fanny says maybe, unless it has to be over Papa's dead body. Why can't you all just stay here?"

"Why, Cassandra Becket," Morgan teased, taking hold of her sister's hand as they descended the wide, curving staircase, "anyone would think you'd missed me. Did you miss me? I was barely gone, you know."

"I know, but now Spencer's taken to teasing me, with you away, and I'm fairly certain that I'll soon have to put a frog in his bed. It isn't fair, being the youngest one. I'm fourteen, Morgan, not a baby. If *I* was old as you, I'd put up *my* hair. But I will never go to London because Papa would pine for me. Why won't he go to London, Morgan? Court says London is a great big bore, so he won't go there, either. But how would Court know that, since he's never been there? Is London a great big bore?"

"Goodness, Callie," Morgan said, as they approached the opened doors to the main drawing room, "you've got a tongue that runs on wheels, you know that? Tomorrow. I'll answer all your questions tomorrow, I promise."

And then she smiled, because there stood Ethan in all his London "fancy" clothes, talking to Eleanor, who was sitting in her usual chair in her usual quiet, passive way. Yet even Ethan seemed to know that impressing Elly was his surest way to ingratiate himself with the Becket family.

"Callie," she asked quietly, "would you please go find someone and ask them to take tea and cakes up to my chamber for my maid? Please?"

"Fanny said you brought a maid. If you have a maid, Morgan, why is your hair down? If *I* had a maid, I'd—"

"Callie, *scoot,*" Morgan said, watching as Ethan bowed and excused himself to Eleanor, then walked toward her, his pleased expression at the sight of her causing her heart to do a small, pleasant turn inside her chest.

She offered her hand to him, knowing Elly was watching, and he bent over it, brought it to his lips before looking at her, seeing her broad smile.

"What?" he asked, wishing to be included in whatever joke she found so amusing.

"Nothing," Morgan said quietly. "It's just that you're so pretty."

Ethan laughed. "Aware as I am that the two of us are enacting a small, civilized play here tonight for the benefit of your family, I should probably point out that that's *my* line, madam. And, I believe, in defense of my entire gender, to tell you that men are never considered *pretty.*"

"But it's true, Ethan," Morgan told him in all seriousness, with all of her usual honesty. "I don't think I'll ever tire of looking at you, or of how I feel when I do."

"And now you're going to tell me we can't disappear for an hour or so without anyone noticing," Ethan said, his voice low, his tone intimate. "Especially now, when all I can think about is untying that damn bow and burying my face in your hair."

"I should tell Louise your reaction, then maybe she'd understand why I refused to let her tie my hair in knots on top of my head." Then Morgan had an idea. "Hmm…perhaps she does know."

"Pardon me?"

"Nothing important, I promise. And, unfortunately, yes, we are expected to stay here. You've met Elly, I see. Our papa calls her our *petite générale,* although not in front of her, of course. I have to go say hello to her. Come with me?"

"Yes, of course. Your sister was just about to show me some of her drawings."

Morgan halted in her progress across the large room, looked at Ethan in amazement. "Really? What on earth have you been saying to her? Elly never lets any of us see her drawings, except for Papa."

"Possibly because she's decided that none of her siblings has developed much of an appreciation for art?"

Morgan grinned. "Possibly. Even probably. We're ignorant oafs for the most part. She's our only civilizing influence. Poor thing, saddled with us, but I imagine she didn't have much choice, being the oldest, and with her leg and all. It wasn't as if she could run wild here, like the rest of us."

"Her leg?"

"Shh, not now." She went to Eleanor then and bent to kiss her cheek. "You've got to come to London, Elly.

It's everything you said it was, and the people are even worse than you said, although some are better. You'd love it."

Eleanor shook her head slightly. "I don't think his lordship needs to know my poor opinion of society, Morgan, especially as I know nothing I haven't read, not having visited the metropolis."

"Not even if I share that poor opinion, Miss Becket?" Ethan asked as Morgan sat down on the couch across from Eleanor's chair. He himself took the chair beside the woman he had already perceived to be his hostess. "I'm interested in learning if I'm worse or better than the majority, you understand."

Eleanor looked at Morgan's lover—only a fool wouldn't see that the two were much more than debutante and hopeful suitor. Besides, Eleanor knew Morgan, knew her very well. The girl did nothing in half measures. "I would have to conclude, my lord, that you are both better and worse, or I wouldn't be seeing you here now, would I? Am I correct, my lord?"

Morgan coughed into her hand, aware the inquisition had begun, then stood up to say she needed to check on Cassandra, to make sure the child had done as she'd been asked, as she believed her maid would be better for some tea and cakes. In fact, Morgan had decided it was better for her to leave than to watch as her family put Ethan through hoops, thus showing them all that she had no worries about him acquitting himself very well on his own.

Ethan barely had time to stand up before Morgan had run from the drawing room, and when he sat down again, Eleanor was smiling at him.

"Allow me to explain, my lord, as I'm sure a gentleman such as yourself would never ask the obvious question. We have no servants here. We have…helpers. Paid, and paid well, even by London standards, I believe, but no one gives orders, and no one takes them. We *ask.* And, thanks to my father's feelings on the subject, we all contribute."

"Very commendable, Miss Becket."

Eleanor shrugged her slim shoulders. "Very workable, my lord. My father believes in what is workable. And now," she said, reaching down beside her to lift up a slim leather portfolio tied with black ribbon, "perhaps you'd like to see more of Becket Hall before the sun hopefully rises tomorrow and Morgan can show you herself."

"I would be delighted, Miss Becket," he said, and sat forward on his chair as she untied the bow and opened the portfolio.

Her watercolors were amazingly good, better than some he'd seen on display in London. She'd painted her home from every side, and in several lights—the hall in summer, the hall with a winter storm howling in from the Channel.

As she very carefully turned over each watercolor, Eleanor also very carefully told him the history of Becket Hall, all of the very carefully constructed lies that made up the very carefully crafted history of the Beckets of Romney Marsh.

Ethan listened to the story, which began with a wealthy gentleman shipowner who'd left his sunny, southern island home in order to bring his adopted children and his infant daughter to England, how the discovery of Becket Hall had been so fortuitous for them, and how the crews of their ships had also decided to make the vast estate their new home.

It had the sound of a fairy tale as Eleanor told the story, but Ethan was content to listen, to pretend he believed every word, for he was fairly certain that, as is common in fairy tales, there was at least some truth mixed in.

It was only when Eleanor turned over one of the paintings, then quickly replaced it, that he interrupted her. "Is there something you don't wish me to see, Miss Becket? A work that disappointed you, perhaps?"

Eleanor knew she should ignore what she was certain was deliberate goading by the man, but she was also curious. A child's memory was suspect at best, and she longed to know if what she remembered was really a memory, or just bits and pieces of a faded dream. Could a scene such as she'd painted it look real, even possible?

"I enjoy painting landscapes, my lord," she explained as she turned over the last watercolor of Becket Hall, to expose a totally different one, her family's home no longer her subject. "I even imagine them, then paint them. Like this one."

Ethan leaned closer, to see what was for the most part a landscape, with a large country house in the distance, placed in the midst of a rolling, well-maintained parkland setting. The house itself was white, the design Palladian. And vaguely familiar.

"Very nice. The, ah, the proportions are extraordinary. I feel as if I could reach into the picture," Ethan said and, so encouraged, Eleanor showed him the next watercolor, her curiosity getting the better of her common sense.

This painting, Ethan saw, was obviously the same house in its elevated setting, but from another angle, showing the gently descending rear prospect, again from quite a distance, as if the artist didn't wish to deal with the detail of the structure, but only its general outline.

The parkland, however, was a different matter, and had been imagined in some detail. Ethan could see a large ornamental pond, and even a three-arched stone bridge that spanned its narrower end. The rolling hills in the distance, golden with sunlight. The tall trees, including several plantings of evergreens.

Not Romney Marsh. Not at all anything one would find on Romney Marsh. Or, for that matter, on a faraway, near-tropical island.

Ethan picked up the last drawing, one that seemed to concentrate for the most part on the pond, a few small boats and several white swans gliding effortlessly in the water.

"You know, this looks almost..." he hesitated, not really knowing why he should "...almost real. Thank you so much for showing me, Miss Becket."

"You're welcome," Eleanor said, keeping her head down as she quickly closed the portfolio and retied it. "Thank you for the kind words. I know I'm not very good, but I do enjoy it. Painting, that is."

"Not very good? Why, Miss Becket, if I didn't know you better, I'd say you were begging for compliments."

Eleanor lifted her incredibly well sculpted chin, turned huge brown eyes on Ethan. "You don't know me at all, sir, do you? Ah, and here are more people you don't know, my lord."

Ethan got to his feet as four men of varying ages and appearance entered the room, their united front very obvious, perhaps purposely so.

Within minutes, he'd learned that the intense, almost brooding dark-haired one was Spencer, the taller dark-haired one with the fair skin, friendly smile and startlingly compelling eyes was Rian, and that the scowling one with the thick mane of dark blond hair and a short but full beard was Courtland Becket.

Three very individual-looking gentlemen; four, if he added Chance Becket into the mix. Not related by blood—Ethan already knew that—yet they all seemed to have the same alertness about them, and their confidence was nearly palpable. Rather like well-seasoned soldiers—confident, yes, but ever watchful, vigilant. Formidable.

But when Ethan bowed to the patriarch of the clan, he knew he had met a man who stood very much on his own. He was tall, whipcord lean, and with the greenest eyes he'd even seen. Ainsley Becket's coal black hair had begun to go gray at the temples and his tanned skin carried more than a few lines, but the man was far from old, and definitely far from careless.

"My lord," Ainsley said with a slight inclination of his head, and Ethan responded with a bow of his own, then held out his right hand.

"I've brought correspondence from your son, sir," Ethan said, feeling the need to establish his credentials…considering he was already outnumbered four-to-one, and the storied Jacko had yet to make an appearance.

"Interesting, thank you," Ainsley said, his head tipped very slightly to the right, those green eyes faintly narrowed as he looked intensely at Ethan, assessed him. "I will, however, delay the pleasure of reading the letter until after I've spoken with my daughter."

"Certainly, sir, I—" Ethan didn't bother finishing his sentence because Ainsley had already turned his back on him and was in the process of leaving the room. So he turned to smile at the brothers instead. Was it correct to smile at a pride of lions, hoping they'll soon lose interest?

Spencer now had his head tipped slightly, perhaps in an unconscious imitation of his adopted father, and ran his fingers through the mass of unruly black curls that would have seemed effeminate on any man who wasn't so very clearly male. He stepped closer to Ethan.

"You know, my lord," he said, "there is a law in pirate lore that states that if at any time a man meets with a prudent woman, and that man offers to meddle with her, without her consent, he shall suffer present death. Interesting, yes?"

Ethan refused to so much as blink. "Fascinating, Mr. Becket," he said, then added, "that you know so much about pirate lore, that is."

Spencer took another step forward, only to have Courtland grab his arm. "You've made your point, Spence, and with your usual grace. Let it go."

"Fine," Spencer said shortly. "You stay here and be polite. I'll take my dinner in the kitchens."

Rian Becket came up beside Ethan and handed him a glass of wine he'd poured at the drinks table. "Don't mind Spence. He's always on the lookout for a fight."

Ethan accepted the glass. "Thank you. I'll be careful not to provoke him."

Courtland shook his head. "Difficult to do, my lord. Someone else *breathing* is often enough to provoke Spence. Our father is in the process of buying him a commission. If he's so angry, he might as well direct that anger toward Napoleon, yes? And now, my lord, although you will be making any appeals to her father, perhaps you'll tell us your intentions toward Morgan. Eleanor, if you'll excuse us?"

"Certainly," Eleanor said, getting to her feet. Ethan hadn't realized how petite she was, as she'd already been seated when he'd entered the room. Petite, yet regal, and with a fragile beauty that he'd already decided cloaked a strong mind and a will of iron. "I've already arrived at my own conclusions. My lord." She curtsied to Ethan and then headed for the hallway, and he didn't allow his gaze to linger on her slight limp.

"Now," he said, turning back to Morgan's brothers. "Fire away, gentlemen, but know this. I *will* marry your sister, if we have to outrun the lot of you Beckets all the way to Gretna Green."

"Ha! That's not what we're asking," Rian told him, grinning. "She can have you if she wants you. We want to know how you're going to *tame* her."

Ethan relaxed at last, because here, at least, he felt he stood on solid ground. "Why, by *not* taming her, Mr. Becket. I'm many things, but I'm not an idiot."

CHAPTER TWENTY-FIVE

MORGAN SAT WHERE SHE'D been directed to sit, and looked at Ainsley Becket. "I know what Chance wrote in his letter to you, Papa. I read the letter. I thought I should tell you that."

Ainsley looked at his daughter, saw the apprehension and courage in her eyes. "Your stay in London was short, but eventful. I expected no less, Morgan. As for your suitor, I'll trust my own judgment, if you don't mind."

"But Chance said—"

"I know what he wrote, Morgan. He sees you as a child. Brothers, especially loving brothers, are prone to such shortsightedness where their sisters are concerned."

Morgan subsided more fully into the leather couch. "I suppose so. I still can't imagine Chance and Julia rolling around together, and yet they're expecting their first child this coming winter." She shrugged. "It's all rather mind-boggling."

Ainsley coughed into his fist and got to his feet. "Honesty, Morgan, is not always a virtue. Now, as dinner is to be served soon, I suggest you go find this beau of yours and direct him to my study, as he says he has something for me."

Morgan nodded, also getting to her feet. Could she ask the question she'd never asked, had never before thought to ask?

"Papa...how did my mother die?"

Ainsley Becket was rarely shocked, and even more rarely showed shock when he experienced it, but now he sat down behind his desk once more as he asked, "Is there some reason you need this answer now?"

She walked over to the desk, half sat on the edge of it. "I'm not sure. I've really been afraid of her, I suppose, afraid that I was like her, and I didn't want to be like her. You know, Papa, like mother like daughter? But...lately, I've realized that I don't know who she was, that I've been judging her without knowing her."

"I see. And possibly judging yourself as well?"

Morgan lowered her head. "Possibly."

"Ah, Morgan, I should have realized. I'm so sorry. I've been lost in my own misery for so long, too long. Tell me what you want to know."

"Her name, I suppose. Why she sold me. Why she sold me to you. And what happened to her. I should know what happened to her, shouldn't I?"

Ainsley picked up the letter opener in front of him, held the ends with his fingers. "I am ashamed to admit that I never knew her name. She chose me, I believe, because I was known on the docks and seemed to be at least slightly respectable. She wanted what was best for you, Morgan, and knew she couldn't give you anything but poverty and a future that matched hers."

Morgan nodded again, sniffing back unexpected tears. "How did...how did she die?"

"I only heard the story, but supposedly, only a few months after you came to us on the island, she attempted to say no to the wrong person." He put down the letter opener and stood up, placed his arm around Morgan's shoulder. "That was a long time ago, and none of your responsibility. None of your legacy. Do you understand?"

Morgan leaned into him for a moment. "I used to wonder if you were my father. But I knew that was silly of me."

Ainsley kissed the top of her head. "Ah, but if that were true, sweetheart, you'd have so much more to worry about, wouldn't you?"

She smiled up at him. "Yes, you're quite reprehensible, aren't you?"

Ainsley was happy to see her smile. "That I am. But, Morgan, I would be honored to have been your real father."

Morgan hugged him. "You are, Papa." Then she pushed away from him and stood up, took a deep breath. "And you're going to say yes to Ethan, aren't you? I'll have him, either way, but I'd really prefer your blessing." She held out her hands. "No, don't answer me. I know *you* trust my judgment."

And then she was gone, off to tell Odette about her dangerous man, so that when Jacko entered through the other door to the study, the one that had been left slightly ajar, she had no idea her conversation had been overheard.

"Your judgment," the man said, settling his still muscular bulk into the couch, just where Morgan had sat. "So, Cap'n, in your judgment, telling her that

Perdita was weaving drunkenly in the dirt outside her crib, yelling for somebody to drown her whelp for her, wasn't the truth Morgan needed to hear?"

Ainsley poured himself a glass of wine. "What do you think, Jacko?"

"Me? I don't think. Where's our fancy London dandy?"

"Why, your fancy London dandy is right here," Ethan said, entering the study, "and for what it's worth, you did the right thing if you fed Morgan a bag of comforting moonshine, Mr. Becket. Morgan is Morgan. It doesn't matter who or what gave birth to her, and she's beginning to realize that."

When neither man spoke, Ethan pulled Chance's letter from an inside pocket and laid it on the desk. "My apologies for eavesdropping, gentlemen, but the door wasn't quite closed. And now, Jacko is it? May I say that Morgan's description of you did not do you justice and I'll beg you not to crush my hand as I offer it, and that we three then get down to business."

Jacko looked at Ainsley. "He's got starch, I'll say that for him."

Ainsley only nodded, as he was reading Chance's letter. Once finished, he handed it to Jacko, who grunted as he struggled to pull a pair of spectacles from his pocket and place them on his nose.

"Before we deal with your mission, my lord—"

"Ethan, sir. I would be honored if you'd call me Ethan."

"Ethan, yes, thank you. Before we deal with that," Ainsley said, gesturing toward the letter Jacko was reading, his mouth moving as he concentrated on each word, "perhaps you'd like to tell us more of Jacob's heroism, as I understand you are the only witness to the event, other than Morgan, who has already told me she was on the ground and didn't really see much of anything."

"Jacob is a hero, sir. He protected Morgan to the best of his ability. Lord only knows what would have happened if he hadn't acted when he did. As it was, I arrived on the scene too late to do anything but watch."

"Starch, and smooth," Jacko said, at last putting down the letter. "Doesn't lie, Cap'n, doesn't tell the whole truth. You have to admire a man who can do that without a blink."

Ainsley looked at Ethan for a long moment, then said, "You're right. The boy is a hero. Morgan…she shot the man, didn't she?"

"Sir, do you really want me to answer that question?"

"No, I suppose not. I'm told the man was most likely French, and after whatever it is you're carrying. I'll have words with both you and Chance at some point concerning putting Morgan in danger, but for now, what can we do to help you? Sunday night is not that far away."

"Saturday, sir," Ethan corrected as he sat down beside Jacko. "I thought it best to allow Morgan to think the *Marianna* is dropping anchor here Sunday night, and Chance agreed. Everything happens some time tomorrow. If past experience is any indicator, the *Marianna* will arrive here at any time between noon and midnight, and be just as quickly gone again. We have enough to occupy our minds without wondering when Morgan will pop up out of nowhere, offering her help."

Ethan felt his breath leave him as Jacko grabbed him

by the shoulder, pulled him into a one-armed hug that had the potential to crack ribs. "Starch, smooth *and* smart! By God, Cap'n, put him in a skirt and *I'll* marry him!"

Three hours later, after the other Becket men had joined them and they'd all taken their dinner on trays brought to the large study, Ethan was on his way upstairs, happy with the plan for the following evening and wondering how much of the goodwill he'd established would be forfeited if he sought out Morgan's bedchamber.

When he realized, in the space of two seconds, that he didn't much care what anyone thought, he turned to his left at the head of the staircase and counted down five doors on the left, his valet having already done the necessary reconnoitering for him earlier.

The chamber he entered was large, as was, he supposed, every room in this enormous house someone had been so eager to sell just as the Beckets were so eager to buy it.

He saw Morgan sitting at her dressing table, her back to him, and walked over to her, bent to push back her hair and press a kiss against her throat. "Tell me something, my love, and don't attempt to spare my feelings. Do I look gullible?"

Morgan put up a hand to hold him where he was, enjoying their combined reflection in the mirror. "You look handsome. Even dangerous. But gullible? No, I don't think so." She turned on her chair and kissed him on the mouth. "You don't taste gullible, either. Why?"

Ethan pulled her to her feet, appreciating the sight of her in the pale yellow dressing gown. "No special reason. I missed you at dinner."

Morgan shrugged. "I know you and Papa and the boys had things to discuss. I was kept busy enough myself, answering questions from my sisters, most especially Callie. If Chance and Julia intend to sponsor her come-out, please don't suggest that we'd rather do the honors. I thought my ears were going to fall off, she talked to much, asked so many questions. And she's quite disappointed in me that I hadn't visited Astley's Circus to see the horses. So I told her you could make Alejandro fly, and now we're committed to that tomorrow morning. Tomorrow morning, by the way, means Callie will be beating on my door by eight o'clock. I hope you don't mind."

Ethan relaxed. Eight o'clock would be just fine. Any later than midafternoon, and he wanted Morgan fully occupied somewhere away from the beach. Ainsley had already guaranteed him that Eleanor could be counted on in that area. "I don't mind at all, and Alejandro will be thrilled. He loves to show off for the ladies."

Morgan slipped her arms up around his neck. "I also hope you weren't teasing me, because I also want to see him fly."

"Then I suppose Alejandro will just have to be at his best tomorrow. As for tonight..."

Morgan began backing toward her turned-down bed, still with her fingers laced tight behind Ethan's neck. All she'd ever wanted, all she'd ever needed. When she held him, she held all of that, and more she couldn't even have dreamed existed. "You have tricks of your own? Perhaps you could show me one or two of them?"

Ethan scooped her up into his arms, laid her on the

bed and quickly joined her there. “You know, imp, I had a life before I met you. I very nearly remember it. But, by God, I could no longer have one without you.”

CHAPTER TWENTY-SIX

SATURDAY MORNING DAWNED wet and dreary, a circumstance that threatened the planned outing on the shore but did not deter Cassandra from begging, cajoling and in the end convincing Morgan and Ethan that "a little damp never melted anyone."

Wearing pattens to keep the damp from their feet, Morgan and Cassandra stood on the beach at noon, once the rain had stopped, their capes wrapped around them as a heavy gray sky warned of more rain at any moment.

"I can't believe you talked the two of us into this ridiculousness, Callie," Morgan said, turning her back to the breeze coming in from the Channel. "Oh, look, we're not the only idiots," she said, pointing up to the stone terrace, where it seemed everyone in Becket Hall, from the patriarch to the scullery maid, had lined up to watch the spectacle. Even Jacob, his arm in a sling, was there, watching. "Did you run through the halls, ringing a bell and shouting out that everyone was to come see Alejandro fly?"

"Certainly not." Cassandra grinned at her sister. "Although I may have mentioned to a few people that Ethan says his horse can fly. I may even have heard that Spencer wagered Rian five pounds that it isn't so."

"Oh, wonderful, Callie," Morgan said, turning her back on the terrace to look toward the distant stables. "Here they come."

She watched as horse and rider picked their way down to the sandy beach before cantering toward them.

Alejandro looked magnificent, his head held proudly, his mane and tail truly marvels. What a cheeky beast! A prince among horseflesh, and well aware of that fact.

But it was Ethan who captured Morgan's attention, and held it. Their night together had been even better than the first, which she had believed impossible.

She had once felt confident that nothing could be as exhilarating, as freeing, as riding her mare, Berengaria; the sound of the mare's hooves hitting the turf, harness jingling, the soft, fast puffs of the animal's breathing. The world around them grown small and yet infinite at the same time.

Now it was Morgan and her Ethan making their own world, the sounds of that world being soft sighs and whispered words, and even surprised and delighted exclamations cut off by long, drugging kisses.

If Morgan loved the feel of Berengaria's strength below her as she straddled the mare, last night she'd learned the rapture of straddling Ethan, riding him, feeling his strength, meeting that strength with her own. So aware, so joyous, so cognizant of being alive. Free, unhampered by any earthly chains. If flight were indeed possible, she and Ethan had flown last night....

"Morgan?" Cassandra pulled at her sister's sleeve. "Why are you smiling like that? You look silly."

"Hush, Callie," she said automatically, her attention

still centered on Ethan. He wore a dark brown Carrick coat with several shoulder capes, capes that flapped in the wind just as did the coattails that rested lightly on Alejandro's hindquarters. He wore his blond hair severely pulled back and secured at his nape, so that his fine, cleanly planed features were what captured her attention.

Was Odette on the terrace, or peeking from one of her windows? Did she see the colors? The brilliant red, the sun-bright yellow? How did anyone *not* see them? Odette might say that Morgan was surrounded by the same colors, but Morgan couldn't see those, wasn't sure if she could believe in them. What she could believe was what her own eyes told her.

Mostly, she believed in what her heart told her. *This is your man, and he is yours.*

"I will not hush," Cassandra protested. "He *is* gorgeous."

Morgan smiled at her sister as horse and rider stopped not ten feet from them and Ethan dismounted. "Cassandra Becket," she said, "you're entirely too young to say things like that, let alone think them."

Cassandra rolled her eyes in fourteen-year-old disgust. "The *stallion* is gorgeous, Morgan. Honestly, if I grow up to be silly, please have someone lock me in my bedchamber and toss the key in the Channel."

While Morgan bit her lips to keep from laughing, Cassandra went to Alejandro, who had just obeyed Ethan's command of, "Alejandro, bow."

Ethan smiled at Morgan as, one by one, he put the willing animal through his paces, his own gaze firmly on Morgan. He moved beside her and whispered, "I've had an idea. We'll travel to Tanner's Roost until the banns can be read, and return here for the ceremony. *Maman* won't say a word against that plan, or even blink at the manner in which we entertain ourselves until we can stand in front of a vicar. Your village does run to a vicar, doesn't it?"

"It does. Although I probably should point out, my lord, that you have as yet to ask me for my hand in matrimony."

Ethan was genuinely surprised. "I haven't? Good God, I haven't, have I? Yes, well, there's no time like the present. I'll just go down on one knee and—"

"Ethan, get up," Morgan told him, giggling. "The whole world is up there on the terrace."

"Good. Witnesses. But if you're quite sure it can wait?"

"Quite sure. Besides, the sky's starting to spit."

"I'm confident that's some local saying, and more than colorful. But I agree, we're going to be rained on very shortly." He turned to call Cassandra away, as she'd been standing with Alejandro, stroking his neck and whispering to him. "Move back now, and Alejandro will show you his best trick. I do hope someone remembered to bring a carrot, because he fully expects to be rewarded."

"Me, I did! I've got three," Cassandra said, holding up the carrots she'd taken from the kitchens. "Now make him fly."

"First I'll use one of these to bribe him," Ethan said, taking a carrot as he approached the horse. "I apologize, my friend, but I know you understand that there are times when it is important to distract the ladies with bits of brilliance."

Alejandro quickly disposed of the carrot, then turned his teeth-baring smile on his master.

"Yes, yes, your modesty is always so humbling, you miserable hulk of bones," Ethan told the horse, then backed away from him, standing a good ten feet clear of the animal.

"Will he do it? Did you ask him? Do you cast a spell on him? Is that how it's done?"

"Callie, quiet," Morgan warned her, then took a deep breath, her own anticipation as high as or even exceeding that of her sister.

"First, the *courbette,*" Ethan said, one eye on the horizon, where gray skies met gray sea. "Alejandro—courbette!"

As Morgan watched, openmouthed, and Cassandra danced in place, clapping her hands, Alejandro reared upright, pawing at the air, then proceeded to actually *jump* in place four times on his hind legs before gracefully assuming his previous position. Cassandra ran forward, to give him another carrot.

"Magnificent," Ainsley Becket said, having come up behind them without anyone noticing. "Where on earth did you get him? I've heard of these horses, but I didn't think pureblood Andalusians were even allowed to cross the Channel."

Ethan had been expecting the question. "As it happens, Ainsley, I was traveling on the Continent a few years ago and was fortunate enough to be able to assist someone with a particular problem. Knowing of my love of horseflesh, the man gave me Alejandro in the way of a thank-you."

Ainsley nodded. "As Jacko said, not a lie, not the full

truth. He very much admires that talent in a man, and I agree with him. Therefore I won't ask you to confirm or deny that your *travel* was in the way of clandestinely assisting in the safe removal of some of the world's most treasured horseflesh from Bonaparte's attention, as I heard was the case a few years ago."

"That would probably be best, sir, thank you."

"He still didn't fly, Morgan. He jumped, beautifully, but he didn't fly. Ethan said he would fly," Cassandra complained.

Morgan looked from Ethan to her papa, and realized that there were some things men knew and women could only guess at…at least until a woman got her own man alone. But it was already clear to her that Ethan's current mission may have begun with a request from this Marianna person…but it had not been his only mission during the war.

Obviously, the two of them were going to have some very *long* talks at Tanner's Roost, and she wouldn't be the only one with secrets to share.

"If you'll excuse me, Ainsley," Ethan said with a slight inclination of his head. "I believe your daughter wishes to see Alejandro's last remaining trick."

He motioned for Cassandra to come stand beside him, and called to Alejandro, who immediately lifted his head at the sound of his master's voice. "Alejandro, good boy. Time to impress the audience, Alejandro, all right?"

The horse actually nodded his proud head and, behind him, Ethan could hear Cassandra giggle.

Ethan shot his arms straight up into the air and held them there. "Alejandro—*capriole!*"

From a complete standstill one moment, the magnificent stallion jumped nearly five feet straight up into the air, giving out a mighty kick of his back legs, his front legs tucked beneath that strong chest. His magnificent tail flew outward even as the sheer velocity of the jump caused his mane to fan into the air above his head, almost like a peacock spreading its feathers.

Alejandro seemed to actually hover in the air a moment, but when Morgan blinked, the stallion was once more standing quietly on the sand, looking more than a little pleased with his performance.

"My God." Ainsley shook his head. "I've seen drawings, of course, but nothing that even vaguely compares to this. Are you using him for stud?"

"Not yet, no. There were promises made, you understand, not that I could find a purebred Andalusian mare in England in any case. Until now, I hadn't seen a mare I believed worthy of crossbreeding. Berengaria, however, seems the exception. Morgan?"

"Oh yes," Morgan said, uncaring that her excitement was all but palpable. "What a magnificent combina—"

"Sails, Cap'n," Jacko interrupted, a little breathless, as he had run down from the terrace. He handed Ainsley a spyglass, a second one to Ethan. "That your *Marianna,* boy?"

"I doubt it," Ethan said, raising the glass. "She's not due yet. Wait…yes, that's her."

"And she's not alone," Ainsley said, pointing beyond the *Marianna.* "French flag. You can only play the same game so often, Ethan, before someone else wants to play, too. We're only fortunate the Waterguard dislikes patrolling when the weather is less than fine. Jacko."

"Right here, Cap'n, awaiting your order."

"A crew to the *Respite,* now. Hoist anchor, turn her and open the gunports. We couldn't hit anything from here, but a show of force should be enough to send the Frogs running. Cassandra, up to the house, *now.*"

Ethan turned to Morgan. "Morgan, up to the—oh, never mind."

"Thank you, Ethan," she said, taking the spyglass from him and training it out over the Channel. "She wasn't supposed to be here until tomorrow night."

"Perhaps Marianna misunderstood."

"Misunderstood? But surely you and Chance were quite specific when you—" She lowered the spyglass to look at him. "Oh, you'll pay for that, Ethan Tanner."

He grinned at her. "Can I suggest a suitable punishment? *Later?*"

Morgan shrugged, lifted the glass to her eye once more. "Sounds promising. As long as you don't try to drag me away now that everything's begun."

"I'd need a full team of horses for that feat," Ethan said, and the moment was over.

Ainsley was still speaking, talking to himself, or possibly to his sons, who had also come down onto the beach—save Courtland, who was already on his way to the *Respite* at a full-out run, as if anticipating his father's orders.

"She was out too far. Why would she have gone out far enough to catch the attention of the Frenchman? Not that he'll come much closer once he realizes he's outgunned."

"Never has come within range, not a single one of the bastards we've seen this past year or more," Spencer said. "Took Morgan's fancy man over there to bring this one so close, and to force us to show our guns. We should have sunk him months ago."

"Would that be the French ship, or me, do you think?" Ethan asked, leaning down to whisper the words in Morgan's ear.

"He means the ship, as well you know. Papa was careful to have the *Respite*'s design meant to disguise the existence of gunports. And Spence is right. These French ships been a thorn in our sides long enough. No one really expects an invasion anymore, but they like to wear on our nerves. Ah, look. He's turning away, probably to go back to patrolling out of range…and lying in wait for when the *Marianna* heads out once more."

"A fine frigate your friend sails," Ainsley commented, following the *Marianna* with his spyglass long after a glass was needed to see it clearly. "She's flying the Union Jack, which is dangerous in itself, but makes sense in these waters. Ah—some slight damage to the mainmast. Seems they did more than play with the Frenchman. Rian, Spencer, gather a crew. See to having the damage repaired. That ship must be ready to leave with the evening tide."

Someone had taken Alejandro's reins and was already leading him back to the stables. Everyone, it seemed, was jumping to or running off, or whatever it was men under the cool, decisive command of Ainsley Becket did, and Ethan was quite impressed. There might not, as Eleanor had said, be a hierarchy of servant and master at Becket Hall, but when itch came to scratch, there was no question as to who was in charge.

Morgan slipped her hand into Ethan's as they watched the progress of the *Marianna,* until the French ship had reassumed its accustomed role of patrolling the English coastline from a safe distance, only the tops of its sails still visible.

"He won't go far, just as Papa said," Morgan told Ethan. "Your friend will have to sneak out of here again somehow, and that means the *Respite* will have to become a part of this. Our sloop's faster than anything the French have yet to put in the Channel. Lead the way, cause a diversion. And maybe finally put one of those blasted Frenchmen on the bottom."

"Yes. I imagine they play havoc with any smugglers operating in the area," Ethan said, watching as the *Marianna*, now safe, began to drop anchor alongside the *Respite*, both the larger and smaller vessels riding in what had to be a natural, deep harbor not clearly visible from the shore. Whoever had picked this location for Becket Hall had chosen well. Carefully.

"Yes, you have no idea how—" Morgan glared up at Ethan. "You won't be happy until you have all my secrets, will you?"

"Probably not. Come along now, they've put down a longboat and I really should go greet Marianna. Cap'n?" he asked, falling into Jacko's way of addressing the man who was most definitely a captain, on sea or on land.

Ainsley lowered the spyglass at last. "I'll be in my study with my charts. Have the woman and her captain there as quickly as possible, please, along with the boys. And yourself, of course. That cylinder of yours had better be important, Ethan."

"I doubt that it is, sir," Ethan told him frankly. "But getting my friend safely back to America is very important. You do understand that there are many who'd consider her an enemy of the Crown. The minister will deny any knowledge of her if she's captured."

Ainsley nodded in agreement. "Then, Ethan, let's get her here, and let's get her gone."

Morgan was in a hurry to reach the area of the shore where the longboat was heading, eager to see this mysterious Marianna who had "chosen the better man."

As they neared the landing spot, she could see the occupants of the longboat. "Why, they're all Negroes. Your Marianna keeps slaves? Odette won't like that, not at all. None of us will like that."

"American ships are being stopped, Morgan, remember, and any considered to be English sailors removed and forced to join the British Navy. With her very unique crew, mostly from the West Indies, I believe, Marianna has escaped the problem. But from my understanding, they are all free men. Marianna is…she's very much her own person, and not afraid to stand up for her beliefs. You'll like her, really."

Morgan decided to withhold judgment until she'd spoken to the woman, who was just now being helped onto the shore by one of her crew. It was difficult to see her at first, as her head was well-covered by the hood of her cloak, but once she was onshore, and turned to thank her crewmen, the hood fell back, revealing the woman's face.

"Here, Abraham, if you please," she said, untying

the laces holding her cloak and handing it to a tall, ebony man who looked capable of breaking in half anyone who so much as looked at the woman too hard.

Marianna was slim of build, and rather tall, with an erect posture that put the lie to any notion that long weeks at sea had fatigued her. She wore a dark divided skirt beneath a long blouse tied with a deep blue sash at her waist, the blouse so white it nearly glowed. A man's shirt? Morgan wondered, as the sleeves were rather long, and hung almost completely over her hands, and the open, upturned collar reached past her chin.

Her hair had been cropped short, streaked by the sun, and tousled as if she woke in the morning, ran her hands through the uneven spikes, then thought no more of the matter.

She'd seen her share of summers, but her blue-green eyes didn't seem to suffer for the slight lines around them, and her jaw had softened only marginally. There was an air of serenity about her, as well as one of sadness. Most surprising was her very pale skin, barely touched by the sun.

She had been and, although well past her first flush of youth, remained a remarkably beautiful woman, Morgan decided.

A remarkably beautiful woman who at the moment was clinging to Ethan, happily calling his name and then kissing him on both cheeks.

Ethan returned Marianna's embrace, then gently disengaged himself in order to introduce the woman to Morgan. "Marianna, my fiancée, Morgan Becket. Morgan, please allow me to introduce Mrs. Marianna Warren."

Marianna looked from Ethan to Morgan and back again, her grimace almost comical. "Oh, my. Your fiancée, Ethan? And here I was, hanging on you like some limpet." She smiled at Morgan. "I'm sorry."

"Oh, no, Mrs. Warren, don't be. I know he's mine."

Marianna's eyebrows shot up as she looked at Morgan in amazement. "Really?"

Morgan shrugged. "Well, he's not yours," she said, and then could no longer hold back her grin. "Welcome to Becket Hall, Mrs. Warren."

"Marianna, please," the woman said as all three of them began the rather long walk to the terrace, the very large Abraham following a few paces behind them. "We've some damage, I'm afraid. The English were becoming too curious so we left the harbor, and then we got turned about a bit in the mist and suddenly the French were too close. I'll be happy to get back on the open sea."

"I'll be sorry to see you go," Ethan told her as he motioned for the ladies to precede him up the stone steps to the terrace. "I don't think you'll be carrying back what your Federalist friends hoped to see."

Marianna's shoulders slumped, if only for a moment. "Women should run countries, do you know that? Women with sons. Women with daughters. Women who understand that sacrificing children is totally without glory, and that no battle, no matter how soundly won, can ever be called a true victory. There would be much more negotiations and many fewer wars if women made the decisions. But no. Old men make wars, then keep themselves safe and pretend to care as the young are sent into the slaughter. And I'm sermonizing yet again, Ethan, for which I apologize."

"I like her. So much so that I won't even mention our own Elizabeth, or Catherine the Great, or even Cleopatra," Morgan whispered to Ethan as they made their way along the terrace, to the French doors standing open at the opposite end.

"I appreciate that, imp," he answered, before looking to Abraham. "Our host wishes to speak with you as well, Abraham."

"Is that so, sir?" Abraham asked, his large white teeth showing as he grinned widely.

"You're Mrs. Warren's captain, aren't you?"

"To hell and beyond, sir, that I am, and for her good husband before her."

Abraham hadn't said much, but the song in his speech made Morgan smile. The lilt in his voice was the lilt in Odette's, and she longed to ask him where he'd been born.

But others matters were more important, a fact she noticed the moment she saw her father's face. She quickly stepped behind Abraham, who could probably effectively block out the sun, let alone hide one female who didn't wish to be noticed, then told to go away.

Ainsley, who had been leaning over one of the large tables, studying an equally large chart, looked up incuriously as they entered the room.

Morgan saw the slight squint as her father's eyes narrowed, saw the way that, just for a moment, his lips seemed to compress tightly before they relaxed into a small smile. "Please, come in, make yourselves comfortable," he said as he stepped away from the charts. "I am Ainsley Becket."

Marianna stepped forward at once, her right hand

outstretched. "Then you are the man I wish to thank, Mr. Becket. Thank you for that show of force as we made for your lovely harbor. I'm Marianna Warren."

Ainsley felt the warmth of her skin, the fragility of her long, slim hand in his. "Warren?" He looked to Ethan. "Isn't that strange. I hadn't known our guest's full name before now, had I? Warren. Shipbuilder, merchant trader. Richard Warren, from Hampton Roads, I believe."

"My late husband. You knew Richard?"

"I did, if only by reputation. A fellow trader, you understand. My most sincere condolences, madam. I had no idea he was gone."

"Murdered, yes. But that's a sad story for another day. You've seen the damage to my ship?"

Ainsley didn't answer immediately. He was too shocked at his response to her. He hadn't had a thought for another woman since Isabella was taken from him more than a dozen long years ago. And this woman was so different from Isabella, who had been small and rather softer—an exotic, warm-blooded girl, actually, who'd never been allowed to reach her full potential. Isabella had laughed and sang and danced. This woman was all elegance, all business.

Ethan noticed Ainsley's small confusion, and said, "One of Mr. Becket's sons is already gathering men to make repairs, Marianna. Excuse me, please, and I'll fetch the cylinder. Morgan? Would you care to go with me, perhaps find some tea and cheese and cold meats for Marianna and her captain?"

"Find some tea and cheese and cold meats," Morgan repeated in a singsong voice once she and Ethan were out in the hallway. "Why is it always women who are relegated to such matters? I'd wager Marianna Warren doesn't fetch cheese and meat. And what's wrong with Papa? Did you see him? He was very nearly at a loss for words."

"Marianna Warren is a beautiful woman, imp. Or hadn't that occurred to you?"

Morgan stopped dead in the hallway. "But…but he's never…"

"Don't worry, Morgan. Marianna leaves tonight."

"I'm not *worried.* Just surprised. And, once she has delivered the cylinder with our government's response, there will be a war?"

"You'd probably have to apply to someone with more knowledge than I on that topic, but yes, I think there will be a war. America is still 'those upstart colonists' to many in England. Now, see if you can get someone to make up a tray for Marianna and Abraham, and I'll go unearth the cylinder, all right?"

"Aye, aye, Cap'n," Morgan said, saluting him rather sarcastically before watching him head off toward the staircase. "Be a lady, Morgan, do *lady* things," she grumbled as she retraced her steps past the study, on the way to the kitchens, her head down, watching her skirts kick out in front of her with each long stride.

"Miss Becket? Excuse me, Miss Becket?"

Morgan turned to see Abraham standing in the shadows. "Oh, hello. Is there something you need?"

"Yes, miss. You have a *mambo* here with you, miss? I saw the *aizan* hanging on the lintel of a door beneath the terrace. A *humfo* door, yes? You have a *mambo?*"

Morgan opened her mouth slowly, just as slowly said,

"...Ah, yes. Yes, we have a *mambo.* A very powerful *mambo,* Abraham. *Marassa.* Our Odette is one of twins."

Abraham nodded. "I understand. I, Abraham, am *dosu.*"

Morgan racked her brain for the meaning of *dosu,* and then remembered. The first child born after the birth of twins, a girl being a *dossa,* a boy a *dosu.* The one who unites all the powers of the twins so that he is more powerful than they. More powerful than Odette.

Odette subservient to someone else. Morgan could barely imagine such a thing.

"You...um, you wish me to fetch her to you?"

Abraham seemed to grow even taller, larger. "This is not my land, not my place. I would go to her. We need speak of the safekeeping of my mistress."

"Then please to come, great *hungan.*"

Morgan nearly jumped out of her skin at the sound of Odette's voice, and hastily backed against the wall, so that she was not standing between this powerful voodoo priest, this powerful priestess.

They made quite a sight, the pair of them. Abraham in breeches that fit his muscular thighs like a second skin, Odette in her shapeless dress and threadbare carpet slippers, her graying hair tied up in a checkered bandanna.

"I have been waiting weeks for you, great *hungan,*" Odette said as they passed by Morgan as if they'd forgotten her presence. "A peasant feast only, I fear, but a groaning board bent beneath your favored *afibas* and *rapadous.* There is also *trempé,* to slake your thirst, if that pleases you."

"That it does, woman."

Abraham then slipped into some sort of patois, and

Odette followed his lead, their voices growing more quiet as they turned a corner in the hallway and disappeared.

"Well, I'll be damned...."

Morgan, her nerves stretched taut, yelped at the sound of Ethan's voice, and whirled around to beat her fists against his chest. "*Don't* sneak up on me like that!" Then she pressed her arms to her own chest and took a deep breath. "My God, I've never seen Odette like that. And she knew he was coming. Did you hear that part?"

Ethan tapped the silver cylinder against his thigh. "I did hear that, yes. I'm not going to think about any of it right now, but I did hear it. And, now that Abraham seems to be well taken care of, have you arranged for anything for Marianna to eat?"

Morgan pulled a face. "As long as nobody says anything important until I'm back," she warned, then trotted off toward the kitchens.

Ethan shook his head and returned to Ainsley's study, to find that both he and Marianna were bent over the charts, seemingly as comfortable with each other as old friends.

"I think that's workable, Ainsley," Marianna said, straightening, one hand to the small of her back. "But I'll say again, there is no need for you to put you and your people in any danger. We've been outrunning the English for nearly two years now. The French as well. We fly so many flags from the *Marianna,* I sometimes forget which one to raise. All we need is to get into the open sea."

Ainsley folded one of the charts, then looked at her. "And you've never had a problem?"

"Only the once," Marianna admitted with a smile.

"But we were prepared. Half the crew put themselves into chains below decks, a few sturdy casks of not very pleasant smelling refuse were opened to the breeze. Nobody is anxious to board a slaver. Especially one that has been spotted just as a sail-wrapped body is being tossed unceremoniously into the sea."

Ainsley's smile was unabashedly admiring. "A ruse worthy of a master, Marianna. My compliments. But now, if you'll excuse me, I would like to inspect your ship for myself. Please remain here, and enjoy whatever refreshments my daughter manages to collect for you. Ethan," he murmured, making a quick signal with his hand, "perhaps you'll join me for a moment?"

Ethan handed the sealed cylinder to Marianna, and then followed Ainsley out onto the terrace. "Is there a problem, sir?"

"You mean other than that I dislike the idea of watching a woman sail into the open sea with little protection, her mission already decided to be fruitless in any case? That is what you said, isn't it?"

They walked slowly along the length of the long terrace, both with their hands clasped behind their backs, their gazes on the two ships in the harbor in front of the village. "It is my opinion, yes. Some want peace, some on both sides. But more are committed to war, and the French would be delighted to have England's forces divided along two fronts. That's why we met that man at the inn. He wanted to intercept any communications. I only wish I knew how he knew about the cylinder."

"A question for another time, I'm afraid, although it

seems obvious the War Office is leaking secrets somewhere. In any case, by my best reckoning, we'll be at war with America by summer. Spencer is badgering me to buy him a commission, but I don't want him fighting in America. It's the little corporal who threatens us, not America. They much prefer to be left alone on their side of the Atlantic. Young countries have to be more careful of conflict arising from the inside rather than the outside, and we've lost one war over there. Do we really need a second lesson in their devotion to their new land?"

"Have you traveled in America, Ainsley?"

The older man turned his head to train his narrowed gaze on Ethan. And when he spoke, the change of subject was startling, and very telling. Clearly, there were places Ethan should not attempt to go. "Eleanor showed you her watercolors."

"Why, yes, she did. Her views of Becket Hall were remarkable."

"And the other watercolors?"

Ethan wasn't sure what he should say, what Ainsley Becket needed to hear. "Her imagination is quite lively. I could almost believe I've seen such a place. Of course, England has so many grand country houses, doesn't it, and Eleanor tells me she's never been away from Romney Marsh."

"That's all you have to say on the matter?"

"All that I imagine you wish to hear, yes," Ethan responded carefully, and then decided to change the subject yet again. "I'm glad we have these moments alone, Ainsley, as I believe in repaying favor for favor.

The minister had a rather strange request for me just before I came here."

They were at the bottom of the stone stairs now, and heading across the uneven ground toward the beach. "And this request?"

"I'm not sure," Ethan admitted, "as it was withdrawn almost as quickly as it was presented. Probably when his lordship realized who he was speaking to, and recalled his long-held opinion that I'm by and large worthless. He'd asked me to keep a keen eye out for news of free trading in the area. Oh, yes, and French spies. He included those as well."

"He did, did he?"

"Yes, he did. Perhaps he already knows of a problem at the War Office? He mentioned that Chance had done some very good work on the subject last year, but when I suggested he then send Chance back for another look-round, he said he couldn't. That there were rumors… and then we were interrupted. In any case, he didn't charge me with the mission."

"And from what he said you deduced exactly what, Ethan?"

"I deduced, Ainsley, that I love Morgan very much. I deduced that she loves her family very much, and that I would not do anything to jeopardize anything or anyone Morgan loves." Ethan glanced toward the *Marianna*. "Ah, they are busy out there, aren't they. Do you think she'll make the tide?"

"I have every confidence, yes."

Ethan looked at Morgan's father. "Enough confidence to allow me on board the *Respite* as we escort the *Marianna* beyond danger?"

"Have you ever been involved in a battle at sea?"

"No, sir."

"But you want to sail aboard the *Respite*."

"I have my uses, Ainsley."

Ainsley patted Ethan's shoulder. "Yes, I think you do. You'll be under Court's command."

"Not yours?"

"I don't go to sea, Ethan. Not anymore."

There wasn't anything Ethan could think of to say to that, so the two continued on in silence.

A companionable silence between two men who understood each other. Or, if they didn't quite completely do so, were content with what they knew.

CHAPTER TWENTY-SEVEN

THE SPITTING RAIN HAD turned to a wind-lashed downpour, and dark came early to the coastline—weather excellent for keeping the Waterguard snug and dry in their quarters and their ships anchored. The starless night was no aid to navigation, and only those supremely confident in their abilities would hazard out into the angry waters of the Channel.

It was a challenging night, even for the local free traders, whose long experience had ingrained every bit of shore, every possible current so deeply into them that they sailed more by instinct than anything else.

Free traders like The Black Ghost Gang.

Fitted with its black sails—a remnant of earlier days, another place, another time, another life—and with not a single lantern visible onboard, the *Respite* had slipped out of the small harbor at Becket Hall shortly after dark under Courtland's sure command, the able Jacko sailing with him.

And Ethan with them both.

Precisely one half hour later, the *Marianna* had raised anchors and followed.

Morgan had remained on the terrace, partially sheltered by a deep window embrasure, candlelight from the drawing room spilling out onto the terrace. She was wrapped in Ethan's Carrick coat, ignoring the wind and rain, unaware of the damp. Occasionally she'd rub at the spot on her chest where her *gad* had rested until she'd hung the chain around Ethan's neck, warned him that he'd damn well better come back to her, held him tightly for long moments, then let him go.

Men do what men do, and women wait.

Her sister Fanny thought that ridiculous, and had said as much, at some length, until Eleanor had quietly told her that nobody really needed to hear more of her thoughts on the matter, most especially her belief that Rian wasn't as yet prepared enough for such a dangerous mission.

Fanny had gone to her chamber now, probably to stand at the window with a spyglass as she watched for Rian's return.

But Morgan couldn't go inside. As long as she and Ethan were sharing the same dark sky, the same wind and lashing rain, she was connected to him. She had to be there to see what she didn't want to see, to possibly hear the last thing she wanted to hear. The flash of gunfire, the sound carried over the water.

"Morgie?"

Morgan turned to see Jacob had joined her in the window embrasure. He wasn't wearing a coat, and was soaked to the skin. She hadn't spoken to him since…since that night, and the morning that had followed. She didn't want to speak with him now. She had room in her heart, her mind, only for Ethan. "You should be in bed, Jacob, nursing that wound."

He nodded, his young features tight. "That's the

thing, Morgie. The wound, I mean. Everybody keeps asking me what happened. But I don't remember, not much anyway. I saw that Frog pointing his pistol at you, I remember that. I remember yelling, and running, and trying to get my own pistol out…"

Morgan didn't know what to say, so she said nothing, but just kept staring out to sea.

"Maybe I was holding the pistol when he shot me? Maybe my pistol just went off by itself when I fell? What do you think, Morgie?"

She took a deep breath, let it out slowly as she looked at him. He was still her friend from her childhood, but now everything had changed. Some bridges, once crossed, can't be crossed again. "Does it matter, Jacob? Whether you aimed well, or shot him by mistake or the whole episode was just good luck, you saved my life. That's what I'll always remember, always thank you for doing."

Jacob tried to scrub the rain from his face. "I should be dead, Morgie. I wanted to die. What I said to you… what I did? His lordship says we have to find ways to…to live with our mistakes, but that we can't always make up for them."

Morgan put down the hand she'd been using to shield her eyes from the rain and looked at Jacob. "He said that to you? When?"

"Right after he knocked me down. Or maybe before. I don't remember." He pulled out his bottom lip, exposing the gap in the middle of his bottom teeth. "He knocked out my tooth for me, too, so I'd feel better. I've no worries about how you'll go on, Morgie, not with the earl. He's a good man."

Morgan shook her head. "I just want to forget what happened, Jacob. There was fault on both sides, you know. I thought of you as my childhood friend. But I teased you, used you. I'm not always a nice person, Jacob. Maybe I only got what I deserved that night."

"Oh...oh, no, Morgie. I've always known what you were doing. I've always known the likes of me would never be the one for you. But I could see you and his lordship looking at each other, always finding reasons to touch each other, and I knew what was going to happen in that inn. I just kept sitting, and drinking, and after a while I started thinking maybe I was wrong, and why wouldn't you want me?"

"Jacob, don't blame the drink. I don't want to talk about this anymore. There was wrong on both sides and now we need to...to find ways to live with our mistakes." Then she smiled. "But I'm glad Ethan knocked out your tooth. That was very kind of him."

Jacob smiled, shook his head. "Sheila likes how I look now, like I've lived some, she says. She says I'm a hero."

"Sheila?" Then Morgan remembered the young girl who worked as one of the maids. A pretty girl, slight and blond. As different in appearance from Morgan as day was from night. "She's sweet on you, Jacob?"

"Mayhap." Jacob shifted from foot to foot, half pleased, half embarrassed. "Is that all right?"

Morgan was already looking out into the darkness again. "I think that's more than all right, Jacob. Now stop thinking so much and go get some rest, all right?"

"You're not coming in? It's hours past midnight, Morgie. No matter what, the *Respite* won't be showing up until morning, if that."

"I know. But I think I'll stay out here. Just a while longer."

"I'll watch with you. His lordship wouldn't want you to be out here all alone."

"Jacob, I really want to stay here by myself."

He peered at her through the darkness. "It won't ever be the same between us, will it, Morgie? No matter what we say, it won't ever be the same."

Morgan sighed. "Nothing stays the same, Jacob, but that doesn't mean we can't be friends. It's just… different now."

"*Different,*" he repeated, nodding. "I suppose it is. Maybe that's the part of finding ways to live with our mistakes his lordship talked about?"

Morgan felt incredibly sad. "Yes, I suppose it is. We're still us, but now we're different. I'm sorry. Be good to Sheila, Jacob. That should go a long way toward making things right."

Once Jacob had gone, Morgan wiped at the rain on her face and began to pace the stone terrace, unable to stand still. She felt like a caged beast, one that could only breathe and truly live, once Ethan had returned. Once she'd held him, once she knew he was all right.

How she loved him! Had she told him she loved him? He had to know, didn't he?

Again her hand searched for the *gad* that wasn't there, even as her mind searched for prayers she barely remembered.

Only hours later, when she could no longer ignore the wet and cold, did she climb the stairs to her bedchamber, where Louise was waiting for her.

The maid didn't say a word, but only helped Morgan

off with the Carrick coat before wrapping her wet hair in a towel and guiding her to a chair. The maid knelt in front of her, helping to strip her of her clothes, and only clucked her tongue a time or two when she noticed that Morgan's teeth were chattering.

Morgan fell asleep beside the fire as Louise brushed her towel-dried hair, but awoke in the first false light of dawn, a pillow beneath her head and a blanket twisted around her legs.

Ethan.

She raced to wash and dress in her blue riding habit, because the buttons were all in the front, and quickly dragged a brush through her hair, barely taking time to pull on her boots before racing down the front stairs and out onto the terrace. She lifted a hand to shield her eyes from the bright sunlight now just beginning to reflect off the water.

"Not yet, Morgan," Ainsley said, lowering his spyglass. "With dawn coming, I imagine Courtland took the risk of lying helpless in the water as the sails were changed. We can explain being on the water, if necessary, but not those sails."

In other words, their larger plan may have met with brilliant success in the long run, but in the short run a single detail could bring them all down. That sobering fact kept father and daughter quiet for long minutes, even as the sky brightened and gulls began their daily aerial survey of the wide shingle beach.

And the minutes dragged on. Became an hour.

"Papa? Do you think they met with any trouble?"

"Difficult to say. But nothing Courtland and the men couldn't handle, I'm sure. Ah, good morning, Eleanor."

"Good morning, Papa," Eleanor said, then smiled at Morgan. "Going out for a ride, Morgan?"

"No, I—what are you doing out here?"

"Worrying, along with everyone else." She raised her arm, pointing toward the horizon. "Is that a sail?"

"Where?" Morgan stood on tiptoe, knowing that was a silly, useless thing to do, and shaded her eyes as she squinted toward the horizon. Her heart was pounding, her breathing uneven. Where she had always felt confidence when the Black Ghost Gang rode, now all she could feel was fear. How did her papa stand it, each time Courtland and the others went out on a run? "I don't see anything, Elly. Papa, do you see any—oh, wait! There! *There!*"

"Morgan, stay here," Eleanor said quickly. "I know you want to run down there, but you really should remain here and—"

Morgan didn't hear why Elly thought she should remain on the terrace, and she didn't much care, either, as she ran down the stone stairs and onto the rough stones that separated Becket Hall from the sand and water.

Only when she'd reached the hard-packed wet sand and turned toward the small village that had been built for the men and women who had come with them from the island did it occur to her that Eleanor might have been warning her away in case there were injuries aboard the *Respite*. Injuries, and worse.

Morgan stopped on the sand, her breathing now ragged with fear rather than exertion, and waited as the sloop tacked toward the natural harbor.

"Be all right, be all right, please be all right," she

murmured over and over again as the *Respite*'s anchor finally appeared, sliding into the water, and men climbed into the rigging to lower the white sails.

A lifetime later, as Morgan walked slowly, hesitantly toward the village, the first longboat made its way back to shore, loaded with the men from the *Respite.*

Morgan walked faster, faster, and then broke into a run when she saw Ethan climb out of the longboat, walking the last few yards through the thigh-deep water.

"Ethan!"

He looked up just in time to see Morgan running toward him full-tilt, her long dark hair flying out behind her as she launched herself at him, clinging to his shoulders, wrapping her legs around his waist.

He spun in a circle, mostly to help balance himself, and allowed Morgan's kisses on his face, his hair, his throat, before she leaned slightly away from him, still with her legs clamped around his waist.

"You're bleeding," she said, touching her fingers to his temple.

"Nothing fatal, Morgan," he assured her as she looked to be torn between worrying about him and wanting to beat on him for daring to worry her. He'd both hoped for and had expected no less from this woman; his woman. "Some wood splintered thanks to a lucky shot from a French cannon and hit me, that's all. I'm fine. We're all relatively fine, and Marianna's safely on her way home, the Stars and Stripes already hoisted high. An amazing sight. It was all amazing."

"There was a fight? You were shot at?"

Ethan wanted to remind Morgan that he'd been out on the water all night, and he wouldn't mind if she stood on her own now, but she was wiping at his face, bemoaning the streaks of smoke and gunpowder.

And then he nearly staggered to the ground as Spencer Becket walked past him, delivering a considerable slap to his back as he said, "Well done! Welcome to the family, Ethan. Morgan, for God's sake, get down off the man. You look a proper idiot."

Morgan dropped her feet onto the sand, but didn't let go. "Spence approves? What did you do, Ethan?"

"Nothing nobody else did," Ethan told her, grinning. "God, Morgan, it was magnificent. We laid back, waited for the *Marianna* to make her break into open water, and then swooped down on the Frenchman when he showed himself. Cut him off, turned him, chased him halfway to hell, and then took him down. Courtland was magnificent, you should be very proud of your brother, all your brothers. Jacko kissed Court on the head when it was over, and then someone broke out some rum for everyone."

Morgan looked at this man she loved, and sighed. "Oh, God. And you're happy, aren't you? Nearly delirious with it. I suppose you'll want to do this again, won't you?"

"If the occasion rises, yes," Ethan told her, then became serious. "At the moment, however, we have something else to discuss, as I seem to remember a proposal we're still lacking."

"Good God, man, what are you doing!" Morgan glared down at Ethan, who had gone down on one knee in the wet sand, and then at the crowd of men and women from the village, all of them congregated on the shoreline, and most of them looking at her and Ethan.

"Get up you idiot," she warned quietly. "Everyone's watching. Oh, God, here come Papa and Eleanor."

"Good. The more the merrier," Ethan told her, taking Morgan's hand in his as he smiled up at her. "And now, Miss Becket, having the permission of your esteemed father—and Spencer—and cognizant as I am of the dubious honor I am bestowing on you, will you marry me?"

"I can't believe you're doing this," Morgan said, her gaze meeting that of Jacko, who was grinning at her even as he used a large handkerchief to wipe grime and sweat from his face.

"Neither can I, imp, so hurry up and say yes, before I change my mind."

Morgan looked down at him. "You wouldn't dare."

"No, I wouldn't. Say yes, Morgan. I love you more than I need my next breath."

"I love you, too, Ethan Tanner," Morgan said quietly. "Yes, I'll marry you. I'll even live in your drafty castle. Now stand up and kiss me."

"I can see I'll be hen-pecked for the next fifty years, if I'm lucky," Ethan said, getting to his feet once more. His hands cupping her face, he then did as he'd been ordered, as Morgan slid her arms up and around his neck and he gathered her more fully against him.

There were a few cheers, a faint spattering of clapped hands, and then everyone went back to their own business as the sun rose more fully into the sky, as gulls laughed overhead—even as Morgan and Ethan slipped away, hand-in-hand, not to be seen for the remainder of the day.

EPILOGUE

MORGAN HALF-SAT AGAINST several pillows looking down at Ethan as he lay propped on one elbow, using his fingertips to draw out the battle on her bare belly.

"...so when the Frenchman made his move for the *Marianna,* Court gave the order and we cut straight across...here."

Morgan giggled. "That tickles. Now, where was the Frenchman?"

"Right here, beside your navel. Pretty little thing, that."

"The French ship?"

"No." Ethan smiled up at her. "Your navel. I like the way your belly is so flat, and then there's this surprising little hollow, just here..." He laid his palm on her belly, dipped his middle into that hollow, moved his fingertip in small, light circles.

Morgan closed her eyes for a moment as something tightened inside her. Pleasurably. "You...you were telling me about the battle."

"Hardly a battle, darling," Ethan said, his attention straying even as he bent to place a kiss between Morgan's full breasts. "But feel free to consider me a hero if that makes me more attractive to you."

Morgan pushed him onto his back and rolled over with him, to brace her arms on either side of his body. "How attractive did you want to be? Because I think you've been *attractive* three times so far, and the sun hasn't gone down yet. Should I also mention that I'm ravenous?"

Ethan pulled her close, began nibbling on her earlobe. "I heard knocking earlier. Do you think anyone's worried about us? After all, we might starve."

"Knocking?" Morgan pushed herself up, grabbing the bedsheet that had come undone earlier. She slipped to the floor, wrapped the sheet around her body. "Someone left food out there for us, I'm sure of it," she said, walking barefoot to the door to the hallway.

"I was wondering about your sudden modesty. But don't tell me you're going to step into the hallway like that."

Morgan grinned at him. "Why not? Besides, everyone is down at dinner by now. Still," she added, one hand on the door latch, "you might want to cover yourself. It does you no good to lie there looking so very good, because I refuse to climb back in that bed until I've had something to eat."

Ethan pulled up the coverlet. "Fickle woman. You'd probably sell me to a traveling tinker in exchange for a joint of beef."

"You *are* a joint of beef," Morgan said, then felt herself blushing as she depressed the latch and opened the door, hoping to see that someone had indeed left a tray in the hall for them.

But there was more in the hallway than the tray.

"Hello, Morgan," Callie Becket said as she sat cross-legged on the floor, munching on a chicken leg she'd obviously purloined from the covered silver tray in front of her. "There weren't any more legs in the kitchen after dinner. You don't mind, do you? I like legs best."

Morgan glared at her younger sister. "Cassandra Becket, you are too old to pretend you're a child and too transparent to tell a lie with any hope of being believed. Why are you really out here? What do you want?"

Cassandra bent her head forward so that her light brown curls hid her face. "There was nowhere else to go. Eleanor is off helping Odette at the village because Bertie Cassel broke his leg in the rigging last night. Rian and Fanny have their heads together like always, and Court and Papa are in the study talking to Mr. Eastwood, who just arrived from London. There's no one to talk to and nothing to do, and if you weren't going to eat the chicken leg, why shouldn't I?"

She tossed back her curls as she looked up at Morgan defiantly. "Besides, what are you and Ethan doing in there all day? I asked Court and he just told me to go away."

Morgan was caught between sympathy for her sister and embarrassment, with a bit of hunger thrown into the mix just to help make everything more complicated. "Callie, not now."

The girl got to her feet, still holding the chicken leg. "Not now, Callie. We're busy, Callie. Oh, *grow up,* Callie. Well, you know, Morgan, I'm almost fourteen and I think I am grown up, and I think it's time you all realize that I am, because some day I'm going to be even older, and then you'll *all* be sorry!"

Morgan stuck her head out into the hallway to watch as Cassandra stomped off down the hallway, her curls bouncing, the large bow at the back of her gown hanging crooked and bedraggled.

"Poor little thing. Not a child, not a woman. I should get dressed and go after her," Morgan said as Ethan, clad only in his breeches, reached past her, picked up the tray, then closed the door. "But I don't know what to say to her. We'll take her to London one day, won't we, Ethan? I should tell her that. I mean, if I'm going to be a countess, I should be able to find my own sister a suitable husband."

Ethan put down the tray and lifted the silver dome, his own stomach reacting to the smell of roasted chicken. "It probably would be good to get her away from Becket Hall at some point," he agreed, ripping off the remaining chicken leg and holding it out to Morgan.

She looked at the thing and shook her head, her appetite gone. "We're leaving now, one by one. Some day Papa will be all alone here, in this great pile. He and Eleanor, of course."

Ethan wiped his hands on a serviette after putting down the chicken leg and spared only a moment to look at the thing wistfully before taking Morgan's hand and leading her back to the bed. "Why Eleanor?" he asked, watching as Morgan climbed back into the bed, the sheet still wrapped around her.

"Because that's the way she wants it, I suppose. I don't think she cares where she is. Oh, I've seen her look at Jack Eastwood from time to time when he comes here to talk to Papa—he handles the sale and delivery of our goods in London, you understand. But that's all she does. Look. And he doesn't look back, so what does it matter? But Chance is gone and Spence is gnawing at the bit, wanting to go fight Napoleon. Rian and Fanny will leave one day—anyone with a single eye in their head knows those two will be together one day, even if the world would say that's wrong."

Ethan joined her on the bed, playing with a heavy lock of Morgan's hair that had fallen forward onto her sheet-clad breast. Any discussion of the sort of *goods* this Jack Eastwood sold in London was for another day, although he'd be willing to wager that those goods included tea, silk and French brandy. "Darling, are you trying to say that we should stay here? Because you know that's impossible."

Morgan snuggled into his side. "I know. I went to London, but I always expected to end up back here. And now I won't. It's strange, that's all. It's always been just us, just the family. I've never known anything else."

Ethan kissed her forehead. "We'll make our own family, Morgan. And our children will come to Becket Hall. Ainsley will never be alone. I promise."

Morgan smiled up at Ethan, blinking back ridiculous tears, silly tears, because she was happy, really happy, and had no reason to cry. "Papa's been alone for a long time, Ethan. I don't ever want either of us to be alone the way he's alone."

Ethan wasn't sure what Morgan meant, but there would be time for talk, for explanations. Years, decades. Together. He drew her more firmly into his arms, overcome with love for her, a feeling far removed from the physical passion they'd shared earlier. "Then, darling, we'll just hang on to each other, very tightly. And I promise, I will never let you go…."

* * * * *

The Beckets of Romney Marsh
continues with
BEWARE OF VIRTUOUS WOMEN
by Kasey Michaels.
Available May 2006 from HQN Books.

CHAPTER ONE

1813

ELEANOR BECKET SAT IN her usual chair near the fire, bent over her embroidery frame.

Her sisters Fanny and Cassandra, the latter still downstairs only because their papa had retreated to his study and didn't know she'd left her bedchamber, were playing a card game they'd invented together, and neither of them quite knew the rules.

Morgan Tanner, Countess of Aylesford, sister to the three and quite happily pregnant, sat with her legs up on a Chinese hassock, wiggling her slipper-clad toes in delight, for the slippers were new, and she rarely saw them. At least not while standing up and attempting to peer straight down.

A log fell in the large fireplace in the drawing room where they sat, and all four women momentarily looked up from what they were doing, then settled back to passing the time as best they could.

"They're fine," Eleanor said a few minutes later in answer to the unspoken question that had been hanging in the room all evening, and Fanny agreed that, of course, they were.

"Just enough mist over the water to hide the *Respite,* not enough to hamper them. And the moon couldn't be more perfect," Morgan said, looking toward one of the large windows and the dark beyond. "Callie, stop chewing on your curls. You'll end up with a hair ball in your belly. Odette will pour castor oil down your gullet, and there will be no lack of volunteers to hold you down."

Fifteen-year-old Cassandra Becket used her tongue to push the light brown corkscrew curl from her mouth, then frowned at its damp length. "I can't help it, Morgie. I'm nervous."

"And hours past your bedtime, as it's nearly three," Eleanor pointed out, taking another stitch in her embroidery, pleased that her hands were steady. "You too, Morgan."

"Me? I'm pregnant, Elly, not delicate. In fact," she said, looking down at her stomach, "I'm about as *delicate* as a beached whale."

Fanny giggled. "Maybe if you didn't *eat* so much…?"

Morgan reached down behind her and drew out one of the small silk pillows she'd placed there to make her comfortable, then launched it at her sister's head.

Fanny neatly caught the pillow, then stood up, pressed it against her own flat stomach. She bent her spine as far as she could, still holding the pillow to her, and began walking across the room, her feet spread wide. "Do I have it right, Callie? Enough of a duck waddle to look like our dear, sophisticated countess?"

Callie considered this, then said, "Perhaps if you had first stuffed your cheeks with sugar plums?"

Eleanor smiled as she continued to bend over her

embroidery. It was so good to have Morgan home with them after so many months away, but if her baby didn't come soon even Eleanor would be harboring a few fears that the girl would simply explode on her own, and not need Odette's midwifery.

"What was that? Fanny, Callie, sit down and be quiet. I think I heard something. Elly? Did you hear it?"

Eleanor stood and walked over to Morgan, gently pushing her back into the chair. "We don't want to appear to be too anxious, Morgan. It's bad enough we're all sitting up with you, just as if we don't expect them to be fine at all. Ah—now I hear it, too. They're back. Everyone, do your best to appear unconcerned."

Fanny and Cassandra had already picked up their cards again, and Eleanor was once more bending over her embroidery frame as the Becket men entered the drawing room to catch Morgan in the middle of a prodigiously overdone yawn.

"Oh, look who's back," Morgan said, "and none the worse for wear. Although, darling, could you possibly manage to wipe that ridiculous grin from your face?"

Ethan Tanner, Earl of Aylesford, pulled at the black silk scarf tied loosely around his throat and lifted it up and over his mouth and nose. "Better, darling?" he asked, then bent down and kissed her rounded belly. "Up late, aren't you, infant?"

"Are you referring to me or the baby? Come here, let me hold you. I know you were enjoying yourself romping about playing at free trader, but I haven't had a peaceful night waiting for you."

Eleanor watched, happy for her sister's joyfulness and yet somehow sad at the same time, as Morgan yanked down Ethan's mask and grabbed his face in her hands, pulling him close for a long kiss on the mouth.

"At it again, Ethan?" Rian said as he stripped off his gloves and accepted the glass of wine Fanny had fetched for him. "I think I should point out that the damage is already done."

Cassandra giggled, which drew the attention of Courtland Becket. "Been chewing on your hair again? And what are you doing down here at this hour? Get yourself upstairs where you belong."

Eleanor hid a sympathetic wince as Cassandra's pretty little face crumpled at this verbal slap and the child plopped herself down on one of the couches to sulk.

Didn't Courtland know how desperately Cassandra worshipped him? Or perhaps maybe he did, poor man. "Court? Does Papa know you're back?"

"He does. We came up the back stairs from the beach," Courtland told her, pouring himself a glass of claret. "And, before you ladies ask, the run was completely uneventful."

"You may say that, Court," Ethan said, sitting perched on the arm of the chair, holding Morgan's hand. "If it's uneventful to you that we had to evade the Waterguard and make land two hours behind schedule." He lifted Morgan's hand to his mouth, kissed her fingers. "God, but it makes your blood run, darling. I'll have to do this more often. Can't let everyone else have all the fun."

Morgan rolled her eyes. "Yes, of course. There's nothing like a good smuggling run to liven your exceedingly dull and boring married life. You should go out on every run, really. And don't you worry, I'll be sure to tell our child what you looked like before the Crown hanged you in chains."

"Ha! I think we've all just been insulted, Court," Rian said, pushing back his sea-damp black hair as Fanny looked at him, her heart in her eyes. "As if the Black Ghost could ever be caught."

Eleanor picked up her needle once more, not bothering to follow the lively exchange of jokes and verbal digs that were so commonplace in this rather wild, always loving clutch of Beckets. Like little boys, the men were still riding high on their excitement, and the girls were all more than willing to play their happy audience, even if that meant poking a bit of fun at them.

Was she the only one who saw beneath the surface of that banter? Saw that Fanny believed herself in love with Rian, and that Cassandra's devotion to Courtland was much more than that of a youngest child for her older brother and staunch protector?

This was what happened when you lived in the back of beyond, isolated from most of the world. Siblings in name, but not by blood, as the Beckets had grown into the healthy animals they were, problems had been bound to arise.

But not for her. Not for Eleanor. She was the different one, the odd Becket out, as it were. The one part of the whole that had never quite fit.

Perhaps it was because she had been the last to join the family, and as a child of six, not as an infant or even as experienced as Chance and Courtland had been; already their own persons, older than their years when Ainsley Becket had scooped them up, given them a home on his now lost island paradise. She had landed more in the middle, and had been forced to seek her own identity, her own place.

And that place, she had long ago decided, had been with Ainsley Becket, the patriarch of the Becket clan. She had made herself into the calm one, the reasonable one, the quiet voice of sanity in the midst of so many more earthy, hot-blooded young creatures who eagerly grabbed at life with both hands.

The others would leave one day, as Chance had when he'd married his Julia, as Morgan had when she'd wed her Ethan. Spencer was also gone, his commission purchased, and he'd been in Canada the last several months, fighting with his regiment against America, much to Ainsley's chagrin.

No matter how loving, how loyal, one by one the perhaps odd but yet wonderful assortment of Becket children would leave Becket Hall. Much as they loved and respected him, they'd leave Ainsley Becket alone with his huge house and his unhappy memories of the life he'd loved and lost before fleeing his island paradise and bringing everyone to this isolated land that was Romney Marsh.

But she'd stay. She and Ainsley had discussed all of that, in some detail. She would stay. As it was for Ainsley, it might be safer for her to stay.

Eleanor watched now as Rian recounted the night's smuggling run to Fanny, who listened in rapt attention. As Courtland gave in and let Cassandra fuss over him, even try on the black silk cape that turned the sober, careful Courtland into the daring, mysterious Black Ghost. As Morgan and her Ethan whispered to each other, their heads close together, Ethan's hand resting casually on her belly.

Eleanor put aside her embroidery and got to her feet, barely noticing the dull ache in her left leg caused by sitting too long, her muscles kept too tense as she'd held her worries inside by sheer force of will. Her siblings, everyone, believed her to be so calm, so controlled… and never realized how very frightened she was for all of them, most especially since the Black Ghost had begun his nocturnal rides to aid the people of Romney Marsh.

She left the drawing room unnoticed, her limp more pronounced than usual, but that would work out the more that she walked. By the time she reached Ainsley's study, it would barely be noticeable at all, which would be good, because her papa noticed everything.

The door to the study was half open and Eleanor was about to knock on one of the heavy oak panels and ask admittance when she heard voices inside the large, wood-panelled room.

Jacko's voice. "And I say leave it go. Cut our losses and find other ways, other people. There's always enough of the greedy bastards lying about, willing to get rich on our hard work."

Eleanor stepped back into the shadows in the hallway, realizing she'd stumbled onto a conversation she wouldn't be invited to join.

"True enough, Jacko," Ainsley agreed, "but we must also deal with this now, or else face the same problem again. Jack?"

Eleanor's eyes went wide. *Jack?* Her breathing became shallow, faster, and she pressed her hands to her chest. He was here? She hadn't known he was here. He must have arranged for a rendezvous with the *Respite* off Calais, then sailed home with them.

Jack Eastwood's voice, quiet, with hints of gravel in its cultured tones, sent a small frisson down Eleanor's spine. "Ainsley's right, Jacko. Someone got to these people, and if they did it once, they can do it again. Two men dead on the other side of the Channel, most probably as an example to the others, and the rest now understandably too frightened to deal with us. My connections on this side of the Channel are also shutting the door on me, on us. This is the last haul we'll get, the last we can deliver anyway. Much as I want to keep the goods running, I want to find out who did this to us, who discovered and compromised our connections."

"And eliminate them," Ainsley said, his voice low, so that Eleanor had to strain to hear. She could picture him, sitting behind his desk, his brow furrowed, his right hand working the small, round glass paperweight she'd given him this past Christmas. "I thought we were done with bloodshed when we rousted the Red Man Gang from Romney Marsh."

Eleanor heard the creak of the leather couch, and knew Jacko had sat forward, shifting his large, muscular frame. "You think it's the, Cap'n? It's been two years since we trounced them, sent them on their way. You really think they're back?"

"Who else could it be? Perhaps it's time to put a halt to all of this."

"Cap'n, you don't mean that." The leather couch protested again, and Eleanor stepped back further into the shadows as Jacko's large frame passed in front of the open door.

She'd known Jacko since the moment he'd found their hidey-hole, his wide smile and deep laugh so frightening to the child she had been. Julia, Chance's wife, had once confided that her first thought when she'd seen Jacko was that the man would smile amiably even as he cut your beating heart from your chest.

But Jacko was loyal to Ainsley. Fiercely so. And if Eleanor hadn't learned to love the man, she had learned to trust his loyalty, if not always his judgment.

Ainsley was speaking again. "I do mean it, Jacko. We only began this to help the people here, protect them from the Red Men Gang. A laudable reason, but not one of us suspected the enterprise to grow as it has. We're bringing attention to ourselves, from London, and most probably from the Red Man again. Moving some wool and coming back with tea and brandy, helping these people survive. That was the plan, remember? Now we control most of the Marsh. Someone was bound to notice."

"So you withdraw your protection, leave everyone to find their own suppliers, their own landsmen, their own distributors in London? You watch as they run up against the Red Man on their own, and then bury a few more bodies, add a few more widows and fatherless children to the Marsh. Is that what you're saying, Ainsley?"

Eleanor held her breath. If Ainsley put a stop to the Black Ghost Gang they'd all be safe…but Jack Eastwood would never visit Becket Hall again.

"No, that's not what I'm *saying,* Jack. It's what I'm

hoping. A selfish return to our quiet existence for my sons, my men and, yes, for myself. But we all know that isn't possible, at least not until the war is over and wool prices hopefully climb again. Tell me more of your idea."

Eleanor stepped closer, not wishing to miss a word.

"All right. As I said, someone is trying to cut off our head *and* our feet—our contacts both around London and in France. After this last shipment, I have no one lined up to buy our people's wool, and no one to sell the goods we, well, that we *import.*"

"You've been sloppy? How else would anyone know your contacts?"

Eleanor heard the hint of distaste in Jack's tone. "No, Jacko, I don't think I've been…*sloppy.* I think someone else has been very smart. Why confront us here on the Marsh, on the Black Ghost's home ground, when cutting off our head and feet is so much easier than hitting at our well-protected and well-armed belly? And I think it all begins in London, not France. I've been watching and I have some ideas, which is why I traveled to France and why I'm here now."

As Eleanor listened, Jack further explained his conclusions, and his plan.

No one in France had any reason to stop the flow of contraband either into or out of that country. To the French, profit was profit, and they'd deal with the Red Man, the Black Ghost, the devil himself, as long as that profit was maintained. If the French were nothing else, they were always eminently practical.

Which left London. More specifically, Mayfair, the very heart of the *ton.* Bankers and wealthy cits, industrialists, were also suspected of acting as financial backers to the smugglers, but it was common if unspoken knowledge that many an impecunious peer had staked his last monies on a smuggling run and then suddenly found his pockets deep again.

And Jack had an idea where in the *ton* he should look to find the people who had the most to gain if the Black Ghost Gang was rendered impotent.

"I've narrowed my search down to three men," he said. "Three gentlemen who have had happy and yet inexplicable, unexplainable reversals of fortune in the past few years. We all know the major profits from smuggling go to people at the very top of society."

"People with the money to put up to buy contraband goods in order to resell them at ten times the price, yes," Ainsley interrupted. "But these men you speak of? You said they've had reversals of fortune, which is not the same as having amassed a fortune the likes of which we know can be gotten. That would put them somewhere in the middle, wouldn't it? High placed minions, the slightly more public face of the true leaders, but still minions."

"True. But if we can get to them, hopefully we can get to the person or persons at the very top," Jack said. "And I'm willing to wager that whoever that is, he's also the brains behind the Red Men Gang. They may not be here in Romney Marsh anymore, but they're everywhere else, like a large red stain spreading over the countryside. No one makes a move without them, and if anyone dares, they're mercilessly crushed. You, Ainsley, you and your sons and Romney Marsh? You are all that stand between the Red Man Gang and complete domination of the smuggling trade in the south of England."

Jacko spoke up. "All very well, Eastwood, and you've made your point. But we're here, not about to budge, and you're only one man. Let's hear more of this plan of yours."

"I'm getting there, Jacko. You know I've bought a house in Portland Square, to go along very nicely with my estate in Sussex. I'm an extremely wealthy man, thanks to you, Ainsley, and you aren't the only one who sees the merits in planning for a more…conventional future, a life after we're done with our adventure. I think it's time I inhabited that house and made, well, a rather large but concentrated splash in society."

"To get you close, you have to be noticed by these men you suspect," Ainsley said quietly. "You interest me. Go on."

"I think my way in would be through the gambler in the group, Harris Phelps. He's the most reckless, and the most stupid. He's taken to wearing a scarlet waistcoat and always betting on the red, saying it's his lucky color."

"Damn," Jacko muttered. "Sounds like we're being beaten by an idiot. That stick in your craw as much as it does in mine, Cap'n?"

"On the contrary, Jacko. It's always comforting to know you're smarter than your enemy, as long as you don't make the mistake of becoming overconfident, always remember that even idiots are successful at times if only by mistake. Go on, Jack. I imagine you plan to get close with this Phelps person, and through him, with the others?"

"I intend to lose a lot of money playing at cards with Phelps, yes," Jack said, and Eleanor bit her bottom lip, smiling at the cleverness of the idea. Lose some money, bemoan his shrinking pockets, wish for a huge turn of luck…and then appeal to his new friend for some way to increase his fortune.

"You're that sure Phelps is your man? That you'd put your own money on the line?"

"Yes, Ainsley, I am. I won't always lose, either, not once I've firmly hooked our fish. Which, if I'm lucky, should be quickly enough to have only a two or three week interruption of our runs."

"You've always been a dab hand with the cards, I'll give you that."

"You gave him a lot more than a dab of your money, Jacko, as I recall the thing," Ainsley said, and Eleanor pretended not to hear Jacko's low string of curses.

She remembered when they met Jack, and how. A gambler, that was Jack, a gentleman of breeding but little fortune, living on his wits. But that had all changed the day, two years past, when he'd ridden up to Becket Hall with Billy slung face-down across his saddle after rescuing him from a pub in Appledore, where a deep-drinking Billy had had the bad sense to accuse a man of cheating when he had no friends present to guard his back. Jack had stepped in, saved the sailor from a knife in the gullet, although both he and Billy had each suffered several wounds.

During his weeks of recuperation at Becket Hall, Jack had done more than strip Jacko of five thousand pounds as they'd passed time playing at cards. He also had gained Ainsley's thanks for the rescue of one of his oldest friends, Ainsley's trust and, with that trust, a future.

And never once in that month had he said more than "Good morning, Miss Becket," or "Good evening, Miss Becket," to Eleanor.

She cocked her head toward the doorway, listening as Jack explained more of his plan. "I get close to Phelps, who will bring me close to the others, close enough that I can find ways to bring them down, each one of them. But I need that initial entrée into society. I discussed this with your son-in-law as we crossed the Channel tonight, and he's agreed to give me a letter of introduction to his friend, Lady Beresford. I'm now a gentleman who has spent much of his time these past years on his plantations in the West Indies, happily visiting my homeland."

"That should be enough to gain you at least few invitations. Chance could help you there, too, except that he and Julia plan to remain at his estate with the children until the end of summer, now that he's left the War Office," Ainsley said. "All right. What else? You have the look of a man who isn't quite finished saying what he needs to say."

"No," Jack said, "that's about it. The rest is just details I'll need to handle on my own."

"Such as?"

"I'm thinking I may need a wife."

Eleanor clapped her hands over her mouth, hoping no one had heard her short, startled gasp. Then, once back under control, she stepped closer, anxious to hear what else Jack might say.

"Wives go a long way in making a man appear respectable. It's not enough that I play the rich, amiable fool. I believe I need a wife as well. Most especially a wife who listens with both ears to other men's wives. Hiring an actress to play the part is chancy, but also worth the risk, I believe. Phelps's wife, for one, has a tongue that runs on wheels. Ask her the right questions, and I may get answers that will help me."

"I can see you believe this Harris Phelps to be the weakest link," Ainsley said. "Who are the other two?"

"Sir Gilbert Eccles is one. But the fellow who most interests me is the strongest of the lot. If he's not the head of the Red Men, then he is very close. Rowley Maddox, Earl of Chelfham."

Before Eleanor could clap her hands to her mouth again, someone did it for her, and she was pulled back against the tall, rangy body of Odette, the one woman in the Becket household who knew every secret, the Voodoo priestess who had come to England with the Beckets so many years ago.

"Ears that listen at the wrong doors hear things they should not hear," Odette whispered to Eleanor. "Come away child."

"But Odette—you heard? *The Earl of Chelfham.*"

"I heard. You want nothing to do with this man. You decided. We all decided."

"I know," Eleanor whispered fiercely as she looked toward the half-open door. "But this is…this is like *fate.* And I only want to *see.* Is it so wrong to want to see?"

"You want the man, *ma petite,*" Odette told her, stroking Eleanor's hair with one long-fingered hand. "He's the temptation you don't want to resist."

"You mean Jack?" Eleanor sighed, realizing protest was useless. "There's no future in lying to you, is there, Odette? *You* see everything."

The woman's face lost its smile. "Not everything, little one. Never enough. But I do know your papa won't approve."

Eleanor wet her lips with the tip of her tongue. "I know. But this is my decision to make, Odette, my chance. If I don't take my chance, I'll have the rest of my life to regret it. Years and years to sit by myself with my embroidery, my paints, my music. Sit and watch everyone else live their lives, while mine just slowly, quietly runs out, like sand slipping through an hourglass. Don't you see? I have to do this."

"Born a maiden, not prepared to die a maiden. Yes, I see."

"*No,*" Eleanor whispered fiercely, then sighed. "Yes, yes, that, too. And why not? I've tried being a paragon, and it's lonely, Odette. It's a lonely life. I want to hold more than other people's children. That's a dream, only a dream. But the Earl, Odette? He's real. How can I hear what I just heard, and walk away?"

Odette looked at her for a long time, and Eleanor returned that gaze as steadily as she could, until the older woman sighed, shook her head. "I'll be ordering more candles, I suppose. A bonfire of candles burning for you Beckets."

Eleanor impulsively hugged the woman, neither of them comfortable with such physical displays of affection. Yet Odette put her arms around Eleanor's shoulders and held her tightly for a moment before pushing her away, using the pad of her thumb to trace the sign of the cross on Eleanor's forehead.

"Thank you, Odette," Eleanor said, then squared her slim shoulders and walked into her papa's study to confront the man who had been coming to Becket Hall for over two years, and had never noticed her, never noticed the quiet one in the corner.

He'd notice her now…

"A shame Morgan is married," Jacko was saying. "She'd be perfect, you know. Right, Cap'n? Fire and spirit, that's Morgan. Give her a set of balls and—Eleanor." Jacko looked to Ainsley, who had already gotten to his feet.

"Eleanor? I hadn't expected you to be up and about this late at night. Is there something you wanted before you retire?" And that, she knew, was Ainsley's way of reprimanding her. Two quiet, polite questions, both meant to send her scurrying off, because she most certainly wasn't welcome here at this moment.

She could hardly hear for the sound of her blood rushing in her ears, and she seemed only able to see Jack Eastwood, who had slowly unbent his length from one of the chairs and now stood towering over her.

"I…I'll do it," Eleanor said, still looking up at Jack, at the lean, handsome face she saw nearly every night in her dreams. The thick, sandy hair he wore just a little too long, with sideburns that reached to the bottom of his ears. The slashes around his wide mouth, that fuller lower lip. And his eyes. So green, shaded by low brows; so intense, yet so capable of looking at her and never seeing her.

His look could be best described as constrained; quiet, reserved, even vaguely disinterested. Yet she knew that appearances could be purposely deceiving, and felt sure the man was actually of mass of barely-leashed power behind a careful façade. There was emotion there. He simply hid his feelings deep inside, and Eleanor didn't know if she most longed to know why he hid those emotions, or if she only wanted him to look at her, see her, feel safe to relax his careful shields with her.

"Eleanor..." Ainsley said, stepping out from behind the desk. "I'll assume you heard us, but—"

"I said, I'll do it," Eleanor interrupted, still looking at Jack Eastwood, still half lost in her daydream—she, who rarely dreamed, and only about Jack. "I'll pretend to be your wife, Mr. Eastwood. Go to London. Be your ears and eyes around the women. You can't buy loyalty, no matter how high the price. I'm the logical choice, the only logical, safe choice."

Jack quickly looked to Ainsley as if for help, then back to Eleanor, shaking his head. "I don't think your father approves, Miss Becket."

Was the woman out of her mind? Look at her. A puff of wind would blow her away. All right, so there was a hint of determination about that slightly square jaw she held so high on the long, slender stalk of her neck. God, even that mass of dark hair seemed too heavy for her finely-boned head. Yet she had the look of a lady, he'd give her that. Refined. Genteel. A sculptor's masterpiece, actually, if he was in a mood to be poetical, which he damn well was not.

The large-eyed, delicately constructed Eleanor Becket reminded Jack mostly of a fawn in the woods. Huge brown eyes, vulnerable eyes. But that limp? London society could be cruel, and they'd smell the wounded fawn and destroy her in an instant.

Would she stop staring at him! Stop making him feel

so large, so clumsy, so very much the bumpkin. The skin tightened around his eyes, drew his brows down, and he stared at her, tried to stare through her. Scare her off, damn her. He had enough on his plate, he didn't need any more complications. Certainly not one in skirts.

At last she looked away, to speak to her father. "Papa? You do see the rightness of this, don't you? No one knows me, and when the need is past, I will come back here to live in quiet retirement, as we've always planned. Mr. Eastwood, should he choose to stay in society, can certainly find some explanation for my disappearance. A divorce? Death?"

Eleanor abruptly shut her mouth, knowing she had gone too far. Keep in the moment, that's what she must do, not muddy up the waters with thoughts of consequences.

"We'll speak later," Ainsley said, taking hold of her shoulders, to turn her toward the door.

"No, Papa," Eleanor said in her quiet way, holding her ground. "We'll not speak at all, not about this decision, which is mine. Mr. Eastwood? When do you wish me to be ready to leave?"

Jacko yanked at his waistband with both hands, pulling the material up and over his generous belly. "Always said there was pure Toledo steel there, Cap'n, and you know it, too. She knows what's for. Probably the smartest of the bunch, for all she's a female. Let her go."

Jack narrowed his eyes as he looked to Ainsley, to the grinning Jacko and, lastly, to Miss Eleanor Becket. Smartest of the bunch? Toledo steel? He doubted that.

And yet her gaze was steady on him, and he recognized determination when he saw it. "Ainsley? We could leave tomorrow afternoon. Spend a night on the road while I send someone ahead to alert my staff in Portland Square?"

It took everything she had, but Eleanor did not reach out to Ainsley when he retreated behind his desk, sat down once more, looking very weary, and older than he had only a few minutes earlier. "Tomorrow will be fine, Jack."

Jack was ready to say something else, something on the order of a promise to take very good care of the man's daughter. But Jacko slung a beefy arm across his shoulders and gave him a might squeeze against his hard body, and the breath was all but knocked from him.

Jacko's voice boomed in his ear. "We trust you, see? That's the only reason you're getting within ten feet of our Eleanor here. We're all friends here, too, aren't we? Remember that, my fine young gentleman. You saved that fool Billy, and I'm grateful, so I don't want to have to tie your guts in a bow around your neck."

"No, Jacko, you don't, and neither do I want you to have to try," Jack said when the big man released him, feeling as if he'd just been mauled by a large bear. He shook back his shoulders, bowed to Eleanor. "Miss Becket, with your kind permission?"

She inclined her head slightly, then watched as Jack brushed past her and left the study before turning to her adoptive father. Waiting.

"Rowley Maddox," Ainsley said at last. "Of all the names the man might have said..."

"Should we tell him, Cap'n? In case he has to watch out for her?"

"No," Eleanor said quickly. "Tell him, and he won't let me go. I *have* to go."

Ainsley nodded his agreement, then added, "We don't know, Eleanor. Remember that. We can suspect, but we don't *know.*"

"No, Papa, but we've always wondered. I know what we decided, what we both felt best, that the past is in the past and won't change. But I can't look away from this chance. I just can't. I've lived too long with the question, we both have."

"And you'll take one look at the bugger and have all our answers?" Jacko shook his head. "Maybe we've all been stuck here too long, if any of us believes *that!*"